Instinct: An Animal Rescuers Anthology

Executive Editor: L. J. Hachmeister

Associate Editor: Sam Knight

Cover art by **Alessandra Pisano** – alesspisano.com
Design by **Nicole Peschel** – Source 7 Productions, LLC
Executive Editor – **L. J. Hachmeister** – triorion.com
Associate Editor – **Sam Knight** – knightwritingpress.com
Published by **Source 7 Productions**, LLC Lakewood, CO

Table of Contents

Dedication

This anthology is dedicated to Scott Cromer and all the wonderful folks at Lifeline Puppy Rescue.

Thank you for all the work you do to save lives.

The Gold Standard

A Will Hawthorne Tale from Bowescroft

By A. J. Hartley

Right off the bat I should say that I didn't like the dog. It wasn't anything personal. I'm just not a dog person. I prefer my companions to have a bit more conversation and a bit less in the stink and teeth department. I should also say that the feeling was mutual. As the others fawned over the great brute, it stood there glowering at me as if determining if it would prefer me raw or lightly broiled.

Renthrette and Garnet had brought it home. Naturally. They said it would make an excellent watchdog, but really, they just liked its fur, which was white, and its eyes, which were blue, and its teeth, which were massive.

Also, they liked that it scared me.

"It's just a dog, Will," said Renthrette, pulling her sword from its sheath and rubbing its edge with a greasy rag. "What's the big deal?"

"I don't trust large animals," I replied. "You know that."

Getting me to ride a horse had required the kind of effort usually reserved for redirecting rivers.

"Being only a small animal yourself," she replied with that wicked little grin she wore when she thought she was being witty.

"Hilarious as ever, Renthrette," I said. "But the others won't let you keep it anyway, whatever I say. We've barely had work in a month, and that beast will cost as much to feed as I do."

"Maybe we should keep the dog and drop you," she replied. "Or feed you to it."

"More sparkling repartee. Excellent."

"Well, at least the dog has a use."

"Which is?"

"It's an imposing guard," she shrugged. "If people try to break in it will bark loudly and scare them off. Do you think you could learn to bark, Will?"

"I have proven myself more than useful to this little band of outlaws, thank you very much."

"Look at those ears though!" said Renthrette, rubbing the dog's head so that it half closed its eyes and grinned at me triumphantly. "So soft and cute. It's really too bad you don't have ears like his."

"Stop. I'm, laughing too hard," I said flatly.

"I'm enjoying myself," said Renthrette. "I have a new adorable pet."

"So, you are enjoying yourself at the expense of your old adorable pet," I said, batting my lashes winsomely.

She rolled her eyes.

"His name is Durnok," she said, "after the ancient wolf god."

"You shouldn't name it," I cautioned. "You're only making it harder on yourself."

"Why?"

"Because," I said very slowly, "the others won't let you keep it."

They let her keep it.

I argued, but the great brute padded around snuggling up to them, and they smiled at each other and rubbed its head till even I knew the battle was lost. Then it curled up at Lisha's feet like the world's most lethal rug, eying me in a smug sort of way and growling softly if I made any sudden moves, which Renthrette and Orgos thought hysterically funny. I managed a few growls of my own but when I did so the dog's hair stiffened and it developed the kind of sudden stillness which promised bloody death soon after, so I stopped. That made Orgos laugh all the louder.

"What is with you and the dog?" he demanded when he had recovered. "And don't give me *that I don't trust animals* thing. We've been through too much. What I think is that you resent the dog because you'd rather it was *your* belly Renthrette was rubbing..."

I told him to shut up and when he started laughing again, I threw a bread roll at him, missing badly and startling the elderly woman who had come in to make up the fireplace, making Orgos laugh all the harder.

We were waiting on a job. More specifically, we were waiting for a man with information on a job. I was waiting to get paid. The man in question was one Rasnor Rains who we had never actually met because he was far too important to deal with the likes of us, but he had sent a handful of assorted flunkies to handle the details of our assignments. And the money. This was job five and, we surmised, the most important one to date.

So far, we had escorted a Lazarian spice dealer, whose breath could strip varnish, and his five camels, which smelled so bad they left you longing for the simplicity of varnish stripping, a wine merchant with a cargo of a sweet russet vintage he absolutely refused to let me sample (twice), and a Cherrat silversmith whose entire cargo fit in the hampers of two mules. The last job had been the shared harvest of a village some thirty miles from Bowescroft: three wagons of rice in sacks.

Pretty gripping stuff, right? In each case our job was to handle fees to guards (bribes), make sure the cargo made its way to the right collection point (different each time) and oversee the transit of said cargo from a distance which balanced inconspicuousness with the necessary immediacy required by actual combat. Fortunately, everything had gone smoothly so far. So much so, in fact, that I had started to think we were being overpaid; not a thought I have often had since I started putting my life on the line for money. That thought evaporated when we were given the details of our fifth and final cargo. It was gold. Not just gold though. It was gold from the Blackbird mine, which meant it was Empire property, but it wasn't being handled by Empire operatives, which meant—in turn, as it were—that it was stolen.

Now, don't get me wrong. I am quite happy to lift anything I can from the Empire and will sleep like a babe the night that I do. Why? Because the Empire is a brutal, soul crushing machine that flattens the world beneath it like a mill stone and anything I can do to be a thorn in their side, I'll do. I'll hold my hand up to that. The problem is that if they see me hold my hand up, they'll cut it off, along with other assorted bits to which I am (in every sense) attached. So, acting as armed escort for whoever had stolen from the Empire made me, shall we say, uneasy.

When I say the gold was *stolen* from the Empire, I don't mean someone broke in, fought off a hundred heavily armed troopers, and made off down the alley with a couple of sacks. That wasn't how things worked. This was what you might call *creative accountancy*. Someone on the inside filled in a form, made some completely believable errors in basic arithmetic and quietly siphoned off a stream of ready coin into a corner where, officially, it didn't exist. With the right connections, it was just a matter of marks on a few papers and a few inspectors being paid to look the other way. In other words, it was good old-fashioned corruption. But conceptual theft—robbing someone of numbers in a book—becomes a very different beast when those imaginary numbers have to become actual money. Then we get the aforementioned sacks which have to be sneaked down the alley.

Which is where we came in.

The minting process requires a lot of heat: all that melting of precious metals followed by a cooling process Orgos says is called annealing, repeated multiple times before the blanks are ready to be stamped into coins. This means that the mint consumes wood and coal at a massive rate, and produces tons of ash every week, but since the Empire knows how to turn everything—and I mean everything—into gold, the ash is carefully carted away and sold on to make soap, fertilizer and God knew what else. The poor sods whose job it was to collect the ash, sweep it into crates and haul it away, were only one step up from the miserable buggers who carted out the night soil. In some ways, the ash haulers had it worse since the blokes who handled the contents of the latrines didn't have to worry about it still being hot enough to seer the skin off your hands, or roast your lungs from the inside if you made the mistake of breathing in. Actually, I suppose inhaling is best avoided in both professions, but you know what I mean.

Anyway.

All this skin blistering and lung searing meant it was clearly Our Kind Of Job. Lethal *and* illegal? Sign us up.

The gold would be still in its ingot form, carefully stashed within one of the smoking heaps of ash and, under cover of our lowly task, we were to make off with enough to buy someone a house. Possibly a village. And if it sounds like the smart course of action (instead of turning over our trove to our employer in return for fifty pounds in silver) would be to hightail it out of there with all that raw wealth in our saddle bags, don't think I hadn't already made that suggestion.

"And do what with it?" sneered Garnet.

"Spend it!" I said. "Obviously."

"It's bars of gold, not coins," said Orgos.

"Sell it then!" I replied. "We'd make a fortune."

"We'd get killed," said Mithos, ever the ray of sunshine.

"We're just cutting out the middleman," I replied.

"Who will come after us," said Garnet.

"And do some cutting of his own," said Renthrette, completing her brother's thought before he could have it.

"We don't have the connections, Will," said Lisha. "Unminted gold is carefully regulated. We'd need to be able to show provenance."

"Where we got it," said Orgos helpfully.

"I know what provenance means," I snapped. "But we're making a fraction of the profits despite doing all the work!"

"Welcome to real world economics," said Orgos, returning to the dagger he had been sharpening on a whetstone.

I slumped to the table.

"It's just that there will be So. Much. Gold," I managed.

"For which we'll be paid," said Mithos.

"After which we will walk away with all our fingers and toes still attached," added Orgos, eyes on his blade. "Won't that be nice?"

"Assuming we don't burn them off rooting through the red-hot ash," I grumbled.

"Right," said Renthrette, "because what our employer wants is that we risk melting all his gold. The ingots will be hidden in old ash. *Cold* ash."

I muttered mutinously into the tabletop, opening my eyes to see the great white hound watching me with the canine equivalent of wry amusement.

"And you'll be helping how?" I demanded.

The dog gave me a blank look, but Renthrette rallied to his defense as if I'd kicked him.

"He'll be our watchful companion, won't you Durnok?" she said, brightly at first, then in her best gruff doggie voice. "Yes, you will! Good boy, Durnok. Ignore silly Mr. Hawthorne. What does he know about anything? That's right Durnok, he knows nothing! Stupid Will. He's an idiot, isn't he, Durnok? Isn't he? Why don't you bite his leg?"

"We should get our gear loaded," said Lisha. "Raines will be here within the hour."

Rasnor Raines was our contact at the forge, the man responsible for the creative accounting and, to all intents and purposes, our employer, though—for obvious reasons—he didn't know our real names. He was the one who would be strolling off with the Empire's hard-extorted cash minus the ten per cent grudgingly pushed in our direction. The son of a gold smith who had combined his father's skills with a talent for finance, Raines had been in business in Bowescroft for a little over a decade. In that time, he had upgraded his facilities—and his contracts—twice, finding his way onto the Empire's payroll four years earlier. Whether he had pulled this kind of stunt at their expense before, I couldn't say. Maybe I'd ask him when he showed up.

I rethought that the moment I saw him. I wasn't sure what I had expected—some kind of mild mannered and soft-spoken accountant-type, I suppose—but that was not what we got. Rasnor Raines was at least three quarters pirate, complete with eye patch and gold teeth. The remaining quarter also had a vaguely nautical feel though it was all stuff that lived under the surface. His skin was oily and his hair—braided into three thin rat tails—was yellow and lank, and hung down like the tentacles of a squid. His eyes were fishy too, not bulbous but blank, unfeeling and impossible to read. He would have made a good card player, assuming they played cards under the sea.

The dog didn't like him. It grew stiff and watchful the moment he showed up, and its hackles prickled in little waves as he sat at the table and started talking in a low rasping voice without inflection. His eyes moved without interest or concern from hound to us, to the papers he had brought with him, sliding languidly back to the dog when its guttural snarl became impossible to ignore.

"Don't mind Durnok," said Renthrette, fractionally embarrassed. "It takes him a moment to get used to strangers."

Raines shrugged, uninterested, and went back to his outline of our mission.

"You'll need to be positioned here as soon as the gate opens at four," he said, pointing at his makeshift map. "If you're late, you'll have to take your place in line with the other ash haulers and they'll want to know who you are. There's a community amongst these low lifes, and you'll stand out. Park your wagon behind Franklin's cotton warehouse on Low Street. Bring wheelbarrows to move the ash and move fast. Take only from vat 4. The ingots will be bagged. You'll need to be loaded and gone in a half hour. That's when the guard arrive. I'll be making a show of opening for the day then, which means we need to be closed and you need to be gone well before."

I made a sour face at Orgos. Four in the morning? This job just kept getting better. Raines caught my glance.

"Or you can sleep in and get arrested on the spot," he said, his hard little shark eyes meeting mine and holding them. "Then I can say I've never seen any of you before, and you can take your chances in court."

He flashed his sharp little fish teeth in a kind of mechanical smile. We all knew how the courts handled people suspected of trying to rob from the Diamond Empire.

"We'll be there," said Mithos.

"And you'd better be at the meet that evening," I remarked, feeling the need to stand up to him a little. "With our money."

He gave another impassive shrug as if my concern was unworthy of his attention, but he said, "Ten-o'clock in the alley behind the Clockmaker's Arms on the corner of Jarvis and Hessian. Don't be late then either."

And then he was up and leaving, leaving a single coin on the table to pay for our food and drinks and five more "As a taste of things to come."

That rather changed things. I hadn't liked the man, but you couldn't argue with gold. I picked up one of the coins and examined it closely, looking for that hint of brass which might make his generosity less impressive.

"Gold," I pronounced. "Solid and as pure as I've seen in a long time."

"He is a smith," said Lisha cautiously.

Something in her tone caught my attention, and I looked up to find the others looking still and thoughtful.

"What?" I said. "He's the real deal. His money certainly is. What's the problem? We show up—admittedly earlier than I would like, but still—we load a wagon, and we take it to a pub where we get paid. Simple."

"The dog doesn't like him," said Renthrette.

I laughed but she turned an acid glare on me.

"I was serious," she said.

"So was I," I shot back.

"You didn't say anything," said Garnet, always helpful.

"No," I agreed as if this was obvious, "I didn't need to. My seriousness was in that dismissive laugh, so full of scorn and derision."

"Meaning?" said Garnet.

"Meaning the dog doesn't get a vote," I clarified, "because *it's a dog.*"

"Dogs can be excellent judges of character," said Garnet pensively.

"Is there evidence for this preposterous claim?" I shot back.

"He didn't like you," said Renthrette, as if that proved it.

"That's not the point," I scoffed.

"What is the point?" asked Mithos with his patented *your-stupidity-is-starting-to-annoy-me stare.*

"That we are the thinking, talking, ruling mind of our little band of warriors and we don't take advice from dogs."

Orgos leaned forward, one hand massaging his jaw thoughtfully.

"He's right," he said. "The dog *didn't* like him."

I was so caught up in that "he's right" stuff that I almost missed the tail end of the remark, and it was a moment before I realized that the "he" who was right was not me but Garnet. Which is never true.

"What?" I exclaimed. "Are you serious? You are going to trust a dumb animal over me?" Garnet glared murderously, so I qualified my rhetorical question. "I meant the dog. A dumb animal *and* Garnet."

"And me," said Renthrette.

"And I'm starting to lean that way," Orgos added, grinning brightly at me.

"Of course you are," I snapped.

"Mithos?"

Lisha had said nothing so far, drawing vaguely with her finger on the table where the wine had splashed. Her question made the others go quiet and watchful. Mithos considered the dog for a moment, then nodded very small and solemn like a judge agreeing that, on the preponderance of evidence, the large man who had been found covered in the victim's blood and yelling, "He got what he deserved" should be released immediately.

It was enough for Lisha.

"Then it's settled," she said.

"You're joking!" I yelled. "This is insane! We are changing our entire plan, our basic attitude to this whole situation because *the dog didn't like him*? It's madness. And if Raines is so obviously untrustworthy, what exactly do you think he's doing paying us?"

Lisha nodded.

"A fair question," she said. "Thoughts?"

"Say he's been milking the Empire for a while," Mithos ventured, putting his mug down. "Someone has gotten wise to him, or he fears they might have."

"So, he's looking for someone to blame," Orgos joined in.

"Right," said Mithos. "He'll pin the accountancy stuff on some lowly clerk on the inside, but he needs outsiders to be caught red handed with the gold."

"Enter us," said Renthrette. "We show up, load up our wagon, only to find a couple of platoons of the Empire's finest blockading the street."

"Raines expresses his amazement at us and loyalty to them, hands over the expendable clerk and," Mithos concluded with a self-satisfied shrug, "life goes on."

There was a thoughtful pause and Orgos took a sip of his ale.

"So, we don't go," I said. "We pocket his money—serves him right too—and we make sure we are nowhere near Low Street at four in the morning. Shouldn't be too hard."

Mithos tipped his head on one side, his eyes narrowed in thought. It wasn't a look I liked.

"Right?" I said, trying not to sound desperate. "Stands to reason. Hello?"

"Or," Mithos mused, "we take the opportunity to repay a scoundrel for his bad faith and leave the Empire's nose out of joint in the process."

Orgos put down his mug and grinned widely. "I like the sound of that," he said.

"What?" I demanded. "No. That has a terrible sound. It has the sound of people being arrested and tortured, people being creatively executed, people a lot like us. It is not a good sound."

Lisha turned her gaze on Mithos.

"You have an idea?" she asked.

And, as it happened, he did. It was an awful idea almost certain to get us all killed, but it was an idea, and—perhaps predictably—they liked it. Even the bloody dog.

So, we went. First, we sat up till everyone else in the inn had gone to bed, eating and planning and trying not to throw up with terror, though that last one might just have been me. Then we went, picking our way across town in the dark like suicidal moles.

There was no curfew in Bowescroft like there was in Cresdon, but the Empire kept sentries at the gates and patrols around the streets. The soldiers stopped you or didn't if they saw you, depending on their mood. There was no curfew, but their default position was suspicious with a side order of hostile, and they were always armed to the teeth.

Our fiendishly clever plan to outsmart the evil gold smith was to show up precisely where he had told us to at the very time he had instructed. Genius, right? But—and this is where it got really good—I was to go in alone.

Why me, you ask, as—believe me—did I?

"Because we don't know what you'll find when you get there," said Mithos levelly, "and you are good at thinking on your feet."

"What the hell does that mean?" I exclaimed.

"It means you lie like other people draw breath," said Renthrette nastily.

I gave her a wounded look.

"It means," said Orgos, grinning, "that you, my friend, can talk the hind leg off a donkey and then persuade it to enter a dancing contest."

I frowned and Lisha leaned in, her dark eyes serious.

"We need someone who is good at improvising," she said. "Someone who can stall and who can convincingly play innocence."

"And idiocy," Renthrette added.

Lisha ignored her with difficulty.

"You're an actor, Will," she said. "A storyteller. In this situation, that's what we need."

"I'm gonna get killed, aren't I?" I said, matter-of-factly.

"You're not going to get killed," said Lisha. "We'll be on hand and, to make doubly sure, you can take Durnok."

"The dog?" I exclaimed. "You are sending me into a trap where a dozen Empire troops will be lying in wait, spears at the ready, but I'll be fine because I've got the bloody dog that tries to bite my hand off every time I look at it?"

"Him," Renthrette corrected. "Not it. He's not a thing."

And that was that.

So, at precisely four in a dark, cold morning, I sidled unhappily up to the side door of Raines's forge, took a breath, and rapped imperiously on the wood in the manner of a man who didn't want to be kept waiting. A thin fog hung between the silent, ramshackle warehouses and workshops, and the place felt ominous, as if I was being watched by eyes I couldn't see. At my side the big white dog stood still and silent as the street, its breath clouding like the fog. I listened, and heard nothing inside the forge, and gave the dog a nervous glance. The thin chain leash chinked, and the great beast looked up at me, its cool blue eyes meeting mine expressionlessly.

"Just you and me, dog," I muttered.

It continued to watch me with those frank, animal eyes, till I felt uncomfortably transparent, and looked away, just as I heard the snap of a bolt. The door cracked open. A glimmer of lamp light showed a heavily shadowed face peering out. I didn't know the man.

"Ash transfer," I managed. "Vat four."

"You're early," said the door keeper. He sounded curt, irritated. "And where's the rest of them?"

"On their way with the barrows."

"You don't have a barrow?" he snapped.

"Like I said, they are on their way."

"I'll let you in when they arrive," he said. The door started to close but I jammed my foot in the gap.

"We don't have a lot of time," I said. "I need to get started. Get the paperwork signed off."

The shadowed face creased into bafflement.

"Paperwork?" he parroted scornfully. "What paperwork? You're a garbage hauler! You come in with a barrow, you cart out the crap and you leave. There's no paperwork!"

"Basic commodity exchange practice," I said blandly, easing into my role. "Your trash for my labor, signed and quantified according to pre-agreed upon terms as set down in certified contractual documents like these which, conveniently enough, I have here for your perusal."

I gave him a suitably bureaucratic smile and produced a sheaf of closely worded papers.

He opened the door another inch so he could give the paper a disbelieving stare.

"What the hell is that?" he muttered, his eyes wide and anxious.

I pushed them into the light of his lamp, confident that his being able to see them better would not ease his mind. His gaze wandered vaguely around the documents, an unfocused and random movement which made my heart sing a little song of joy. He couldn't read.

"There's been some sort of mistake," he mumbled, his eyes still blank. "This isn't how things are done. You come in, you cart away the crap, you get paid. No papers, no signing."

He pushed the documents back toward me, but I tutted smugly and shook my head.

"No can do," I said. "See?" I added, flipping the pages at random and pointing to a numbered paragraph, "according to the terms of this subsection all traffic between the parties of the first and second part must accord with all printed citation, vis-à-vis said contractual agreement, and be ratified by signatures at the moment of transactional completion. More than my job's worth to forego the legal niceties. Let me in and we'll find a nice light spot to go over the terms and, assuming you are in agreement…"

"I can't do this," he said.

It wasn't defiance so much as panic. He was out of his depth and knew it, but he was also worried. I played a new card.

"Perhaps if you consult with Mr. Raines…"

As soon as I said the name, the door man blinked and his already mounting anxiety ratcheted up a notch like a spurred horse. He licked his lips and his eyes flashed about. Another minute and he'd be sweating, despite the cool morning air.

"No!" he sputtered. "Mr. Raines said he wasn't to be roused till seven. You were going to come, and I was going to help, and he was to be left out of it completely."

He said it like a child reciting something learned by heart, like he was reminding himself.

And there it was. Mithos and the rest had been right. We were being set up, and this poor dolt at the door was Raines's fall guy. If the Empire weren't already there, they'd be arriving any moment. I needed to be elsewhere and quickly, but there was—maddeningly—something

I had to do.

"Just initial each page," I said, "and I'll load up your ash."

"Initial?" he said stupidly.

"First letters of your name, or whatever mark you use in place of a signature."

"Can't you just take the ash and go?" he wheedled.

"The moment this is done," I said, forcing a smile.

I could feel the minutes ticking away, could practically hear the regular stomp of marching sentries coming toward us, but I pushed my impatience down and tried to look casual. He was sweating hard now, and his furtive glances around were getting more frequent and more worried. I didn't know what Raines had told him, but he knew he was sliding toward trouble with each passing second, even if the worst he could imagine was a furious boss kicking him out of his job.

Trust me, I wanted to say, *it is far worse than you know.*

So, he squinted at the papers he couldn't read and, with my careful prompting, painstakingly scratched his little ham fisted cross, tongue poking out between his teeth in concentration, on the first page, then the second, then the third…

Suddenly he glanced backward into the darkness of the shop.

"What was that?" he said, more to himself than to me.

"Let's just get this done, shall we?" I said.

He hesitated, listening, his eyes focused on nothing, then shrugged and turned back to me.

"Every sheet?" he muttered pleadingly.

"Front and back," I said.

When it was finally done, he pushed the door wide.

"Now can you please just get it and go?" he begged.

"My colleague with the barrow hasn't arrived…" I stalled.

"You can borrow one of ours," he snapped. "Over there. That's vat four at the end. Just load it up and get out. Here."

He thrust a dusty shovel into my hands.

"All right," I said. "No need to be rude."

"You don't know Raines," he shot back, his guard dropping. "If this doesn't get done just how he said…"

"What?" I asked.

"He'll…" But he didn't want to say. "He's just not a man you want disappointed, all right?"

I gave him a careless shrug and turned to the ash vats.

It was smoky and hot inside, the forge lit by a handful of oil lamps which gave the place an amber cast with pockets of deep shadow. The dog didn't want to go in, and I couldn't really blame him, but we had no choice.

I gave the leash a tug, and he made a chuff of protest but followed me in. The door keeper eyed the animal warily, keeping his distance. Inside was a huge leather bellows, studded with brass and worked by a hand crank. Anvils of various sizes littered the flagged shop floor and the walls hung with pincers and hammers of every imaginable size. The soot-stained walls were stone, presumably to reduce the risk of fire, and it was clear how well they insulated the place. I could feel the inside of my nostrils scorching. I breathed through my mouth and could taste the ash on the air, a fine, bitter powder. I turned aside to cough and spat on the ground.

"Quicker you get done, the quicker you can get outside in the air," said the doorman without sympathy. "Vat four."

"I know," I shot back, my annoyance real.

"There was supposed to be a team of you," he said shoving the oversized wheelbarrow into my midriff. "If you don't finish on time, Mister Raines will be…"

"Disappointed," I finished for him. "Yeah, you said."

"I have to get the fire going," he said. "Yell when you're done."

And he disappeared behind the forge, glad to have better things to do.

I looped the leash over the horn of an anvil and climbed down into the vat. The dog watched me but did not object, though it sniffed the air uneasily. The ash looked pale and gray, but I could feel the heat of it on my face. I spat again, my throat beginning to burn, then thrust the shovel in and began to spade the hot fine powder into the barrow.

It was miserable work. Each stab of the shovel raised a stinging ash cloud that clung to my sweating face and hands. Somehow my labor didn't seem to reduce the ash heap at all, and what I had thought would take no more than a couple of minutes had started to feel like it would take most of the morning.

"You not done yet?"

I turned and saw Garnet with a barrow and shovel of his own, the red-faced door keeper showing him in, fidgety and anxious as before.

"What kept you?" I demanded as Garnet patted the dog's head absently, then dropped into the vat beside me in a cloud of ash.

"Here now, aren't I?" said Garnet. "This is all you've done?"

"It's hard," I said, trying not to sound pathetic and failing.

He ignored me, shoveling at twice my speed just to make my inadequacy clear. My throat was parched.

"You don't have something to drink, do you?" I asked the doorman.

"Just finish up and go," he snapped.

"Rude," I observed to Garnet. Or the dog. It made little difference.

Ten minutes later we had both barrows fully loaded and were straining to force them out into the street. The air was blessedly cold, but there was so much ash stuck to my skin that I could barely feel it. The dog led the way, glad to get out of the stifling forge, but as soon as it reached the street it stopped, froze in fact. It was rigid, mid stride, head cocked and hackles up.

Something was wrong.

"Garnet," I said warily.

"What?" he replied, his breathing labored. His barrow was rather fuller than mine.

I glanced down the street. On the corner I could see our wagon parked, waiting. The figure sitting at the front looked like Renthrette. There was no sign of the others.

There was a shout from somewhere beyond the wagon, an answering one from somewhere behind us, and suddenly the silent, empty street was full of noise and people. Soldiers. Diamond Empire troops: at least a dozen wrapped in gray wool night cloaks and wearing iron helmets. They carried full body shields marked with their garrison number and business-like cut-and-thrust swords, and they swarmed toward us. We, having nowhere to go, stood exactly where we were and tried to give them no excuse to kill us which, historically speaking, wouldn't take much.

An officer emerged and started barking at us not to move (which we weren't doing) if we valued our worthless lives (which we did). The dog growled and one of the troopers with a halberd-like spear materialized beside us and pointed the spiky business end at the animal. Ignoring all warnings to the contrary, Renthrette leapt down from the wagon and came sprinting over, yelling the dog's name with such unreasonable ferocity that the guard with the halberd took a step back, his eyes on her. Another produced a bow and nocked an arrow.

"Not another step!" bellowed the officer.

I raised one hand to stop Renthrette and cautiously reached out to the dog with my other. I patted the beast on its head gingerly, and the snarling stopped.

"Empty those barrows!" ordered the officer as stillness returned.

A couple of the soldiers elbowed Garnet and I out of the way and pushed until the barrows overturned, splintering under their own weight. Ash and cinders, some of them smoking hot, spilled onto the cobbles and billowed up in clouds which doubled up the soldiers and left them coughing and spitting. The officer was annoyed.

"Get on with it!" he roared.

Humbled, and with dust encrusted hands clamped over their mouths, the soldiers began a desultory search, raking the ash heaps with the tips of their swords. There was an expectant hush, broken only by the creak of the forge's front door. The doorman, terrified and miserable, stumbled out, shoved by the bigger man who emerged after him.

Rasnor Raines stood in the doorway, barely suppressing a smirk as he took in the unfolding scene.

"Morning officer," he remarked conversationally. "Anything I can help you with?"

"Everything seems to be in hand, thank you," the officer replied pointedly. He was on his dignity and wanted the civilians to keep out of it. Raines wasn't that kind of civilian. He strode purposefully over to Garnet's barrow, pulled a knife from his belt and plunged it into the ash heap. He moved it around, came up with nothing and tried a few alternate spots. He got up, unperturbed, and came over to me. His eyes met mine and his upper lip curled into a scornful and self-satisfied smile.

"Got something for me?" he inquired.

"Some ash?" I suggested. "Though it will cost you. And the embers are extra."

His amusement turned to irritation, and he pushed me aside, setting to a sifting of my spilled barrow with increasingly baffled gusto.

"Where is it?" he demanded without looking up. "Where the hell...?"

There was an embarrassed silence from the troops. A couple exchanged glances, and the officer took a step toward me.

Raines leapt suddenly to his feet and got in my face.

"What have you done with it?" he demanded.

"With what?" I answered guilelessly.

"My...er," he began, then corrected himself, "the *Empire's* gold."

I served him a blank look and took a moment to let it land.

"Gold?" I said. "We are garbage haulers. Not a lot of gold in our line of work."

"Why you thieving little..." he spat. He made a lunging movement toward me but one of the guards put a hand on his shoulder. It was more caution than restraint, but it did the job. For now.

Renthrette stepped quickly between us, not to save me, you understand, but to make sure the petulant gold smith's rage couldn't redirect at the dog somehow. Soldiers bustled and shouted, the dog barked, the officer roared, and eventually we were all peeled apart and shunted aside at sword and spear point.

I raised my hands in surrender, as did Garnet. Renthrette—ignoring her guards—stroked the bristling hound, and Raines shouted more furious bile and assorted accusations, some of which included the hapless door keeper, whose puzzlement had hardened into resentment. For a long moment that was all there was: stillness and tension from everyone else, and Raines shrieking his ass-covering lies and accusations at us, the soldiers, and his surly employee.

And then it was like a light went on in the door keeper's head. He frowned once more, deeper this time, and stared at Raines as the tumblers of the lock which had kept his brain from working for years finally clicked into place.

"Wait," he said stupidly. "Me?" He glared at Raines who gave him the kind of dull amazement which would have been the same if the question and had been asked by the dog. "You're saying I've been stealing from you—from *them*," the door keeper continued with a wary glance at the Empire troops, "for months and working with these idiots? I've never seen them before in my life."

His dull outrage was so clearly honest that the soldiers flashed more uncertain looks at the officer, who hesitated, then nodded his command.

"Search the wagon," he ordered.

A pair of soldiers, glad of something definitive to do, bustled off down the street. The rest of us stood in watchful silence, and there was a profound sense of the story changing. The officer and his men had come on stage sure of their roles, clear in their minds as to how the crisis would build and resolve, how they would go through their lines until gratefully receiving the audience's applause. Suddenly it looked like they were in the wrong play, as if the whole stately tragedy they had dutifully rehearsed had somehow turned into a comedy full of twins and women dressed inexplicably as boys.

"Nothing," said the troops shame-facedly as they returned from their search of the wagon. "No gold."

Well, of course there wasn't. Raines's gold was nowhere near here. It had been liberated via the back entrance by Mithos, Orgos and Lisha while Raines slept upstairs, and I kept the illiterate door keeper busy at the front. By now it was heading to the other side of the city along with everything we owned from the inn. Assuming we got through the next few minutes, we'd be living elsewhere for a while. I said nothing and tried to look mildly interested.

"Gold?" said Garnet stupidly. "Don't know anything about any gold."

I glared at him. This was not the time for him to start dipping his toe into the noble thespian arts. That was my department.

"Personally," I said, turning to the officer, "I'm offended that humble laborers like our good selves can't go about their business without being falsely accused..."

"Yeah, yeah," said the officer, waving me into silence. "No gold," he said to Raines. "You said these people would have it. They don't, but it's still gone. Which makes me wonder if..."

"It was him," said the door keeper, whose resentment had hardened into decision. He pointed at Raines, then took two long steps toward him, index finger still aimed like a crossbow, and prodded him squarely in the chest. "I knew there was something funny about the way he always insisted on doing the final cash count alone, the way he always kept two sets of books."

The officer's face tightened, and his eyebrows slid up into his hair. Raines stared at the doorkeeper in horrified disbelief. The look was as good as a confession.

"Two books?" said the officer.

"Oh yes," said the doorkeeper. "There's the one he has in the office which anyone can see, and the other he keeps under the loose floorboard in his bedroom, that he thinks no one knows about."

There was another loaded silence. I was starting to like the doorkeeper. He wasn't very clever, but he was a positive well of useful spite.

"Show them," said the officer, nodding to the guards holding Raines. The doorkeeper led them inside.

"This is outrageous!" Raines protested, recovering some of his haughty righteousness with difficulty. "I am a respected citizen and a pillar of the community! For five years I have been a loyal servant of the Empire..."

"A long time to have been skimming profits," I agreed conversationally.

His mask of innocent indignation slipped, and his eyes slid after the doorkeeper as if he had just realized he was no longer under guard. He moved quickly after them, shouting about the violation of his privacy and threatening various kinds of legal action if anyone "planted" anything.

That would be his defense. And somehow, we'd find ourselves in custody, "temporarily detained" until the facts of the matter had been made plain to the authorities… Except that by then they'd figure out we weren't who we said we were, and then they'd start asking around, and all manner of things might come out about us and our activities, all of them—from the Empire's insensitive and close-minded perspective—bad.

So, I went after Raines and the dog came after me. It was madness, but I had no choice. Renthrette tried to follow, but the officer, who had been momentarily caught off guard, had recovered in time to throw an arm across her path. Two of the Empire troopers quickly blocked the door, but I was already in, rushing after the spitting, cursing Raines, the great white hound at my heels.

The doorkeeper led the soldiers through the hot and smoky workshop and up a flight of timber steps to the living quarters above. They moved with hasty determination, men on a mission, and we came behind like the tail of a comet which was, for reasons I couldn't begin to explain, extremely pissed off. By the time we reached the top of the stairs the door keeper was already on his hands and knees, prizing a floorboard free.

Raines bellowed his inarticulate fury, but the doorkeeper sat up grinning maliciously, a little leather-bound volume in his hands.

"Very interesting," he said, flicking through the pages. For all his glee, he wasn't really looking at the book, and I remembered that he couldn't read.

"I'll take that," I said adopting my previous, officious manner.

He hesitated, uncertain, then held it out toward me. Raines lunged like a pouncing cat, snatched it and barreled back down the stairs. Being the closest to him, it was me who gave chase before the guards knew what was happening, me who leapt the last step and landed awkwardly on the workshop floor, and me who was the first to realize what he was doing as he reached the forge, wrapped a towel around his hand and yanked open a venting shutter in the steel smelter.

There was a great belching and a lance of pressurized fire shot out toward the stairs. I dived under it, rolling and falling badly on the stone flags as the jet stabbed at the guards. The second soldier shrunk back, but the one at the front was less fortunate: the flame caught him squarely in the chest. As he twisted away, screaming, his cloak became a torch which filled the stair well with a sheet of fire. By the uneven blaze of the firelight, I saw Raines turn to the front door where more guards were fighting their way in, saw the calculation in his eyes, as he reached for another of the great shutters on the smelter and heaved it open.

There was another roar as the vent clanged open, another tongue of flame flicking out like some caged beast testing its new freedom. The guards hesitated, and Raines moved to the great bellows and began to pump. The flame creature at the heart of the smelter roiled and swelled, spewing white-hot heat from the open vents. I felt my eyebrows crinkle and singe, smelled burning hair over the hot wood and metal, and I shrunk away from the furnace, half closing my eyes.

He turned back to the stairs, assessing his options. One guard had dragged his burning comrade back up to the door keeper in the bedroom, but the staircase itself was already on fire. There was no way in or out that way.

Raines pushed the shutter facing that way closed, then gave another yank on the bellows. The jet of fire blasting toward the front was bigger, longer, more intense than ever. The guards ducked back, and in that instant he made his move, thrusting the incriminating book into the heart of the furnace, then ducking behind the smelter and heading for the back, the very door through which Lisha and the others had liberated his gold not so very long ago.

I knew they would be long gone, knew that Garnet and Renthrette couldn't reach me from the front, knew that with the fire raging untended, the building wouldn't last much longer. The air was dense with hot smoke. Even as I watched it thickened like fog so that the inferno at the heart of the smelter only showed in occasional flashes of orange. My breathing was thin and ragged. If I waited much longer, I wouldn't be able to walk, even if I could find my way out.

But Raines would be waiting. I was the only person who could stop him getting away, and I had made an impression. He wouldn't leave before he was sure I couldn't go after him.

I sucked in air, coughed half of it out again, spitting, lightheaded, then forced myself as close to upright as I could manage. Face half buried in the crook of my left arm, right arm held fumblingly in front of me, I slunk around the smelter. Navigating as much by the feel of heat on my skin as by sight, tripping on tools and jarred by the edge of work benches, knowing that the smoke was getting to me, that I was getting weak and unsteady, I blundered toward the back of the shop.

The fire was spreading now. It rolled and rumbled low and purposeful all around me and the air had turned sour. Soot and cinders swirled around the cramped workshop, burning the skin of my arms and neck, but I peered through the gloom and could see the back door only yards in front of me.

But no Raines.

And then I realized. I spun on the spot to face the smelter and there he was, behind me, his hands on the remaining vent shutter, poised to send a fiery blast right at me. I couldn't move, couldn't get out. He knew it too, and something mad and vengeful flashed in his eyes, bright as the firestorm at the heart of the furnace.

Then something else was moving, something big and fast, something whose white fur smoked and kindled as it leapt like it had emerged from the smelter itself; a beast which drooled molten metal, a hell hound whose eyes—even in the crimson and amber of the fire light, burned blue.

Durnok.

The dog pounced, slamming into Raines and throwing him back against the smelter. He shouted in surprise, and I heard the hiss of skin against the smoking heat of the steel, but by then the smoke had forced the air from my lungs and I collapsed, wheezing, gasping, feeling the fire in my chest as if I had swallowed it. The world went dark.

And then, somewhat against my recent run of fortune, it went light again. And cool. I was on my back, and I was, improbably, alive. I rolled, gathered myself onto my knees and retched, hacking and spitting black slime onto the ground.

"Classy," said Renthrette. "These theatre types are such sophisticates, don't you think, Garnet?"

Garnet's face swam into view, and he gave me an appraising look.

"A study in elegance," he remarked.

I sat up, a rope of gray drool trailing across my chest.

"I'm alive," I said. "Unless you two idiots are my special hell, which is not beyond the realm of possibility."

"You're alive," Renthrette confirmed.

"I got out!" I gasped. "How did I…?"

But Renthrette's broad and knowing grin told me all I needed to know. As if to make the point, a wet muzzle thrust itself into my face and licked me.

"The bloody dog," I said, trying to escape and failing. "The dog saved my life and pulled me from the forge before the building collapsed."

"Correct," said Garnet, matching his sister's grin.

"And his fur got singed," said Renthrette in her talking-to-a-baby voice, "and will take weeks to grow back properly just to save smelly old Will. Isn't that right, Durnok? Isn't it? Aren't you a brave boy?"

"Is there another burning building someone can put me in?" I asked.

"There is not," said Garnet.

"And are we under arrest?"

"We are not."

I sat up, putting one hand gingerly around the great hound's head in a way which was supposed to be friendly, and checking the street for any sign of the Empire soldiers. The forge was a blackened ruin, and the officer and his men were all gone.

"And are we…" I ventured, "by any chance, a bit richer than we were yesterday?"

Orgos loomed over me, lowered his face toward mine, and whispered.

"As a matter of fact," he said, "we are."

"Yeah?" I said.

Lisha squatted beside me and grinned at Mithos.

"Yeah," she said.

I sat up, braced myself, and turned to the great hound.

"Who's a good boy, Durnok?" I said, matching Renthrette's tone. I ruffled the dog's fur and his tail thumped rhythmically against my leg. "Who's a good boy? That's right. You are."

Author Bio

A.J. Hartley is the bestselling writer of mystery/thriller, fantasy, historical fiction, and young adult novels.

Look for more Will Hawthorne short stories and check out A.J. Hartley's full-length adventures in *Act of Will* and *Will Power*. His most recent novel is *Burning Shakespeare*.

Visit https://ajhartley.net for more information.

to do something.

"Jon... Hey..." I took a step toward him, just as the dog's eyes jerked from me to something over my shoulder.

My entire body went cold, as if the temperature had dropped by a dozen degrees. I stopped in my tracks, and with a sense of growing dread, I turned to see what was lurking at my back.

Standing at the end of the aisle was a woman with fiery red hair. She was wearing a green dress with lace at the sleeves and throat. Her face was deathly pale, and when she raised a finger to point at me, I got the distinct impression that I'd just been marked.

"Who...?" My voice dried up as a rustle came from behind me. Terror kept me from looking, though I desperately wanted to. Was Jon rising from where he lay, intent on scaring the life from me? I wouldn't put it past him, though it seemed odd considering what Duke had said about him being in a foul mood.

The retriever barked once, breaking me from my fear-induced paralysis. The sound must have been the dog moving. I took a quick step toward the pointing woman, not quite sure what I was going to do. The dog ran past me, and for a moment, I thought the retriever might be attacking her, but when she came to a stop at the woman's side, and the women laid a hand on her head, I realized that the scary woman must be her owner.

"I'm sorry," I said. "I didn't know anyone was in here."

I chanced a look back.

Jon Luckett was gone.

I blinked at the empty space, shocked by his sudden disappearance. I stared blankly at the space for a good couple of seconds, wondering how he'd snuck away so quickly, before turning back to ask the woman.

But like Jon Luckett, both the woman in green, and the golden retriever, were gone.

"Are you sure we're going the right way?"

I paused at the intersection with a frown. Was I? It was hard to know for sure considering how quickly I'd come through the maze the first time. And now, with Detective Cavanaugh trailing behind me, I was feeling a smidge self-conscious.

"I think so," I said, taking a left.

Light played over the corn, casting shadows that seemed to move in between the stalks. More than once, I swore I saw the golden retriever, only to find it to be a clump of dirt, or a stray shadow cast by the flashlight Cavanaugh was holding.

We'd been checking the corn maze ever since I'd discovered what had looked to be Jon Luckett's body. He had yet to appear, alive or dead, nor had I seen hide or hair of the dog, or the ghostly woman, since.

"And you said he was dead?" Cavanaugh asked from behind me.

"I didn't check his pulse or anything, if that's what you're asking."

"You do know this is a Halloween event, right?"

I scowled at him. Of course, I knew.

"There's likely a rational explanation to what you saw. It wouldn't surprise me in the slightest if he was messing with you."

"And how would he know I was coming?" I asked, more embarrassed than annoyed. The more I thought about it, the more I realized that Cavanaugh was right, and Jon Luckett's apparent death was probably a joke played at my expense.

Cavanaugh didn't have to answer. The noise his arm made as it brushed against the stalks was answer enough.

We reached another intersection and I stopped. "I think this was it."

"You think?"

"It's hard to say for sure, but this looks like it." I pointed. "He was lying over there."

Cavanaugh played his flashlight over the spot I'd indicated. It looked like any other dead end in the corn. "I don't see anything."

"And the woman was over here." I walked over to where I'd seen the ghostly woman in green, making sure to peek around the corner there, just in case she was crouched on the other side, waiting to jump out at me.

No one was there.

Minutes passed with both Cavanaugh and I scouring the area for any sign of Jon or the woman. There was no blood, no torn cloth, or even tufts of dog fur. This section of the maze looked like every other section. I even parted the corn in the hopes of spotting something— a body, perhaps—hidden behind the stalks, but there was nothing.

Cavanaugh tipped back his hat to rub at his forehead. "Let's head on back. Mr. Luckett is probably already mingling, having a laugh about his prank with the others."

I doubted that, but what else could we do? There was nothing here to find. "All right." I kicked a small rock, only to find it was connected to a larger stone beneath. My toe throbbed all the way back through

"His dog died?" I asked, heart breaking at the thought of losing a pet, while, at the same time, alarm bells started clanging in my head.

"She did." Courtney actually sounded sad about that, which shouldn't have surprised me, but it did. "Goldie always had health issues. You would have liked her." She glanced at me. "Still, it came on suddenly, caught them both by surprise."

"And what happened to Annie?"

"Jon never liked letting Annie out of the house, which meant Goldie was her closest, if not only, companion. She kept her sane, I think." She handed back the photo and turned away. "Annie never recovered after Goldie passed. The way I heard it, she died a few days later of a broken heart."

Nothing moved in the corn. The sign still hung from the rope, barring entry, which meant… What exactly? I assumed Jon was the one who'd put it there. He must have entered the maze, thinking he'd seen his dead wife and dog, and then…?

I had no idea what to think. I didn't believe in ghosts, whether they were human or animal. I mean, spirits, sure. If we're talking about a feeling, or the residual affection that remained once a loved one had passed. But a legitimate, pale and creepy ghost?

There had to be some other explanation.

My family was still wandering the grounds, seeing ghosts of their own, but those were the sheets-with-eyeholes kind. I'd spotted Detective Cavanaugh on my way over to the corn maze, but what could I tell him? If I tried to explain my ghost theory, he'd laugh and tell me to get some sleep.

So, with a quick glance behind me to make sure I wasn't being watched, I ducked under the rope barrier, and entered the corn maze.

I walked carefully, listening for any sound that might indicate I wasn't alone, but it was hard. Screams and laughs and the general murmur of dozens of voices speaking at once made it almost impossible to discern much outside of my own passage. I checked every intersection, every dead end, yet, no matter how hard—or where—I looked, there was nothing to indicate Jon or his dead wife and dog had passed through.

Instead of turning back, however, I kept going. The maze had to spill out somewhere, didn't it? Every step took me farther away from the entrance and the safety of the crowd. The hair on my arms was standing on end, and I was clenching my teeth against a shock I wasn't sure would come.

More than once, I thought I saw eyes peering at me through the corn, or a light breeze would cause the stalks to sway and rustle, giving the impression of movement. I desperately regretted not dragging one of my kids along. Or perhaps Manny, though he'd tease me relentlessly for my nervousness. Anyone would do, really, just so long as I wasn't alone in a place my hindbrain kept warning me was haunted.

It did make me wonder if there was more to Annie's death than merely a broken heart. Ghosts didn't manifest if the person—or, apparently, animal—died peacefully. Or did they? I only had stories and movies to go on here.

I took a step, and I was no longer surrounded by corn. The maze spilled out into a section of Jon's farm not being used for the Howl-O-Ween event. A few barns were scattered across a field, and fence blocked off most of them. A roped off path led back around toward the front of the maze, and I imagined when it was open, someone would be back here to greet those who completed the journey.

But, for now, I was alone.

I tugged my phone from my back pocket, happy that I'd remembered to take it from the cup holder of my van where I always left it, and checked my bars. Two. It should be enough. I did a quick Google of both Jon and Annie's names, but came up with little more than what Courtney had already told me, and a short article mentioning Annie's death. Apparently, Jon had a brother who'd died when he was just a kid, and Annie had a sister named Lana who lived out of state. That wasn't much to go on.

"I'm being stupid," I muttered, shoving my phone back into my pocket. Jon was playing a prank; he had to be.

I had just started to wind my way back around to the front of the corn maze when I saw a glow coming from the equipment barn.

The glow was faint. My heart hitched as it moved, and a shape crossed from one end of the open doorway to the other.

A shape in a green dress.

My brain screamed at me to run, to flee back through the maze, but my feet were frozen to the spot. The glow persisted a good ten, twenty seconds, and then winked out.

I should get Detective Cavanaugh.

But if I did that, I *knew* I'd drag him all the way out here only to find nothing but an empty barn full of tractors and sharp objects. You know, the sort of stuff you'd find in a horror movie.

I took a step, but it wasn't back toward the maze, nor was it on the path back around front.

Despite my trepidation, I was headed for the barn.

With every step, the night got that much darker. I pulled my phone back out of my pocket and flipped on the flashlight app, using it to light my way. There wasn't much to see now that the glow was gone. No more shapes passed across the doorway, no sounds drew my attention. I felt alone out there, and the thought wasn't as reassuring as it should have been.

"Hello?" I called as I neared the barn. And then, because I couldn't help myself, "Annie?"

I didn't expect an answer, figuring that whatever I'd seen was likely long gone. So, when someone stepped out of the barn, I couldn't stop the scream that ripped from my throat like a live thing. I stumbled back and lost my grip on my phone. It fell to the ground and flipped so that the flashlight was pointing down, casting the area in gloom.

The woman was mostly as I remembered her from the corn maze, though she was diminished, as if she'd lost a foot of height, and about ten pounds around the hips. She was still pale, red-headed, and was wearing the same green dress I'd seen her in earlier. And she still scared the life out of me.

"Who are you?" I asked, too terrified to pick up my phone again. The woman wasn't glowing, meaning I could only see her by moonlight. Did ghosts glow? I mean, she *was* glowing when I'd seen her in the barn, so why wasn't she now? "What did you do with Jon?"

"You shouldn't have come here."

I jumped at the sound of the woman's voice. There was no spectral quality to it, no airy gasp of words. She sounded, well, human.

"Who are you?" This time, my voice didn't tremble.

"I didn't bring her here. She came on her own."

I was confused at first, but then realized the woman in green wasn't addressing me.

She was looking *past* me.

I whirled around to find another woman wearing the same green dress. This was the one I'd seen in the maze, the one who'd pointed at me. At her side, the golden retriever stood, happily panting.

"What's going on?" I asked. "You're not Annie."

"No," the woman by the barn said, almost sadly. "I wish you wouldn't have seen this. It wasn't supposed to happen this way."

"Where's Jon?" Quite suddenly, I was positive I didn't want to know. These Annie's weren't ghosts, nor was the Goldie in front of me. But Jon Luckett? I didn't think he was so lucky.

"We don't have to," the woman with the dog said. "She doesn't know anything."

"She saw us. We do."

The woman by the barn tossed something aside. It took me a moment to realize it was her phone. It was likely the source of the glow I'd seen.

But none of that mattered anymore. In place of her phone, she was now holding a knife.

Protests flew into my head, but I didn't bother uttering them. What good would saying, "You can't do this," or, "I won't tell anyone" do? Those phrases didn't even work in movies.

The woman with the knife took a step toward me. There was nowhere for me to go. And even if I did run, how far would I make it before one of them caught me? Or the dog? I was, for all intents and purposes, surrounded.

Still, I took a step back, toward the golden retriever and the woman there. As I did, the dog growled low in its throat.

"Get her under control, Cam." Moonlight glinted off the knife as the woman took another step my way.

The growl grew deeper, more sinister. I was afraid to so much as twitch, lest the golden retriever leap at me.

"Why?" I asked instead. "Why do this?"

"Jon killed her." The knife-wielder paused her advance to answer. "He had to pay for what he did to Annie."

"We just wanted to scare him." This from behind me. "We didn't mean for him to die, not really."

"He didn't just keel over on his own," I said. "You must have done something to him."

"He deserved what he got." Another step my way. "He killed Annie. Murdered her. He used Goldie as an excuse, and no one bothered to look too closely, but I know what happened."

"You could have taken your concerns to the cops." I shuffled back a step but stopped when the dog growled again.

"I tried. My sister…" The woman with the knife took a deep, trembling breath. "It doesn't matter. Jon got what he deserved. He refused to admit it, but I *know*. I won't allow my life to be ruined because you saw me here tonight."

This time, when she took a step toward me, she raised her arm, knife in hand and poised to strike.

The growl that followed caused me to cry out, thinking I was going to go down under both the knife, and the weight of an angry canine.

Instead, a golden streak shot past me, toward the woman intent on killing me—Annie's sister, Lana. She screamed as the dog latched onto her arm, and together, they went down.

I spun around, thinking the other false Annie would be coming at me, but she was just standing there, hand to her mouth, eyes wide.

So, instead, I went for my phone.

"Call her off!" Lana screamed. Her knife was on the ground at her side, and the golden retriever's mouth was latched around her forearm, but even in the dark, I could tell she wasn't biting hard enough to draw blood. "Cam! Make her stop!"

"I...I can't." I could hear tears in Cam's voice. "And I don't think I should. I don't want anyone else to die because of us."

Neither did I. I hit a button and brought the phone to my ear, keeping a close eye on both of the women and the dog. "Manny?" I asked, relieved when he answered on the first ring. "Find Detective Cavanaugh. There's been a murder..."

Jon Luckett had thought he'd seen a ghost. Two of them, in fact. He'd followed what he believed to be his dead wife, as well as her beloved golden retriever, into the corn maze, and there, he'd met his end.

I got the story from Detective Cavanaugh later. Apparently, Annie's sister, Lana, had recruited her best friend, Cam, to help prove Jon had murdered Annie. They bought a dog that looked like Annie's old dog, and then they dressed up in her favorite dress, before they headed for the Howl-O-Ween event to enact the plan.

The whole incident was on Lana's phone. She'd set it to record what she'd hoped would be a confession, but instead, it caught her growing anger at Jon's denials, as well as her eventual breakdown, and subsequent act of murder.

It was hard to say what happened then. Both Lana and Cam had refused to talk about it, so all Cavanaugh had was the recording. All we know for sure was that Lana's anger caused her to attack Jon, and choke him to death, all while Cam begged her to stop.

I kind of felt bad for Cam, since she was only at the party to help create the illusion of a ghost, not to participate in a murder. Her presence allowed "Annie" to disappear around one corner, and then appear somewhere else.

Jon *had* fallen for it, but he never did admit to killing his wife. Did that mean he was innocent of the crime? I'm not sure anyone will ever know for sure.

And then there was the golden retriever.

Lana and Cam might have gotten away with the murder if it had been just the two of them. Unfortunately for the women, the golden retriever named, not surprisingly, Goldie, had gone for help the moment she realized Jon was injured.

And I was the lucky one to spot her.

"You're a good girl," I told Goldie from the front seat of my van. She'd heard it at least a hundred times since I'd taken possession of her after Halloween night. She'd likely hear it a hundred more over the coming months, and hopefully, years.

Normally, I would have had someone else with me as I dropped Goldie off, but I wanted to do this one alone. She'd saved my life, and if Jon hadn't had the life strangled out of him, if Lana would have let up, even just a little, she likely could have done the same for him. It was what she was trained to do; to be a rescue dog. It was something neither Lana nor Cam knew when they'd bought her.

I pulled into the driveway and got out with a mixture of sadness warring with joy. If I thought I could handle keeping a dog and a special needs cat, along with the constant stream of foster pets I took in, I might have kept her.

But for as much as I appreciated Goldie and wanted to keep her as my own, there was someone else who needed her more.

The front door opened just as I helped Goldie from the back of the van. The moment Lisa Edmonds saw her new pet, she dropped to her knees, eyes brimming with tears.

Goldie didn't hesitate. She knew why she was there.

Carefully, but with a wagging tail, she went to Lisa and allowed the older woman to gather her into her arms. As Lisa wept, Goldie licked away her tears, causing Lisa to laugh the first heartfelt laugh she'd probably had since her husband and beloved dog had passed.

I slipped quietly away, not wanting to interfere in the moment. Seeing the joy in Lisa's eyes was thanks enough, and I knew right then and there I'd done the right thing. Lisa had been saved from the sadness that had threatened to overwhelm her.

But the credit wasn't really mine.

It was what Goldie was trained to do.

Author Bio

Alex Erickson is the author of both the Bookstore Café and the Furever Pets mysteries. As E.S. Moore, he's written the Kat Redding urban fantasy series, which is currently out of print, but will hopefully rise again.

When not writing, he can be found gaming, listening to loud obnoxious music, and, well, that's about it. He lives in Ohio with his wife and son. And while he doesn't have a dog to save the day, his three cats would happily watch if something were to happen to him before going back to their naps.

You can find him online at: alexericksonbooks.com

Dog

By D.J. Butler

Which daughter is sick?" Billy Redbird asked.

"The older one. Sunitha." John Abbott patted the pocket of his raincoat and heard the tablets rattle. "I'm bringing home some medicine Ruth wants to try. I don't know. The other pills didn't work."

They stood in thin rain on a narrow street in the Bowery. In just a few more paces, they'd reach the intersection where they'd split and go their separate ways. They were coming from the evening lecture of their Zaphon professor, Tzaark. The wolf-lizard had blinked and yawned his way through a facilitated discussion about not ignoring the spiritual dimensions of any non-human you encountered.

The lecture series on first contact scenarios was a bit of an outlier in John's accounting degree, but he was taking it because he was applying for a job with the Sarovar Company, to leave the Sol system and work as an accountant and become one of the fabulously rich Sarovar Traders. Billy was a few years younger than John and was getting his undergraduate degree in biomechanical engineering.

"The tea?" Billy asked.

"She couldn't get it down."

Billy cocked his head to one side. "You hear that?"

John heard the soft battery of the rain. He heard the hissing wheels of a passing rickshaw and the hum of a hovercar taxi. Halfway down the block, shouting from a third-story window, and from the corner sang the beckoning whistles of the evening's first streetwalkers, prowling around the green canvas eaves of a Brazilian bodega.

"Sounds like New York to me," John said. "Sounds like I want to get inside and see my daughters."

"You don't hear a dog?" Billy asked.

John listened again, and then he did hear an animal sound. "How can you tell it's a dog? I just hear whimpering."

"Yeah, but it's a dog's whimpering." Billy followed his ear to a pile of junk leaning against a cracked brownstone. A chair missing one leg leaned against a table that only *had* one; cardboard boxes and plastic sacks lay heaped about. Billy squatted and looked beneath. "Here, girl."

John crouched, balancing by resting his knuckles on the wet concrete slab of the sidewalk. He could see a dog, sitting on its haunches. In the darkness, he couldn't make out much. The dog looked like a Labrador puppy but squashed. Some kind of mutt, probably. "Is he bleeding?"

"She," Billy said. "Yeah, I think she has a cut across her belly and her hind leg."

"People can be really rotten," John muttered.

"Might have been another animal," Billy said. "Or an accident. Plenty of sharp things to impale yourself on in Manhattan without someone doing it to you on purpose."

"If she cut herself on barbed wire, it still means some idiot left barbed wire where a dog could get to it."

"Here, girl," Billy said.

The dog whimpered.

"Doesn't your name mean 'Dog'?" John asked. "I mean, not Billy. The other one. She should come right to you."

"My other name is Waagosh. It means 'Fox.' But you make a good point."

Billy pulled a pouch from under his shirt, where it hung on a leather thong. Holding it close to his chest to shelter it from the rain, he shook a little of the contents into one hand, and then replaced the bag.

"That smells like tobacco," John said.

"It is tobacco," Billy told him. "It's very good tobacco, cured in a traditional fashion, with no added chemicals." Then Billy sang words John didn't recognize. Presumably they were in his native tongue, Ojibwe, and they sounded long and hypnotic. Then Billy reached forward and placed the tobacco on the ground in front of the dog.

"I'm trying really hard not to crack a joke here," John said, "because I feel like something's going on that I want to respect."

"Maybe you were going to say the dog doesn't smoke." Billy turned his head and grinned. "Jokes are okay. The spirits aren't offended by jokes."

"So…tobacco?"

"I'm giving a gift."

"To the dog?"

"To the dog's spirit. Animoosh. To honor the dog and show her we have good intentions. Come to us, Animoosh. Good girl."

Abruptly, the puppy bolted forward. She ran right past Billy's tobacco, and past Billy himself, and threw herself on John. Caught off-guard, John managed to grab the dog in both arms and then collapsed backward, sitting in a cold pulled on the sidewalk. A rickshaw sloshed a wave at him as it passed, missing, but spattering a ricochet of fine droplets against his cheek.

He dreamed of darkness. He couldn't see walls around him, but he felt them, and he sensed that they were closing in. He was running, and the ground beneath his feet was rocky and irregular, so he stumbled.

He skinned his face against an unseen rock wall.

In the darkness, he heard rhyming, drone-like chanting in an unknown tongue.

"Sunitha!" he cried. "Sunitha, where are you?"

"Dad!" Her voice was distant. It echoed and receded even as he heard it.

"Sunitha!"

She didn't respond. In his heart, he knew that she was gone. Worse than that, he knew that she had died alone.

John woke up in a cold sweat. His body stank of sour fear, and cold gray morning light seared his eyeballs.

"John!" Ruth stood over him, shaking him by the arm. "John, wake up!"

John took a shuddering breath and tightened his shoulders before releasing them, trying to drive out the fear. "I'm awake," he said.

"Mom," he heard Sunitha say. "Dad."

John turned, and he and his wife together looked at their oldest daughter. Ellie squirmed in the top bunk and lowered her head over the edge of the mattress to be part of the conversation, too.

Sunitha sat up, leaning against the wall. Her color was back to normal, she wasn't sweating, her eyes were open. She even smiled.

And Dog lay sprawled out across her lap, head on her hip. Sunitha scratched the dog behind her ears and around her shoulders. A long mohawk of golden fur stood up along the beast's spine.

"Dad." Sunitha wore a slightly dazed smile. "She says she knows you."

"Yes," John said. "Yeah, I brought her home last night."

"Her name is Animoosh," Sunitha said. "She doesn't like to smoke."

John fought to keep his jaw from falling open.

Ruth laughed, a slight hysterical note to her voice. "No dog likes to smoke."

"We're keeping her, right?" Sunitha asked.

"We're keeping A-Ni-Mooth," Ellie said, repeating the name in big, loud chunks.

"We don't really have the room," John said. "My plan—"

"We're keeping her," Ruth said. "Of course, we're keeping her."

Author Bio

D. J. Butler is an American speculative fiction author. His epic flintlock fantasy novel *Witchy Kingdom* won the Dragon Award for Best Alternate History Novel in 2020. *Witchy Winter* won the 2018 AML Award for Best Novel and the 2018 Whitney Award for Best Speculative Fiction, and *Witchy Eye* was a preliminary nominee for the Gemmell Morningstar Award.

For more information, go to: davidjohnbutler.com

Safe Place

A Talons and Tethers short story

By Eliza Eveland

I crack open an eye at the sound of my boy shuffling about. It's early enough that the room is still dark, but he doesn't light a candle. There was a time when he would have been afraid to walk around the palace in the dark, but those years have long since passed. Now, my bones are weary and my joints ache in the morning chill, but I lift my head and thump my tail against the floor just the same.

In the deep shadow, I hardly recognize him. He's gotten taller, leaner, stronger. We don't play ball as much as we used to either. It's just as well. I don't have the energy I used to, and my eyes aren't as good as they once were. I know his smell, though, and even if it's changed a little through the years, it makes me happy. He smells different from the humans around the palace, like the first autumn frost on leaves and wet earth, but all elves smell a little more like the wild world than the stone buildings humans make.

He pulls on his heavy socks, and his boots, but it's not until he reaches for his bow that I know why he's gotten up so early. "Come on, Brick," he whispers as he passes me on the way to the door.

That's what he calls me, and I call him Boy, even if he is more a man now. He'll always be my boy.

My joints creak and pop as I rise, but I shake out the stiffness and follow him. We're going hunting for rabbits, or maybe pheasants. I hope it's rabbits. They're more fun to chase.

The big hallway is empty except for a few men in iron suits. They help me guard my boy, and sometimes they have treats. I nose the one at the door, checking his pockets just in case he has one.

"Mornin', Prince Faelyn," says Orin, patting my head. "You're up early."

My boy sighs. "I was hoping to slip out before you got here. Can you just pretend you didn't see me?"

"King Crow will kick my ass all the way to Greymark if I let you go out hunting alone." Orin digs into his pocket and brings out a dry cracker. Not my favorite treat, but

I'm starving, so I take it.

"I won't be alone. I have Brick."

I wag my tail and puff out my chest. *See, Orin? I can guard him, too.*

Orin sighs and crosses his arms. "I know he's a war hound, but he's not a very good one, Faelyn. He's getting up there in years, you know."

Rude! I try to hack up the cracker on his boot, but it's stuck in my throat.

"Please, Orin? Cover for me just this once. It's not like I can't handle myself, and I'm just going out to Mercia's estate. I'll be within sight of the estate walls the whole time, and I'll be back before lunch. I swear it!"

Orin huffs out a breath, considering us for a moment. He looks down at me. I wag my tail and try to look cute. "Don't make me regret this," he says and turns his back, pretending to examine the ceiling. "My, what lovely masonry. I've never noticed."

While Orin is busy examining the rocks, we sneak away.

There are more guards at the mouth of the castle, but we don't go that way, instead slipping out a window in the library. There's a little ledge there that gets slippery when it rains, but it's been dry lately. My boy leaps down to the ground and turns around, holding out his arms for me to jump. I go without hesitation, and he catches me with a grunt.

"Are you getting fatter or am I just getting weaker?" he says as he puts me down.

What is it with people being rude to me today? It's called muscle, Boy. All hounds have it. You should try getting some.

He snorts and replies, *You keep telling yourself that, old hound.*

I don't talk mind-to-mind with my Boy as much as I used to. He wants to keep his powers secret, though I don't understand why. There are dozens of mages in Brucia, even a special school for him to go and learn more about his magic, but my boy doesn't like schools. He doesn't like people telling him what to do, or when to do it, or why. Once upon a time, before I knew him, he was raised as a slave in an elven war camp, and he says there was enough ordering about in that job for a lifetime.

Carefully, quietly, we make our way through the little courtyard on the side of the palace, and he hoists me over the squat stone wall. Jumping down makes my joints ache, but I shake it off. Once we're free of the palace walls, he pulls up his hood and we hurry on our way. Human guards, with their inferior sense of smell, only have their eyes to rely on, and they will only see a man and his dog out for a morning stroll. We go to the stables where I catch a fly and eat it while my boy is saddling Toffee, his favorite horse.

Morning, hound, says Cinnamon, the old mare. *Thanks for getting that fly for me. I've been swatting him all night.*

I grin and let my tongue loll out of the side of my mouth proudly. *Ah, if it isn't the war hound. I wondered what that stench was.*

I know that voice. With a snort, I lift my attention to the rafters where a black and white tomcat carefully crawls along one of the high boards. *'Lo, Tom! How did you get out this time?*

Tom Whiteshanks is an inside cat, but he's not very good at it. He gets out a few times a week, usually to come chase mice or pigeons. I sometimes help.

He grins down at me. *I got into the mage's workshop. He always keeps a window open in there when he's brewing potions.*

Your boy is going to miss you.

Tom sighs and rolls his eyes. *For the last time, hound. Isaac is not my boy. He is my servant.*

I quirk my head and perk my ears in doubt. *Are you sure he sees it that way?*

He feeds me, collects my droppings, and showers me with love and affection. What else would he be?

Tom gives a lazy stretch, tail twitching. *What's yours up to?*

We're going hunting! I think. My tail thumps loudly against the floor, sweeping errant bits of hay back and forth. *You should come with us! It'll be fun! There are rabbits and birds and all kinds of weird things to sniff and pee on!*

He pauses licking his paw to look down at me, whiskers twitching. *Good gods, hound. Have you no decency at all?*

Nope! I pant. *I don't even know what that is.*

Clearly, Tom replies dryly and goes back to licking his paw.

So, does that mean you'll come with?

Not today, hound. Today is the day I finally catch that white mouse that's eluded me in here, and then I plan to nap in a sunbeam.

Tom has been trying to catch that white mouse for weeks. I'm pretty sure he's actually caught it twice and just let it go so he'll have an excuse to visit the horses every day.

Faelyn has Toffee saddled and leads him out of the stall, signaling we're ready to go.

Enjoy your sunbeam, I say to Tom as my boy mounts the horse.

Enjoy your pissing on things, Tom replies as I trot out of the stables behind my boy.

I follow Toffee and my boy along in silence, enjoying our walk through the brisk morning. Most of Brucia is still asleep, but there are people beginning to wake in the deepest parts of the city.

The faint glow of lanterns bleeds through windows into the street at the bakery and my stomach growls at the smell of fresh dough. We pass the butcher who sometimes has treats for me, but his window is still dark. No treats this morning.

At the gate, the guards stand around like sleepyheads and don't even notice the elf prince and his war hound as we trot on, passing under the stone arch and across the drawbridge into the wide, wild world.

There, nothing sleeps. Crickets sing in the tall grass off the dirt path. Field mice scurry around looking for somewhere to hide. I track a beetle for a little while, nose to the ground, until it sprouts wings and flutters away. Then I have to run to catch up with my boy.

When we reach the Y in the road, he takes Toffee to the right. I pause, the fur prickling at my neck. *Mercia's estate is the other way.*

"We're not going to Mercia's estate," Faelyn says.

My stomach complains. It would've been breakfast time when we arrived, and Mercia and Aryn have no shortage of children willing to drop me scraps.

Where, then? I ask, trotting up behind Toffee carefully. I don't want to get kicked.

"Don't worry, Brick. I've got some snacks for you in my bag."

As hungry as I am, snacks aren't my biggest concern. I can guard my boy just fine against most things, but what if something goes wrong? I'm not as young and spry as I used to be. No one will know where to look for us if something happens.

I'm on high alert as we veer off the road and into the high grass. It's too early and too cold for snakes to be about, but the world seems to have gone silent, as if the crickets and mice can sense a predator I can't see or smell.

The twinge of color in the sky deepens, brightening to a tapestry of pink and orange. The shadows become shallower and soon the grassland stretched out before us is bathed in the gold light of dawn.

I bound through the tall weeds, knocking dew from the plants, and kicking free fluffy white balls of flower seeds. Some of the seeds stick to my fur, but the rest dance in the sky before flying off. A yellow butterfly lands on my nose and I try to catch it, but it flaps away.

A little further on, I catch the scent of two rabbits and start to lead my boy to their hiding place. When he doesn't follow, I spin around and bark excitedly, but he keeps riding, disinterested in my find. In fact, he seems disinterested in everything around him.

It's like he's got somewhere else to be, but that's not how hunting

A wave of chuckles floats around the circle.

"You move one muscle, and you'll die where you stand!" Faelyn shouts, bow trembling. "I'll kill you where you!"

"You and what army, boy?" The man in black gestures around with the knife. "You're all alone out here. No guard. No one to protect you."

"I'm not alone! There's a whole unit of guards in the forest there. They'll be back any moment."

I quirk my head to the side. That's a lie. No guards came with us. Faelyn made sure of that. The only thing in the forest is…me? Surely, he doesn't mean me, though. I'm only one old war hound.

The man in black and his friends look around nervously. If only it were true. A whole unit of guards might scare them away, and my boy would be safe.

And then I get an idea. If my boy can lie to protect someone he loves, maybe I can do the same thing.

I slide back out of sight, puff out my chest and turn my snout to the sky before letting out an undulating howl.

"What in the nine hells is that?"

"It's nothing. Keep your wits about you."

"Sounds like a demon!"

I snarl and scratch at the dirt, before running through some thick bushes to make them rustle. There's a small tree that I put my paws up on to shake it. The trunk snaps under my weight and the branches go down.

"Have you ever met my father?" Faelyn says, his tone warning. "He's the biggest elf you've ever seen. Seven feet tall with eyes like burning coals."

I find another tree and run up it, making it bow and bend. The wood snaps and cracks like thunder.

"At the Battle of Brucia, he killed a hundred men, three at once with a single swing of his sword," Faelyn continues.

"That's crap. He's just another elf," spits the man in black.

"He's king of the elves," replies a nervous man.

I peek through the leaves and see the man in black threatening one of his own with the knife now.

"And what does the king of elves have?" says the man in black. "Gold, stupid, and lots of it. He'll pay through the nose to get his boy back. You want to be rich? Or a coward?"

I claw my way through some more brush, making it shake loudly. Several pheasants flee and take to the air. I howl again, this time lower and louder.

"That's no demon, Viktor. That's a Molossus war hound!'"

"Shut up!" roars the man in black. "It's one stupid dog! Are you really going to piss yourself over one mutt?"

"Wherever the hound is, his master's sure to be close by," Faelyn warns, stepping closer. "My father commands a whole kennel of hungry hounds. You know they eat your face first. And then your balls. They like the soft bits best of all."

I rake at the tree bark with my claws, snarling and growling, trying to sound as mean as I can. Then, with heavy steps, I stomp to the edge of the forest, sitting in a deep shadow where my black fur blends in and only my eyes peer out. I flash my teeth and bark menacingly, letting the drool go everywhere.

"Mother have mercy!" shouts one of the bandits. He drops his weapons and bolts, climbing onto his horse and galloping away.

Once one breaks and runs, most of the others follow. They mount their horses. I chase after some, snapping at horse hooves, barking and snarling all the way. As soon as they see me, even more run, and soon it's just the man in black holding his knife to Will's throat.

Will rears back, smashing his skull against the man's nose and throwing an elbow into his ribs. On instinct, the man in black grabs for his bloody nose, and lets Will wriggle away. I pounce the man in black and knock him to the ground. With two big paws on his chest, I pin him to the ground and lean down to growl. My boy leans in, an arrow pointed at the man in black's nose.

His hands shoot up to cover his face. "All right! All right, already! I get it! You win. I lose. Now call off your hound!"

"Swear you'll leave us alone!" My boy shouts.

When the man doesn't reply right away, I move a paw to his throat. He makes a very satisfying choking sound before I let up.

"I swear to leave you be and let you go," replies the man in black. "Just get this monstrous beast off my bloody chest!"

You should shoot him, I say to my boy.

Does he smell like a lie? Faelyn asks.

I sniff the air before huffing out a disappointed breath. *No.*

Faelyn hesitates only a moment, just long enough that I think he might let the arrow go. Instead, he takes a half step back. "Release him, Brick."

With a frustrated snort, I back off and let the man rise.

He dusts off his black shirt. "You might have gotten lucky today, prince, but the Brotherhood has long memories and casts a long shadow. This isn't—"

I interrupt his pointless speech by lifting a leg to pee on his foot. He shrieks like an offended eagle and scrambles away.

"You're dead, you hear me?" he shouts, climbing onto his horse. "You and everyone you love." He rides a circle around us shouting, "Trinta never forgets!" before galloping off.

Faelyn drops his bow and throws his arms around Will, squeezing him tight. "I thought I lost you."

"You'll have to try harder than that," Will quips and squeezes back.

They part and Faelyn drops to one knee, arms outstretched. "Come here, boy!"

He doesn't have to tell me twice. Panting, I bound across the space between us and throw myself into his arms hard enough to knock him over. Laughing, he falls to his back, and I tackle him, licking his face. For a minute, I feel like a puppy again as we wrestle, and he's back to being my boy. It doesn't matter that we've gotten older, and things have changed. We're still best friends, and nothing—not even time or whatever he has going on with Will—can change that.

My boy finally manages to get free, and I crash to the grass laying on my back, my tongue lolling out of the side of my mouth.

He lies panting in the grass next to me a moment before he says, "I'm sorry about earlier, Brick. You were just trying to play."

It's all right, my boy. I turn my head and look at him. *We're still best friends?*

He smiles and pats my head. "Best friends forever."

Will comes over and pulls Faelyn to his feet. With a serious voice he says, "We can't keep doing this, Faelyn. You have to tell your father about us."

The joy on my boy's face lessens, but he's not sad. The air smells more like worry.

"I know."

"He'll understand," Will promises.

"But what if he doesn't? It's different when you're a prince." My boy picks up his discarded bow and picks some stray blades of grass from it. "And what about the Runecleavers? I'm promised to one of them."

"It will all work out, Faelyn." Will wraps his arm around Faelyn's. "Do you want me to come with you?"

Faelyn sighs and looks down at me. I wag my tail, hoping it's the reassuring gesture he's looking for.

"No," says my boy after a minute. "It might be easier for him if it's just me. And if things don't go well, I can always come find you."

Will nods. They hug and kiss goodbye and then my boy gets back on Toffee, and we head for home.

Later that night, I lay on the rug in my boy's room while he has a long, quiet talk with his father in the next room.

The king hugs my boy after, squeezing him tight. "If he makes you happy, then he's welcome here, Faelyn. That's all that matters to me. Will's a good man. I'm glad you found someone worthy of your heart."

There are more words, more hugs, and some tears, but when the elf king gets up to leave, my boy is smiling again, and it's good to see. I'd trade all the ducks and fish and rabbits in the world to see him smiling.

I lift my head and wag my tail as the king comes past.

He stops to give me a few pets. "Take care of him, boy. He still needs you."

I do my best! I say, but it comes out to him as a quiet, "Ruff!"

When the king is gone, and the lights are out, my boy pats an empty space on the bed and invites me up. It's been a long time since he let me sleep in the bed with him, but we cuddle up that night, and when he's fast asleep, I crawl down to my spot at the end of the bed to keep watch. I may be old, and my joints may be sore. I can't run and play like I used to, but I can still sleep with one eye open, and protect my best friend while he sleeps.

I make a vow that night. Wherever I am, that will be his safe place. Whether it's on the road, at the lake, or around the castle, I am my boy's safe place, and that will always be true.

Author Bio

Eliza Eveland (she/they) is a coffee addict living in woods of West Virginia where fairies are real, and magic grows on trees like vines.

Eliza writes real, relatable characters in fantastic worlds that just happen to have wings or pointed ears and a little bit of magic.

Author website: elizaeveland.com

Facebook Group: facebook.com/groups/616062436341571

TikTok: tiktok.com/@elizaeveland

George and KitKit Save the Witches

By Faith Hunter

Author's Note: Based on "My Dark Knight", a short story set in the Jane Yellowrock world, but from the critters' point of view.

KitKit watched human-witch-kitten called Angie standing in open doorway. Angie-kit waved her hand in front of pride alphas, called the Mama and the Daddy. She pushed power-magic into the room where the Mama and the Daddy witches slept. Angie had much magic-power. It was in many shades of greens and yellows to KitKit's eyes. Power was to make the Mama and the Daddy pride alphas sleep.

This was, "Not allowed," according to the Mama. This was "Oh, Angie. I'm ashamed of you," *bad*. This was the smell of an alpha swatting a kitten. Though the alphas were lax in using their claws, to KitKit's way of thinking.

KitKit was the Mama's familiar though the Mama did not understand or accept this. And because there were four witches in the den, and only one KitKit, she had to leave her alpha-witch and follow the little witch.

Angie was not silent like KitKit. Humans, even witch-humans, were noisy no matter how silent they tried to be.

KitKit followed, cat-silent. She sent ahead warning to George the Stupid-Dog. *Angie is coming. Angie did bad thing.*

KitKit had allowed George the Stupid-Dog to communicate head-to-head in the cat way. Cat familiars were not allowed to share with stupid dogs, but it had to be done to protect so many foolish human-witches.

Angie inched forward, around the reclining sofa, past the unlit Christmas tree and the wrapped boxes that KitKit had not been allowed to tear open and play with. KitKit smelled and saw George the Stupid-Dog and the smaller-male-human-witch-kit called EJ on the sofa. Both were awake in the dark.

"Hey, Sissy," EJ said.

Angie made a little squeaking sound and stopped. KitKit laughed in cat laughter by twitching her tail tip. It was funny.

A bright light hit Angie's face.

"Turn that off," Angie hissed like a cat. The light went out.

KitKit moved to a corner and watched.

Angie used her magic to see in the dark and spotted EJ under a blanket in the Daddy's spot. EJ giggled. Angie frowned.

"You're a son of a witch on a switch." Which was the Mama's swear words, in the same way a hiss was KitKit's swear words.

EJ giggled.

"How did you know I was up?" Angie demanded.

"You's magic was singin'"

"Magic doesn't sing. It sparkles."

"Sings. And the magic from the woods is singin' louder. It hu'ts my ea'us."

KitKit raced to the window. There had been magic on the hill behind the house all day, different magic from the residue of death magics that had killed everything alive there. This was fresh magic. This was *danger*. And the alphas would not listen no matter how KitKit yowled and talked and stared at the magic on the hill through the windows. KitKit not could make them understand, even when she scratched the Daddy.

For some reason, they couldn't see it and they had refused to listen to their own kits, too, when the little-ones said magic was on the hill.

The Mama and the Daddy said nothing was there. As KitKit watched, it grew brighter. It was *big magic*.

"It sings like a wolfie and a bird and the bells in the church," EJ said.

George the Stupid-Dog joined KitKit and the human-witch-kits at the window. George growled, a deep menacing vibration. KitKit hissed and arched her back.

George the Stupid-Dog put his head against KitKit. *I will watch the kits. You wake the biggers.*

Biggers is what George the Stupid-Dog called the Mama and the Daddy alphas.

"A wolf?" Angie asked.

"Yup. And a bird and bells."

Angie said, "It shines the color of Uncle RickyBo. That might make it a were-animal."

It was not a were-creature, or even any kind of normal animal. KitKit and George knew this. KitKit raced to wake the Mama and the Daddy.

GEORGE

Dog eyes were not as good in the dark as cat eyes, but George's nose

kill and eat the bad magic behind the house. And KitKit would stop the Mama Bigger's death magics. It was going to be fine.

"Oh dear," Cia said. "I had hoped Shaddock was mistaken about an emergency."

George whuffed. His Lincoln Shaddock had sent them. This was better and better.

Puffing, the children reached the *hedge.* "Hey, Ant Liz and Ant Cia," EJ said, waving.

George did not know why the humans were called ants, except that Lincoln Shaddock called them so, and Angie liked Lincoln. George liked Lincoln Shaddock too. He was the best vampire. George wished that Lincoln Shaddock was here with the Edmond vampire.

Angie straightened her nightclothes and wrapped EJ and George in the blanket they had dragged with them, petting them both equally. George liked being petted. He shared some of his slobber with her hand.

Liz said, "EJ. Angie, is there some reason you called a vampire instead of family?"

Angie scowled. Edmond smiled. Edmond showed a bit of fang. George thought KitKit would like Edmond.

"The attack isn't witch magic," Angie said, her smell defiant and stubborn. "It's a were-creature or something else, and I didn't want you to get bit by a werewolf or something."

"Big teefs to eat you with!" EJ said.

"Ah," Liz said, still composed. "Next time, please call us too."

"Yes, ma'am," Angie said, lying, by her scent. *Why did Angie need to lie?*

The second car pulled up and Angie transferred her antagonism to the new vehicle.

"*Who's that?*"

A dark-haired witch emerged from the car.

"Melodie?" Cia called out.

George caught her scent and growled deep in his throat.

Danger . . .

Angie said, "Mama said not to talk to people I don't know."

"Angie," Liz said sharply. "Manners."

But Angie's anger smell grew worse as the third witch approached. And George nudged her hand, adding his low growl to her worry. This witch was bad, bad.

Melodie said, "I'm sure the child has been through a lot tonight. I'm Melodie Joy Custer-Luckett from the Custer witch clan, Angie. I'm renting a room from your aunt Elizabeth while I finish a course at the university."

The witch lied. The stink of it filled the air. George bumped Angie but the young witch only petted his head.

The danger witch added, "I was studying late and saw you rush off, Liz. I'm a paramedic. I thought I should follow."

Angie's smell said she didn't like the Melodie witch. He nudged her again. *You are right. Do not trust this one.*

Angie said, lying also, "It's a pleasure to meet you, Miz Melodie."

She elbowed her brother, and EJ pulled a slobbery finger out of his mouth to say, "Pweasure meet you." And stuck his finger back in his mouth.

Why did Angie lie? KitKit would know. George wished KitKit was here. Lying and secrets were cat things, not dog things.

"Edmund," Angie said, sounding very grown up, "Ant Liz, Ant Cia, Miz Melodie, we must break the ward and save my mama and my daddy. And KitKit."

"Breaking an Everhart ward will be difficult," Melodie said.

But she smelled of…*hunger.* Like a dog who wanted to steal a treat.

Liz and Cia nodded, but Angie's scent went smelly like lemons at Melodie's words.

Edmund had been listening and his scent was full of caution and a predator's alertness. George would not want to make Edmund mad.

"Sissy, I havta peepee," EJ whispered. "And I'm hungwy and cold."

"We'll be free soon," Angie said. She tucked the blanket tighter around them, to give EJ some heat.

George promptly pretended to fall asleep, drooling on EJ's leg. Bassett Hounds were wonderful droolers. He drooled and drooled, fooling all the witches and even the vampire.

The visitors discussed the "situation," as they called it, and looked at the pictures Angie had sent Edmund. Liz said, "Tell me what happened, Angie Baby, and very carefully, walk me through what you did to make such a strong ward."

"I messed up," Angie said. Angie described what had happened, emphasizing the colors of the magical working and EJ piping in with its sound—a drum beating slowly.

George drooled.

"You twined the magics together," Cia said. Her scent was worried. Like the smell of a squirrel when a hawk was near.

"Yes," Angie said. "It's what Mama and Daddy do to our magics when they bind 'em so we can't use 'em."

"And you can see the magics? The energies they use to bind you?" Melodie asked.

"It's why it's so easy to get out. But this is different. Mama and Daddy and KitKit are all frozen."

Liz asked, "Could she have triggered a temporal disengagement?"

"Or a temporal deactivation," Cia said.

Those big words sounded very, very bad.

Melodie said, "Temporal... You Everharts are an interesting bunch." Her scent was stronger. Full of hunger.

"I gotta peepee!" EJ said. "I gotta peepee noooow!"

"First thing, then," Liz said, "is to get my favorite nephew out of the protection ward so he can go potty."

"He's your only nephew," Angie said crossly, smelling of jealousy. "And I gotta use the bathroom too."

"Alrighty then," Cia said. George opened one eye to see Cia witch unwinding a ball of string and starting to trace a protective circle.

EJ muttered, "Hold it. Hold it. Hold it. Hold it. Sissy, I gotta go now!"

"You'll need three of us. Where do you want me?" Melodie asked Liz.

Smell of hunger, hunger, *hunger* rising. *Danger*, George thought at KitKit.

There was no answer. And then, slowly, KitKit thought back, *Betrayal. She. Wants. All. The. Tuna.*

KitKit loved tuna. She was telling George that the Melodie witch was trying to take everything.

Yes, he thought back.

Let. Me. See, KitKit thought, so slow.

He opened both eyes to see. Bassett Hounds did not have very good eyesight, so he breathed in to verify everything he saw.

"North is here," Liz said, walking to a different spot, "so each of you to the side in a triangle pattern." The witches sat and closed the circle, the powers flaring into place with a flash of light.

George had seen and smelled an Everhart witch circle open. But this one smelled different. Not right.

Very. Bad, KitKit agreed.

"Oh my..." Melodie said, staring all around. "I've never seen anything like this. Do you Everharts do this kind of"—her hand made little circles in the air—"working often?"

Hunger, hunger, hunger. She wanted it all.

"No. But there's always a first time," Liz said, smelling grim. "I've never seen one so tangled. Cia, Melodie, can you determine the first step?"

"The strand from the top of the *hedge*, perhaps?" Cia said. "Except we'd never get to it."

"No. But Angelina can reach her end. Angie," Melodie said. "Do you see the energy strand trailing from the *hedge*, one you twined into your smaller ward?"

"Yes," Angie said.

Melodie said, "Good girl. Reach up to where it touches the top of your portable circle and, gently, tweak it loose."

Angie smelled of worry. She knew the Melodie witch was lying. So did the Edmund vampire. But he frowned and nodded at Angie.

Angie reached up and tapped the top of her magics. George didn't watch her. He watched the Melodie witch and tried not to growl.

There were sparks and flickers of color over George's head.

Melodie's hunger smell continued to rise, and she kept glancing at Edmund. The vampire knew he was being watched, though he pretended not to. KitKit should be here.

She could keep all the lies straight.

"Question," Edmund said to Melodie. "If the small ward falls, won't the children be caught in the same temporal displacement as their parents?"

"Angie, stop!" Liz said.

George liked Edmund. He would mark the vampire's shoes and pants to show his approval first chance he got.

Angie's fingers stopped moving.

For an instant, Melodie's lips flattened. Her pores emitted the sour stink of frustration, on the night air. She lowered her head and schooled her expression to concern, but George was Bassett Hound. He could not miss the scent change.

Edmund said, "If Angie peels away the power she is drawing from the *hedge of thorns*, might that also destabilize the entire ward, resulting in a release of energy?"

Cia said, "We could have blown up the entire hillside."

"We'd have been fine under our own circle," Liz said, "but at the very least Ed would have been toast and the kids would have been stuck or killed."

"I gotta peepee! I gotta peepee now!"

"Elizabeth," Edmund said to Liz, "what would happen if the children simply pushed their small ward through the larger one?"

"We'd have... I don't know. Cia?"

"I gotta peepee!"

"I think...the smaller ward would peel away and the kids would be free?" Cia said.

"But—"

"Good. We're coming through," Angie said.

"No!" both twins shouted.

George pulled his short but powerful legs under him. Angie touched the edge of her protective shield against the outer ward.

I gotta peepee! I gotta peepee! I gotta peepee!" EJ's voice shrilled.

Angie shoved the small shield hard against the larger one. George helped. Angie smelled of effort and fear sweat again. The edge pressed through, and she and EJ and George followed. Her small ward did not explode. It was too strong. Stronger than the house ward.

Angie smelled proud but her ants smelled mad. "What?" she asked.

George growled very, very low. Dogs did not growl at family, but the ants smelled mean.

"You disobeyed us," Liz said.

"I been studying the wards and how the energies worked. I figured it would be okay."

"I gotta peepee!"

Angie's magics made a cracking noise and fell in sparks. EJ jumped upright, his feet tangling in the blanket; he nearly fell. Edmund caught EJ and carried him behind a tree.

"I get to peepee on the tree? Sissy, I get to peepee on a tree!"

Edmund stepped back around the tree looking amused. George followed the little boy. He had to peepee too. And check the mail. Other dogs had peed here. The smells were...amazing. He had not been outside the ward in... Not ever. There were so many wonderful smells. He smelled EJ's peepee and then peed himself in the same spot to show he owned EJ, and then he started smelling everything everywhere.

Angie said, "He is such a paaaaaain."

George smelled magic. Strong bad magic on the wind. And guns and gun powder.

He looked up. Barked. Raced to Angie. Barked again. No one listened to him.

Scratch. Bite. Kill, KitKit thought.

Melodie raised her hands. She shot at Edmund. With a gun.

Edmund said a *bad* word and dove back on top of EJ, pushing him to the ground.

George saw lights and smelled strange smells as Liz threw magics at Melodie.

Edmund popped beside George and Angie, moving fast, the way vampires did, so fast the air popped. Edmund picked them up and raced behind the tree where EJ was hunkered down.

As fast as his powerful legs could, George leaped on top of EJ's butt. Edmund smelled dangerous and George liked his blood smell. Edmund was a good predator. Maybe better than KitKit.

Edmund said, "Angelina. Stay. Behind. The tree." The smell of vampire magic rolled out over them, what the witches called vampire mesmerism. George should have barked and resisted, but he was suddenly so sleepy.

More gunshots rang out.

The vampire was gone with a small pop of sound.

George blinked his bad eyes. He was supposed to be doing something.

Angie petted George and EJ, who snuggled up against her, muttering sleepily about wanting a hamburger. Thankfully, the blanket was warm, and the smell of little-boy peepee and George pee was a happy smell.

Angie muttered something, broke the compulsion.

George whuffed in surprise. The Edmund vampire was a strong vampire, to put them all under his mesmerism. If KitKit was here, she would have known it was happening and she would have scratched the vampire with her claws. George was ashamed that he did not know the vampire was using his magic. Next time, he would know, and he would bite the vampire.

Angie duck-walked on short legs like a Bassett Hound around the tree to see better.

George walked around the tree to smell better. Sweat, anger, magic, desperation, and *hunger* were hot on the air.

The twins hit the Melodie witch with magic. They tackled her, restrained her, and left her. Melodie smelled unconscious. Everhart witches were excellent fighters. Even KitKit would approve. Snowflakes began to fall. George had never seen snow. It was beautiful!

Good. Witches. Happy. Freaking. Snow. But. We are. Dying, KitKit thought at him.

Liz asked, "Why would she shoot you?"

Edmund's scent changed. It was deadly. Predator ready to kill. He said, "Perhaps I was the greater threat. Take me down and then take down the less powerful witches."

Liz snorted like a Bassett Hound. It was a glorious sound. "Greater threat? I don't think so. We were prepared, you weren't. And what good would it do to take us down?"

"I assume that this particular witch is working with the humans attacking the ward," Edmund said. "There have been tales of black ops government groups and even of private armies kidnapping witches for personal use."

Liz secured the unconscious witch's ankles and said, "Fangheads too. Witches for the power, bloodsuckers for the blood."

George heard something with his beautiful ears. He whoofed softly.

Edmund whirled. "Movement cresting the hillside. The two back there may have backup."

"Melodie's gunfire alerted them," Liz said. "Damn."

"Keep the children safe," Edmund said. He was gone with a soft pop.

Liz made a fierce face and smelled of deadly anger. It matched Edmund's. "Give no quarter," she shouted.

Angie's family witches grabbed up EJ, George, and Angie, and raced behind their car. It was fast and George's middle was sore. But that was better than being dead. The witches set up a protective, *warming* working.

EJ rolled over and George drooled on EJ's back. This was nice. He did not like winter cold, and EJ was warm and smelled of the wonderful scent of pee that had splattered on his clothes.

Angie lay down, her scent confused, her face scrunched up in the way that George had learned meant she was thinking dangerous bad thoughts. He licked her face. She pushed him away and he thought she didn't even notice the lick.

He followed Angie's gaze to the top of the magics that protected the house. The *hedge of thorns* ward of energies. The energies had spiraled up to the high center of the *hedge's* dome in whirls. The energies looked like something KitKit made when she got into the yarn basket.

Angie sighed, smelling of sadness, but her eyes focused something dangling from the top of the dome.

George followed her eyes to see a small strand, glowing yellow with magic. On the other side of the ball of magics was a lightless strand of death. He didn't know why, but he thought this was a dangerous thing for her to be looking at. He nuzzled her hand and she petted him, which made him happy but also worried him.

The darkness of the death magic strand wiggled slightly and grew just a little.

Angie frowned harder and her scent changed again, smelled like she did when she was going to do something that the Biggers thought was foolish and bad.

From high on the hillside came the sound of gunfire. Then someone screamed and stopped. Edmund's fury-smell came to them on the wind with dead-human smell. *Good. They are dead,* he thought at KitKit. *Much evil human blood.*

George heard the back door of the house-den open. Evan the

Bigger, smelled of his own blood and the scent of…shock? Bitter and sharp like bad cheese. George had never smelled such a smell. The Bigger had been bleeding when he crawled away. But if the Mama Bigger was still in the frozen ward with KitKit, what did that mean about the Daddy Bigger being free?

"Evan," Edmund said.

"My children?" the Bigger gasped.

"Safe."

"Update me," the Bigger gasped.

George raised his head. He smelled witch blood. Evan Bigger was damaged. Angie said he hit his head. George had not noticed. He had been derelict in his duty. KitKit would be mad. Worse, Lincoln Shaddock would be disappointed.

Edmund told the Bigger everything.

Evan Bigger, his voice harsh and parched and tired, said, "They were…going to kill us."

"Yes."

"I'm not a violent man," Evan said, "but…"

"They will not trouble you again," Edmund said. "My military and tech team are analyzing the people and the device. They will be dealt with."

"Good." Mixed scents of self-loathing and satisfaction came from Evan Bigger on the steady wind down the hill, tart and acerbic. "What did he tell you?

"He is with a group called DTP. Death to Paranormals. Starting with the Everhart/Trueblood family. There are two more warriors and two 'suits' over the hill in a van. We must assume they will be along presently."

Gunfire rang out. George smelled more blood. Vampire blood.

He heard the sound of bodies falling. He whoofed softly.

Gunshots echoed from the hill.

Too fast for him to react, Angie broke the warming ward and reset it, leaving EJ and George safe. George barked, but no one noticed. He barked and yowled and howled. No one noticed or cared. Angie scrambled around the car and froze at the sight of Liz and Cia on the ground, twitching beneath magics that writhed like red snakes. They had been attacked and George hadn't noticed this either.

Melodie struggled to get loose from the straps on her ankles.

Angie raised her hands and hit the evil witch with *sleep*. Melodie fell over.

George whuffed, proud of his human. So very, very proud!

Angie ran to her twin witch ants who smelled just alike underneath, and on the surface of different soaps. She studied the energies trapping them. To George's eyes the *trapping* working was all squiggle lights, but witch Cia was turning blue. She wasn't breathing. She was dying. So was Liz.

George whuffed again. *KitKit! Witch twin is dying!*

Get me free. She sounded faster. KitKit the familiar was making progress in breaking the death magics, but not fast enough.

I cannot get to you! You are trapped, he thought.

Idiot dog!

Angie took a deep breath and shoved her hands into the energies all around her ants. She jerked as if she had been hit with a human fist. She shook. Bit her tongue.

George smelled Angie's blood. He raised his head, panting. Worried.

Angie directed the energies attacking her ants down into the earth. He had no idea how, but she drained the magic into the ground. She fell over. Cia sucked in a breath. Liz groaned and sat up, coughing.

George barked and barked and fought out of the blanket until he was on top of EJ, protecting his small human witch.

Behind the house, George heard Edmund speed up the hill. He tackled a human that George had not smelled. Downwind. *Danger!* The sniper's rifle skittered off a rock, firing a shot into the sky.

George heard a crack as Edmund broke the shooter's neck. Like a human wringing a chicken's neck. Vampire and human blood carried on the wind. George knew that Edmund was feeding from the paralyzed human's neck to heal. The sound of his footsteps burdened by extra weight told George's beautiful ears that the vampire carried the still-breathing human down the hill. He dropped him. By the smells, Edmund then healed the Bigger. The Daddy Bigger was still alive; his blood smell was strong.

George heard as Edmund called Lincoln Shaddock. *Finally,* they called the Mama Bigger's sire. Though the Mama Bigger did not know she was part vampire because she did not have a Bassett Hound nose.

Evan Bigger staggered around the house to Angie and sat heavily on the inside of the ward. "We don't have good options, Angie. You, EJ, and I will go home with your aunts, and we'll try tomorrow—"

"No." Angie crossed her arms over her chest just like Daddy Bigger did when he was being alpha. "Mama's death magics are growing. They'll kill her and the baby by morning."

George asked KitKit if that was true and KitKit said, *Yes. I am dying.*

Daddy Bigger smelled of tears. "We have to stop it now. But none of us knows how, Angie."

"I do." She pointed up. "We have to find a way to get up there and unravel the knot of death and heaven." Daddy didn't reply. He just shook his head.

Edmund said, "Evan, you have a concussion."

Whatever that was.

Edmund also said, "Shaddock is taking care of the bad guys on the other side of the hill."

George lifted his wonderful nose into the air and sniffed. Lincoln Shaddock was here! Lincoln Shaddock should kill and eat the bad guys, though no one asked him. But things were not fixed yet. KitKit was dying. He hated KitKit. But he wanted her back.

This was confusing.

"The top of the *hedge* is twenty feet above the roofline," Edmund said.

George thought Edmund must be seeing through the Daddy Bigger's magic blood to know this.

"The *hedge of thorns* feels slightly warm," he said, "with a faint vibration. I can leap and climb to the top, provided the *hedge* is as solid at the top as here."

"Even if you got up there, over the house, in the air," Cia said, her voice rough and hoarse, and her body smelling of exhaustion from the spell Melodie witch had hit her with, "even if the *hedge* held your weight and didn't fry you like bacon, you aren't a witch. You can't unravel the working."

"Hell," her twin said, "I don't think *we* could."

"The *hedge* won't hold more than two hundred pounds," the Daddy said.

"I can do it," Angie said.

"No, Angie. You can't," Liz said.

"That *isn't* happening," Daddy Bigger said.

"In a moment of panic," Edmund said, "Angelina merged all of these energies. I fear that if this temporal deactivation explodes, time-warped-space and broken death magics might destroy the surrounding area. Might perhaps result in worse consequences."

Liz cursed. Daddy looked mad. George had no idea what that meant.

Angie said, "Edmund can carry me up the *hedge*. I can pull the threads through and unravel all but the last strands. Then we can slide back down with me holding them. On the ground, I can pull them. The *hedge* and the temporal *thing* should fall."

She tilted her head, watching her family. She smelled satisfied, the way a pack leader smelled when they were right and expected the others to bow down and show bellies in submission.

Edmund said, "You figured that out on your own?"

She sighed. "Somebody hadda. It's my fault."

"You didn't do this on purpose, Angie Baby," Cia said. "If your mama hadn't drawn on the death magics, they wouldn't have been there to get tangled up in your shield."

"If Mama hadn't used them, then EJ and me woulda watched Mama and Daddy die."

Daddy Bigger sucked in a breath and smelled of bitter fear.

Edmund said, "As viewed from a military perspective rather than a personal one, Angie is correct. It will take all of us to stop this, and only Angelina can untangle the energies."

Daddy started to argue, but he stopped, staring at Edmund. "You swore to protect my family."

"Even to my undeath. Yes."

Cia said, "Angie needs food and water first." She went to her car and brought back a bottle of water and a banana. She smelled angry.

Angie ate and drank and went behind the tree where EJ had peed. When she was done, Edmund held out a hand and Angie placed her small hand into his.

Edmund adjusted Angie on his back, wrapped her arms around his neck, her legs around his waist. "Hang on tightly."

She did. He stepped back several yards, toed off his shoes, and raced at the *hedge* fast, fast. Fast as a vampire possibly could. Air popped.

George raised his head and watched and smelled. The vampire loved Angie. This was a good thing. A good love.

Edmund sped up the side of the *hedge*. At the top of the magics, he stopped and swung Angie off his back, sitting her on the slightly curved dome of energies, the blanket that had kept George and EJ warm, around her. George hadn't noticed when it was taken.

Full of fear and courage, Angie said, "Can we run like that when I'm not scared and cold?"

Edmund chuckled. "If we succeed, Angelina, I will take you on a full moon run. For now, can you untangle the magics?"

She pressed her fingers against the energies of the original ward and pressed through them, her tiny fingers twisting back and forth. She pulled a strand of yellow energy up and up and had to stand on the dome of energy to continue. Edmund steadied her to keep her from slipping, and still she pulled the energy strand through the small opening she had made. She tossed it and began another.

Much time passed.

George went to pee again. He snuffled the wonderful smells near the road. Rat, raccoon, opossum, weasel, squirrels, bird—and vampire and Angie in the air, up high. More time passed as George snuffled, and sunrise had begun to tint the sky gray when Angie sat back from the opening, leaning against Edmund's legs in exhaustion.

George raced closer to the *hedge* on his stubby powerful legs and watched.

Angie held her hands in front of her. He saw flashes of light and pulses of power in them, though there was nothing real to focus on.

"I'm done," she said. She spoke so softly that George knew the others didn't hear. Only his beautiful ears heard. "Being an Everhart is hard."

"Why is that?" Edmund asked.

George knew. Power is dangerous.

Hurry, KitKit whispered.

"We have to save the world sometimes. Like Ant Jane."

"Ah. That is indeed a heavy burden. Do you have the strands you want?"

"I have two. I can't ride down on your back. You can carry me like a bride!"

"Oh, Angelina." Edmund said, sounding sad and…depressed?

Angie said, "We're never gonna get married, are we?"

"It is unlikely," Edmund said gently, helping her to stand.

"I woulda made a beautiful bride."

Edmund choked back a laugh and lifted her into his arms. "Coming down," he shouted, and leaped. His bare feet caught the surface, skidding along the frozen energy.

He dropped to his backside when the angle became too great to maintain balance. They hit the ground at a run.

"Twenty minutes until sunrise," Liz said. "Cutting it close, fanghead."

Edmund set Angie on the ground and said to her, "Give me one minute to get in back to take out the time-frozen humans there. Then I want you to say, 'One, two, three,' and yank the strands of magic on three."

He looked up. "Cia and Liz will rush in the moment the magic falls and help your mother. Evan, you'll have to carry Angie to safety. Are you up to it?"

"Yeah. I can do that."

But George thought he smelled weak, as if he was about to die.

want to know what differences he saw in me. His whipcord-thin build had filled out, but he was still wiry. Lean…like he was hungry.

His taste in fashion hadn't changed, though. Ratty jeans, scuffed boots, holey tee. Very James Dean.

"Only for the weekend." A smile flavored his tone. "What are the odds?"

None to none.

Damn it, Auntie.

She must have gotten fed up with my one-woman cold war and decided it was time for a truce.

"Well, I have to be going." I eased on the backpack. "See you around."

As I brushed past Corbin, he gripped my upper arm in a light hold.

"That's the thing." He wet his bottom lip. "You make sure you don't. See me, that is."

"I'm a busy girl with a full social calendar."

As the eldest daughter of the alpha pair of the Savannah, Georgia, gwyllgi pack, I had a full-time job in defending my title as gamma, or third. Many of the gwyllgi credited my high ranking to nepotism. Until I kicked their hairy asses.

"Hmm." He stroked his thumb down the inside of my arm. "What are you doing now?"

"Save our oceansss," Keet, the tattletale, sang. "Oceans. Oceans. Oceans."

"The aquarium?" Corbin grinned, the corners of his smile sharp. "I love the aquarium."

As I stared at his teeth, prickles raced up the side of my neck.

The night of my high school graduation, I drank enough liquid courage to attack him with my mouth. No one would call what I did to him a kiss, and the cringeworthy details had been burned into my memory.

His frown when I sashayed over to him. His startled expression when I sat on his lap. His grunt of surprise when I claimed his smooth chin in a passionate nightmare of miscalculation that resulted in him laughing at me, scooping me into his arms, and carrying me home, where he tucked me into bed.

Like I was still a stupid little kid with a raging crush on him.

Which was exactly how I felt.

Crushed.

The shame wasn't helped by the fact he up and disappeared the next night, as if he couldn't wait to get away from me.

"Whatever," I huffed, sounding totally mature and not at all like a pouting teen. "It's a free country."

Corbin fell in step with me as I exited the house. "Mind if I drive?"

"I have a truck." I dangled my keys in his face. "Feel free to drive yourself, though."

The spit dried in my mouth when I saw what he was driving. A 1969 Ford Bronco painted reef aqua with sharp white trim, a pristine white hardtop, and gleaming white leather seats.

"One last chance to change your mind," he breathed in my ear. "Sure you don't want me to drive?"

That model and paint combo was one I had obsessed over for years, and I envied him for owning it.

"I'm good," I mumbled, failing to tear my gaze from his ride. "See you there."

With vampire strength, Corbin removed his hardtop and carried it into the garage while I watched, leaving his Bronco open to the cool night air.

"Vroom. Vroom." Keet scratched at the plastic bubble. "Vroom. Vroom."

Removing the backpack, I stared him down. "Really?"

He broke into garbled Transformer noises, another beloved franchise of his, that cemented the request.

"Do you mind if Keet rides along?" I heard the betrayal in my voice. "I can strap him in with a seat belt."

Corbin took him, placed him in the back, and secured the pack before turning back to face me.

"Come on, Eva-Diva." Corbin opened the front passenger door. "Please?"

"Don't call me that." I fisted my keys until they cut into my palm. "I'm not a kid anymore, Corbin."

Nostrils flaring, he rasped as the jut of his fangs grew more pronounced behind his lips. "You've cut yourself."

Turning my hand over, I saw he was right. I had been too angry to feel the bite of the metal.

"I'm gwyllgi." I flashed him the already closed wound. "It's not like I'm in any danger from a scratch."

Eyes darker than a starless sky, Corbin strode toward me. "I'll be the judge of that."

His strong fingers braceleted my wrist, and he brought my hand to his nose. No. Not his nose. His mouth. He bent his head, ensnared my gaze, and glided his tongue across my palm.

I forgot how to breathe, how to think, how to do more than gawk as he cleaned my skin of blood.

"Well, look at that." He rubbed his thumb down the pink seam. "You were right."

While I was dumbstruck, he shepherded me to the Bronco and lifted me into the copilot seat.

I let him strap me in with a kind of wonder, a near certainty I was dreaming, and then he shut the door.

The metallic slam broke the spell he put me under, jarring me out of my shock, but the vampire was quick. He slid in behind the wheel, cranked the engine, and spun out before I could fumble the catch open on my seat belt.

Manic laughter trailed us as Keet fluttered, enjoying the wind cutting through the tiny breathing holes in the clear plastic.

When I acknowledged how much I enjoyed my long hair snapping in my face, I felt like a traitor to my pickup, which Dad handed down to me when I turned sixteen.

"Is that a smile?" Corbin cut his eyes toward me. "Having fun yet?"

"No," I lied, smothering a dopey grin resulting from riding in *this* car with *this* guy.

"You've always been a crap liar, *Eva*."

"You don't know me well enough to say that."

"I know all kinds of things about you." He pitched his voice low. "Like how your lips feel on my skin."

Mortification shot my hand to the door, and I closed my fingers around the latch. Jumping wouldn't kill me. Even if the asphalt shredded my skin and impact broke bones, I would survive it. I would rather that, rather a semi hit me, than have this conversation with Corbin. Ever.

"I made a fool of myself, and I'm lucky the guy whose lap I fell into didn't take advantage."

"That's how you want to play this?" The steering wheel groaned beneath the clench of his fingers. "You want to pretend you didn't brush off every boy who spoke to you on your way to me?"

"I was drunk. I don't remember what I did or didn't do. That's how drunk works."

A growl vibrated in his chest, and the wild heart of me thumped harder, until fur brushed the undersides of my skin in warning the beast wanted out. A crimson veil drew across my vision, and I had to focus my breathing to hold on to this form.

"I remember." He stared out the windshield, his voice a thready whisper. "Enough for the both of us."

The rest of the trip passed in silence, minus a fart sound here or there from Keet and the random burst of birdy laughter.

This time of night, the doors to the Clarice Lawson Oceanic Research Institute had just opened, and lines weren't long. It helped that the entire building was warded against humans. Only the paranormal community was welcome at the area's largest attraction.

Seeing as how the aquarium was named after Uncle Linus's mother, who funded the project, he finessed a lifetime pass for me the year it opened. Another bonus of Aunt Grier being Clarice Lawson's daughter-in-law was that no one batted an eye when I brought Keet in to spend quality time among the fishes.

Corbin, who rarely spent time in Savannah, was doomed to the ticket line or hitting a kiosk.

Smiling as I walked up to the door, scanned my card, and entered the cool building, I left him behind without a hint of guilt. "You want to hit the shark exhibit first?"

I preferred the leafy sea dragons, but Keet loved sharks. And penguins. God, the penguins.

After he saw an African penguin at the aquarium's grand opening, he became obsessed with them. The live webcam of their enclosure became his new favorite TV show. He refused to fly for a year and took up waddling as his primary mode of transportation.

For hours each night, he swam in the pool at my parents' house until he worked up the nerve to dive and swim underwater. African penguins held their breath for four minutes max. Keet, being undead, had a poor sense of time. He also didn't require oxygen. His laps tended to last twenty minutes.

"Bum, bum, bum, bum," Keet began, alarming the patrons around us. "Do, do, do."

When we passed under a splashy banner for The Little Guppies Show, he belted out his favorite song.

"Save our oceansss." His claws raked the plastic bubble. "Oceans. Oceans. Oceans."

The song came from the animated 4D show for kids, which included live elements to surprise the audience. Water sprays, rumble seats, and flying mylar streamers. The latter, he always stole and nested in until they got so ratty Aunt Grier tossed them.

"I have to buy tickets, remember?" I headed to a kiosk. "It's not movie time yet."

"Bum, bum?" Keet pouted. "Do, do?"

"We can see the sharks while we wait," I assured him. "Maybe you'll see that big stingray you like too."

With a show ticket in my pocket, I joined the queue for the people mover that carried patrons through an acrylic tunnel bisecting the floor of the shark exhibit.

"You still like vanilla?"

A groan poured out of me as I glanced over my shoulder to find Corbin holding two soft serve ice cream cones. With so many people, and so much perfume and cologne, I hadn't smelled his approach.

Vanilla for me. Pineapple for him.

Always with the pineapple.

And yes, I was aware how sad it made me that I had memorized his favorite, well, everything.

"I'm on a diet."

"Gwyllgi don't diet." He thrust the cone into my hand as we rode into the exhibit. "Try again."

Shifter metabolism burned calories off as they touched our lips. That, and a genuine love of good food, meant he was right. Gwyllgi were eating machines. More so than the sharks swimming above us.

"I'll take your ice cream," I said haughtily, "but only because my parents taught me not to waste food."

A chilly rivulet tracked over my fingers, and I chased the drop with my tongue before stealing a few of his napkins to protect me from more spillage. "There. I'm eating it. Happy?"

The way he watched me lick my lips caused a lump to form in my throat.

"Not even close," he rumbled, invading my personal space, "but it's a start."

As I faced forward, determined not to embarrass myself again, a warning prickle stung my nape.

A low growl poured into the tunnel, and patrons scattered like leaves on the winds of a hurricane.

Puffing out my cheeks, I kissed my peaceful evening goodbye and turned to identify the problem.

Bastian Crowley.

I should have known.

And he'd brought his brothers, Mathieu and Ormand, with him.

"Eva Kinase," he roared. "I challenge you for your rank as gamma."

"You want to do this here?" I ate my treat with forced nonchalance. "Now?"

"You used your witchy magic on my brother," he accused. "Otherwise, he would have beaten you."

Thaddeus Crowley had challenged me yesterday, right after I ate enough tacos to send myself into a food coma. I had to wonder if he had done it intentionally. Jerk. The joke was on him. I never lost a challenge, or my dinner. Or my lunch. Or my breakfast, now that I thought about it.

What can I say? Momma didn't raise no quitter.

Before we were done, I had broken his right leg, his left arm, and probably his tailbone.

But I won. I always won. I was a Kinase.

Daughter of an alpha. Granddaughter of an alpha. Great-granddaughter of an alpha.

I might be a dynastic aberration, but I refused to be a failure.

"I'm a gwyllgi, the same as you." I hated airing our pack's dirty laundry in public. "I have no magic."

Plenty of folks wondered, and I couldn't blame their curiosity, given my peculiar life up to this point.

Mom almost miscarried me after a challenge gone wrong. Aunt Grier, her best friend, used necromancy to save me. That would have been fine, if her magic hadn't also tweaked my biological clock, setting my development on fast forward.

I was born early, right after Mom's first trimester, but at the length and weight of a full-term baby. They might have explained that away too, with a joke about how much Mom ate during her pregnancy, if the trend hadn't continued.

I grew weeks within days, months within weeks, years within months.

I was the flower girl at Aunt Grier and Uncle Linus's wedding, but at two and a half, I passed for twelve.

At the age of five, I was done growing, leaving me in a body frozen between twenty and thirty.

Mentally and emotionally, I developed a step or two behind my apparent physical age, earning me freak status and making me a one-of-a-kind oddity. I was twenty-five next week, and my outside matched my inside. For now. No one knew why I'd stopped growing or if I would start again.

As much as my family hated to admit it, I'd accepted I was living on borrowed time years ago.

Maybe that was why I got hung up on Corbin in the first place. He was a Deathless vampire, the only one of his kind in existence, as far as anyone knew. A true immortal, unlike the other vampire types. It was less lonely knowing another weirdo was out there.

"Witch," Bast snarled. "I bet if I set you on fire, you'd burn."

"Um." I crunched through the cone. "I hate to break it to you, but literally anyone would burn if you set them on fire."

A huff of laughter reminded me Corbin was getting a firsthand look at the ugly side of my life.

"Who're you?" Bast turned on Corbin. "Are you with the witch?"

After polishing off his cone, Corbin took his time wiping his fingers and then his mouth clean.

"I'm the guy," he said, "who just scored a front-row seat to watch you get your ass kicked."

"Big talk from a bloodsucker," Mathieu sneered. "Want a turn with me when he's done with her?"

"Nah." Corbin bared his fangs, sharp and deadly, in a smile. "I'm here as a spectator."

As much as it galled me to ask Corbin, I did it. "Will you agree to act as an impartial witness?"

"I would, but I can't." He rolled a shoulder. "I've never been that where you're concerned."

Unsure what to make of that, I decided I didn't want to ask and be told the reason he couldn't be impartial was he viewed me as a little sister to protect.

"Canvass the crowd and pick a lucky soul for us?" I wanted this done by the books. "Bast, we need to pick a spot that's not the conveyer in the shark exhibit."

I cut him off when he attempted to talk over me. "There are children present. I won't risk harming innocents."

Most paranormal species were indoctrinated to violence and bloodshed from an early age, but I didn't want to scar those with more delicate sensibilities.

"Okay." He tilted his head back, watching the giant ray swim overhead. "I've got just the place."

Forethought on his end did not bode well for me, but I sucked it up and let him have his way. "Lead on."

I fell in behind the Crowley brothers, not trusting them at my back, and shot my folks a text.

Bastian Crowley challenged me at the aquarium. Mathieu and Ormand are with him.

Kick ass, baby girl. Mommy loves you.

A flush prickled up to my hairline, but I couldn't stop my smile.

Love you too.

Within minutes, Corbin returned with a young woman who gazed up at him with wide blue eyes.

Ugh.

The idea of him with other women always put me in a violent temper, so maybe this was a positive.

"This is Paula," he rushed out her credentials. "She's a warg, and from out of state, so there should be no conflicts of interest."

Our pack had interbred heavily with wargs, diluting our blood enough to escape Faerie rule, but that was centuries past. As long as she wasn't from a Georgia pack, I had no problem using her.

Paula took one good look at me and cringed back a step. "Hi."

Damn my Southern manners.

I wanted to rip out her curly blonde hair and strangle her with it, but I shook her soft hand, and mine came back smelling of magnolias and a foreign pack that would suit my purpose just fine.

"Thanks for doing this." I forced a smile. "With any luck, I won't hold you up long."

"I totally understand." She ditched Corbin and fell in step with me. "I'm from Florida, the Iglesias pack."

She rolled her eyes. "I'm five rungs down the ladder, and the boys can't stand it. They pick fights with me less now that I've whooped all their asses at least once, but cornering you in public, on a date night?"

Her upper lip curled. "That's as low class as it gets."

Cue feeling bad for all the nasty things I had been thinking about her.

He was doing it again. Burrowing under my skin. Warping my common sense. Making me territorial.

I had to yank him off my heart like a juicy tick on an itchy dog.

"I agree." Genuine warmth seeped into my grin. "I'm gamma, under my parents. You can imagine how that goes."

"Oh." A grimace twisted her adorable features. "That's got to suck."

"Yeah."

We passed through a door labeled *Employees Only*, and the fishy scent of the aquarium grew sharper. Metal stairs painted glaring white led us up two stories, by my estimate. "No matter how many times I prove my worth, there's always someone who doesn't believe I've earned my spot."

Or who thought I wielded mystical witchy powers to get it, which was beyond ridiculous.

Aunt Grier was a necromancer. Had her magic mutated me in utero, that was what I would have become—a necromancer. Not a garden-variety witch, but whatever.

If I tried beating the ignorance out of people, I was more likely to kill them than cure them.

"I'm sorry," I told her, "for the abundance of dickweasels in your pack."

"I'm also sorry for the abundance of dickweasels in your pack."

Our easy camaraderie made it simple to picture how this might have been my life, had I been born without necromantic intervention. I could have had friends in my pack, friends in other packs. My status as the eldest child of the alphas would have elevated me rather than made me a target with a flashing sign on my back. But without Aunt Grier, and her magic, I wouldn't be standing here.

"Here, fishy, fishy, fishy. Here, fishy."

Paula jumped at the voice and only then noticed my backpack. "What is that?"

"My aunt's parakeet." I shrugged out of the pet carrier. "Corbin, do you mind holding Keet?"

We had reached the top, where more grates formed a platform over a massive tank filled with...sharks.

Well, that explained why Bast confronted me in the tunnel. A hint of things to come.

"Oh," Corbin grumbled, "so you do remember I'm here."

As if I could forget. His presence was a warm tingle down my spine, impossible to ignore.

Once Corbin was in possession of the carrier, bubble facing out, Paula peered in.

"Oh. I see him." She laughed. "He was hanging upside down from the top."

"He's weird like that."

"Here I was wondering if clear backpacks were new and trendy. I always miss those memos."

"Trendy? Me? No." I snorted. "Whoever's in charge of fashion deleted me from their newsletter too."

I tolerated jeans, tees, and undies. I hated socks, shoes, jackets. I preferred strappy camisoles with shelf bras, though I didn't require one, sadly, and breezy athletic shorts with panties sewn in.

Simple. Painless. Efficient.

Glamourous, I was not.

Plus, it was easier to get bloodstains out of basic clothing. Or to replace it without breaking the bank.

"Anytime, princess," Bast taunted. "I don't have all night."

"That's my cue." I rolled my shoulders. "Paula, if you have a phone, I would appreciate you filming this."

Technology made it easy for wins and losses to be credited without dispute.

For that reason, I filmed *everything*. Then I sent the tamer bouts to my folks, who watched the clips at home while eating popcorn and cheering me on from the couch. Sometimes they invited friends over, really made a party out of it, and left me wishing I had never been born.

Corbin had no parting words for me, but he did hold my stare until I broke away to face Bast.

"You challenged me, I even let you pick the location, but the choice of weapon is mine."

"I can beat anything you've got." He snorted. "Are your claws manicured too?"

"You've got to be kidding me." The tips of my fingers were a horror show of chewed nails and torn cuticles. "Do you even know what a manicure is?"

Paula's soft laughter did nothing to calm Bast's raging temper, and he released a vicious growl.

"Shift." I anchored my hands on my hips. "I'll give you a five-second head start."

"Keep it." His upper lip quivered, and spittle dotted his chin. "I can beat you without it."

"Need me to hold your clothes?" Paula checked with me. "You don't want to lose them in the water."

"Gwyllgi keep what they wear during the shift," Corbin answered for me. "Handy, right?

"For real?" She gaped at me. "So unfair."

"It's a fae thing." I winked at her. "Thanks for offering, though."

Crimson magic splashed up Bast's legs in a red wave that crested his shoulders, climbing until it coated him. As the viscous liquid drained away, his human shape did too, melting into a muscular form that was half bull mastiff and half Komodo dragon. His burnt-orange fur gave way to heavy scales in strategic places, and needlelike teeth filled his mouth.

The change was much gentler to my kind than our warg ancestors, faster too, but he wasn't me.

Not to brag, but I came from a long line of female alphas. I might be crap at living in my human skin, but I knew my worth on four paws.

On the edge of my hearing, Corbin counted down from five, as if he couldn't help himself.

When he hit one, I gave myself over to the magic, and it splashed, crimson and vibrant, around me, pulling me down into my gwyllgi form.

I wasn't winning any beauty pageants like this, but I was a beast. Literally.

"I've never seen a gwyllgi shift," Paula whispered to Corbin. "Never seen one in person either."

"She's beautiful, isn't she?" Corbin had the balls to sound proud, like he had anything to do with it. "Wait until you see her move. She's like greased lightning."

The praise earned him a twitch of my ears. I couldn't be hearing him right. How would he know? He had never seen me fight. Never watched me shift, either. I had only let him see me in this form a handful of times, aware of how off-putting the odd blend of canine and reptile could be.

The only way he could have that knowledge was if…Mom and Dad let him watch the videos.

As proud parents, I could picture them doing it, but why would he ask to see them in the first place?

Bast finished his change, and his rage at me for beating his time tempted me to roll my eyes. This guy, and his brothers, had been pack since before my birth. He knew me. He knew what I was capable of. Why my speed still offended him, I had no clue.

As Mom was fond of saying, *You can't fix stupid.*

And she had tried, for my sake, until it became clear her intervention only made me appear weaker, an easier target for when my parents turned their backs. To survive the pack, I had to make it on my own.

For the sake of the recording, I stood my ground and let Bast strike first, a punishing rake of his claws down my side.

The low snarl rippling through the room sent a hot shiver down my spine, and my ruff stood on end. Corbin knew better than to interfere. All his posturing accomplished was distracting me. The urge to snap my teeth at him twitched in my neck, but I couldn't afford to take my eyes off Bast.

When Bast circled for a second pass, a nip and run, I let him get close then snapped my jaws shut on the side of his throat. I shook him until he yelped then spat him out on the grate. Had we been on two legs, it would have qualified as him crying uncle, but the murderous glint in his eyes warned he had no intentions of taking the out I was willing to give him.

"What the hell?" Mathieu grunted. "Is that…bird shit?"

"A sparrow must have gotten in," Ormond muttered. "Like they do in grocery stores."

Oh, God, no.

Keet.

That was the last thing I needed, but I was stuck.

Shift and yell at the bird, and Bast would eviscerate me in my softer, pinker human form.

Let the bird dive-bomb them, and I was in real danger of them killing him.

Well, he couldn't technically die, he was already dead, but if we lost his body parts, we would have to source new ones, and I did *not* want to grave rob for a parakeet.

Using my distraction to his advantage, Bast slammed into me, knocking me closer to the platform's edge.

Annoyed with myself, I snapped my teeth at him and forced myself to ignore Keet.

Him, we could reanimate.

Me?

Not so much.

I was hard to kill, all shifters were, but it wasn't impossible.

Bast pivoted on the ball of one wide paw and charged me again.

There was no finesse, no style, just brute strength. With his strategy stuck on repeat, I didn't bother altering mine either. Lazy of me, I know, but it had been a week. Mom would tan my hide if she watched this one. Bast was smaller than me but bulkier through the shoulders, and he was mean. His bites struck bone. I had no issue with him tiring himself out on wasted feints if it kept his teeth away from my throat.

Our fight developed a familiar rhythm.

Bast rushed in. I tore a chunk out of him. He retreated.

Rinse and repeat.

The next battering-ram-style attack shoved me back, and my hind feet slid across slippery metal.

Faster than I could regain my balance, Bast whipped around and hammered me again with his shoulder.

Clarity slapped me as my legs skated out from under me.

Bast had been herding me, and I was too slow on the uptake to recognize his ploy until it was too late.

Frigid saltwater stole my breath when I splashed into the tank.

"Eva."

Corbin's enraged bellow shocked me out of my stupor, and I blinked stinging eyes to find the sharks circling me, curious about their guest. A flurry of movement drew my attention away from my fellow predators, and I cringed when I spotted the milling crowd of visitors standing in the acrylic tunnel.

As they gasped and pointed, I could only pray they saw my scales and figured I was a new attraction.

Then the phones came out, flashes went off, and I accepted my parents were going to kill me.

If they didn't die laughing first.

My paws hit the gritty bottom of the tank about the time my lungs began screaming for air. The sides of the enclosure were textured at eye level with rock and coral for the sake of the viewing window, but the upper sections were smooth and painted a cool blue.

Gwyllgi couldn't swim, which, yeah. Ironic. You would think we could dog paddle at least, but sadly not. Our dense muscle mass and solid build meant we were heavier. Factor in our head size, and weight that tended to be disproportionate to our bodies, and we couldn't hold our heads above water on four legs. Wherever we got our scales, it wasn't from a long-lost aquatic ancestor. Gwyllgi sank like freaking rocks.

To shift, abandoning the agreed-upon weapon of teeth and claws, would award Bast the win.

I would rather drown in front of an audience than forfeit to that dickweasel.

A second disturbance scattered the sharks, and my stomach dropped when a yellow bullet shot straight for me.

Keet, in full-on penguin mode, nibbled the fur on my nose, yanking me toward the faux coral reef I'd noticed earlier. I let him guide me—it was that or die bald—and climbed them. There, painted the same eye-tricking blue as the upper tank, was a metal ladder bolted to the curved side.

Hallelujah.

Pulling myself up, paw over paw, was about as much fun as it sounds. The narrow rungs on the reinforced stainless-steel ladder weren't meant for gwyllgi paw pads, and the lack of oxygen was fire in my lungs. Black dots twinkled in my vision before I hit what I estimated to be the halfway point.

Keet pecked and clawed at my vulnerable face to keep me motivated on the climb, drawing blood that perked the sharks' interest.

As it turned out, that proved even better motivation than having a wannabe penguin attack out of love.

When my head broke the water, Matthieu yelled, "Bast, she made it out."

Within seconds, Bast guarded the ledge, snarling and snapping at me. I couldn't climb over or past him, and my limbs trembled from exertion. As much as I didn't want another dunk, I didn't see another way.

Slinking down a step, until the water almost closed over my head, I let Bast overextend to reach me for a finishing bite then sprang up and sank my teeth deep in his throat. He dug in his paws, his claws finding purchase in the grates. I was stuck, I didn't have enough leverage, and I couldn't stand here all day.

Lungs expanding with fresh oxygen, I let go of the ladder. My punishing grip, and weight, drew Bast in after me. He panicked as we sank and flailed several yards, but I was primed for when I touched down on the reef.

Within minutes, Keet had caught up to me, and I hustled to escape his encouragement.

This time, nothing obstructed my view of the platform, and I climbed out then flopped onto my belly. Panting and coughing up water, I blinked to clear my blurry vision in time to watch Corbin run to me.

"Now we wait." Paula exhaled with relief. "Either he climbs out, or he doesn't."

Sides heaving, I lay there while Keet, who had caught a ride on my back out of the tank, cleaned my fur. I grunted when he wedged his sharp beak between my gleaming scales, but I lacked the energy to snap at him, even when his intense grooming hurt. A hazy part of my brain wondered if that wasn't the point.

Passing out mid-challenge from repeated oxygen deprivation was probably not wise.

Smart little bird, that Keet, I'll give him that.

"You okay?" Corbin sank to his knees near my head. "Am I allowed to touch you now, or…?"

Baring my teeth, I wanted to spit he wasn't allowed to touch me *ever*, but all I could do was growl.

"Leave her," Paula advised. "From what she told me about her pack, we don't want to risk her win."

Maybe I could edit out that last part before my folks watched this, and they would see it. After my swim, they would demand a copy to gauge how much damage was done and what reparations must be made.

With a nod, he broke into a smile. "You were amazing."

Ears flat to my skull, I curled my upper lip to show him teeth.

"I was five seconds away from diving in after you," he murmured, then grinned when I chomped the air an inch from his nose. "It would have been legal. I asked Paula. The reason you slipped was Bast, or one of his brothers, greased the grate." He held up a vial. "It was clear, scentless. That's why no one noticed. My money's on treadmill lube. It reminds me of the spray I have for mine back home."

That he had collected evidence to make my case before saving me was…weirdly sweet.

"Can you believe Keet?" He huffed out a laugh. "How did he not get eaten?"

Nostrils flaring, I scented the air, but I couldn't detect him.

Now that I thought about it, I hadn't felt or seen him since Corbin began his vigil either.

A whine left my raw throat as I shoved to my feet, my body working overtime to heal the damage, and I did what I always do when Keet escaped his cage at Woolworth House for unsanctioned hide-and-seek.

Where is the absolute worst place he could have gone?

Body trembling with exhaustion, I rose and wobbled over to the ladder.

Sure enough, a yellow dot swarmed Bast, guiding him onto the reef and up the hidden ladder.

The sharks were moving past agitation to aggression, and I couldn't blame them. We had been splashing in their pool, bloody, for too long. I waited until Bast's head broke the water then cleared a path for him to haul himself onto the grate, grateful that even without Corbin's findings, Keet's involvement couldn't be held against me since he had elected to assist us both for his own mysterious birdy reasons.

As Bast choked and gasped, I pressed a paw down on his windpipe. He smacked a back leg against the metal in a tap out, but I didn't trust him to honor it. I applied more pressure, until his eyes bulged, and his kicking became frantic. Only then did I hold the stares of each of his livid brothers and release him.

Crimson magic splashed bright and hot over Bast as he shifted into a soggy lump of man who regretted his pick of venue, if his wild expression as he scrabbled away from the tank was any indication.

Eager to get my voice back, I embraced the change and returned to two legs.

"Keet?" I coughed a few times, my human throat tender. "Where is he?"

"Still in the water." Corbin checked with Paula, who nodded it was over. "I'll get him."

"Thanks." I forced myself to swallow the next brutal coughing fit, straighten my spine, and unleash my dominant nature. "You've had your fun and your five seconds of fame with the tourists, Bast. It's over."

A row of employees with sharp glowers crowded their own much smaller, private viewing window.

I was willing to bet they'd appeared the second I hit the water to ensure we didn't harm their animals.

"Take your brothers and go," I ordered him, "while I make nice with the aquarium staff."

Mathieu and Ormand hooked their hands under Bast's arms and hauled him to his feet. They carried the wobbly instigator strung between them, their expressions tight, a wet trail zigzagging behind them.

"Um, Eva?"

With the threats removed, I turned to Corbin, whose pale skin had taken on a greenish tint.

"We've got a problem." He pointed to a banana-yellow feather floating in the water. "I don't see him."

"You've got to be kidding me." I rubbed a hand over my face. "That bird will be the death of me."

Corbin and I scanned the sharks as they passed, but they all gave off a *nothing to see here* vibe.

None of them had the decency to have a feather stuck between their rows and rows of teeth, telling us which one was guilty.

The staff door swung open, and a tall woman with a blunt haircut prowled over to me.

"Eva." Miss Lacy, a vampire older than the dinosaurs circling below, frowned. "The shark tank? Really?"

"She had no choice." Corbin stepped in. "I'm sure you could see that, safe behind your acrylic wall."

"What happened was reckless, thoughtless," she clipped out, "and dangerous to the animals."

"Corbin." I cut him off with a slice of my hand through the air. "Miss Lacy is right."

Miss Lacy, because she had been my favorite tour guide when I was a kid. That was how we knew each other, and that was why, after years of listening to her talk about shark conservation, she expected better of me.

"Of course I'm right," she huffed, then drew me into a hug. "Now, unless my old eyes were playing tricks on me, your aunt's familiar was just swallowed whole by our tiger."

Withdrawing from her embrace, I asked, "Do we wait for him to pass, or…?"

"That would not be ideal." Her thin lips pressed together. "The stomach acid would digest everything but the feathers, perhaps the beak. We'll have to hope that…" She leaned over the tank. "Ah. The matter resolved itself. Classic gastric eversion. Do you see?"

The tiger shark had barfed up its stomach.

Not only the contents.

The entire thing.

A pink and pulpy mass hung out of his mouth, along with everything it had eaten lately. Including one pissed-off parakeet, who kicked off its forehead and rocketed toward the surface in a huff.

It did make me wonder, though. Tiger sharks were garbage cans of the sea. They ate everything. License plates, tires, a suit of armor, wallets, cameras, coins, fur coats. And once, a chicken coup. With chickens in it. I mean, *how*? Whatever we tossed into the water, they gobbled down.

Except, apparently, undead parakeets with savior complexes and aspirations to penguindom.

"Keet." I scooped the bird out of the water and examined him beak to tail. "You're in big trouble."

Miss Lacy placed her hands on my shoulders and aimed me toward the stairs, her request clear. She left us with that not-so-subtle hint then went to speak to Paula. Likely, she wanted a copy of the video for their records in case the animals suffered any trauma from the experience.

"Bum-bum, bum-bum, bum-bum-bum-bum."

"Yes." I rolled my eyes. "I saw." I cuddled him close. "There are probably already videos posted online."

Uninterested in being soothed, he kicked free of me and lit on my wrist.

"Keep our oceans cleaaan…" He hopped up my arm. "Oceans, oceans, oceans."

"I don't recognize that song." Corbin frowned. "Do you?"

"Oh, yeah." I reached in my pocket and produced a soggy ticket. "It's for The Little Guppies Show."

"That sounds…interesting."

"He won't leave until he's watched it."

"I can take him, if you want to head home and shower."

"I'm already here." I shrugged. "Might as well stick it out to the bitter end."

Also? I was terrified Keet would get ideas now that he had successfully penguined with sharks. Corbin wasn't used to babysitting the little troublemaker. I would feel better if I kept my eyes on him.

"I'm going to buy dry clothes from the gift shop. Then we'll get tickets." The one in my pocket was worthless. We had missed the showtime. "Sound good?"

"Whatever you want," Corbin murmured. "I'll follow your lead."

I didn't trust his tone, his implications, or the shivers blasting down my spine.

We took the stairs, careful of the wet spots, and waited at the bottom for Paula to join us.

Ever the showman, Keet entertained us by hanging upside down then swinging from my middle finger.

"You missed your calling." I scratched Keet's earholes. "You must have been a bat in another life."

"That was amazing," Paula gushed as she caught up to us. "You're a beast when you shift."

A sour taste coated the back of my throat. "Thanks?"

"She's fierce," Corbin agreed. "Her coloring is unique too." He swung his gaze to mine. "She's beautiful."

Paula glanced between us, a grin splitting her cheeks. "Where do I send the recording?"

I gave her my email addy for the video and got her number in case a statement was required from either party, or the aquarium.

"I'm in town for the week." She ducked her head. "Want to grab lunch one day?"

When I hesitated, Corbin elbowed me in the ribs, and I blurted, "Sure."

A flush burned in my cheeks, flashing me back to Mom setting up playdates with packmates' kids.

"I'll call you tomorrow," she offered shyly, "and we can set something up, okay?"

"That sounds great."

I smiled as she returned to her group, then I elbowed Corbin. "Really?"

"She seems nice, and you could use a friend besides me."

"You're not my friend." I paused in stuffing Keet into his carrier. "Well, that's one mystery solved."

"Hmm?"

"Keet escaped by picking at a seam. He unraveled a section of the zipper and wiggled through."

There was nothing for it but to keep wearing him and pray he would behave.

Ha.

Yeah.

I couldn't even think that with a straight face.

Leaving Corbin to birdsit while I bought new duds and changed, I emerged from the gift shop itchy from the salt, but dry.

At the kiosk, Corbin took point, flirting with the older woman. "Two tickets to your next show, please."

"One started not five minutes ago." She blossomed under his

attention. "You haven't missed much."

"That sounds perfect." He hit her with his megawatt smile, and even *my* knees wobbled. "How full is it?"

"This early," she said with a wink at me past his shoulder, "it's almost always empty."

Relief at having a moment to collect myself without spectators trumped her insinuation. "Thank you."

An usher met us at the door and guided us to prime seats using a flashlight he trained on the floor.

Gwyllgi had near-perfect night vision, but I appreciated the escort if for no other reason than he kept me from being alone in a dark theater with Corbin.

Exhausted from my ordeal, I removed the carrier, slumped into my chair, and set the pack on my lap. I angled it to ensure Keet had a perfect view of the screen then let my head fall back. Beside me, Corbin settled in, sprawling his legs until our knees bumped. I cut him a glare out of the corner of my eye, but he was too busy pretending the singing fish pals on screen were a blockbuster movie to notice.

Ten minutes into the thirty-minute show, I was falling asleep. As much as it galled me to admit, Corbin's presence at my elbow allowed me to let my guard down and close my eyes.

As my breathing leveled off, I registered shuffling footsteps behind us and resented other latecomers would be invading our territory. That meant I couldn't afford that nap after—

A line of fire cut across my throat, and I dropped the pet carrier onto the floor. Stretching out one leg, I kicked it under the row ahead of us to protect Keet from getting stomped as we fought off our attackers.

Vicious snarls rose beside me, explaining why Corbin hadn't leapt to my rescue. He was caught in the same trap, a garrote cutting off his air. Unlike made vampires or Last Seeds, he required oxygen.

The width of the seats meant our attackers had made a fatal error. In my case, anyway. The backs were deep and curved inward. I was pinned, for the moment, but I had room to wiggle my right hand through the gap up to my meaty forearm, relieving the pressure on my windpipe.

As soon as I had that barrier against suffocation in place, I thrust my other arm through the hole on its side. The thin wire cut into my skin as I flexed forward, and the man behind me hit the chair with a thud. That gave me slack to duck under the garrote and free myself.

Hands planted on the armrests, I kicked off the floor and flipped myself over my seat and my opponent. I landed on his heels, shoved him forward, and he flopped over the chair to land on his butt on the floor. He must have hit his head, because he sat there stunned for a beat until he slumped sideways.

With Ormand out of the way, I turned on Corbin's attacker. Mathieu. He retained his punishing grip on the silvery wire, torn between finishing what he started or helping his brother.

Nice girl that I am, I made the decision for him. I cocked my arm and punched him in the side of the head so hard, he staggered back from the blow, but he kept his grip on the garrote's wooden handles.

As Mathieu fell, Corbin let himself get dragged over the back of his chair to avoid decapitation.

They landed one on top of the other, but Corbin was still caught.

Before Mathieu regained his senses, I punched him again, right in the nose. His eyes rolled back in his head, and I claimed the garrote from his limp fingers. I lifted the wire gently, but Corbin hissed as the metal released his throat.

"Back off," Ormand snarled, rising from between the rows with Keet's backpack in hand. "Or I finish what the tiger started."

"That's a fight you really don't want." I sank my nails into my palms. "Leave him out of this."

Gaze locked on mine, he ripped the pack open, ruining it, and groped the bottom. "Where did he…?"

"Save our oceansss," Keet shrieked, diving straight for him. "Oceans, oceans, oceans!"

The parakeet went straight for the eyes, clawing and raking until Ormand screamed and cursed him.

Coarse hands clamped over my neck from behind and squeezed until I saw stars. Mathieu. Again. I stepped back, hooked a leg through his, and yanked it out from under him. He fell, but he took me with him. I landed on top of him, sinking rapid elbow strikes into his muscular stomach, but his grip held firm.

A loud squelch preceded a spray of warm blood that hit the top of my head and rained on my face.

"Are you okay?" Corbin lifted me off Mathieu with vampire-quick reflexes. "Can you talk?"

Healing the damage would only take a few minutes, but I held my throat and shook my head for now.

Glancing behind me, I found Corbin had stomped Matthieu's skull in with his boot.

I swung my head toward him, shock pounding through me, but an odd light filled Corbin's eyes.

"He hurt you." A feral ruthlessness carved his expression. "He had it coming."

No words came to mind for the brutal display of violence that would do any gwyllgi proud.

Pack life kept my hands covered in blood. I had killed, and I would kill again. Those were the hard truths anyone ranked above middling in any shifter pack accepted as inevitable. But just this once, I had a white knight, and it was…

…nice.

"Save. Our. Oceans."

Corbin turned his attention to his phone, and I was grateful for the excuse to look away.

"Keet?" I spun around, searching for him. "Where did he go?"

We followed the sound of sobbing to where Ormand knelt, his hands covering his face. Blood seeped between his fingers, and he wept while Keet tore skin off his busted knuckles, the parakeet rubbing his face in crimson rivulets.

And, yeah, that was Keet, bathing in the blood of his enemies.

Thank God he was on our side.

"You ambushed Eva," Corbin snarled, "and she's not crying about it."

The big man got to his feet, weeping blood through his fingers. "Where's Matthieu?"

"Dead." Corbin made no bones about it. "Give us any more grief, and you'll be next."

The thread of eagerness in his voice, the desire for more violence, was unlike the chill man I had known. I couldn't call foul, not when I was smeared in others' blood, but he had always hidden his vampire side. I wasn't sure what it meant that he let me glimpse it now. I wasn't even sure he meant to let me see.

Throwing his head back, Ormand unleashed a mournful baying noise from his human throat.

His face was a patchwork of fine scratches and Keet-sized bite marks. His eyes, well, there wasn't much left of them until he had time to regenerate.

Blinded by rage, and the aforementioned lack of eyeballs, he charged us. He smacked into an aisle seat with his hip, bounced off, and kissed the floor at my feet. Fresh blood spread in a puddle under his chin, and I figured he must have bitten off his tongue.

While he lay there, sobbing quietly, Keet lit on his head and began plucking out hairs.

I really, really hoped Keet didn't find any tongue and bring it home as a souvenir/snack.

"That bird is something else." Corbin stared at the crimson stain. "He's got a bloodthirsty streak."

"I would never say this to Aunt Grier's face, but, at the end of the day, the little guy *is* a zombie."

Had he been any bigger than a parakeet, say, a macaw or cockatoo, we might have been in danger of him cracking open someone's skull with his beak and eating their brains.

"That's harsh."

"Hey, I'm just keeping it real." I slid Corbin a smile. "Or should I say, Keeting it real?"

"That's terrible." A soft laugh huffed out of him. "I can't believe you went there."

"I thought it was funny."

"Well, you were just strangled. Twice. It probably restricted the blood flow to your brain for too long."

"Very funny."

"I thought so."

Grateful for the empty theater, I debated on the best course of action, considering there was a fatality.

"I've already texted the cleaners." Corbin bobbed his shoulder. "Mathieu attacked a sentinel." He gestured to his spattered shirt. "Plus, I'm a vampire. That's how we do things."

Cleaners were the fixers of the supernatural world. They made evidence of paranormal activity vanish. It was a stretch to call this their jurisdiction. Gwyllgi handled their own problems.

But I was tired. And Corbin was being nice. So, I was willing to bend, just this once.

"Thanks." I managed not to choke on the words. "Drive me back to Woolly?"

I wanted Keet safe behind the bars of his cage while I unwound from our adventure and confessed all to Aunt Grier before the internet—or Miss Lacy—tattled on me.

"What kind of date would this be if I didn't end the night walking you to your door?"

"This isn't a date." I ignored the uptick in my pulse I was sure he heard. "You also have a room at Woolworth House, so…it's more like me walking you to your door."

"I'll take it."

"Exit to the left," Keet chirped. "To the left, to the left, to the left, to the left."

"The emergency exit," Corbin murmured. "Good idea." He frowned down at Keet. "What about him?"

With his backpack ruined, I was forced to resort to how I carried him when I was a kid. "I got this."

Corbin went ahead, scouting the hall leading out of the building, while I tucked in my shirt.

"I had to ditch my bra," I told Keet. "Don't get any ideas while you're down there."

Gently, I slid him into the neck of my shirt, and he nested on the fold of material above my waistband.

After taking one last look around, I joined Corbin, whose proud smile hadn't budged all night.

Determined to ignore that, to ignore *him*, I led the way to the garage and called for the elevator.

We rode up in silence, which was nice, minus Keet yanking hairs out of my navel.

That freaking *hurt*.

The Bronco was impossible to miss, or maybe it was my infatuation that made it stand out to me.

"Get you a girl," Corbin whispered in my ear, "who looks at you like Eva looks at 1969 Broncos."

"I'm sure that won't be a hardship for you." I elbowed him. "1969 Broncos? Now those are rare."

Ones that had been fully restored to my exact dream specifications anyway.

Gah.

I should have said yes when Uncle Linus offered to buy me one for my sixteenth birthday, but no. I had to be proud and have principles and blah blah blah at him about earning my own money and how much sweeter the reward would be.

Sixteen-year-old Eva had been a total and complete idiot, in my humble opinion.

As I opened the passenger-side door, I caught movement out of the corner of my eye.

Bast.

And whoa boy was he pissed. He must have heard the news about Mathieu from Ormand.

About to untuck my shirt and pray to God Keet didn't decide to tour Savannah by moonlight, I jerked to a standstill when that same glitter of madness sparked in Corbin's eyes. He leapt onto Bast, knocking him flat on his back. Bast's skull hit the concrete with a dull thud, and crimson spread under his head.

Corbin kept going, hammering away at him, until Bast was a smear on the parking deck floor.

The frantic beat of my heart drew Corbin's attention, and he stared in a daze at what he had done.

"Here." He tossed me the keys to the Bronco. "I should go."

"Corbin." I fumbled to catch them. The blood made them slick. "What are you…?"

Slinky as a cat shifter, he jumped onto the metal railing, then leapt into open air.

"Corbin." I raced for the edge. *"Corbin."*

Old-growth oaks obscured my view, but patrons scattered from his fall or my screams or both.

There was no point in searching for him. I wouldn't find him. I tried that once. Okay, a million times.

A covert ops vampire knew how to disappear when the situation called for it, but why did this one rate? There had been no formal challenge to protect Bast, and there could be no doubt he was out for blood. Security footage would corroborate our story.

Corbin had no reason to run. The sentinels, and the pack, would rule in his favor. So why vanish on me?

The manic gleam in his eyes was new. So was the flirting. What had changed? Him or me?

"Pepperoni," Keet mumbled through my shirt. "Sausage. Ham. Bacon, bacon, bacon."

Despite parakeets being omnivores, Keet was trending toward carnivore in his old age, around fifty.

"Okay." I eyed the keys in my palm. "I'll order a pizza, and we'll race the driver to Woolly."

In the Bronco. That Corbin had left in my care. I wanted to vomit from the responsibility of driving it.

Careful not to harm Keet as I strapped on my seat belt, I slid the key into the ignition and noticed a silver charm on the loop. A dog tag. The kind soldiers wore. One side held Corbin's information stamped on its battered surface. The other side…

Happy eight belated birthdays since the last time I saw you.

My chin misses you.

I do too.

Tears smudged my vision, and my throat grew tight.

"Pepperoni," Keet demanded, yanking on my shirt. "Sausage."

"I'm on it," I assured him, wiping my eyes dry. "I need to make some calls first, okay?"

The cleaners had to be made aware there was another body for them to collect.

Out in the open.

Where anyone could see.

Such was paranormal life, but sheesh.

Think of the children.

With that formality observed, I dialed Rollo, the pack enforcer on duty, and requested he dispatch a packmate to guard Bast's remains. On second thought, I requested a tarp to spread over the body too.

While I waited on the promised enforcer, I placed the pizza order to prevent Keet from mutinying.

As I fit my fingers into the indents made by Corbin on the steering wheel, I measured my hand against his much larger one. I could almost imagine the metal was still warm from his skin.

Lost in thought, I startled when Marly, one of the top enforcers, arrived to claim the scene.

With a dip of my chin, I put the Bronco in reverse and made my way out of the parking deck.

As I passed beneath the trees, I shrugged off a prickle of awareness that warned I was being watched.

"Thank you," I whispered, allowing the wind to catch the words and fling them into the cool night.

"Welcome, welcome, welcome." Keet wriggled against my stomach. "Pizza, pizza, pizza."

Stuffed crust wouldn't solve all my problems, but it was a good start.

Until I figured out what had changed with Corbin, well, at least I had Meat Lovers' Supreme.

And a 1969 Bronco in reef aqua that smelled like leather and copper, vampire and…possibilities.

Author Bio

USA Today best-selling author Hailey Edwards writes about questionable applications of otherwise perfectly good magic, the transformative power of love, the family you choose for yourself, and blowing stuff up. Not necessarily all at once. That could get messy.

Author website: haileyedwards.net

Social Platform #1-Facebook Group-
facebook.com/groups/1965693747023964

Social Platform #2-Twitter-twitter.com/HaileyEdwards

Helpful

A story in the universe of Blood Trails

By Jennifer Blackstream

*T*hat dog *mummy just moved.*

I stared at the embalmed beast under the glass case before me, my tail swishing back and forth over the museum floor. There. The bit of loose bandage on the right of the small bundle with the vaguely canine-shaped head. It had definitely moved. Fluttering as if in a breeze.

But there was no breeze under the glass.

The dog had definitely moved.

"Majesty."

The woman's voice was quiet enough, but there was a sharp edge to it that made me glance to the side, more out of curiosity than anything. The colors of the Embalmed Animals of Ancient Egypt exhibit surrounded me in a veritable sea of red and gold that smelled of sand and long-dead musk. My witch, dressed as she was in her red trench coat and brightly colored leggings, looked oddly at home.

Though, based on her expression, she wasn't enjoying the exhibit.

She took a step closer to me, bringing her within five feet of my spot in front of the moving dog mummy. "Please, don't do anything…"

I was still learning to understand human speech, but after only a few months, I'd developed a remarkable understanding of the witch's facial expressions and tone. Right now, she was making the "Did I Leave The Stove On" face. Since she hadn't cooked today, that expression probably meant she was having trouble putting her thoughts together.

I tilted my head to show her I was still listening despite the prolonged pause. It was okay if she took her time. I didn't mind waiting.

Helpful cats like me never minded waiting.

She raised a finger in the air and pointed at me, as if that would help her focus. Maybe it did.

"Don't do anything."

It sounded like the same words but this time there was a finality to her tone, as if the thought were finished. My tail twitched in frustration. I'd hoped she'd use one of the words I knew. Like *food* or *bedtime.* I liked those words.

"You should make him leave," came a higher-pitched female voice from somewhere under the witch's hair. "He's going to cause trouble."

My ears pricked forward. It was the pixie's voice. The tiny pink creature that spent most of her time flitting through the air around the witch, complaining and...*sparkling.*

I'd almost caught her yesterday...

The witch's eyes narrowed, reading my intentions before I'd even realized I was staring. Before she could say anything, a child's voice pierced the air behind her.

"Mommy, it's a kitten!"

Kitten. That meant me.

A child I recognized as the one who'd been dragging her mother around like a dead bird since the exhibit had opened suddenly bent to scoop me up. I went limp to avoid injury, watching the floor fall away as the small child hefted me into her arms with the wild abandon that would fade as soon as a less helpful cat taught her to be more cautious around strange animals.

Coincidentally, she'd lifted me just high enough to see the tiny pixie hiding underneath the witch's hair...

Sparkle, sparkle.

Peasblossom narrowed multi-faceted pink eyes at me, staring me down.

I meowed.

The witch flinched, then closed her eyes and took a slow, deliberate breath.

"Olivia, put that poor animal down," her mother ordered, apparently not inclined to address the issue of what a kitten was doing inside the Cleveland Museum. "I thought you wanted to see the mummies?"

Mummies. That was the word the curator kept using when she talked about the display. I turned back to the canine I'd been examining before the witch interrupted me. I blinked.

The dog mummy was gone.

"It's empty," the little girl complained, putting me down. She shuffled over to the stand. "What's it say?"

Her mother frowned as she squinted at the plaque under the case. "Basenji were a type of dog breed prized by ancient Egyptians. So prized that they were often mummified after death and buried with their owners so they could continue serving their masters in the afterlife." She glanced up at the empty case.

I looked around the room, my tail lashing as I watched for some hint of loose bandages trailing from behind one of the large potted plants. The dog mummy had escaped. I would find him. I was good at finding things.

I'd found the witch.

Lots of times.

The witch stared me down as Olivia and her mother moved on to the next mummified animal—a bird of some kind. Now she was making her "Did You Eat All The Honey" face she usually reserved for the pixie. Only she was looking at me.

"Was there a mummy under that glass when we came into the room, Peasblossom?" she asked without taking her eyes off me.

"How should I know? What do I want with a mummified dog?" The pixie tugged on the witch's hair. "Let's go to the cafe. Maybe they have honey."

Honey. I knew that word too. The pixie wanted to eat.

"You had enough honey with breakfast." The witch was still staring at me, but she flicked a hand over her hair as the pixie continued to tug. "Peasblossom, you can't still be hungry."

Hungry. That meant food. But she was using her "no" tone.

The pixie hated the "no" tone.

The ensuing argument was enough to distract the witch, so she forgot about the dog mummy, and I trotted along behind her as she left the Egyptian room, continuing her search for whatever it was she was here to find. She didn't share many details with me, but that was okay. I was here to help, whenever she needed me.

Up ahead, a strip of tattered bandage disappeared around a corner with a sharp jerk.

I shot forward. Claws extended, I brought my paw down on the yellowed bandage, anchoring it to the floor.

"What are you doing?"

I looked up, finding myself face to face with the dog mummy. He looked bigger now that he wasn't wrapped up like a caterpillar in a cocoon, its limbs bound tightly to its body in a way that could only be managed with a subject that was deceased. Now that he had legs to stand on, I could see he was tall enough that I'd be able to walk underneath him without brushing my ears against his stomach. One of his pointed ears had escaped the bandages, as had his thick, curled tail. He was a brown and white dog with a pointed snout that looked somehow familiar.

It took me a moment to realize I'd understood what he said. *All* of what he'd said.

"You speak cat?" I asked, impressed.

The canine wrinkled his nose as much as the bandages would allow. "I speak all languages. I am a messenger."

"You're dead," I pointed out. "You must be *very* helpful if you're still delivering messages." I puffed out my chest. "Helpful like me."

A gap in the bandages over his face gave me a glimpse of one chocolate colored eye narrowed in focus. "Yes," he said finally. "I am. Who are you and what do you want?"

I resisted the urge to look down at the bandage still caught in my claws. "I want to help. Naturally. I'm *very* helpful."

The dog tilted its head. "Are you The Finder?"

His words reached into my mind, back into my memories. A woman's voice echoed inside my head, speaking from the past. *"Find her."*

He'd said Finder not Find Her, but I wouldn't hold a mispronunciation against him. He was a dog attempting to speak cat, after all.

"Yes," I answered graciously. "I am."

The dog stared at me for a long minute. He looked a little ridiculous, if I were honest. What with most of his body being bound in aged, unraveling bandages except for his legs poking out. His fur was a bit patchy, and his flesh a bit emaciated and blackened, but not bad considering how long he'd been dead. He took a step forward, and when he moved, he did so with more strength and grace than I'd have expected from a mummy.

"I am Bas. I have been sent by my master to find an amulet called the Nine Lives. It is a small pale green ceramic cat on a leather strap."

"It sounds like a collar," I observed.

Bas's ears flattened, letting more of the bandages slide off. A human passing by stopped short, his eyes bulging as he raised one shaking hand to point at Bas. I glanced over at the man as he started babbling and pointing, his head swiveling to look at the other humans passing by. The crowd immediately began giving him a wide berth, with mothers pulling on their children's arms to keep them from stopping to stare.

You could always tell the humans sensitive enough to pick up on the Otherworld.

"It is not a collar," Bas said evenly, ignoring the security guard approaching the hysterical human. "It is an amulet. And it is very powerful."

"Is it *your*...amulet?" I asked.

"No. It belongs to a sorcerer, an associate of my master, Ra. He created it to give himself nine lives."

"Why?" I asked. "Humans don't know what to do with the one life they have, why ask for eight more?"

"It's just something humans do," Bas said, a hint of exasperation creeping into his tone. "It doesn't matter. When he finished with his eighth life, he decided he would use the final life to recharge the amulet and pass it on to someone deserving, someone who would use it to help others. Unfortunately, the man who was supposed to have it, lost it somehow. So the sorcerer asked my master to send me to fetch it."

"He used one life to charge an amulet that would give someone else nine lives?" I spoke slowly so Bas would have a chance to hear that he wasn't making sense.

"Power given costs less than power taken," Bas said, using the same voice the witch used when she explained something to the pixie. Slow, with the sort of cadence that said the words were replacing violent urges.

I blinked slowly as a weight slid over my body. As if I hadn't slept in days and it was catching up with me all at once. I shook my head. The magic was building inside me again.

"Are you all right?" Bas asked.

"Yes." I took a deep breath. "So, the amulet was stolen and you want help finding it. Because you're a messenger, not a finder."

Bas shifted his weight on his mummified legs, making his bones creak. "I *could* find it. I know where it was, where it should be. I could track it that way. But Seth mentioned to my master that the Finder would be at the museum and would offer to help. If you are the Finder, you can make this task go more quickly."

The magic pulsed inside me, and I swallowed it back. "Seth?"

"One of the gods." Bas paused. "Usually he isn't so helpful."

"But I am," I reminded him. "Helpful, I mean." The magic pulsed again, stronger this time. "I need a moment. If you'll excuse me..."

"Time is not on our side," Bas said firmly. "The sorcerer said that whoever stole the amulet has already burned through one of the lives. We must find it before he burns through the rest."

"Burned?" I leaned all my weight on my front paws, trying to keep from falling over as I looked for the witch. The magic was for her. I needed to go to her.

"Used. It's what made the sorcerer check in on him. It's how he discovered the amulet was not where it should be. He believes

119

someone has stolen it and is using the power of the 'lives' the amulet grants as an energy source for other spells."

My stomach hurt. And my paws hurt. So much magic. Where was that witch?

Bas eyed me with what must pass for concern in canines. "Are you sure you're all right?"

"Fine. Just need to give something to my witch. One moment."

"But—"

I lurched to all fours and trotted in the direction I'd last seen the witch, ignoring the sputtering dog mummy behind me.

I found her standing in the room next to the one Bas and I had been talking in. She was speaking with a man who looked like he'd just eaten something very sour. The witch held up a figurine to show him, something black and shiny that looked like a man holding some sort of weapon. She was saying something to the sour man and nodding at the figurine. The man glanced down at the object even as he turned his body as if he'd walk away. He was making the "I'm Not Eating That" face.

The witch spotted me coming toward her and her entire body tensed, no doubt preparing for the surge of magic I was bringing her. If I were honest with myself, she wasn't great with magic. More often than not, she caused a lot of trouble with the energy I gave her. But I'd promised the pale lady that I would be helpful. Always helpful. And she'd been very specific that I was to use my magic to help this witch.

"Majesty," the witch said, a warning in her voice.

She always spoke my name with such gravitas. Such respect. It made it easier to forgive her shortcomings.

The power inside me swelled. It crackled in the air, tickling my nose, and I sneezed.

The magic left me in a whoosh, heading for the witch. When I opened my eyes, the witch was still standing there, as was the unpleasant looking man.

The figurine in her hand was gone.

No, wait, it was back again.

No, now it was gone.

I frowned. How was making the artifact disappear and reappear helpful?

I shook my head and turned to go back to Bas. The witch would figure it out. She always did. The important thing was, I'd given her the help she needed, even if I didn't understand it. And now it was time for me to help Bas.

When I returned to the dog mummy, he was staring at me with a look on his face I couldn't quite read.

"What?" I asked.

"Did she call you Majesty?"

"Yes."

Bas closed his eyes and let out a heavy sigh. "Then the worship of your kind still continues. Perfect." He opened his eyes and shook his head, causing more of the bandages to loosen. "Humans have learned nothing."

I waited patiently for him to return to the task at hand.

"Anubis was dog-headed, you know," Bas muttered. "But that wasn't good enough for the humans. Jackal-headed, that's what they say now. It's insulting."

Suddenly, his entire body tensed, every muscle tightening until he looked very much like the dried mummy he'd been when I first saw him. I reached out a paw to touch his chest, relieved when his eyes refocused, and the tension left him in a visible whoosh.

"We have to hurry," he said grimly. "The sorcerer just sent me a message. The amulet has burned through two more lives."

"What does that mean?" I asked.

"Death," Bas said gravely. "Or something worse."

It took some convincing to explain to Bas that letting me ride on his back was the quickest way for us both to get to our destination. The mummy dog ran with the speed of a feather in a windstorm, and it was only after I pointed out that he could either carry me, or wait for me, that he agreed to let me ride. As unhappy as he was with our traveling arrangement, he was even more unhappy when we reached our destination.

"Cats," he spat.

I rose up on my hind legs so I could look over his head at the sprawling yard before us. Cats, indeed. Apparently, our theft victim was an avid cat lover. My feline brethren were everywhere, dotting sunny patches on his lawn, lounging on the windowsills inside the house. And when the door opened and an old man I assumed to be the victim emerged onto the porch, he even carried a cat on one shoulder. The cat on his shoulder was young, as young as I looked. And he was clinging to the old man's sweater with the tenacity of a youth determined to hold the high ground over his fellow felines. Literally.

"This has to be a joke." Bas shook his head. "A horrible, horrible joke."

Amulet Theft Victim left the door open behind him—apparently so his furry friends could come and go as they pleased—and walked down the porch steps to retrieve a package the delivery man had left by the garage door. It didn't seem to annoy him that the delivery person hadn't carried the package all the way to the front porch. A tolerant man, then.

Bas raised his nose to sniff the air. "I can smell the amulet, but the scent is faint."

"There might be a faster way to track it. I held out a paw. "Excuse me," I said, speaking to one of the cats meandering over the lawn. "Excuse me, might I have a moment of your time?"

The cat, a regal calico, turned to look at me, and her expression softened when she saw my youthful face. "So polite for one so young. What brings you here?"

I recognized a mothering instinct when I saw one. I tucked my front paws together, making my feet look even tinier, and tilted my head so the sunlight caught my blue eyes just so. "The man who feeds you. He had an amulet. A piece of clay shaped like a cat?"

"Yes," the calico said, nodding. "I believe his granddaughter gave it to him, though where she got it, I couldn't say. He was very sad to see it go missing. He's worried the tiny human will think he didn't like her gift."

I didn't know much about magic, but I was willing to bet the man's granddaughter had had nothing to do with making that amulet. More likely the sorcerer had delivered it himself, in a guise that would make an old man not only accept the necklace, but treasure it.

"So, he didn't know it was magic?" Bas asked.

The calico gave him a small smile. "He's only human."

"We want to get it back for him," I said, indicating myself and Bas. "Do you have any idea where we might find it?"

Another cat approached from behind the calico. This one had sleek black fur, and a piece of his ear was missing. He stopped when he heard our conversation, and his ears flattened against his head.

"The trinket isn't missing," he corrected me. "It was stolen."

"Stolen?" the calico echoed. "I didn't see anyone."

"You were sleeping," the black cat informed her. "But I wasn't. I saw him take it."

"Who?" Bas demanded.

The black cat shot Bas a dirty look, then turned to me. "It was the mailman."

A low growl rumbled in Bas's throat, and more of the fur on his neck pushed through the bandages, making him look larger. "The mailman. Of course."

"Someone you know?" I asked.

"I know his kind." Bas looked down at the black cat and took a step forward. "Where can I find this mailman?"

"He doesn't come here anymore," the black cat scoffed. "He's a thief, isn't he? He's not going to come back here after what he did. Not when he stole such magic."

Bas blinked. "You knew the amulet was magic?"

Every feline in hearing range stared at the dog mummy, and I cleared my throat.

"We're cats," I said, trying to be gentle. "You think we wouldn't feel that level of magic?"

"Stupid dog," the black cat muttered under his breath.

Bas tensed, and I dug my claws into his back in a silent warning not to anger my brethren. One wrong word and the yard full of cats would become a yard full of enemies with razor sharp claws and eight lives to burn.

Blessedly, at that moment, footsteps sounded on the sidewalk behind us. Bas turned his head, then immediately pivoted so quickly that if I hadn't already had my claws out, I'd have fallen off. I had a split second to observe that dead dogs must not feel pain, and then I was holding on for dear life as Bas charged up to a woman approaching Amulet Theft Victim's mailbox.

The woman came to an abrupt halt, then rocked back on one foot, her right arm rising to protect her face. She didn't lose her grip on the envelopes in her grasp, and she didn't run, but I could see the fear in her eyes as she stared at the large dog bearing down on her.

"Bas," I snapped. "Sit!"

Bas did not sit. But he did come to a dead halt to swivel his head around to stare at me as if I'd paid a grave insult to his dearly beloved grandmother.

"She's the mail carrier," I pointed out to him. "Perhaps she knows where her predecessor is now. We need to find a way to communicate with her."

Bas wrinkled his muzzle in disgust and looked up at the mail carrier. After taking a steadying breath, he spoke.

"The mailman you replaced. Where is he now?"

The woman's jaw dropped, her eyes bulging. She still didn't let go of the mail. "You... Did you just... You talked."

I lowered my face to my paws, a sudden headache forming between my eyes. The woman was doing that stuttering thing the witch did sometimes. I didn't have to understand what she was saying to know that Bas was going to make the human crazy. It would be the human in the museum all over again, with the eye-bulging and the babbling. We'd never get the information we needed. How was I supposed to *help* him if he insisted on being so—

The headache blossomed, flowing up and out with enough force that I was certain it would take the top of my head and my ears with it. There was no holding onto it, and the magic poured out of me like root beer from a shaken soda can. I collapsed onto Bas's back, blinking furiously to try and stay conscious. When I finally opened my eyes, the mail carrier was still there, and so was Bas.

Only now there was an elephant standing next to the mail carrier too.

I froze. Well, if the talking dog hadn't done it, the elephant would. I should have brought the witch. Though, she hadn't done much better, as I recalled. There'd been that rhinoceros inside the house…

To my surprise, the mail carrier instantly relaxed, shoulders slumping so rapidly the bag of mail nearly slid off her shoulder.

"I'm dreaming." Her voice was higher now, and she was smiling so big I could almost hear laughter. "I knew it. Knew I had to be dreaming." She shook her head and looked down at the letters in her hand, glancing through them before looking up at the address on the house. "It's the stress," she told Bas. "That's what it is. New route. Faconi didn't give notice, you know. He inherits a bunch of money from some aunt and—bam!—he's gone."

I frowned. Now she was making the "My Keys Were in My Pocket The Whole Time" face. She'd said a bunch of words I didn't know, but one sounded familiar. *Dreaming.* Dream. Dreams. The witch used that word when she talked about the woman at the hotel. The sorceress.

I didn't think this mail carrier was a sorceress. Maybe she thought Bas had made the elephant?

Regardless, she clearly seemed to be feeling better, so once again, my magic had been an immense help. "What's she saying?" I asked Bas.

The dog ignored me. "And where has he gone?"

Where. I knew that word. He was asking her where the thief had gone.

The woman snorted. "We're not that close. But my money's on that fancy neighborhood on the south side. Faconi was always going on about how he'd have a mansion there someday."

She shook her head and kept walking toward the Amulet Theft

Victim's mailbox. Bas started to turn, but suddenly seemed to notice the elephant. He tensed, then stared down at me.

I looked back at him. If he wasn't going to ask, I wasn't going to volunteer.

He must have been in a hurry, because he deliberately turned away from the elephant. "You said you can feel magic?"

"I'm a cat."

He waited, as if I hadn't just answered his question, then seemed to realize I had. "We'll go to the neighborhood then, and you tell me when you feel the magic."

I flattened my ears against my head. "I'm not a scent hound. The amulet isn't so powerful it's going to radiate magic in giant waves I can feel just walking through the neighborhood."

"Then we'll go to the neighborhood, and I'll try to catch the amulet's scent, and you try to feel for the magic. If he's burned through three of the lives already, then he's done something big. It shouldn't be hard to find."

He took off without waiting for a response, and had I been a less helpful cat, I might have leapt off his back and made him circle around and ask me nicely to continue. But being the exceptionally helpful cat I was, I dug my claws into the bandages over his back, deep enough that I felt mummified flesh, and held on as he began that supernaturally fast run in whatever direction the mail carrier had indicated.

I felt the magic as soon as we entered the neighborhood. The feel of it made my fur stand up and my nose itch. I tugged at Bas's flesh, and the dog mummy trotted to a halt.

"I think I smell something," he said, lifting his nose in the air.

"No need." I pointed with one paw, leaning over so Bas could see me, and Bas followed my gesture to a large mansion on the corner at the intersection of two pristine streets. All the houses in this neighborhood were grand, but none of them came close to the monstrosity radiating magic like a field of four-leaf clovers.

It was the ugliest mansion I'd ever seen. The front of the building looked as if someone had taken two different—ugly—mansions and smashed them together. The left was red brick, curved to look like a medieval turret. The right was pale stucco, half of which drizzled down the front of the house to make it look like a termite mound. The east side of the house was made entirely of windows, giving it a modern look in complete contrast to the medieval-style door.

"That mansion was created with magic," I said, trying to look away.

"Then that's where we'll find the amulet."

Bas loped toward the house with the confidence of someone completely unconcerned at the prospect of confronting a human and his magic amulet that created mansions. I was about to ask Bas if he was certain he was up to the task, but then I remembered what he'd said. Seth—a *god*—had told him I would help. And I was *very* helpful. Perhaps Bas had the ability to use the magic I channeled, just like the witch.

No wonder he's so confident.

Getting inside the house wasn't difficult. One of the windows on the side made completely of windows was open, and Bas wasted no time plunging inside, into the solarium within. He padded forward a few feet, then paused to listen.

There. Voices coming from the second floor.

Bas crept up the stairs and stopped just outside a door that was partially open. I could hear a man's voice inside. He was using the "I'm the Boss, and I'll Smack You If You Don't Start Cooperating" tone. Another voice responded, lower and more raspy than the first. It didn't speak long enough for me to get a feel for its attitude.

Whatever the second voice had said made Bas freeze. For a second, I had to press my paws harder into his back to reassure myself he was still here, still flesh and blood and not turned to stone.

"What's wrong?" I whispered.

"That voice." Bas shook his head, as if he couldn't believe it. "I know that voice. It's Rayaan."

"Who's Rayaan?"

Bas didn't look at me. "But he was locked away. Sealed in a cave. No one should have been able to find him."

I dug my claws into his back. "Who's Rayaan?"

Bas stiffened his legs, pushing himself to stand straighter as if he were staring down his opponent now. "A very powerful djinn. And that fool has released him."

"I'll raise it for you," Rayaan promised. "I'll raise the whole ship, with every last gold coin and every last jewel."

I climbed up to sit on Bas's head so I could see what little of his expression was visible beneath the bandages. The raspy voice was speaking again. This time, it sounded like the voice the witch used when I was under the bed and she was kneeling down beside it waving a can of Tuna. The Tuna Offering tone.

"I don't need you." The sound of a hand striking a heavy leather-bound book punctuated whatever Faconi had said. "I've been studying magic for years. I can raise the ship myself."

Magic. I knew that word too.

Bas snorted. "Faconi fancies himself a wizard."

That explained the "I Can Carry All the Groceries Myself" tone.

"You are no wizard," the djinn said, a hint of a sneer creeping into his voice. "I sense no power in you. You will never raise the ship without me."

The djinn was using the "You're Going to Drop the Milk Again And I'm Not Helping You Clean It Up" tone. Apparently the djinn didn't agree with Faconi's view of himself as a wizard. *Wizard* was another word I knew.

"I didn't need you to build this house," Faconi said smugly. "With this amulet, I don't need your magic to get what I want." A rustling of paper. "I've been studying this book for years. All these spells. And now I finally have the power to make them work."

"A true wizard wouldn't need the amulet," the djinn mocked. "Every human has the potential to learn magic. But not everyone has the skill. *You* don't have the skill. You can memorize the spells in that book all you like, but the fact is, you're no different from someone who hears a song and believes they can sing because they've learned the lyrics, and they remember the tune."

Bas snorted in agreement with whatever the djinn had said.

"Shut up," Faconi snapped. "The point is, I don't need your help."

"You needed me to find the ship," Rayaan countered.

"I needed your *knowledge*. Your experience. Which is why *I* summoned you into that book, with everything you know written out on its pages for me to peruse as I have need. You are a resource, not an ally. I have plans—big plans. And now that I know where to find the *Flor de la Mar*, I'll have all the money I need to finance them."

I shook my head. Based on my experience with the witch and her pixie, the wizard was no doubt attempting a spell while the djinn criticized his technique. If this were the witch and the pixie, I'd smell burning potion soon.

"That amulet won't last forever." Rayaan's voice turned sweeter, sliding back into the Tuna Offering tone. "I could make you powerful. Make you a true wizard, with a limitless—"

"Spare me your pathetic attempt to trick me into releasing you. I'm no fool. I didn't need you to build this mansion, and I don't need you to do this."

Bas jerked his head up, fast enough that I nearly tumbled to the floor. "He's going to burn another life. I have to stop him!"

"Wait!" I blurted out. "Don't—"

Bas bolted forward, hitting the door to the bedroom hard enough that it smacked into the wall with a fur-raising bang. He snarled as he paused just long enough to get his bearings, his gaze quickly finding Faconi.

I knew it was Faconi because he'd clearly been to the Halloween shop and had chosen "Middle-Aged Wizard" as his costume of choice. He was wearing an honest-to-gods robe, complete with hood, in a shade of crimson that the witch outright refused to put in the washing machine for fear of the Red Die. He had resisted the slouched pointy hat, but had apparently caved in to the desire for a staff. The large piece of wood was taller than he was, making him look even more like a child playing dress up.

Less humorous was the book lying on the desk beside him. It looked brand new, but the pages were covered in red ink that dripped and shimmered in a way no mundane ink would have done. The pages rustled even though there was no breeze in the room, and when the pages moved, I swore I heard someone—or something—breathing.

The wizard had enchanted it somehow. Or…trapped something inside it?

Faconi gaped at the mummy dog, but only for a second. Then he snatched the book from the desk and ran toward a closet door at the back of the room, looking very much like a man intent on escape. I hung on for dear life as Bas took off after the wannabe wizard, mummified bones creaking as he ran. Ahead, Faconi tore open the closet door and ran inside as if it were an exit to the outdoors. Bas did the same, and I squeezed my eyes shut, waiting for the inevitable moment when the canine's skull would meet the back wall of the closet.

The impact never came.

There was no wall. There was no closet. The door that should have opened to reveal a row of poorly fitting sweaters, instead opened to reveal…a lake.

I had a split second to register the fact that Bas had run out into empty air, and then we were both falling. Bas hit the water first, sending a spray of freezing water over my face a split second before I too was lost in the dark blue depths. The cold stole the breath from my lungs. Water dragged at my fur as it tried to force its way into my nose and mouth. Energy roared to life inside me, riding a wave of adrenaline, a desire to survive and protect whatever lives I had left.

The power blossomed out and up, exploding in a wave of force that pushed me a few inches deeper into the water. Warm tears leaked from the corners of my eyes. I was going to drown.

A mummified jaw grabbed me by the scruff of my neck. Seconds later, I was being held in a fierce grip, my face finally above water. I sputtered and coughed as I twisted in Bas's grip, searching for the wizard who'd led us on this miserable chase only to leave me to die in the lake.

Before I could locate my prey, Bas dropped me. Panic seized me, and I dug my claws into his bandages, trying not to let my head slip under the water again. Furious, I opened my mouth, ready to demand an explanation.

Bas spoke first. "You have taken something that doesn't belong to you. Give it back, or be hunted down like the cowardly thief you are."

He wasn't talking to me.

"Who are you?" Faconi demanded.

I clung to Bas's back, staying close to the surface of the water. I didn't think the wizard had seen me. That could be to our advantage. I looked around, finally spotting the middle-aged man standing at the water's edge. *Who*, he'd said. I knew that word. He wanted Bas's name.

"I am Bas, messenger of the gods. I was sent with a message for you. The amulet is not yours. Give it back now so that I might return it to its rightful owner. If you force me to take it from you, I make no promises that you'll survive the experience."

The wizard's face twisted into a sneer. "Tell your master the amulet is mine now."

Bas bared his teeth. "I'm not leaving without it."

"Then you won't leave." Faconi pulled the book from under his arm and flipped it open. "And you won't tell anyone you found the amulet."

I didn't need to understand what he'd said to know what he'd meant. He planned to hurt Bas, and he was opening the book for a spell to do it. Bas swam madly for the shore, but Faconi was already reading from the book.

I reached inside myself, searching for the magic, for some sign it was building again. I'd never had any control over it before, never tried. The pale lady had been very clear that the magic was to help the witch. She'd said the magic would happen when it was needed, my job was just to be there. To be helpful.

There. The magic. I felt it inside, like the flicker of a small candle flame. I concentrated on that dancing bit of light, concentrated until it grew bigger and bigger, the flame beginning to crackle and burn in earnest. Power flared out from my body in a warm rush of blessed heat—

Heat that was abruptly extinguished as the muted blue sky darkened to an ominous grey and a torrential downpour covered the lake and the banks around it.

The wizard didn't stop chanting. He leaned forward, using his body to protect the book as best he could.

Bas floundered for a second as the rain made the surface of the lake rough and choppy, and I let out a miserable mewl as tiny waves tried to drag me off the mummified dog's back.

Bas was still five feet from shore when the wizard's spell struck him in the chest.

The bolt of purple energy drove into Bas's body, expanding inside him in a wave of violet before concentrating in a single spot in his throat. Bas made a horrible choking sound, floundering in the water. It was all I could do to stay low enough on his back that the wizard couldn't see me, but not so low that I drowned. The wizard held out his hand, then flung it skyward. The purple light inside Bas flew up and out of his mouth, then exploded in a shower of purple sparks.

I had no idea what the wizard had just done, but he wasn't sticking around to explain himself. He ran around the edge of the lake, onto a bridge I hadn't seen when we fell in. The bridge was a contraption of rickety wood that started with a single step just outside the door we'd fallen through before curving around what looked like the face of a cliff and extending over the very edge of the lake. That was how the wizard had left the portal without falling into the water, while we'd missed the sight of the bridge entirely. I stared in growing horror as the wizard ran over the bridge and up the curved steps to the still-open door that led to the bedroom closet.

He darted inside and slammed the door shut behind him.

Bas regained his composure and determinedly swam to the edge of the lake, climbing out on trembling legs and forcing himself to keep going until he left the reach of the rainstorm. I dropped onto the grass with a gasp, sucking in a breath of air that wasn't heavy with rain.

"What did he do to you?" I asked.

Bas didn't answer right away, his jaw twitching as if he were grinding his teeth. Finally he shook his head and opened his mouth.

I waited.

No sound came out.

Bas's eyes widened. He opened his mouth again.

Still nothing.

Suddenly I remembered the bright purple light in Bas's throat. The way the wizard had flung it into the sky, and how it had burst. My tail fell. "He took your voice."

Bas's snout wrinkled as he pulled back his lips to bare his teeth, and his hackles rose.

"It's okay," I told him. "I'll help you."

He darted forward. I jerked back just in time to avoid being caught in his jaws when he snapped them closed in the space I'd been a moment before.

"Bas!" I stared at him, every muscle in my body tense, ready to run. "I'm trying to *help* you."

Bas stared at me as if I'd grown a second tail. He looked out at the lake, deliberately glancing up at the rainstorm.

I didn't look. I was pretty sure I knew what he was getting at.

"I don't tell the magic what to do. I put the magic out there, and it helps people. The wizard kept his concentration, that's not my fault. It's good magic." I lifted my chin. "I'm helpful."

Bas snorted. A sound so filled with disgust, it almost made me flinch.

All I wanted to do in that moment was find someplace warm and dry where I could clean myself off and have a nice nap. My muscles hurt, and my tail felt like it had a kink in it from the force of expelling all that magic in such a short time span. The witch usually comforted me when I felt like this. Petted me and said things in a soothing voice that was almost as welcome as a scratch behind my ears.

But the witch wasn't here. She wasn't here to help Bas.

But I was.

I looked up at Bas and opened my mouth.

The mummy dog snarled and snapped his jaws again, putting his mouth close enough to my face that I felt his hot breath.

He was so *angry*.

Tears blurred my vision, but I blinked them away. "I *am* helpful. I'm going to help you get out of here."

For a second, I thought he'd jump on me. Thought he'd give into the violent urges I could see behind his eyes, take a swipe at me with his huge paw, or snap at me again with his sharp teeth. But he didn't. Instead, he turned his back on me. He walked away.

He *dismissed* me.

Defiance rose inside me. No. No, he was wrong. I was helpful. The pale lady had told me so. I'd helped the witch lots of times.

I narrowed my eyes. And I would help Bas too. Whether he liked it or not.

My claws dug into the ground as I tensed my body, coiled my energy until every muscle was a loaded spring. Without a sound, I leapt forward, hitting the ground at a dead run. Bas didn't hear me coming, and this time when I dug my claws into his bandages, I put a paw on either side of his neck, with my bottom legs digging into his back bandages for purchase.

Bas snarled in fury and spun around, but it was too late. I had kitten-sharp claws, and he was covered in convenient bandages—as well as skin the texture of beef jerky. I let him try to dislodge me for a minute or two, then raised my voice.

"The longer you take to listen to me, the more lives that wizard is going to burn through."

Bas snapped his jaws closed, dragging his breath over his teeth in a sound that made my fur stand on end. I ignored him, focusing instead on scanning the cliff face on the other side of the lake. Cliffs usually meant caves. And caves meant shadows.

I stared grimly at the rock as I dug my claws in deeper, tugging at Bas until he broke into a run. I used my claws on either side of his neck to guide him toward the cliff face, searching for the cave I needed to get us out of here.

I was helpful. And I would prove it.

The pale lady had showed me the path through the darkness. Showed me the shadowy plane with all its twisting roads. Sound traveled differently here, she'd said. It echoed and moved. Everything said in the shadows got back to her. The pale lady had spoken cat— with the aid of magic—and I remembered every word.

Bas snarled and tried to buck me off when we entered the cave, but I wasn't so easy to lose. The witch couldn't hide from me, and Bas couldn't shake me off. I was *helpful.*

The shadows closed around us, and I blinked my eyes, seeing the shadow plane as the pale lady had taught me. And this time, I didn't just look for the path that led back to the bedroom and the human wizard. This time, I spoke.

I called into the shadows, giving my voice the feline lilt that no other living creature could manage. I screamed a battle cry. I called for aid. Called those I knew would come. They would come because we'd been family. Taken in by the same kind woman. The one who'd eventually delivered me to the witch.

As the pale lady had told her to do.

I didn't wait for them, just trusted they would come. Trusted they would follow my voice into the shadows. The pale lady would hear. She would open the path for them. I believed.

The pale lady had said she was helpful too.

The closet in the wizard's room might have been enchanted, but the closet of the room next to that one was full of mundane darkness. And Bas was angry enough that the flimsy sliding door didn't stand a chance. He hit the door like a battering ram, barely slowing enough to get his bearings before tearing out the door and around the corner into the room with the wizard, the desk, and the enchanted closet.

The human wizard gaped at us as we burst into the room through the same door we'd entered the first time. "You," he spat at Bas. "How did you get back here?"

Bas ground his teeth, resisting the urge to try and speak—refusing to give the wizard the satisfaction.

So, I answered for him.

I leapt onto Bas's head and hissed.

Another hiss sounded behind me. Then another. Then a pair.

I purred.

They had come.

The wizard took a hesitant step back as my allies filed in behind me. To my right appeared a pair of Siamese cats with beautiful blue eyes, pale bodies, and dark chocolate brown coloring in their ears, tails, and legs. They stepped forward in tandem, their eyes trained on the amulet around the wizard's neck. Faconi shifted back and forth, but the two sets of blue eyes followed the amulet with unerring focus.

To my left, a tortoise shell cat paced forward until he was level with me, then stopped and stood with his head cocked to the side. He stared at the wizard for a moment before moving three inches to the left. Then he sat. Waiting.

A rough meow that was more like a cough came from farther back, announcing the arrival of my most intimidating ally yet—a huge alley cat with a knot at the end of her tail so big it looked like a mace with a curved handle. Most of her ears were missing, and one fang stuck out of her mouth even when it was closed. She had bald patches here and there on her body where the flesh was too thick with scars for the fur to grow back, and her face bulged on the left side as if the bones of her face had been broken and hadn't healed properly. She looked hungry.

"Get the amulet," I told my fellow felines. "He stole it from a man who cares for our kind."

A group hiss rose from my brethren. The wizard ignored us, focusing on Bas.

"Go back to your master, and I will let you live. You and your minions."

Every cat in the room stiffened.

It didn't take an understanding of human speech to recognize we'd been insulted. The way the wizard had curled his lip when he looked at me and my brethren and used the tone the pixie used when she looked at a plate of steamed vegetables said it all.

No doubt as outraged as we were by the grave insult his feline allies had been paid, Bas leapt for the wizard with his mouth open, sharp teeth bared, his muscles underneath my paws tightening as he fired himself like a mummified rocket. Faconi tightened his grip on his staff and swung it at Bas like a club. The blow struck Bas's jaw, and one of his teeth chipped off and flew to the side, skittering over the floor. Bas crashed to the rug just short of the wizard, and I leapt off to avoid being crushed as he threw himself into the roll and came up on his feet again.

I landed in the exact spot the tortoise shell cat had been standing before he'd moved.

Faconi was about to find out that none of us were as ordinary as we looked.

The alley cat leapt at Faconi, her jaws closing around the staff before the human could wind back for a second strike. The ball-tailed feline looked like a thirty pound cat, but she had the weight and the strength of an animal ten times her size. Which Faconi discovered when he tried to raise the staff and shake her off, only to narrowly escape dislocating his shoulder for his efforts. He released the staff with a confused grunt.

"Release me." Rayaan's raspy voice slithered from between the pages of the book. "I will help you. I am worth more than just my knowledge and memories. My power could be at your service."

"No!" Faconi snapped.

The Siamese crept toward the human, parting to flank him where he stood just in front of the desk. A paw touched my shoulder, and I turned to see the tortoise shell cat gesture for me to follow him. I did as he beckoned, sitting in a spot he indicated on the corner of the bed.

The bed sat perpendicular to the desk, and my new position put me closer to the wizard than I would have liked, but I'd heard stories of the tortoise shell cat's abilities. His gift of future-sight. Nothing grand, but just enough that if he told you where to be—or not be—it was best to listen.

Faconi wrapped a hand around the amulet, chanting in that same rhythmic tone he'd used earlier. Blue energy rose from the amulet, crawling down his arm, to his shoulder, and across to his other arm raised high in the air. The blue light expanded, taking form—a humanoid form with cloven feet and large horns curling out from its head. When the light faded, a crimson-skinned devil stood beside the wizard, forked tail lashing behind him, a hideous grin stretching his mouth wider than any humanoid mouth should, revealing rows of razor-sharp teeth.

"You're wasting your 'power,'" Rayaan taunted. "Free me and you won't need to use up your precious *limited* resources."

"This is a devil from the regions of Hell," Faconi said without taking his eyes off Bas. "It will not only fight for me, it will lead me to hidden treasure. I won't need to raise the *Flor de la Mar*. I waste nothing."

The devil twisted its body, lashing out at Bas with its tail. Bas snapped his jaws closed, catching the writhing limb in his teeth. With a hiss, the devil jerked his tail closer, dragging Bas close enough to bring its claws down on the mummy dog's face. The bandages fell away from Bas's left eye, along with a chunk of dried skin. The devil cried out in delight, but its joy was premature. Bas responded to the attack with a swipe of his own claws, and he caught the devil across the throat. Black blood trickled down the devil's bare chest, and it screamed a gurgling sound of unholy rage.

A feline whine made me look toward the Siamese. One of the pair had taken his eyes off the amulet and was creeping toward the devil. I leaned forward, fascinated. The twins' secret was perhaps the one I'd most wanted to see in action. I'd heard they were the vessels for ancient ghosts—royalty, no less. Something about an ancient duty to preserve the spirits of their masters. I'd never seen the spirits myself…

Until now.

A smoky form rose from the male Siamese's body as he got closer to the devil. I stared at the image of an old man dressed in fine silks, his head bald, and his eyes full of ethereal silver light. The ghost chanted in a smooth, lyrical language that made the devil snarl.

Apparently, Faconi couldn't see the ghost. He didn't react at all to its appearance, nor did he seem to find the Siamese creeping toward his summoned devil a threat.

No wonder he'd needed the amulet to power his spells. He had no sensitivity at all. He had no idea his precious devil was about to be dismissed.

The wizard snatched his staff off the ground where the ball-tail had dropped it, and now he pointed it at Bas. I flattened my ears. No matter how many attacks he suffered at the hands of my brethren, the human seemed convinced Bas was the only threat. That getting rid of him would make his "minions" go away.

Minions. I remembered that word now. The witch used it sometimes when she was angry.

It was a dismissive word, used for the people in the fight who didn't matter.

Energy rose with my anger. Anger at being ignored. Anger that this human had taken what wasn't his, was using it to hurt people. Hurt Bas. Bas who was *helpful.* Like me. I concentrated as hard as I could, focused as hard as I could.

Nothing.

I hissed in frustration, glaring at the wizard, trying to make that anger *do* something.

Claws pressed down on my tail from behind me, digging past flesh and into the bone. I screeched.

A fountain of gems shot forward like a razor-sharp rainbow. And thanks to my position, they were all headed straight for Faconi. The tortoise shell cat made a sound of satisfaction as he removed his claws from my tail, watching as the gems sliced into the wizard. Shallow cuts mostly, but they bled. A lot.

The wizard's mouth moved, but he didn't say anything, seeming caught off guard by the sight of all the priceless gems. He actually twitched as if fighting the urge to drop to his knees and pick up as many as his flimsy pockets could carry.

The alley cat took advantage of the wizard's hesitation and seized the staff in her jaws again. The sudden movement at the bottom of the staff threw the wizard off balance and he stumbled and fell to the floor. The Siamese that had still been focused on the amulet took her chance. She darted forward, her delicate jaws closing over the string just above the small clay cat.

There was no guardian as tenacious as a Siamese. Rumor had it, centuries ago a pair of Siamese had been tasked with guarding a precious chalice. So intense was their diligence, the sheer force of their concentration, it had left the feline—and her descendants—with the crossed-eyes her breed was known for.

Now she used that same intensity, that same determination, as she pressed her teeth together, sealing her jaws closed over the strap. Her sharp teeth pressed into the worn leather, and with a vicious tug, she jerked the amulet free.

Faconi cried out in dismay as she sprinted across the room and darted under the bed. He swiveled his head around in desperation.

Searching for his devil.

Unfortunately for him, the devil was locked in battle with the ghost of a man who sounded like he'd fought a devil or two before. The musical chanting coming from the ghost's mouth was smooth and confident, beautiful in its simplicity. The devil screamed and slashed at the ghost, but his claws passed through it without so much as distorting the old man's face.

"What are you doing?" Faconi shouted, clearly still not seeing the ghost. "Get the cat! It's under the bed and it has my amulet!"

The devil growled something in a language that made my skin crawl under my fur. It lumbered toward the bed, wincing and hissing as the Siamese carried his ghost behind him, the ghost still chanting, still calm and confident.

The tortoise shell cat darted under the devil's arm as it raced to join the Siamese. The devil crouched down and reached underneath the bed, but if the expression on its face was anything to go by, the tortoise shell cat kept himself and the Siamese with her prize out of his reach.

Suddenly the devil flinched and jerked its arm from under the bed, using it now to shield its face. The ghost's voice rose, gaining power.

"Get the amulet!" Faconi screamed.

The devil snarled—

Then vanished.

The ghost bowed his head, spoke a few more soft words, then drifted away into smoke.

"Rayaan!" Faconi shouted, his voice high with panic. "I release you!"

"Say the words!" the djinn shouted.

I tensed and straightened. *Rayaan.* That was the name Bas had given the djinn. The wizard was talking to the djinn in the book. And Rayaan was using the "Yes, I Promise, Now Give Me the Honey" voice the pixie used when negotiating with the witch.

Faconi shouted something in a language more formal than the first. I recognized a spell when I heard one, had heard the witch often enough. There was a certain cadence to spells that sounded different from regular human speech.

Suddenly a figure erupted from the pages of the book. A figure of smoke and obsidian, with eyes that made you feel like you were falling if you looked into them too deeply. I would have sworn I heard the whisper of sand when the djinn stepped out of the book and onto the floor of the wizard's bedroom. Faconi looked at Bas, a triumphant, evil look in his eyes as he waited for the djinn to destroy his enemies.

Rayaan grabbed Faconi, curling one clawed hand around the wizard's throat.

The wizard's end was quick, violent, and bloody. The spray of the wizard's lifeblood colored everyone but the tortoise shell cat, who'd, of course, managed to stand exactly out of range despite having left the protection of the shelter under the bed.

The djinn faced Bas and began to speak. I didn't understand what he said, but Bas nodded. First at the djinn, and then at me.

The djinn turned to me. When he spoke next, it was in a feline tongue, though a more ancient version with a thick accent.

"I know the divine when I feel it," Rayaan said gravely. "And for this messenger to be blessed with the help of so many of your kin, his mission must be one of great importance."

I raised my chin. "Yes."

"I want only my freedom." The djinn nodded to Bas. "He has no voice anymore. He cannot speak for me of what I did here. But you can. You will tell the gods that I helped you. You will ask them to let me be."

"I will," I answered seriously. "I will tell them you were very helpful. Helpful is good."

The djinn nodded and walked away, disappearing into a puff of smoke before he reached the door.

I went to Bas, and he leaned down to let me onto his back again. That seemed like a good sign he wasn't angry anymore. When he pushed himself to his feet, there was something in the heaviness of the movement. Something more than pain. I'd expected relief if not joy over our victory, but the mummy dog seemed...tired. Or sad.

Sometimes they felt like the same thing.

I would help him, I decided. I knew how to cheer him up.

"Thank you for your help," I told my kin.

"You are welcome, little brother," the alley cat said, licking the wizard's blood from her paw.

"It was good to see you again," the tortoise shell cat said kindly. "She misses you."

"I miss her too," I said, thinking of the woman who'd brought me to the witch. "Perhaps I will visit."

"She would like that," the Siamese said in unison. "As would we."

Bas twitched, obviously ready to leave, so I finished my goodbyes.

He returned us to the old man's house with the same speed as before, and I watched as he trotted up to the front door and pawed at it.

The old man answered the door, this time with a different cat on his shoulder. He looked down at Bas, and the mummy dog rose up, showing the man the amulet.

"You found my necklace," the old man said, the skin around his eyes creasing as he smiled. "Thank you. My granddaughter would have been so sad if she thought I'd lost it."

I would tell my brethren to keep an eye on it. Make sure no one else took it.

"What's happened to you?" he asked, gently cupping Bas's face in his hand and tilting it to get a look at his injuries. "Been to the wars, I see." He nodded and pushed the door open wider. "Come on in then, let's get you cleaned up. I have some bacon in the fridge. It'll do you some good I think."

I'd heard the witch use that tone lots of times. Usually before she cuddled me, petted me until the pain went away. And that word was familiar too. *Bacon.* A very yummy treat, if I remembered correctly.

Bas was in good hands.

I meowed happily as a somewhat bewildered Bas allowed the old man to lead him inside. I wondered if Bas had ever had a human care for him before. Not as a servant or a messenger, but as a beloved family member.

It was an experience I highly recommended.

I left Bas to soak in the love humans reserved for animals and headed for the shadows.

I had a message to deliver.

A month later, the witch once again bungled the magic I so helpfully provided to her. One minute she was chasing some sort of goblin down an alley, shouting at him in her "Stop or I'll Dump All the Honey Down the Sink" voice, and the next the entire alley was covered in pitch blackness. My night vision was excellent, but even I couldn't see in the inky dark the witch fueled with my magic.

I flicked my tail from side to side. I would never understand her choices.

But, I supposed I didn't have to. I was just there to help.

As long as I was in complete darkness, now seemed as good a time as any to check on the amulet. Not that I doubted my brethren's dedication to making sure the old man didn't lose it again, but the old man had mentioned bacon last time I was there, and given his love for cats, there was a good chance some of it would be offered to me.

I walked into the shadows, blinking to see the paths through the shadowy plane. I found the one I wanted, and after a few wrong turns, I found myself crawling out from under the couch in the old man's living room.

Bas's face was the first thing I saw when I crawled out.

"Bas!" I said, racing over to leap onto his back. "You're still here!" I rested my chin on his bandaged head between his ears and paused. "But why are you still here?"

Bas lifted his head, then made a sound. Or rather, tried to make a sound. Nothing came out.

I climbed on top of his head so I could look down into his eyes. "You still can't speak?"

"His master doesn't want him back."

I looked up to see the black cat lounging on the armrest of the couch I'd crawled out from under. He indicated Bas with his chin.

"A messenger who can't speak isn't much good, is he?" the black cat added.

My chest tightened and I flopped down on Bas's head, pressing close in a hug. "I'm sorry, Bas."

Bas shook his head. He looked up at the old man puttering around in the kitchen, then looked down at the floor. I lifted my head enough to see there was a bowl on the floor. A bowl with dog food in it.

With bacon on top.

Bas wagged his tail.

"Oh," I said slowly. I felt my own tail rising, my mood lifting—and not just because there was bacon. I patted Bas's head with my paw. "You have a human now too. That's good. He will take care of you." I paused, then added, "Though I have to warn you, they don't always show their appreciation for your help. You just have to know that they do appreciate it. Deep down."

Bas made a sound in his nose that sounded like laughter, but was probably just an oncoming cold.

I flicked my tail from side to side, glancing back at the dog dish.

"Are you going to eat all that bacon?"

Author Bio

Jennifer Blackstream is a *USA Today* bestselling author of urban fantasy and paranormal romance. She is amazed and grateful to have made a writing career out of a Master's degree in Psychology, hours of couch-detecting watching *Miss Fisher's Murder Mysteries*, and endless research into mythology and fairy tales. She firmly believes that whether it's a village witch deciding she wants to be a private investigator, or a single mother having a go at being a full-time writer, it's never too late for a new adventure.

A fervent devotee of cooperative board games, Jennifer sets aside at least two nights a week for team-based adventures such as *Mice & Mystics*, *Sentinels of the Multiverse*, or *Harry Potter: Battle at Hogwarts*. She uses games with dice-based mechanics to lure in her ridiculously lucky-rolling son and daughter in the hope that they too will develop a passion for cooperative escapism.

Connect with Jennifer Blackstream at jenniferblackstream.com

Fugitive

A story in the world of The Dresden Files

by Jim Butcher

My name is Mouse and I am a very Good Boy. Everybody says so.

When My Friend, Harry Dresden, asked me to guard his little girl while she was at school, I was proud to do so. They gave me a Service Dog Test, which I passed, because My Friend told me to just do whatever the testing man told me to do, so I did.

Now I am a Service Dog, and I wear a magic vest that makes everyone think I am very important to my Maggie, so they let me go everywhere with her. That is the best, because My Maggie can become very uncertain sometimes, and it is always good to have a friend to sit with you and wag his tail when you are not certain.

I carefully nosed forward one of the flash cards from United States History that read 'This US President could write two letters at once in separate languages.'

My Maggie was already dressed for bed in one of her father's t-shirts that read 'Don't Make Me Put You In The Trunk. It's Already Crowded In There.' She was a tiny child with dark hair and dark eyes.

She crinkled up her nose, frowning at the card and guessed, "Benjamin Franklin?"

I made a grumbling sound.

"I can't help it, I like him best," Maggie said. "Maybe John Adams?"

I lay down on my side and moaned.

Maggie giggled at me. "Ronald McDonald?"

I rolled on my back and made an exasperated noise. Terrifying Hamburger Clowns had nothing to do with the American Revolution—and there was a quiz tomorrow.

"You take class way too seriously, Mouse," Maggie told me. "It's Jefferson, everyone knows that one."

I sat up and said, "Woof," in my most approving tone so that My Maggie would know she had gotten the answer right. My Maggie was a very intelligent student, but she sometimes wanted to do other things more than she wanted to do school.

I loved school! I learned so many things! Like Reading! And Math! And Science! I got to go to class with all the other kids and everyone petted me!

I think if more dogs realized how much fun school was, they would all want to go.

My Maggie and I worked on the American Revolution quiz until lights out, and then My Maggie got into bed, seized her flashlight and her comic books, and got under the covers with them.

I lay down in front of the door, dutifully ready to snort a warning if one of the nuns came down the hall. My Maggie loved her comics, and even though she was breaking the rules, she always fell asleep in a few minutes, and she did so again tonight.

I dozed off, trusting my nose and ears to tell me if any trouble came.

It did.

At midnight.

One moment, all was quiet. The next, the very air quivered with subtle power. By the time I opened my eyes, a seam had opened in the air, flush against the floor of My Maggie's dorm room. Within seconds, it had widened into a ragged oval of sullen red light and something huge began to haul its way through.

My Maggie was a heavy sleeper, and lay motionless in bed, her cheeks pink.

I got up and prowled to stand between her and the opening gateway. Power radiated from it—but no menace, and I decided to wait and see what was happening.

Slowly, almost impossibly, a great beast emerged from the gateway. Three huge canine heads arose from the red light, and enormous paws thrust forth to drag the great beast into the dorm room. There was barely room for it to fit, and I found myself nose to nose-nose-nose with an absolute monster of a dog, one that radiated sheer metaphysical mass and strength.

I leaned forward carefully, sniffing at the central head. Three heads sniffed back, taking in my scent before they focused on me, and then a deep, resonant voice sounded clearly in my mind.

"Please excuse my intrusion. I am here looking for Mouse Dresden," the beast said, politely enough.

"That is me," I said back, the same way. "I am Mouse Dresden."

"My name," the beast said, "is Cerberus."

"You are famous," I said.

"Yes," the three-headed dog replied. "I need your help."

"I am a Service Dog," I said. "But I think that means I mostly help My Maggie."

One of Cerberus's heads sniffed curiously toward the little girl.

"She is in danger."

My ears came forward at that, very seriously. "Why?"

Two of Cerberus's heads looked ashamed and hung low. "I failed in my duty. A prisoner has escaped Lord Hades' custody. I must track down the fugitive. But I require your help."

"Lord Hades and My Friend know one another," I noted.

"Yes," Cerberus replied seriously. "My Lord believes the fugitive was removed from Hades to harm Your Friend and his offspring. My Lord likes Your Friend, so he sent me to help."

I let out a low growl. "Who would do such a thing?"

"When we find them," Cerberus said, "I will tell you."

I growled again, more thoughtfully. "I cannot go with you. I cannot leave My Maggie unprotected. I am her Service Dog."

Cerberus sat down and pondered this thoughtfully. "What if My Lord provided security for her?" he offered.

"I do not know him," I said. "Or you."

"I swear to you by my noses and tail," Cerberus said, "Your Maggie will be safe."

"Oh!" I said, "that is a different matter, of course."

"Thank you," Cerberus said gravely. All three of his heads turned toward the still-glowing gateway.

After a moment, a cloaked and hooded form arose from the ruddy light, human in shape more or less, but smelling of dark and damp and of slithering scaly things. The figure emanated calm and power, its hooded head looking around the room for a moment before she settled calmly down in My Maggie's chair at her desk and folded feminine hands over one knee. The hood over her head seemed to stir gently from time to time.

"This is a friend," Cerberus said. "She is very protective of women. She will keep Your Maggie safe until dawn."

"Then I must return by sunrise," I said.

"Agreed," Cerberus said. "Let us waste no time finding the trail."

I rose and shook myself, going over to sniff the figure guarding Maggie, marking the scent. She smelled partly like a human, and partly like a snake, and I felt amusement coming from her as I snuffled.

Should anything happen to the little girl, Hell itself could not hide this creature's trail from me.

"What are we tracking?" I asked Cerberus.

The three heads growled from three throats and one chest.

"A monster of the old world," Cerberus rumbled. "The Nemean Lion."

Cerberus turned one wall of the building into red light for a moment and we walked through it, which I thought much more practical than a doggy door. Once through, the Hades-hound shook his massive form and blurred with shadow. When he was finished, he had only one visible head and was the size of a very, very large but very normal dog like me, a black fighting breed, heavy and thick with muscle.

"That is a very good illusion," I said, with a certain amount of insight. My Friend was a wizard, after all.

"Thank you," Cerberus said gravely and began to run. I kept pace with him, which was difficult. I have been doing lots and lots of school, but there is not enough room on the grounds to exercise properly and I had become professionally soft and squishy as Maggie's primary bodyguard and snuggle companion.

"I do not understand," I said. "You can do so much. Why do you need my help?"

Cerberus let out a little growl. "When it escaped Hades, the Lion had help from the outside. And now there is a force at work against me. Not mortal magic, nor divine in the way I have come to know it."

His eyes glanced aside at me. "Something like what you use."

That made my hackles rise. "Oh."

"You know of what I speak?"

I growled in the affirmative. "My Shadow. He is also a temple dog. But he is a Bad Dog."

Both of us shivered at the mere words.

Cerberus flicked his ears. "My claim on the Lion is preeminent. But this creature prevents me from tracking the Lion somehow. I thought you might help balance the scales."

"I like doing that," I confirmed. "But I cannot simply tell you where the Lion is."

My mythic companion slowed his pace as we rounded one last corner, and there before us was the Castle, the blocky stone house My Friend had taken away from Criminal Bad Man. At this time of night, the Castle should have been locked and dim, but instead there were half a dozen men outside with lights, mostly gathered around the large wooden front door, where the sidewalk was lit by a row of several overturned and burning automobiles.

One of them, a large white pickup truck, had a hole in it, through the engine block. The edges of metal around the hole still glowed with heat to my vision, so great had been the force exerted where something small and irresistible had gone through it.

"Here is where the trail begins," Cerberus intoned. "The Nemean Lion has not had a body in millennia. Its shade had to take one to use as a vessel. It is still weak."

I blinked at the cars. "That," I asked, "is weak?"

"Yes," Cerberus said. "In its day, it required the power of Heracles to be defeated."

We both paused in the shadows across the street from the castle as the men shone their lights on the ruined cars and trucks and talked. I recognized two of them—Will Borden, the werewolf who fought beside My Friend in the great battle, and Michael Carpenter, who was just the best human ever, next to My Friend of course.

"I just don't understand it," Will was saying. He was a big man with a small man's height and moved with tremendous power carefully concealed.

"You're sure?" Michael asked carefully. He was a tall man, his hair and beard shot with silver, but his body was still thick with muscle. "You're absolutely sure it was Mister?"

"The door guards said he got out again," Will said with certitude. "Then, bam. He lets out a yowl and takes off down the street. Flipping cars."

Michael frowned. "Could that have been an illusion? Concealing something else?"

Will shook his head. "I don't know. Harry said something about hostile illusions not working near the Castle now that he had initiated countermeasures."

"Did he really say that?" Michael asked.

"No, he mumbled something like, 'I've buggered hostile illusions and veils for the foreseeable future, so if it's there, assume it's real.' Then he shambled off to his room."

Michael sighed and glanced back at the Castle with worry on his face. "It's been a hard year for him."

"Yeah," Will said. "But he's still trying."

He grimaced. "Look. This is Mister. Should we wake him?"

The larger man frowned thoughtfully. "He's in very rough shape. I hate to think of him taking more hits."

"You want us to lie to him?" Will asked.

Michael gave him a faint smile. "No. Never that. Lies, even kind ones, are seeds that sprout trouble."

Will sighed.

"But," Michael said. "Given how shaken up he's been, I doubt he'll be much help to us. We'll start the search now and let him sleep until morning. It's only a few hours until he wakes up in any case. Keep combing the castle and see if Mister turns up. Perhaps whatever the guard saw was some kind of facsimile."

Will nodded with a grimace. "You believe that?"

"It's too early to believe anything," Michael said calmly. "Let's get more information."

"You know who you sound like, right?" Will said with a lopsided smile.

Michael grinned. "He does tend to rub off on people."

"Hey," Will said. "Isn't that your truck?"

Michael sighed and glanced up. "Yes. At least it's insured."

The two of them kept talking quietly as they went back inside, taking all but two of the other men with them. Those two stared at the shattered cars for a moment, glanced at one another, and then stood a little closer together to face the night.

Cerberus turned to regard me seriously. "The Lion's shade took the wizard's cat."

I stared at him for a moment, shocked. "What? Why?"

"The Lion's spirit needed a body. I suspect whoever helped it escape had control of the spirit and directed it to seize the wizard's cat when it got outside."

"But that is Mister. He is my friend."

Cerberus growled and narrowed his eyes. "The cat has been taken by the Lion. And the Lion has made him invincible."

He tilted his head toward the glowing hole in Michael's truck. "See? The cat struck the vehicle with such force that the metal burst. It didn't tear. All the way through the engine, and all the different materials inside."

"I do not care about engines and metal," I said. "I care about my friend Mister!"

Cerberus looked at me steadily for a moment.

"The cat," he said finally, "has been possessed by one of the deadliest creatures my region of the world ever knew. It took the power of a demigod to stop the Nemean Lion back in the day."

He stared at me and said, "The Lion will kill those who have not earned such treatment. It must be stopped."

"I will not hurt Mister," I said firmly. "Or let him be hurt. By anyone."

Cerberus' chest vibrated with a growl so low I could not hear it, only feel it. "What did you say?"

I tilted my head at Cerberus and said, "You have six ears. Did none of them hear me?"

Cerberus was silent for a moment, and then snorted out a breath.

"The Lion's hold on him will be too tight to sever. But perhaps there is a way. I have no particular wish to harm this Mister. But I will do my duty."

"We both will," I said. "My Friend's heart is badly wounded. He needs Mister to help him feel better."

The legendary dog sighed. "I do not know what can be done. But we must find the Lion before it begins harming innocents. You can see how dangerous it is, even weak with hunger."

I stared at the shattered cars. I could smash cars like that if I had to. Mostly. But it would take me time, and the Lion-possessed Mister had done so in seconds.

Cerberus was sober and wary—which implied that the Nemean Lion was a creature at least as formidable as he.

Mister, possessed, was very, very dangerous, and not only to cars or innocent people.

It would break My Friend's heart if Mister hurt or killed an innocent.

And there was only so much heartbreak a man, even My Friend, could take.

And perhaps that was the point. This escape had been no accident, no quirk of fate.

It was an attack on My Friend.

Suddenly I felt like biting someone.

"How long before the Lion is at full strength?" I asked.

"Not long," Cerberus said. "It will regain strength as it kills. If I follow the scent, can you make sure Your Shadow does not interfere?"

"We will find Mister," I said firmly. "And we will save him."

"We will find him," Cerberus agreed, though his voice was cautious. "And then we will see."

Cerberus took the lead, lowered his great blocky head to the ground, and began to course after the scent. He had an excellent nose. I could barely track Mister's passage myself, and my nose was better than almost any dog I knew. But Cerberus was a Big Dog. And also, he had three noses, which I think gave him an unfair advantage.

But still. A dog is his nose, and Cerberus's nose was amazing. He was so much cooler than me, which was awesome.

Almost instantly after we set out, I felt a force working against us—gentle but inexorable, like gravity, pulling against our progress, as if no matter where we ran, we would be running uphill.

Shadowy energy permeated the very air, causing chance to bend against us—it sent a truck belching smoke and stench on the street near Cerberus as he tried to recover the trail. It caused other cars to blare their painfully loud horns distractingly and sent gusts of wind eddying between the buildings to stir up twenty thousand city-scents to hide the trail.

I growled in my chest and the air around me flickered with light as I poured my will against that shadow, increasing my pace to race at Cerberus' right side. This working of My Shadow was meant to harm My Friend, and the very thought had my fur expanding as azure light rippled and sparkled from it. My outrage pushed the light out from my fur into the air around us, expanding to shield Cerberus, enveloping the legendary dog in flickering spectral blue light.

"There!" Cerberus growled. "I have the trail! Well done!"

I barked, sending waves of unseen energy of light flowing like a river out ahead of us, to help make sure no poor humans would suffer a collision with a determined hellhound—and the two of us broke into a tireless—well, mostly tireless—run.

We raced out of the city to the west, passing through neighborhood and park and shopping center in the darkness. More of my will spilled out to bend chance in our favor, so that we passed through the shadows of momentarily flickering streetlights, or between cars so that their lights never shone on us. We passed from city to suburb to ex-urb, racing at a pace far faster than most...well, cars.

The hellhound ran in a straight line. He leapt metal fences and leaned a bit to one side to streak around houses—wooden fences and outbuildings he simply ignored, and we left a trail of holes the size of a small car in those.

"The trail grows fresh," Cerberus told me, and I could readily follow it myself now. Mister had passed this way less than five minutes before. We drew to a halt at the edge of a housing development that was full of bare earth and skeletal wooden frames. Beyond it were rolling fields with occasional groves of trees, where Illinois farmland and rural properties began.

We were out of the city.

"That farm," Cerberus growled. "The Lion is there."

I lifted my nose to the wind and said, "I smell blood."

"Cow," Cerberus confirmed. "The Lion needs to kill. It must have been forced to refrain from killing mortals until it could regain some of its strength from other sources."

In the night, something screamed. Perhaps it was a cow.

I shivered. "What now?"

Cerberus was silent for several seconds before he said, cautiously, "Let us sniff them out first."

Them? Ah, of course. If the Nemean Lion had been assisted in its escape from the outside of Hades, it would be foolish to assume it was alone. A cautious approach seemed most wise.

We ghosted forward, crouched low, noses and ears alert. The farm was a small one, a square divided into quarters. Two were fields, one was pasture, and one held the farmhouse and outbuildings. A winding stream, lined with trees offered the only cover, and so we used it to approach. The wind was in our noses, giving us a good picture of what was ahead, and we crept to within a few seconds' worth of sprinting of the farmhouse and its buildings.

We crouched in the cover of the trees and brush supported by the stream, and I watched as a streak of motion flitted across the pasture and slammed into a third cow. The cow made a screaming sound of pain and staggered, and I was just as glad that I could not see clearly what was happening to the poor beast. It thrashed and kicked and moaned and then slowly went still as the life bled out of it.

After that, a shadow blurred toward the chicken coop next to the farmhouse. Birds screamed, though their sounds ended with little splatting noises—and something very large, with a very big chest, let out a coughing sound that stirred the grass in a wave rolling out from the farmhouse.

"We must hurry," Cerberus said. "The Lion is remembering how to move in the mortal world again."

I inhaled deeply and said, "There are children in the farmhouse."

Cerberus gave me a sharp look. Then he leaned forward, and I could hear the snuffles of his extra noses. "Ah," he said. "So there are. You have a very good nose for that."

"Children matter," I said.

And that was when we finally saw the Nemean Lion.

It was in the form of Mister the cat. Mister was a very large tom cat (but still much smaller than me), with short grey fur and a bobbed tail and with one ear notched from fighting. But at the same time, he was very much not Mister. The moon cast a shadow of the cat that was far too large and far too lumpy and far too dark, and the darkness around him seemed to have a shape of its own—like something that was massive but trapped one dimension over.

"The more blood it spills," Cerberus noted, "the more the Lion will have access to the mortal realm." The hellhound leaned forward, preparing to move.

"Wait," I said. "Watch."

Cerberus glanced at me but waited.

And the door to the farmhouse opened.

A human figure stood in the doorway, covered in a heavy black robe with a heavy black hood. It faced the Lion, holding up a gloved hand in a salute.

And a moment later, My Shadow appeared beside the hooded figure. My Shadow was a temple dog like me, only he wasn't all plump and snuggly. He was lean and strong-looking and there was something about the way he moved that spoke of a hunger he could never fulfill. Dark energy radiated from him.

My Shadow leaned against the robed figure and let out a low growl.

"Oh," I said with quiet dread. "I think that is Cowl."

"What is a Cowl?" Cerberus asked.

"One of My Friend's foes," I said.

"A mortal wizard?" Cerberus asked.

"Yes."

"That is bad," the hellhound said. "This world is not mine. If his will is strong enough, he could trap or banish me."

I flicked my ears thoughtfully. "We must overcome them," I said. "Distract the Lion somehow. I will push him out of Mister."

Cerberus grunted. "Or I could kill the cat and the same thing will happen."

"We will not do that," I said. "I must save Mister for My Friend."

"It is but a cat," Cerberus said.

"I will be a Good Dog and save him," I said.

"For me to be a Good Dog, I must send the Lion back to my master," Cerberus said. "I am a very Good Dog. He always says that."

My Shadow took a couple of steps forward and stared directly toward me.

I held my breath.

"What is it?"

I looked at Cerberus. "He knows someone is out here. He can feel me thwarting his will."

My Shadow sniffed the air, but the wind wasn't with him. He took a few restless paces while Cowl faced the Lion.

"You are freed from eternal punishment thanks to me," Cowl said, his voice resonant and rough.

The Lion paced back and forth, tearing at the earth with its claws casually. Mister's little paws tore furrows in the earth a foot across. It let out a coughing sound and another growl.

"Because if I permitted you to take mortal lives, you'd have attracted immediate attention," Cowl said, his voice annoyed. "There are at least four wielders of Power in Chicago who might have banished you. Continue questioning me and I will do so myself."

The Lion growled and raked at the earth with its back claws. It threw up shovelfuls of dirt as it did.

"I have mortals for you, obviously," Cowl said calmly. "You missed the pigs. Feed. We will discuss the plan when you have done so."

The Nemean Lion let out a snarling sound, turned, and streaked away toward another outbuilding.

This time the screams were truly hideous, piteous, high pitched and terrible.

Cowl turned and vanished into the farmhouse. After a moment, My Shadow went with him, if reluctantly, looking back over his shoulder with his hackles erect.

"Cowl is going to bring out the children," I said. "We must protect them."

"That is not how I am a Good Dog," Cerberus said.

"But it is how I am a Good Dog," I told him.

"By the time the Lion feeds on mortal souls, it will be a very difficult fight," Cerberus said.

"Perhaps we should go bite Cowl and My Shadow first."

"They are behind the farmhouse's threshold," Cerberus said. "I cannot enter without being invited."

"Oh. What if we both go fight the Lion," I said, "while he is in the piggie building."

"Perhaps you can exorcise the Lion swiftly," Cerberus said. "Then we deal with the wizard if necessary. Unless we cannot."

"If we cannot," I said, "the wizard will be there. And My Shadow. And he is skinny and fast."

"Then there is no time to be gentle," Cerberus said, his voice regretful. "I am sorry."

"We must save Mister," I said. "My Friend needs him."

"I am sorry," Cerberus repeated. "The Lion is too dangerous."

I eyed Cerberus.

And I showed him my teeth.

"What are you doing?" Cerberus said. I noted that his shadow, too, was much larger than it should have been. Much larger than me.

"If you will not help me save Mister," I said, "I will help Cowl and My Shadow defeat you."

Cerberus looked indignant. "You will not."

"I swear it," I said, "by my nose and tail."

The mythic dog stared at me, exasperated.

In the distance, another piggie screamed.

"That is different," he said after a second. "There is no time for this. What is your plan?"

"Plan?"

"If you wish to be the Big Dog," Cerberus said, "you should have a plan."

I tossed my head and shook my ears until a plan came. "Very well," I said. "But you must do what I say. And you must trust me. And then we will both be Good Boys."

Cerberus wagged his tail hopefully.

I concentrated and started altering energy to help the plan work.

The first part of the plan was simple. Cerberus dropped his illusion under the cover of night and was suddenly enormous and fearsome. And also, he had three heads. He hurtled across the yard to the building where the piggies were kept and smashed a hole the size of a garage door in the side of it.

From within the barn, there was an enormous sound that was part cough and part snarl, and Cerberus answered with a ferocious series of roaring barks. Piggies began squealing in even greater panic as the sound of shattering wood cracked through the night.

A big machine went flying out one end of the building, some kind of tractor about the size of a truck. It tumbled across the ground and crashed onto its side.

Inside the farmhouse, lights flicked on. The front door, tearing off its hinges with a squeal of protesting metal, slammed flat down onto the porch, and My Shadow stood on it with all four paws, staring intently toward the barn. Umbral energy began to boil off him in roiling waves that a mortal could not have seen, and My Shadow hurtled across the ground toward the barn to join the battle.

He did not see me where I lurked in some nearby brush. That was the trouble with working with dark energy—it tended to blind even those who use it. My Shadow flew across the ground with his own supernatural power and grace, and I was once again sad at what my brother had become.

But though I felt sorry for him, there were also innocent children in danger, and that was more important.

I waited until My Shadow had entered the barn.

Then I picked up the large stick I had chosen and sprinted forward. It was difficult, but I turned my head sideways so that the stick held in my jaws dug into the earth, and I began to sprint around the farmhouse in a circle, leaning so that my paws were on the inside.

The side of the barn exploded in a shower of splinters and shards of broken wood, some of which flew out very fast and went very far.

Cerberus landed on his back, all three heads snarling and biting, while something that was shaggy and looked like one of those saber-toothed cats from the Stone Age, except with an enormous mane, landed atop him. It was grotesque with muscle and power and speed and landed atop him. Cerberus's great jaws raked and tore, as did his claws, but the Nemean Lion did not care. Its hide was invulnerable and where Cerberus's jaws and claws struck, green sparks flew up, but nothing was torn, and no blood flowed.

Cerberus was not to be so easily overpowered, though. The great dog levered its paws beneath the Lion and flung it away, then regained his footing so quickly that it seemed its own kind of magic. Cerberus flung himself in a chest-to-chest clinch with the Lion. The two great beasts staggered back and forth, tearing vast gouges in the earth as supernaturally powerful muscles strained against one another.

But Cerberus was bleeding from marks of claw and fang. The Lion was not.

The doorway of the farmhouse darkened, and suddenly Cowl stood there, all dark robes and dark hood, gripping a wizard's staff in one hand. He stared toward the battle for a moment and then I saw a flash of white teeth in the hood.

"A gift, Lord Hades?" Cowl murmured. "Why bind one when I could have two?"

And he raised his hand and began to mutter beneath his breath. Power gathered around him and began to snake out toward Cerberus.

And that was when I finished the circle, dropped the stick, and touched the furrow in the earth with my nose and a surge of bright energy.

An invisible curtain of my energy leapt up from the circle, rising up to enclose the farmhouse in a dome, and Cowl's Power was snuffed out like a candle on Maggie's birthday cake.

The dark wizard froze and stared at his hand for a moment. Then he drew in a breath and extended it again, snapping a louder word— and nothing happened.

I let a growl explode from my chest and sprinted toward the dark wizard and went for his throat.

I am a Good Dog. But people who hurt children deserve to be bitten. My Friend would agree with me.

Cowl saw me coming at the last second and brought his staff up. He managed to get it between his throat and my jaws, but I overbore him and drove him to the ground with all the power in my body. The breath exploded of him in a huff, and I closed my jaws, shattering the staff as if it had been a dental bone treat.

Perhaps I should have considered that.

A wizard's staff is a powerful magical tool, one that is often used to store Power so that the wizard can unleash it when he is tired or otherwise does not have access to the natural flows of energy in the world. The energy stored in the staff exploded outward and flung me up into the ceiling of the farmhouse.

I hit hard enough to hurt even me, and I fell heavily back down onto Cowl, who let out a weak curse. We both sort of flailed at one another, stunned and weakened. He got his arm between my teeth and his throat, and I bit down, but his robes were enchanted with protective magics, and I could not get my teeth through them.

This Bad Man had attacked My Friend when he was so sad he could not fight. He had endangered Mister the Cat, who I had known since I was a tiny puppy.

So, I clamped down like a vise on the armor, twisted my head and shoulders and hips, wrenched my jaws, and snapped both bones of his forearm like sticks.

Cowl screamed.

He twisted and I lost my grip on his suddenly wobbly forearm. He wriggled out from beneath me and staggered into the farmhouse's kitchen. I followed, still dazed.

He seized a red metal fire extinguisher with his good hand, and suddenly my nose and eyes were full of powder that smelled very bad. I reeled to one side, shaking my head and sneezing uncontrollably to clear my nose. When I could see and small again, Cowl was running out the front door.

"Ash!" he howled.

I chuffed and growled, my throat raspy with powder, but I did not pursue him—for this part of the plan Cerberus was on his own.

My nose had already told me where the children were—locked in a bedroom.

I reared up and threw my whole weight of my body and bright energy at the door and smashed it open. Inside the bedroom, three children, all of them smaller than My Maggie, and with darker skin, were huddled together and sniffling, staring at me with wide eyes.

"Woof," I said encouragingly, and wagged my tail. I probably looked silly covered in all that white powder.

The children just stared at me.

Oh.

They had been with My Shadow. And he looked like me. But he was not me. He was not all squishy and snuggly.

I went into the room and flopped down on my back to show them my tummy, wagged my tail and said, "Woof!"

The largest of the three, a boy, peered at me. "Different doggie," he said quietly. "He's fat. And he has a collar."

"Woof!" I said again and wriggled around encouragingly. Then I got up and went to the broken door, turning in circles and wagging my tail. "Woof, woof!"

From outside, there were more crashing sounds, and Cerberus let out a shrieking bellow of pain and fury. The children heard the sounds and flinched back—and at the same time, I felt the power of the circle I had raised around the farmhouse fray and vanish. Cowl must have scuffed the magical circle and shattered it.

I went to them and began nudging the children with my nose, making encouraging chuffing sounds, wrapping them in layer after layer of bright energy, calling forth courage and banishing fear.

"I'm scared!" said one of the little girls.

The other just cried quietly.

The little boy made eye contact with me for a long second. Then he swallowed, and I felt the power far greater than his small body leap up in his heart as he looked at his baby sisters and said, "We have to get out of here."

"Woof," I said seriously, and bumped him gently to his feet.

"Come on," he said firmly. "Hold hands. We're going home."

He got his sisters up, and made them hold hands, which is always a good thing for humans to do with each other when things are bad. Then he put a hand on my collar and grabbed on, and I walked them forward, my fur glittering with thousands of little blue sparks of bright energy.

I led the children out of the farmhouse, and into a battle of myth and legend.

Cerberus and the Nemean Lion were ripping and tearing at one another. They roared and bellowed and rolled, struggling to keep the upper hand, smashing their way through the little chicken building so that splinters flew everywhere.

Over to one side, Cowl the Bad Man was struggling. He snarled and lifted his good hand, and a bolt of purple lightning leapt across the farmyard with a crack of thunder. It struck Cerberus in one shoulder and tore supernaturally tough flesh from the great dog in gobbets.

Cerberus howled in agony, and as he did, My Shadow darted at him from behind, shadow power wrapped around him in a shroud, and My Shadow went for the legend-dog's hamstring.

Cerberus went down, blood spraying, shadow spreading up his wounded leg, and the Lion landed atop him, raking and tearing with berserk abandon.

I led the children around the side of the house, and out of sight, toward the doors of a root cellar, set at an angle in a block of concrete. Bright power tilted the world so that the doors had not been locked, and I grabbed one of the handles and tugged it open.

"Down here!" the boy said. "Come on! We have to hide!"

He led his sisters down the stairs into the shelter, just as I heard Cowl scream, "Ash! Get the children!"

Lightning flashed and thunder cracked again. Cerberus screamed. The Lion roared in berserk triumph.

I nudged the doors to the shelter shut, and whirled, power shining from my shoulders and the fur around my neck, just as My Shadow came sprinting around the side of the farmhouse and came to a sliding stop facing me, all lean power, with his darkness rolling off him in waves, meeting my bright power in a cascade of little red and blue sparks like a battle line of fireflies meeting halfway between us.

"You," he growled. His contempt was plain. "You have gotten even fatter."

"You are mean," I said back. "They are children. How can you help hurt children? That is not why we were born."

"Simpleton," sneered My Shadow. "Fat, foolish slave in a collar."

"It lights up," I snarled, "so cars can see me at night. Because My Friend cares about me."

My Shadow bared his teeth and took a step toward me. The conflict between our energies grew brighter and more intense, and the grass blackened and curled away from the showers of sparks.

"Run away, brother," My Shadow said, sneering. "The Underworlder's slave is all but destroyed. You cannot withstand us."

"They are *children*," I growled, from deep in my chest. "I have feelings about that."

"They are meat," said My Shadow.

I showed him my teeth. "You," I said quietly, "are a Bad Dog."

The deadliest insult I knew hung in the air in perfect silence.

And My Shadow and his dark power shot forward to kill me.

We met in a shower of clashing energy, made manifest and visible, blue light and dark shadow smashing together along with our fangs, our claws, our bodies. My Shadow was a terrible opponent. Our power was close to equal, the raw source energy of darkness and light from which all terror and hope, all fury and devotion, all lies and truth were created, and I felt his power trying to make me slip and fall—but my own power matched him, and my claws dug firmly into the earth.

My Shadow was strong and swift, but I was stronger and sturdy. He smashed his chest into mine and I fought him off, our jaws dueling for grips on the throat. He almost got me, but the thick ruff of fur around my neck and shoulders made getting purchase more difficult, and I raked at his ears.

We struggled furiously for the space of a breath and then parted, smashed into one another again, and this time I knocked him back. He was on his feet again with sinuous speed that was a little frightening. I did not dare to follow him up for fear that he might slip past me and harm the children.

"Get him, doggie!" the boy shouted, encouragement from behind me, his own little beacon of bright energy adding to my own.

I planted all four feet in front of the door to the root cellar and lowered my head, blue sparks leaping off my fur, while My Shadow prowled left and right. Around the far side of the house, there was another thunderous detonation and the sound of the old car in front of the farmhouse being crushed in the battle.

And then there was a great, mournful howl from where Cerberus fought Cowl and the Lion.

And then silence.

Fires had begun to burn on the other side of the farmhouse, or perhaps in one of the outbuildings. The flames made the shadows behind the farmhouse darker, and my brother grew less visible, his eyes and teeth gleaming.

My Shadow came to arrogant attention, staring at me with his ears flattened back with hatred.

"The Master of the Future comes," my brother growled, breathing hard. "This is your last chance to flee."

In response, I kicked my feet back, throwing up dirt, and did not move.

Cowl and the Nemean Lion came around the corner of the farmhouse. The human wizard was limping and clutched his wounded arm against him in pain, but his back was straight. Rage emanated from him in its own cloud of dark energy, reaching out to My Shadow and causing him to snarl in the same fury. The dark wizard stopped behind My Shadow with the Lion looming behind him, its eyes peering with feline intensity over his shoulder.

All three of them stared at me, and I could feel the weight of their regard like knives pressing against my skin.

"Harry," Cowl muttered, staring at me. "You are an almighty pain in my ass."

The fires leapt higher on the other side of the farmhouse, and the shadows darkened.

Now we came to it.

"Ash," Cowl said. "Nix his aura if you please."

My brother growled, and I felt my bright energy dimming, even as the shadows around him lessened, his darkness and my light blurring and diminishing in tandem.

"Now you die, brother," My Shadow said. "For nothing."

The dark wizard lifted his hand and I felt him gather power for another stroke of lightning—and without my own shield of energy to protect me, I would be helpless against it.

I shook my mane defiantly and said, "You have forgotten two things, brother."

My Shadow paused, suddenly wary.

"First," I said, "that no one tells cats what they may or may not do. Not even wizards."

My brother let out a warning growl, and Cowl paused, suddenly tense.

"And?" My Shadow asked. "Second?"

"I cheat," I said.

Fires appeared at the base of the darkened farmhouse wall behind them. Six fires. Utter, inky, void-black solidity appeared around those fiery eyes, and Cerberus, Hound of Hades, implacable and unyielding warden of the mythic dead let out a growl so deep that it shook the earth.

Cowl whirled.

The three-headed monster dog rose up on its hind legs, and hellfire kindled in three sets of jaws. With a roar, Cerberus swelled in size and power so that his heads were higher than the farmhouse and unleashed three furious jets of deep red and blue flame that shot toward Cowl, scorching the summer grass black for thirty feet on either side of them.

Cowl lifted a hand and cried a desperate word, and the will of the mythic beast, met that of the Master of the Future. Flame cascaded out from the shield the wizard raised, and even the Nemean Lion and My Shadow flinched back from it, suddenly terrified.

"Mister," I snapped. "I know you have been enjoying yourself. It is time to stop playing. Harry needs us now."

And with my brother suddenly distracted, I gathered my bright energy and barked hard and loud, the sound reverberating for miles across the countryside, smashing into the dark spirit possessing my friend the cat.

Cowl whirled to the Lion and screamed, "Kill them! I command you to kill them!"

The Lion flinched away from the sound of my barking, reeling, and in the fury and cacophony of clashing forces the old monster became suddenly insubstantial, a darkness, an idea, a memory.

Here, with the turbulence of forces shaking the air, torn by Cerberus and Cowl and My Shadow, the old spirit could not keep its purchase upon its mortal host in the face of my power, and suddenly the Nemean Lion was nothing but an enormous shadow stretching out from the sturdy, scarred body of the veteran tomcat Mister.

Who looked at Cowl. And then quite deliberately looked away and began fastidiously cleaning one paw.

Cerberus had been waiting for that, and the terrible fire of the underworld swept away from Cowl and over that shadow, burning it away, making it curl up like newsprint in a fire, while the distant roar of the Lion began to fade into an unfathomable distance and depth, burning the Nemean Lion's spirit into the earth, while wave after wave of my own energy washed over it, adding to Cerberus's efforts.

And in seconds, just like that, the Nemean Lion was once again a story, a memory, a piece of history.

"No!" Cowl screamed, pain and frustration welling up.

Cerberus's great jaws closed, and the enormous dog came crashing back to the ground so hard that it shook, trees in the old farmyard swaying.

The Lord of the Underworld's Good Boy stood tall and proud over

Cowl and My Shadow and slowly, slowly bared his three sets of fangs in a triple snarl.

I did too. It was the right moment for that sort of thing.

"Now, brother," I growled, taking a step forward. "It is time for you to flee."

Cowl turned his hood back and forth between me and Cerberus. I could smell the pain rolling off of him.

And sudden fear.

With a curse, he turned and spat a word and ripped open the veil between the mortal world and the spirit realm, rending reality with his will. Then he seized My Shadow by his wounded ear and dragged him forward into the veil and vanished.

The portal sealed itself behind him a second later, and they were gone.

Fires burned in the quiet. The farmhouse began to burn down.

Mister the grey tomcat purred and began arching his back and rubbing it against my chest.

"That is that," Cerberus noted with professional satisfaction. "I am getting *three* treats when I get home."

"I did not know you could breathe fire," I said.

"Yes," Cerberus said modestly. He dwindled from his gargantuan size until he was merely enormous.

"Does it hurt?" I asked.

"Only those who have earned it," Cerberus said seriously. "It was a gift from My Lord, and he is very concerned with justice."

"Oh," I said, and wagged my tail.

There was a creaking sound behind me.

We turned and found the three children peeking out of the root cellar and staring at Cerberus with very wide eyes. Mister walked over to the boy, still purring, and calmly rubbed against himself against the boy's knees. The boy leaned down to pet the old cat. And then the little girls giggled and did too. One of them came over to me and petted my mane, just like My Maggie did.

In the very far distance, my keen ears picked out the wail of emergency sirens.

"It was a good plan," Cerberus said. "Pretending to lose."

"Bad People always look for weakness," I noted. "And once they think they have found it, they cannot see anything else."

"I must go," Cerberus said.

"Not yet," I said seriously.

"But the mortals are coming," Cerberus said. "They will care for the children."

"We have minutes and minutes before that," I replied. "And we are Good Boys."

Cerberus tilted all three heads at me. And then he started wagging his tail.

And in the light of the burning farmhouse, Cerberus and I, and even Mister, spent the remaining time playing with the little ones.

Author Bio

Jim Butcher is the author of the Dresden Files, the Codex Alera, and a new steampunk series, the Cinder Spires. His resume includes a laundry list of skills which were useful a couple of centuries ago, and he plays guitar quite badly. An avid gamer, he plays tabletop games in varying systems, a variety of video games on PC and console, and LARPs whenever he can make time for it. Jim currently resides mostly inside his own head, but his head can generally be found in the mountains outside Denver, Colorado.

Jim goes by the moniker Longshot in a number of online locales. He came by this name in the early 1990's when he decided he would become a published author. Usually only 3 in 1000 who make such an attempt actually manage to become published; of those, only 1 in 10 make enough money to call it a living. The sale of a second series was the breakthrough that let him beat the long odds against attaining a career as a novelist.

All the same, he refuses to change his nickname.

Learn more at: jim-butcher.com

The Unlikeliest Places

A Quincy Harker, Demon Hunter Short Story

By John G. Hartness

Dedicated to Daisy, Gandalf, and Stevie, who rescued me from the darkness inside.

I thought I had the vampire right where I wanted him. He thought he had me right where he wanted me. I was pretty sure I was more right than he was. Then a tornado of tiny knives attacked my right calf with the kind of speed and viciousness I've only found in some of the upper Circles of Hell.

Yes, that Hell. Yes, I went there. Yes, I came back. And yes, the seven pounds of matted gray fur and rage doing its level best to chew through my hamstring was causing more pain than all the demons on the top three Circles ever managed.

I looked down to see a very bedraggled and angry cat with all four legs wrapped around mine, and its teeth buried in my flesh. My jeans did nothing to stop the cat's claws, and it had jumped high enough to clear the top of my Doc Martens before it latched on, so I was getting its whole body weight on four feet's worth of claw, plus what felt like about a thousand needle-sharp teeth.

"Ow, goddammit!" I yelled, shaking one leg. Of course, the second I shifted my weight onto one foot was the precise moment the vampire dove at me, bearing me down to the concrete floor and driving all the air from my lungs. My head hit the floor and stars filled my vision, disorienting me enough that I barely got an arm up before the vamp latched onto my carotid.

Okay, time to focus on the real threat. The cat was hurting my leg, but this undead assclown was going to legit kill me if I didn't stop screwing around. His fangs dug deep into my forearm and one knee pressed on my balls, but despite the growing ball of nausea in my gut and my inability to draw a full breath, I managed to focus my concentration and gasp out, "*Fragor!*"

I hurled my will into the vamp's face, and it went off like a watermelon dropped off a skyscraper. I closed my eyes against the rain of gore and sagged back against the floor as the pressure on my nuts decreased slightly. More like shifted, as the vampire wasn't trying to injure me anymore, he was just dead weight. And soon to be a pile of dissolving goo, so I flung him off me and pulled myself up into a sitting position.

"Mrow?" came from beside me, and I turned to see one of the most disgusting things I'd ever laid eyes on. The fluffy ninja assassin that tried valiantly to cripple me moments before stood glaring at me, covered in vampire brains, blood, and vitreous humor. There were even a couple of shards of fang sprinkled across its fur like confetti.

"Wow," I said to the kitty. "You look like shit."

The cat just hissed at me. I didn't blame it. I probably looked at least as gross, and maybe worse. "So, what are you doing here, puss? This isn't exactly a safe place for man nor cat."

The cat sat down on its haunches and started licking a forepaw, and I swear it somehow managed to extend its middle claw/finger in my direction. Its eyes never left me, though, just stayed locked on me as if waiting for another chance to try and tear my leg to ribbons.

"*Purgatio,*" I murmured, letting my will shape the currents of energy that flow through every space and every creature. The minor spell coursed over me and the cat, cleansing us of the gore and body parts. The cat stood up, turned around in a circle as if confused, then sat back down and resumed grooming, without the rude gesture this time, real or imagined.

Now that I wasn't dripping brains with every shake of my head, I took a quick personal inventory. Nothing broken in the fight, just a few bruises, a bump on the head, and a couple little holes in my forearm. I rolled up my jeans to examine my leg and wasn't surprised to see I was right—the little fuzzbucket did a lot more damage than the vampire. My calf looked like somebody pumped a load of birdshot into it and drops of blood welled up from twenty perfectly spaced puncture wounds.

"It's a good thing I'm pretty much immune to infection," I said to the kitty, who seemed to give not a single shit what I was or was not immune to. "Because if I got gangrene from a cat scratch, Luke would never let me live that down."

My legendary uncle hadn't been in a mood to give me shit about much of anything for the past few months, but I had hope he'd eventually pull out of his grief and get back to his normal, entirely too buttoned-up self.

"Okay, kitty," I said, heaving myself to my feet. "It's been fun chatting, but I've got more bad guys to kill, and I'm sure you've got some vitally important cat business to take care of. So…nice meeting you and all that, and you take care of yourself."

The cat just stared at me through this whole monologue, its yellow gaze unwavering and a little unnerving, if I'm being honest. But I couldn't just sit there all night chatting with a stray cat. There were at least another five vampires somewhere in the building, and with all the noise I'd made, the element of surprise was right out the window.

I stood up and patted my belt and pockets to make sure I still had my gear. Pair of silver-edged daggers on my hips—check. Glock 19 in a shoulder holster under my black motorcycle jacket—check. Awesome vintage "I Broke Wahoo's Leg" T-shirt I found on eBay—check. Plenty of magical mojo and a bad attitude—check.

I was a little bruised, a little bloody, and grumpy as shit after having that much trouble dealing with one middling vamp. So my mind was right, my gear was right, and I had plenty of magic stored up to take on a nest this size. "Let's do this," I said, and started across the expansive lobby to a door marked "Stairs."

And almost fell over as something heavy slammed into my waist. I barely held in a curse as a small, knife-wielding psychopath climbed straight up my back to perch on my shoulder. I looked to the left and saw a pair of yellow eyes framed in a face covered in long, now clean, gray fur. "Mrow."

Looked like I had a helper. Whether I wanted one or not. So I kept heading toward the stairs, adjusting my stride to accommodate my passenger, and ducked my head as the little furball leaned forward and started nuzzling my ear.

Cute cat but distracting as hell. I tried to brush him off a couple times, but that just resulted in holes in my jacket and more rending of my flesh, and there were about to be plenty of opportunities for that, right downstairs.

I'd come to this warehouse in an industrial park on Highway 74 in Marshville, about an hour east of Charlotte, because the workers at a local chicken processing plant had reported monsters attacking them on the night shift for about three weeks. It took a while for the report to make it onto the desk of anyone who would actually give it any credence, then wend its way through the various local law enforcement agencies, up the food chain to the Department of Homeland Security's Paranormal Division, and then back down to my fiancée, Deputy Director Rebecca Gail Flynn, who headed up the Mid-Atlantic Division, covering the Carolinas, Tennessee, Virginia, Maryland, and West Virginia.

I would have expected the main office in D.C. to cover the states surrounding the nation's capital, but I'm not a lifelong bureaucrat, so God only knows where the logic came from. Probably because the paper-pushers in Washington wouldn't know what end of stake goes into the vampire, which is pretty accurate from most of the ones I've met.

So, I got the case of the chicken plant monsters, and after a couple nights of observation, I'd determined that there were indeed monsters of some flavor. The part that sealed it for me was watching a five-foot-tall, ninety-pound woman reach into the back of a cargo van, drag out a carpet-wrapped, human-shaped bundle that must have been at least a foot longer than she was tall, throw it over one shoulder, and walk into the warehouse like she was carrying a sack of potatoes. Either that was the world's most securely wrapped mannequin, or she was way stronger than her frame should allow. So definitely some type of supernatural creature.

It took another day and night of investigation, but I finally figured out what was going on. There were at least four or five vampires living in the warehouse, and they would spend a couple days driving around to local cities and towns, collecting undocumented laborers, unhoused people, sex workers, criminals, runaways, and other folks who typically had fewer and weaker ties to their community, then they'd bundle them up and bring them back to this little patch of gravel and dirt outside Monroe, North Carolina and either feed on them, use them as thralls, or if they met their recruitment criteria, turn them.

It was that last bit that really grated on me. There were already plenty of vamps in the world, we didn't need any new ones. And Uncle Luke had decreed a couple centuries ago that anyone creating new vampires without his permission, which he never granted, was to be destroyed without a second chance.

Yeah, my uncle is kinda king of the vampires. Luke is short for Lucas Card, the name he's been going by most of the last fifty years. A dramatic improvement over the name he used with my dad, which was Mr. Alucard. I always thought that story seemed ridiculous, because who couldn't see that it was just "Dracula" spelled backward? But Dad said people were more trusting in the Victorian era.

Oh, did I forget to mention? My uncle is Count Vlad Tepes, better known as Vlad the Impaler, and way better known as Count Dracula. And my dad? Yeah, he was kinda famous, too. Jonathan Harker? Used to work for my uncle? That's my lineage—the world's most famous vampire and the world's most famous vampire chew toy.

Not to mention my mom, Mina Murray Harker, who my uncle kinda had a thing for, but not in a West Virginia way, since he isn't really my uncle. And me? I'm an experiment in supernatural genetics, proving that when two people who vampires nibble on marry and have kids, their kids get a little extra *oomph* in the genetic lottery.

I'm Quincy Harker, and I'm a part-vampire magic-wielding smartass who's been alive for a century and a quarter and counting. Although if I didn't focus on my surroundings and not let this ball of fur and fury on my shoulder distract me, I might be able to stop counting momentarily.

Me and my passenger reached the top of the stairs, really just an open rectangle in the floor where a stairwell used to be, and I peered down into the darkness. I couldn't see shit. I looked over at the kitty. "You see anything scary, puss?"

The cat jumped off my shoulder, stuck its head down in the hole, and looked back at me. "Mrr-rrr."

Now, I don't speak cat. I didn't know if that weird little chirping sound meant "Coast is clear, tall human," or "You're so screwed. If you go down there, you're gonna get served up with fava beans and a nice Chianti." Probably the latter. In my experience, cats draw a lot of inspiration from the teachings of the great Dr. Lecter.

"Well, kitty, I don't know what that means, so I guess I'm just gonna have to find out for myself." I called up a little sliver of power and shaped it to my will. "*Lumos,*" I whispered, and a sphere of blazing white light flickered into life above my head, illuminating an area at least fifty feet around me.

Now that I looked like a beacon of absolute goddamn hope and glory shining away in the dark of night, I took one step forward, tucked my elbows into my side, and dropped down into the hole in the floor.

The basement level was obviously the vampires' main lair, and it smelled just like you'd expect an abandoned warehouse turned into a haven for bloodsucking parasites would smell—like shit. The stench of rot and waste hit me like a hammer, rolling over me and making me take a wobbly step back wiping my eyes.

"Quincy Harker," a creaky voice said from behind me. "We've been expecting you."

I opened my mouth to say something rude and probably only about half as witty as it would sound in my head, but that's when Graybeard the Furry Nutjob decided to jump down into the hole with me. Right onto my head.

My teeth clicked together painfully, and I stood there for a moment trying to shake the cat off my head, which apparently was hilarious to the vamps in the room, because I heard laughter coming from all sides.

Good. Laugh it up. The more they're laughing, the less they're coordinating an attack. The cat shifted position to sit on the back of my neck, with its back legs draped over my left shoulder and its face and front paws reaching over my right.

"How adorable," a female voice called out from my right shoulder. "The snack brought a pet!"

I didn't even look over at her, just raised my right arm straight out from the shoulder and shouted "*Fuego!*" Fire streamed from my palm, engulfing the vampire who stood about ten feet from me laughing and pointing. Well, laughing and pointing until she was burning and screaming, anyway. She went up like a tinderbox, and five seconds later, there was nothing left but a husk of steaming vampire, which would slowly dissolve into a viscous goo. One down.

I turned around to look at the first voice, the one that knew my name. This was almost certainly the leader, the oldest vampire, the most powerful, and the one who should have known that it was forbidden to make new vampires. He was pretty much the whole reason I was there. Well, him and his whole little nest of kidnapping, murdering assholes. But he was the head asshole.

And he looked the part, too. Most vampires dress normally. Their styles might be a little dated, but they generally make at least a token effort to blend in. The image in popular culture of a vampire sitting on a throne in a tuxedo with a red cummerbund, hair slicked back over a skeletal face, and a cape in the sartorial mix somewhere is a complete Hollywood fabrication.

Except to this guy. He seriously had a throne atop a wooden dais painted to look like marble, and he was wearing the whole outfit, down to that oddball medal Lugosi wore in the movie. I asked Luke once what that was supposed to be, and he just shrugged, saying something about wearing lots of medals through the years. He was a pretty accomplished general, after all.

Well, at least feared, if not all that accomplished. But this dude looked like the version of Dracula that stands out on Hollywood Boulevard and panhandles for tourist photos. Or maybe Grandpa Munster.

The self-styled master vampire, and I was convinced that he probably made everyone in the room refer to his as "Master," rose from his throne, which I now saw was a big office chair with what looked a lot like human bones tied to the arms and back to make it…creepier, I suppose? For a bunch of undead scourges of the night who are supposed to stay hidden, this guy spent a lot of time focusing on his presentation.

I had to wonder who he thought was going to see this shit. I also wondered exactly how intimidated I was supposed to be when his throne creaked and rolled back a couple of inches when he rose.

"Quincy Harker, you have trespassed upon our home, murdered two of my children, and brought vermin into our presence. For these crimes—"

"Wait a second," I said, holding up a hand, palm toward the Dracula cosplayer. "First, I didn't bring the cat here, the cat was already here. And second, I'm pretty sure that the definition of vermin doesn't include cats."

Lugosi Light stood there frozen, his mouth moving but no sound coming out. He'd had a movie in his mind of how this meeting was going to go down, and I'd just derailed his whole train of thought.

"Cat got your tongue?" I asked. I felt a paw thump against the side of my head, but it was worth it. "Then I'll talk. You all know that making new vampires is forbidden, on the orders of Dracula himself. You also know that you've been...indiscreet in your hunting. And grotesquely ostentatious in your decorating." I gestured at the bone throne.

I turned around in a circle, locking eyes with each of the six vampires surrounding me. "So, here's the deal. I'm going to kill your boss vampire here, because he's the one who made all of you. If you run away while I'm busy killing him, and you behave yourselves from here on out, I won't feel much need to go looking for you. But if you interfere in our little dance, I'm going to turn you all into smears on the bottom of my boot before the sun comes up, then I'm gonna go to Denny's and have myself a Grand Slam breakfast while your souls scream in Hell."

Turning like that not only drove my point home, although I'm sure my presentation was made somewhat less intimidating by the presence of a massive housecat sitting on my shoulder, but it also gave me a chance to assess the forces arrayed against me.

They weren't much, as far as an array of forces went—half a dozen college-aged girls, all pretty, all blond, all wearing pretty typical walking around town or campus garb. It looked like my wannabe Nosferatu was more than just a vampire, he was a perv as well. I mean, let's be real. When the age gap between you and your girlfriend is measured in centuries, it gets a little creepy. And yes, I realize the irony of that statement, given that I'm engaged to a human woman who was born close to a hundred years after I first emerged kicking and squalling into the light. But she's *almost* a century younger than me, so I'll take the tiniest sliver of moral high ground here.

"What do you say, kids? You gonna get the hell out, or am I gonna send you to Hell?"

When the first one leapt at me I knew that my negotiating skills were still in top form. The first vampire, a fledgling from the slavering, half-insane look on her face, clad in a faux-vintage Iron Maiden hoodie and artfully shredded jeans, blond hair flying out behind her like greasy streamers, charged me with her hands outstretched to rip my throat out. That didn't go well for her.

Fledgling vampires aren't really all that powerful. They can take out a normal human easily enough, but I think we've pretty well established that I'm not normal, if I'm human at all. But baby vamps only have a little more speed and strength than they did as humans, and while the young woman currently shrieking as she ran at me was apparently pretty athletic in life, she hadn't been dead long enough to get good at the whole vampire thing. And she wasn't going to get any better.

I sidestepped her charge, spun clockwise as I drew one of the big silver-edged daggers from my belt, and slashed through the back of her neck as she passed. I pushed a little extra energy into my strike, because spines are hard to cut through, and I felt her vertebrae part like the Red Sea. It did nothing to halt her momentum, so her body kept running past me for a couple steps even after her head fell to the ground and rolled a few feet to the side. But eventually all things must come to an end, and her torso and limbs collapsed to the concrete.

The rest of the vampires froze in mid-step, stunned at the almost instant death of one of their own. I've seen this a lot over the decades; humans gain some power and decide they're not just strong but immortal. Until someone stronger and closer to actual immortality comes along and instructs them on the realities of their situation—they can still be killed, and if the opponent is strong enough, or skilled enough, it can happen in the blink of an eye. Or even faster, if the open glassy eyes of the dead blond vampire staring up at me from the skull at my feet were any indication.

"Kill him!" the master shrieked, and the remaining five vampires charged me all at once. I wasn't really all that concerned with five fledglings. That I could handle on any given Tuesday. But I did need to keep an eye on the boss to make sure he didn't run for the hills the first chance he got, and I had this fuzzy counterweight throwing my balance off, so it was a little more trouble than I expected. My saving grace was that not only had none of them ever learned how to fight together, odds were pretty good they'd never been in a fight before at all, so I was pretty sure I wasn't going to die. Unless the damn cat opened up my carotid while trying to hang onto its perch.

"Hey kitty, you wanna grab onto my shirt, or even the top of my head instead of the side of my neck?" I asked, thrusting my leg out and cracking several ribs on the nearest vamp.

Damned if the fuzzy freeloader didn't adjust his grip to latch onto my scalp when I asked. It didn't feel any better than him clawing my neck, but at least it reduced the chances of me bleeding to death from cat scratches. Slightly.

The next vamp to get to me had a length of two by four in her hands, a good call since she wasn't strong enough to beat me without caving my head in. But since she obviously wasn't a home run hitter in life, she lacked the coordination to actually connect with the lumber. I snatched it out of her hands, broke it over my knee, and shoved half of it through her chest. Then I swore under my breath, because while I'm definitely strong enough to break a two by four over my leg, and durable enough not to suffer any serious injuries because of it, that doesn't mean it didn't hurt like a son of a bitch. I swear I felt the claws in my scalp dig in a little more, like the little bastard was punishing me more for hurting myself.

There were four baby vamps left, and these women were taking their time, spreading out so I couldn't engage more than one of them at a time, at least as far as they knew. Two charged me from the front, and I called up power into my hands, shrouding them in bright purple spheres of pure magical energy. There was no real "spell" involved, just me channeling the raw power of the earth and all its creatures into twin blasts of pure purple power.

No good reason it had to be purple. I just thought it looked cool. Luke scolds me about being ostentatious, but if the flashiest thing I did in that fight was purple magical bolts, then it would go down in the record books as one of my most subtle encounters ever. Flashes of blinding purple light streaked from the palm of each hand, straight through the chest of each vampire, leaving a softball-sized hole in each young woman's torso. I actually took half a second to bend at the waist and wave at the "master" through one of the holes, just to be a dick.

And of course, that's when things went sideways.

I heard a thunderclap just as I felt a sledgehammer slam into my left kidney. I dropped to one knee, one hand reaching around behind me to feel for holes. No blood, so the Kevlar lining in my biker jacket did its job, but I was going to have one mother of a bruise, and probably a cracked rib or two. I looked behind me and saw the vampire I'd kicked in the ribs grinning at me with a smoking double-barrel shotgun in her hands.

"Now that's not fair," I said when I could draw a deep enough breath to speak. "The critters with the fangs and super-speed aren't supposed to use guns. Those are for us mere mortals." Then I reached under my left arm, drew my pistol, and shot her in the forehead. She dropped like a piano in a Warner Brothers cartoon, and the shotgun clattered to the floor. Three down, one to go.

The last vamp standing was literally shaking in her shoes. I could see it from where I was kneeling. "Last chance," I said. "Run away now, learn to feed without killing people, and never make another vampire, and I won't turn you into a puddle of goo. Stay, and you're never seeing another moonrise."

Her gaze flickered from me to Bone Throne Boy, and I could read the indecision like yesterday's headlines. She stood there, frozen by indecision and fear, until I raised my left hand and made it glow purple again. That made up her mind for her, and she sprinted for the shaft of moonlight streaking in from the hole in the ceiling, leapt up to the first floor, and vanished. I heard the *slap-slap-slap* of her Chuck Taylor high-tops as she hauled ass out of there, hopefully never to be seen by me or mine again.

I don't have anything against vampires, really. I don't even begrudge them their need to feed. I mean, people make more blood, so it's just like donating to the Red Cross. Only a little more directly.

I turned to the throne, smiling at the "master."

"Okay, buddy. Down to you and me. You gonna make it easy on me and just cut your own head off, or are we gonna have to dance?"

Poseur Vamp just smiled at me, like he knew something I didn't. Which he probably did, it being his lair and all. There had already been more vampires here than I knew about, and I wouldn't put it past him to—*OWWWW!*

"Goddammit, cat, what the—"

My words died in my throat as I turned to see what had inspired my furry passenger to dig all its claws deep into my shoulder, spring up on top of my head, then leave bloody furrows in my scalp as it launched itself off my head like a high dive board. I was ready to blast that furball into a stole when I saw it latched onto the face of a vamp five feet behind me. It had its teeth clamped onto the vampire's nose, its forepaws digging into the vampire's ears, and its back claws ripping and tearing at the monster's throat like it was digging for gold.

Kinda hard to be mad at the little monster that just saved your life.

This vampire was a big one, obviously strong in life, and the only other male I'd seen except for the boss. He stood several inches taller than me, and carried at least fifty more pounds of muscle, now augmented by its supernatural strength. But none of that mattered when a tiny Tasmanian devil was pulling a Mike Tyson on both ears.

I chuckled, took two steps forward, drew my silver daggers, and drove the blades deep into the creature's chest, I felt the ribs separate, but the vampire didn't die. No, I intentionally missed the heart with both strikes, so I could pry the sneaky bastard's chest open with my blades, plant my right-hand knife in his guts, and reach into his chest. I ripped his heart out with my bare hand and turned to face the "master."

I tossed the heart to land at his feet with a *splat*. "He won't be needing this anymore, so if you're feeling peckish, we could call it your last meal."

Master Mimicry let out an ear-splitting screech and flung himself off the dais in my direction. He covered most of the fifteen yards between us in a single bound, giving testimony to his strength and cementing my knowledge that he was definitely old enough to know better. I let the knife fall from my left hand, caught the oncoming vamp by the lapels of his tuxedo jacket (yes, I'm serious, the dumb bastard wore a tuxedo to a fight), and rolled back onto the floor, planting my feet in the vamp's gut and straightening my legs. He flew back over my head, and I rolled to my feet.

I've tried to do the whole thing where you roll back onto your shoulders and pop your hips to spring up, but it doesn't always go well, and there was a lot of slippery goo on the floor. The last thing I needed was to bust my ass in front of the master vampire. And the cat. Because the cat had a much higher life expectancy than the vampire.

Master Moron slammed into the concrete but was on his feet in a blink. He did the whole nip up thing, because he gave a shit what people thought of him.

I shoved power through the palms of my outstretched hands and yelled, "*DELEO!*"

This was a new one. I usually focused my energy into fire, or an explosion, or sometimes even a manifested sword. But using the Latin word for "destroy" was one I hadn't tried before. It was effective. Devastatingly so. The master vampire didn't explode, per se, but he definitely fell to the ground in a collection of really disgusting component parts. It was kinda like all the things holding him together into a defined form suddenly gave up the ghost, all at the same time. For a couple seconds, it just rained vampire soup. Disgusting, but really effective. I filed that one away for future use.

With the nest cleared out, I pulled out my cell phone and typed a message. "All clear." Seconds later there was a rush of motors and tires crunching in the warehouse's gravel parking lot, and within a minute a ladder descended into the basement and my boss and fiancée, Deputy Director Rebecca Gail Flynn, walked carefully across the gore-splattered concrete to stand before me.

"Well, this is a hell of a mess," she said, looking around. There was still a glowing sphere hovering over my head, so the basement was as bright as noon, showing all the body parts strewn all over the floor, the walls, and a couple of really gross patches of ceiling. "You let one get away."

"Nah, she took Door Number One," I replied.

"Door Number One?"

"Go forth and sin no more," I said. "I gave all of them but the boss a chance to leave, and if they behave themselves, they can live out the rest of their nights without worrying about me hunting them down."

"Wow," Becks said. "Mercy from the man they call the Reaper? You getting soft on me, Harker?"

"Not bloody likely," I replied. I gave her a hug and a quick kiss, then winced as my newest partner climbed up my back, digging his back paws into my injured ribs along the way. "Dammit, kitty, that hurts!"

Becks laughed and stepped back, looking at the furry psycho currently draping itself over the back of my head with one paw on each shoulder, and its front paws hanging down over my forehead. "Harker, did you…rescue a cat while fighting a nest of vampires?"

I glanced up, the tips of ten little claws and some long gray paw hairs the only part of the cat in my field of view, and heaved a resigned sigh. "No, I think actually he kinda rescued me. I mean, he certainly did more damage to me in the fight than any of the vampires, but he also kept me from getting ambushed by the biggest one. So, I guess he's my cat now."

Becks smiled, a knowing grin that twitched up one side of her mouth. "No, Harker. I'm pretty sure now you're his person. Because if you've ever had experience with cats, you'll know that they own people, not the other way around. Good luck, lover. I have a feeling you're in for an interesting ride with that one."

I didn't bother asking what she meant, because just then the damn cat leaned down and licked my right ear, then bit me, then licked me again, and purred in my ear. Yeah, I guess I was his person now.

What the hell was I going to name a cat?

Author Bio

John G. Hartness is a teller of tales, a righter of wrong, defender of ladies' virtues, and some people call him Maurice, for he speaks of the pompatus of love. He is also the award-winning author of the urban fantasy series The Black Knight Chronicles, the Bubba the Monster Hunter comedic horror series, the Quincy Harker, Demon Hunter dark fantasy series, and many other projects. He is also a cast member of the role-playing podcast *Authors & Dragons*, where a group of comedy, fantasy, and horror writers play *Dungeons & Dragons*. Very poorly.

In 2016, John teamed up with several other publishing industry professionals to create Falstaff Books, a small press dedicated to publishing the best of genre fiction's "misfit toys." Falstaff Books has since published over 150 titles with authors ranging from first-timers to *New York Times* bestsellers, with no signs of slowing down any time soon. In February 2019, Falstaff Books launched Con-Tagion, which has very quickly morphed into SAGA – THE Professional Development Conference for Genre Fiction Writers, held in Charlotte, NC every year.

In his copious free time John enjoys long walks on the beach, rescuing kittens from trees and playing *Magic: the Gathering*. John's pronouns are he/him.

Connect with John at: johnhartness.com

Forever and A Day

By Kelley Armstrong

The only thing worse than finding a dead body is finding part of a dead body. This isn't the first time I've experienced that delight...or the first time the body part in question was a head...or even the first time that head was in my bed.

I wake that sunny Saturday morning, stretching and rolling over to greet my husband, only to find myself staring at a tiny, decapitated mouse head on his pillow.

"TC!" I shout, scrambling out of bed. "What the hell is this?"

There's no sign of the damned cat. Damned matagot, I should say. What's a matagot? I have no idea, despite living in a town founded by fae beings, being married to a half-fae guy, and having fae and Wild Hunt blood myself. Ask any of those fae about TC, and all I get is a dismissive "He's a matagot," as if that explains everything. It explains *nothing*.

Naturally, I've tried to look it up, and what I get is that a matagot is a magical cat of French legend, one that supposedly gives its owner a piece of gold each day.

There is no gold.

If TC could talk, I'm sure he'd say I haven't earned it, despite adopting him from the streets, spoiling him rotten, and saving his life at least once. Maybe he's waiting for a real name, something better than The Cat.

When I shout, footsteps thump up the stairs; Gabriel taking them two at a time. By the time he arrives, though, he's slowed to a stride, as if he just happened to need something up here and *didn't* come running when I yelped.

"Olivia?"

He appears in the doorway. He fills that doorway. Tall, broad shouldered, carrying a few extra pounds around his middle, but he wears it well. He wears his impassive "I am not concerned" look equally well.

I wave at the mouse head on his pillow. "We're feeding him, right? Kibble. Chicken. Tuna. Everything a kitty could want?"

Gabriel wordlessly tugs a tissue from the bedside box, picks up the mouse head and disappears into the bathroom. A moment later, the toilet flushes. Then he returns with a fresh pillowcase, replaces the mouse-head-throne one and drops it into the hamper. Only after that's done does he aim a disapproving stare at TC, who has strolled in behind him.

"You're up early," I say as I swing my legs out of bed.

Gabriel leans over to kiss the top of my head. "I'm making breakfast before I leave."

"Leave?" I reach for my phone. "It's Saturday, right?"

"It is, but I received a call just before five. An old client with a new case."

"Case?" I perk up, making the corners of his mouth twitch in the faintest smile.

"Possibly," he says. "I'm meeting him at the office, where I'll determine whether I wish to take his case."

"Ah. A bit of ethical gray in this one?"

His brows rise.

"Sorry," I say. "Let me rephrase. A bit too *much* ethical gray in this one?"

"With this particular client, I suspect there's very little white mixed into the black…and not enough compensation to overlook it."

According to a recent article, Gabriel is Chicago's most infamous defense attorney under the age of thirty-five. He spent a week with that article on his desk, attempting to incinerate it with his irritation. It was the "under thirty-five" qualifier that annoyed him. I assured him that someday, he'll be the most infamous defense attorney of any age. Marriage is all about supporting your partner's dreams.

I suppose I *should* say that I never imagined myself ending up with a guy who has Gabriel's wayward moral compass. That'd be bullshit. I'm a former socialite. I come from the sort of moneyed world that thrives on ethical gray—they're just better at whitewashing over it.

I prefer this. Gabriel is honest about what he does, and he sets limits and stays within them, no matter how much he's offered. Being half fae, he doesn't see right and wrong the way humans do, but that's an excuse he'd never use. This is who he is, and I'm fine with it, because I've discovered it's who I am, too.

We eat breakfast on the back deck, enjoying the cool spring morning and watching the sun rise over the fence. Then I play 1950's housewife and walk my darling hubby to the front door, kissing his cheek as I hand him his coffee before leaning against the jamb in my silk robe while his Jag purrs from the driveway.

It's a good life. A really good life. The only part I'd change is the damned cat meowing at my feet despite the fact I gave him half my bacon. When he swipes at my bare ankle, I jump.

"Ingrate," I mutter. "Next time, I'm eating it all."

TC stares up at me. Then he pulls my gaze to a bird perched on the oak tree. A single magpie. The hairs on my neck prickle.

One for sorrow.

I snap a shot with my phone. When I check, I have a photo of the oak branch…and no sign of the bird I still see perched there.

An omen.

I hit the phone app and tap the top number. It goes straight to Gabriel's voice mail, as it should, so he's not answering his phone while driving. Ha! No, going to voice mail means he's on a call, probably telling the client he's on his way.

"Hey, it's me," I say. "When you were leaving, there was a magpie on the oak out front. One magpie, which wasn't in a photo I took, and you know what that means. Just be careful, okay? Give me a shout when you get this."

I end the call and stand on the porch, watching the magpie that exists only in my mind.

Gabriel and I don't get what you'd call "gifts" from our fae blood. No invisibility or shape-shifting or magical powers. He has a talent for manipulation, which could come from his bòcan father…or it could just be Gabriel. I have the ability to see omens. Does that include any kind of translation guide? Nope. It's like a warning light on my car, telling me something is wrong without providing an iota of diagnostic information.

TC meows.

"I know, I know," I mutter. "Something's wrong, and it has to do with Gabriel."

I try his number again. Still voice mail. My heart stutters, and I flip to the locator app, with visions of the Jag crashed in a smoking heap, Gabriel trapped inside. It's happened before. Okay, I was driving, but a fae caused the crash, in my defense.

No, there's his little tracking dot zooming out of Cainsville.

I know where he's going, and while I can't catch up with him—the man drives as if he's single-handedly responsible for funding the police charity ball—I *can* meet him at the office. That's better than sitting at home, fretting.

I go inside and head upstairs. In our room, I toss my robe onto the chair, turn toward the bed—

There's another mouse head on Gabriel's pillow.

"TC!" I bellow.

A clatter sounds downstairs. A clatter that is not my little nine-pound kitty. Footsteps pound up the stairs.

I take my gun from the nightstand as someone runs down the hall. I have the gun poised, ready—

Gabriel rounds the corner. "What's wrong?"

I lower the gun as I exhale. "You came back. Good."

His dark brows rise. "Came back? I was downstairs making coffee, and I heard you shout." His gaze moves to the pillow. "Ah, I don't blame you for that." He plucks out a tissue and picks up the head.

"Wait," I say. "You already did that."

"Did what?"

"I woke up and saw the head. You put it into the toilet and changed the pillowcase."

He frowns. "No, I just came up now, and I was going to take this outside, but the toilet is a better idea."

He takes it into the bathroom and flushes it down.

I move into the bathroom doorway. "We already did this, Gabriel. Then we had breakfast, and you left for the office."

His brows knit. "But it's Saturday."

"You got a call."

A moment's more confusion. Then his brow smooths. "I believe I can solve this mystery. You woke up, saw the mouse head, fell back to sleep, and dreamed that I came up to dispose of it. Then you woke up and saw the head again. I have no intention of working today. I'm making breakfast and then spending the weekend with my lovely wife. Come down for coffee. There's no need to dress." His gaze lingers over my naked body. "You look fine just the way you are."

Gabriel leaves. TC hops onto the bed and stares at me.

"Yeah, yeah," I say. "I'm not stupid."

I pull on my robe and head downstairs.

When I reach the kitchen doorway, I stop and say, "Hey, Gabe?"

"Yes, dear?"

He turns, coffee mug in hand, and I shoot him in the foot. He lets out an unearthly shriek and falls, gripping his foot. The Gabriel glamour ripples, giving me a glimpse of glossy skin and wings before the doppelgänger reverts to Gabriel's form.

"Cold-iron bullet," I say, hefting the gun. "Stay on the floor. You even start to stand, and I'll fire again."

"You *shot* me," he says in a perfect imitation of Gabriel's voice. "Liv? Why would you do that? Are you unwell?"

"Cut the shit," I say. "Next time, try learning a little about a subject before you impersonate him. Lovely wife? *Dear*? Hell, Gabriel never calls me Liv, and if I ever called him Gabe, he'd be putting that bullet in me, knowing *I* was a doppelgänger."

"I don't know what—"

"Count of five," I say. "Either you drop the act—and the glamour—or the next bullet goes a whole lot higher. If you don't think I'll do it, then you really haven't researched this mission."

He scowls. The Gabriel glamour ripples and then pops as the doppelgänger takes on a generic human form—a middle-aged white man of average size with brown hair and brown eyes.

TC strolls into the kitchen. The doppelgänger hisses at him.

I don't know much about this German subtype of fae. I've only ever encountered one. They're rare. They're also not known for being terribly bright, which is a boon to the rest of us, reducing the chance they can convince you they're someone you trust.

As I keep the gun trained on the doppelgänger, I phone Gabriel and, again, get his voice mail.

"Hey," I say when the beep prompts me to leave a message. "So, I figured out that warning. A doppelgänger just tried to impersonate you. Can you call me back, please?"

I flip to the tracking app and check Gabriel's dot. He's halfway to Chicago. Still on the phone? Or is something tampering with his phone signal?

I pocket the phone and turn to the doppelgänger. "Who sent you?"

"Someone Gwynn ap Nudd crossed. Someone who should not *be* crossed."

Gwynn ap Nudd. A Welsh king of the fae. Some fae think Gabriel is Gwynn reincarnated. It's more complicated than that, but not entirely inaccurate.

"You mean you were sent by someone Gabriel pissed off." I snort. "You have to be a whole lot more specific than that."

"And if I don't want to be more specific?"

I waggle the gun. Over the next ten minutes, I do more than waggle it, to no avail. The doppelgänger was sent to impersonate Gabriel and spend the morning with me, presumably to keep me distracted, but he only knows his instructions. Like I said, doppelgängers aren't known for being geniuses, and a smart employer wouldn't tell him more than necessary.

Time is ticking. I've already placed a call, and when the doorbell rings, I shout, "Come in!"

Most of the Cainsville elders fly under the radar by taking on the glamour of senior citizens. Young people never notice when the old stay old. Patrick is special…or he thinks he is, which is another thing altogether. He refuses to follow the rule, and he's powerful enough to get away with it. He looks younger than Gabriel, which is disconcerting, considering he's Gabriel's father. We never call him that. He doesn't deserve it, having played no role in Gabriel's upbringing, even to rescue him from a spectacularly shitty homelife.

Patrick doesn't resemble Gabriel. Not surprising, given that what I see is his human glamour. His real form is a whole lot…greener. His fae type has many names—bòcan, hobgoblin, boggart—but the best-known example is Shakespeare's Puck. A wild and capricious creature of the forest. Patrick much prefers his human glamour, which looks like a twentysomething bohemian, the kind of guy you can picture writing in a café. Not far off, since that's what he actually does for a living.

I steer Patrick into the kitchen as I tell him what happened.

Patrick walks up to the doppelgänger. "Who sent you?"

"We've already been through that," I say. "His employer told him as little as possible, and I'm not wasting more time interrogating him when someone wanted me distracted while they go after Gabriel."

"Oh, I can make him talk," Patrick says.

"Feel free. But I'm not sticking around for it."

"You're right. Gabriel's in trouble. We need to go."

"*I* need to go. *You* need to babysit this guy."

Patrick eyes the doppelgänger. "That doesn't seem like much fun at all."

"It isn't about fun." I scoop up my car keys. "It's about Gabriel."

"Good point. In that case, I should go, and you should watch this one."

I start for the door. "Nope, you get the shitty job because one of us owes Gabriel far more than the other."

"And when do I finish paying that particular debt?"

"It's a fae blood debt, meaning it'll take forever and a day."

"That is not a thing, Liv," Patrick says as he stalks after me. "You can't simply make these things up."

"Can. Will. Did." I point at the kitchen. "Watch him. If you get bored, interrogate him."

"Why don't we both go after Gabriel? You just need to tie this one up. You must have something here."

"Handcuffs, but they're not cold iron."

"Then what use are…" He trails off. "Don't answer that."

"I wasn't about to." I open the front door. "Call me if he tells you anything useful."

I climb into the Maserati Spyder—the favorite of my cars. Yes, I have more than one car. A garage full of them, in fact, stored in Chicago. They're an inheritance from my adoptive father, and while I only use the Spyder and a more sedate sedan, I can't bring myself to sell the collection. They're the only tie I have to him, and I hoard them like a dragon with its last pieces of gold. I've reunited with my birth father—the one descended from the Wild Hunt—and in a way, that makes me even more reluctant to cut ties with the man who raised me. Driving his beloved cars maintains a link I don't want to sever.

I'm about to pull from the driveway when a black shape moves on the passenger seat. I whirl, hands rising to defend myself. TC gives me a baleful look.

I lean over him to open the passenger door. "This isn't a joyride, kitty. Out you go."

He stands, as if to leave, and instead stretches out and digs his claws into the leather seat.

"Hey!" I say. "None of that."

He fixes me with another look.

"Fine," I mutter. "You can stay but scratch the upholstery and you're walking back."

Gabriel's office is in Chicago, which is nearly an hour away. I work there, too, as his investigator, and I'm accustomed to the commute, but today it seems impossibly long. I've blown up his phone with enough messages that it's stopped offering the option. I've texted. I've emailed. Nothing.

The last time I checked, his tracking dot was at the office. All I can do is get there.

The doppelgänger referred to Gabriel by Gwynn's name. That's significant. It means whoever Gabriel "wronged" is not only fae, but a fae who knows who he is and knows they don't need to hide their own identity around him. That makes this all the more serious—if fae feel the need to blend, it hobbles their ability to use their powers.

According to human folklore, Gwynn ap Nudd was king of the Tylwyth Teg, the Welsh fae. There are dozens of stories attributed to Gwynn, but one is missing. One very significant story: the tale of Mallt-y-Nos. Matilda of the Night. Matilda of the Hunt.

In human lore, Matilda was a noblewoman who refused to give up hunting when she wed and so was doomed to hunt forever. Nice, huh?

The truth is that she was half Tylwyth Teg and half Cŵn Annwn, the Welsh Wild Hunt. Matilda grew up with the princes of both sides and fell in love with one: Gwynn ap Nudd. Furious, the prince of the

185

Cŵn Annwn—Arawn—called in a blood oath that forced Gwynn to agree that if Arawn could woo Matilda to his side before their wedding day, she'd be his, and the world of the fae closed to her forever.

Not knowing of this pact, Matilda went off to hunt with Arawn the night before she was married. When she saw the world of the Tylwyth Teg closing behind her, she tried to get back to it and died, leaving both men without their beloved, which served them right, really, though it was a shitty thing to happen to Matilda. I can say that with some conviction because I remember it all, having Matilda's memories deep in my brain.

Gabriel is a distant descendant of Gwynn and his living embodiment, with Gwynn's memories, just as I'm the living embodiment of Mallt-y-Nos. As for Arawn, Ricky's a biker with an MBA—and a good friend.

What goes around comes around, especially in fae lore. For now, we have this one sorted, and if this fae is calling Gabriel by Gwynn's name—which the Tylwyth Teg know Gabriel hates—it only means he's being an asshole. Most fae are, at heart. Present company included.

As I fret about Gabriel and try to pass it off as devious plotting, TC stays quiet. We reach the office, and TC finally stirs, bracing himself on the dash to look out the windshield.

"Yep," I say. "Gabriel's car is here."

TC leans into the dashboard, as if only stretching from the long drive and not the least concerned about the welfare of this mere human. Even if said human is very warm on cold nights and, unlike the selfish female one, doesn't kick him off her side of the bed.

I open my door. "Okay, so here's the plan—"

TC hops over me and zooms along the driveway into the alley, where mice might be found.

"Thanks!" I call after him. "Your help is appreciated, as always."

I mutter under my breath. "Damn matagot. No gold pieces, no laser vision, no fire-breathing fury. Some magical cat you are."

I swear his ears twitch as he trots down the alley.

"Just kidding," I murmur. "You did warn me this was serious."

I resist the urge to phone Gabriel again. Instead, I check my gun and slide it into my jacket pocket. Then I step out and stretch. I don't *need* to stretch, but I'm taking my cue from the cat and trying to appear nonchalant in case our fae foe is watching.

The best way to handle this is to play the card I have been dealt. Be what they expect me to be. I might not have the ability to put on a glamour, but I'm fae—I don't need superpowers to be something I am not.

I will be silly blond Matilda, whose only power lies in her ability to cause men to make rash and daft promises.

I head for the door with two steaming coffee cups in hand, having whipped through a drive-thru to collect the props. Black coffee for Gabriel, and a mocha for me. As I walk, I slurp happily and bounce along, the young lawyer's wife in her yoga pants and sneakers and designer spring jacket… The last being perfect for the Chicago wind and also bulky enough to hide my gun.

Gabriel's office is in a Chicago greystone. Like New York's brownstones, only gray. It's a gorgeous building, and we now own all of it, a huge step up from when Gabriel first rented the main level, back when there'd been a meth lab in the basement. He'd had nothing to do with the lab besides helping the owner out of any legal troubles. Yes, at that age, Gabriel had known and employed ninety-five percent of the illegal ways to turn a buck—spending his teen years on the street taught him that—but he drew the line at drugs. That's what happens when you're raised by a mother addicted to everything but proper parental care.

The greystone's front door is unlocked. I throw it open and give a little stumble going in, as if I can't quite manage a heavy door plus two hot drinks. Once inside, I head for the main floor office. I throw open the door and trill, "Honey? I bought treats!"

The answering silence makes my stomach flip, but I keep smiling as I set the coffees on Lydia's desk.

"Gabe?" I call. "It's Liv!"

Earlier, I said that if I ever called my husband "Gabe," he'd shoot me as a doppelgänger. Not entirely true. He'll understand it's a warning. Also, he doesn't carry a gun.

"Are you here, sweetie?" I call. "I saw your car. Ooh, is this a game?"

I swing through his office door. Inside, his open laptop sits on the desk. The screen is locked but not off, meaning he's been away only a few minutes. Just then, footsteps clomp upstairs where we keep the storage boxes. There's a distinct thump, and I can picture Gabriel moving boxes as he hunts for the right one.

That's when I see the open folder on the desk. It's a client file, and on the top page, there's a notation that additional information can be found in a file box. With a business like Gabriel's, it's best not to store everything online, even if it's a pain in the ass to search through boxes.

A coffee mug rests on the visitor's side of the desk. I peer in. It's half-full of cold coffee that hasn't yet skimmed over. Gabriel met his client here and was going through his file when he came across something he needed to access upstairs.

So, where's the client?

No way would Gabriel take him upstairs to the file vault. I slide out my gun and move into the main reception area. Then I tilt my head, listening. Upstairs, there's another footfall and another box thump. Gabriel's still looking.

The blur catches me off guard, damn it, and I'm furious enough about it that I lose a split second of reaction time. There is nothing to hide behind over there, so I wasn't paying attention to that spot…where a fae was apparently using the rare ability of fading into the background, which works until it moves.

As I spin, that blur turns into a woman, her gun rising as mine does.

I stop. Her gun isn't pointing at me. It's aimed straight up, through the old flooring.

"Yes, he's right there," she says. "Coincidentally." Her lips purse. "No, not coincidence at all. You children are so easy to manipulate."

She looks younger than me, with short red hair and a wide mouth. As I watch, the glamour shifts to that of a man in his fifties, stout and wearing an expensive but unflattering suit.

The fae pretends to hold a phone to her ear, "Mr. Walsh," she drawls with a southern accent. "It's been a long time, but it seems I need your help again. No, it'll have to be this morning. At your office."

"Yeah, I get it," I say, still holding the gun as she shifts back to her redhead glamour. "You lured Gabriel here pretending to be one of his old clients."

"Lured you both here," she says with a smirk. "Such simple children. Did you congratulate yourself on seeing through that dimwitted doppelgänger's act so quickly? Oh, no, my dear love is in danger! I must fly to his side! No time to pause and tell the elders what's happened!"

I keep my features schooled even as irritation darts through me. Okay, I was set up. This was *all* set up, including Gabriel being unable to find the right file, I presume, keeping him upstairs.

"Lower your weapon," she says. "It won't do you any good anyway."

"Sure it will. Cold-forged iron bullets."

She puts out her free hand. "Toss one over."

I take one out. She catches it in her hand, squeezes it and then opens her fingers to show no more than a slight reddening of the skin.

"Such children," she says, her lip curling. "Shoot me with that, and it will sting, but I would still have time to shoot both you and your lover."

"What do you want?"

"A little chat."

"Do you know how to use a phone?"

"I wanted both of you, in the same place, out of that cursed Tylwyth Teg town."

I motion around us. "You wanted to speak to us together? Come during business hours. We both *work* here."

"Yes, with that old woman and a constant flow of humans, and even then, you've barely been in this office together in the past week. Are you going to keep questioning me when I'm holding a gun on you?"

I still don't like it. There's more to this, and I've already screwed up once. I don't want to be the "foolish human" again.

But did I *really* screw up? What if I'd realized the doppelgänger wanted me to fly to the office to warn Gabriel? Would I have crawled back into bed and refused to play? Of course not. I'm only annoyed that I didn't see the ploy first.

"Poor little Matilda," the fae continues. "It takes that brain of yours a few extra moments to catch up, doesn't it?"

"I'm not Matilda. Mallt-y-Nos, yes. Matilda, no. There's a difference, and if you came thinking I can do something for you—as Matilda—you're about to be disappointed. Being Mallt-y-Nos means I'm useful to the Tylwyth Teg and the Cŵn Annwn, and nobody else."

"Oh, I have no use for you, Matilda. No one ever did, except those two hapless fools. They were the ones with power. You were just the pretty girl caught in the middle."

"Ouch." I sniff. "You're so mean. I don't think I want to talk to you anymore."

"That's fine, because my quarrel is with the great Gwynn ap Nudd. You are just the means to an end, as you always were."

Her hands fly up, and the glamour evaporates, revealing something barely humanoid, a writhing mass of thorns. She charges. I try to fire my gun, hoping to get Gabriel's attention, but she's inhumanly fast. She knocks it from my hand, slicing my jacket open with her thorns. I dive and hit the floor in a roll. When she launches herself at me, I slam a rolling file cabinet into her. Then I run for the door, because I'm *not* stupid. I don't even know what kind of fae this is—only that I can't fight something covered in thorns.

As I run, I dodge to retrieve my gun. It might not kill her, but it could slow her down. I'm scooping it up when thorns stab the back of my knee, buckling it. As I fall, I twist in outrage. I thought I didn't let her get that close to me...and I didn't. She's still five feet away. She fired the thorns into my leg.

Seriously? What the hell kind of fae is this?

I go to grab the gun again, but thorns hit the back of my other knee, and I fall. There's motion in front of me, and before I can look up, my gun is snatched from the floor.

"Stop," a voice says. A very calm, very deep voice that makes my insides sink in relief. Gabriel. Then I remember the doppelgänger, and I tense, but when I look up, Gabriel's pointing the gun at the fae, not me. His impression is completely impassive, as if he's caught a teen breaking into his office. That look tells me this is indeed my husband.

The fae's glamour returns. "Cold-forged iron won't kill me. I already had this conversation with Matilda."

"Olivia," he says. "Her name is Olivia."

"Oh, she has many names, and I know them all, just as I know yours, Gwynn."

"I'm not Gwynn."

"You think I don't see you in there, Gwynn? I have spent centuries searching, through endless half-fae bastards, catching a glimpse of you here and there, but never enough. Never truly Gwynn. Finally, I find you, and I wait for this week—the only week you gave me—and I had to seethe as those days ticked past. I will not wait for my next chance."

"I have no idea—"

"You cursed me," she spits. "Out of jealousy, you cursed me so I can only glamour myself one week each year. The rest I am *this*." She changes back to that thorny mass. "There is no place for fae to hide anymore, Gwynn, and so I spend my life in the shadows, slinking like a rat."

"I am not Gwynn. I have some of his memories, but you aren't one of them. Not who you are or what you did or how to uncurse you."

"What I *did*? I just told you what I did. Nothing. You were jealous."

He shakes his head. "I have enough of his memories to know jealousy would not be the answer."

She returns her glamour and sneers. "Not the answer? You killed your beloved Matilda out of jealousy. You let her die rather than share her with another."

Gabriel flinches. He might not be truly Gwynn, but there's enough of Gwynn in him to make him flinch at that, even if he knows it's not the truth. The story might be "jealousy" but as with any story, the truth goes much deeper, and while it doesn't absolve him, I have enough memories of Gwynn myself to know that Gabriel is right. Whatever this fae did, she deserved the curse. The quiet and gentle young man Matilda loved grew cold and hard after her death, but he would never have issued such a curse if it wasn't warranted—no more than Gabriel himself

190

would do such a thing.

"You will undo the curse," she says.

"I don't know who you are. I have no idea how to—"

Her glamour snaps off, and she launches herself at me. Gabriel fires twice, but it doesn't even slow her. I try to roll out of the way, only to have thorns pin me down, making me howl in agony. With a roar, Gabriel charges. He's running straight for her. Straight for that writhing mass of thorns.

"Gabriel!"

Something flies past him. A blur of black. It leaps and lands on the fae, toppling her over as she screams.

Gabriel stops short. I wrench out the thorns pinning me down as he runs to help me. The fae is on the ground, shrieking, and all I can see is something black, ripping into her despite the thorns.

Gabriel helps me to my feet. The fae goes still. She's still alive, but blood drips from a dozen wounds, and her eyes roll in fear and pain. And perched on her chest is a black cat.

"TC?" I say.

The door behind us flies open.

"I know who it is," Patrick's voice says. "The doppelgänger mentioned Thiten, and I recognized the name from my books. Gwynn…"

He stops as he sees the scene in front of us.

"Is that your *cat?*" he says.

"Apparently," I say. "Our intruder really doesn't seem to like him."

"TC warned me upstairs," Gabriel says. "I saw him, and I knew if he was here, Olivia was, which meant something was wrong."

"Huh." Patrick walks over to the fae. "She's even uglier in real life."

The fae spits at him but doesn't try to rise, her gaze fixed on TC.

"Thiten," Patrick says. "A very old fae, last of her kind. She lured young women to her home, where they were forced to work until they dropped dead. Gwynn cursed her so she couldn't glamour herself and trick humans."

I walk over and look down at the thorn-covered fae. "Fitting punishment."

TC stands on Thiten's chest, his fur puffed, and I swear I can feel him vibrating with tension. With anger? Or just adrenaline? I bend to give him a quick pat. As soon as I touch him, the world shifts, and I am perched on a castle roof.

I'm on a roof, and I'm holding a black cat. And then I *am* the black cat, and I'm being held by a girl, a scullery maid. The images swirl and merge, the girl and the cat. That's when I realize what we're watching, and my breath catches.

Down below Matilda rides to her final hunt. My chest seizes, and I want to look away, but in this vision, I'm not Matilda. I'm the maid and the cat, and we're watching Matilda, and as the girl, I'm happy for her. She's going to Arawn, where she belongs. Arawn is the right choice, sweetness and sunlight to Gwynn's dark chill.

The maid watches, and she is pleased with herself for not telling her mistress what she overheard about the pact between the young men. Matilda should be with Arawn, and this is—

This is death. That's what comes next. Matilda realizing the world of the Tylwyth Teg is closing to her and trying to ride back. Gwynn is there, shouting at her to keep going, willing to lose her to Arawn rather than see her fall into the fire between them.

Matilda *does* run into the fire. And so does the little maid, black cat clutched in her arms. She runs to warn her mistress, to tell her what she should have said before. She runs, and she falls into the fiery abyss, the cat still in her arms, and when she wakes…

Matagot.

I'm thrown, gasping, from the vision. I look down, and all I see is TC, my vision blurring with tears. This isn't the little maid. It isn't Matilda's cat, either. But there are bits of both here, just as there are bits of Matilda in me.

Endless rebirth. Endless seeking. Endlessly trying—like me, like Gabriel, like Ricky—like us, to make things right.

I forget about Thiten. She's no longer important. Patrick will take her, and the elders will deal with her. As he restrains the fae, I quickly tell Patrick and Gabriel what I saw.

"Enid," Gabriel says. "The little maid was Enid, and the cat was Derog. I remember them."

"I don't," I say wistfully.

"It'll come," Patrick says. "And TC isn't either of them. Not really."

"I know. Still…"

I lift TC onto the desk and bend to look him in the eyes. "You thought you owed a debt. You didn't, but I understand. That's why you found me. Thank you." I stroke the top of his head. "You saved my life, and you are now free of any obligation."

"And me?" Patrick says.

I straighten and look at him. "You didn't save our lives."

He waves at Thiten. "I'm taking a threat off your hands, and not for the first time. We're square?"

Gabriel's brows furrow. He has no idea what we mean, of course. I'm the one who never lets Patrick forget what he did because I'm the one who cares, on Gabriel's behalf.

"Forever and a day," I call as I head for the door.

"Not actually a thing!" he calls after me.

I turn to face him. "Do you want me to stop calling you into adventures?"

"No, but I'd like to actually *go* on the adventure now and then."

I shake my head.

"I'll follow you home," Gabriel murmurs to me. "To be safe. And thank you for coming."

I arch my brows. "Do you ever think I wouldn't?"

The faintest smile tugs at his lips as he leans down to press his lips to mine.

"Forever and a day," I murmur.

"Forever and a day," he says.

We separate, and I see the coffees on Lydia's desk. I lift mine, take a sip and make a face.

"Cold, damn it." I shake my cup at Thiten. "You owe me a mocha."

Gabriel's smile grows a little. "We'll stop at the bakery on the way home. A near-death escape, a captive ancient fae, and a mocha."

"Best day ever."

We head outside. Gabriel goes to his car, and when I open the door of mine, TC is right there. He hops over me onto the passenger side.

I slide in and turn to him. "I meant it, TC. Please don't stay because you feel obligated."

He eyes me, and in that look I see a question, and I have to smile.

"Of course, you're welcome to stay. You are always welcome. Just don't ever feel obligated."

He settles in on the seat.

"Excellent," I say as I start the engine. "Now let's talk about the gold coins."

He gives me a look.

I reach to pat him. "Kidding. No gold coins required. No dramatic rescues required. You have a place to stay, with all the tuna you can eat and all the pets you can endure." I meet his eyes. "Forever and a day."

He stretches out on the seat, and I smile and back the Spyder out onto the road.

Author Bio

Kelley Armstrong believes experience is the best teacher, though she's been told this shouldn't apply to writing her murder scenes. To craft her books, she has studied aikido, archery and fencing. She sucks at all of them. She has also crawled through very shallow cave systems and climbed half a mountain before chickening out. She is however an expert coffee drinker and a true connoisseur of chocolate-chip cookies.

Connect with Kelley at: kelleyarmstrong.com

The Unexpected Dachshund

By L.E. Modesitt, Junior

Rudy was a dachshund. Rudy was a sham.
Rudy came to Nieuwhuis and found there was no lamb.
We were stuck on Nieuwhuis, out of heaven's way.
Building domes on barren clay, under skies so gray...

One fourday night, at least I recall it was a fourday, because it was right after the south end of dome four almost collapsed and the teams had worked for two days straight to stabilize the ground—all because the geo team hadn't caught a tunnel snake's den below the sterilized area—Keryleyn looked across the plastex table at me, and said, "I've been thinking..."

"Yes?" I said warily.

"There has to be more to life than this."

"I agree," I replied, and then I said the most dangerous words a man could utter. "What do you have in mind?"

"They have a few puppy zygotes on the mothership. There's a miniature, cream, longhaired dachshund. His name is Rudolfo..."

"We can't afford whatever they want. Not just the cost...but the food—"

"He's a miniature, Dom. They don't eat much..."

For once, I didn't answer immediately. I just looked into her eyes. That was enough. We'd come to Nieuwhuis under the standard terms, and, at our ages, that meant no children. Ever. But it had been the only chance to escape. At least the air in the gray skies of Nieuwhuis was clean, unlike Old Earth. But there were times when life felt a little empty, and I knew we weren't the only ones to feel that way.

Finally, I said, "How do you figure we can do it?"

As I suspected, Keryleyn had it figured out to the last fraction of a credit, which was good because Rudy cost every free credit we could scrape together, as well as part of our food ration, and that didn't count the sterilized gravel for his box inside the dome.

Almost from the beginning, Rudy wasn't exactly what we expected him to be. We had to wait almost half a year, between the maturation womb and his growing big enough to make the drop planetside. He arrived as a small brownish puppy and was from a reputable breeder, or rather, his zygote came from a reputable breeder, as did most Terran stock.

Since cream dachshunds all start out brownish, how were we to know he wasn't what he was supposed to be? Yes, by the time he was six months old, his coat was turning, but not quite the way we expected. His undercoat was more a golden cream, and the tips of each hair were reddish. And his coat wasn't long and silky soft, like most longhairs. His was medium-length and disheveled, soft but not silky, and just a trace wavy. The other unexpected difference was he had whiskers, sort of a beard—and longhaired dachshunds definitely don't have beards or whiskers. But wire-haired dachshunds do. The only problem with that was, besides the drooping whiskers, he didn't look like a wirehair.

Restricted on our limited data-access time, I finally managed to check the database, and, as well as I could figure, Rudy was most likely a miniature, cream, soft-coat wire-haired dachshund; a variety I'd never heard of. While Keryleyn made a few comments about his not being a longhair, especially after all we'd paid, he was so affectionate, so bright, and so damned cute, there was no way we were ever going to let go of him.

But Keryleyn was right. From the moment he raced around our small quarters, chasing after the balls I got the fabrication team to make out of plastex scraps, until he settled down on his little pallet, he brought a definite warmth and brightness to our lives.

The first time I took him out of the dome was in the evening, when the daylight was dimming. We seldom had true sunsets, because of the high haze-clouds, and it was always quiet on Nieuwhuis, almost spooky-quiet. There were rustles and whispers everywhere, but we could barely hear them. The native vegetation seemed to absorb sound, and the quiet, especially when our teams weren't working and, incidentally, making noise, made the entire planet feel like a well-lit haunted house—not that I'd ever been in one.

But that first time out, I had Rudy on a leash, because he was only four months old, and I didn't want him dashing off beyond the domes into the jangle, that tangled mass of scrawny gray-green growth that wove itself into intricate and unintelligible patterns in places and left inexplicable pathways to nowhere in other locales. Except on the north continent, where there were lizard-like quadrupeds the size of small alligators, but with much longer legs, most of the wildlife we'd observed tended to be small and much of it burrowing, possibly because of the comparative frequency of solar flux-flares.

Rudy was definitely curious, but cautiously so. The first thing he sniffed was the sealant that linked the outer skin of the dome to the permacrete base. Then we took the walkway toward dome five. We were about halfway there when he turned toward the jangle, more than fifty meters away. I kept him on short leash—also from the fabrication shop—but let him investigate the mossgrass that tended to spread from the jangle, even onto sterilized ground, at least until the Terran crabgrass got well-established.

A molecat peered out of the undergrowth, studying Rudy from a distance.

Rudy studied the molecat back, sniffing as he did. Then he whined once and edged back toward me. Even so, the molecat retreated into the jangle.

I was surprised Rudy didn't bark. Keryleyn and I had dachshunds back on Old Earth, and every other dachshund barked. Some enjoyed barking. Some only barked to announce or warn of intruders. But they all barked. Rudy had no interest in barking. He *could* bark—he barked all of three times in his first six months, the first time when Arlena and Pietro came to our quarters.

Arlena practically squealed "He's so cute!!!"

Pietro laughed and slapped the wall.

Rudy gave one short bark and then planted himself at Keryleyn's feet. She picked him up and said, as she held him, "They're friends." Then she set him down.

After several sniffs, especially of their boots, Rudy agreed.

Rudy just wasn't interested in barking. He was also extremely sensitive to loud noises. In fact, they frightened him incredibly. In that respect, it might have been good that Nieuwhuis was a quiet planet, although I often wondered why that was so, or if possibly the native fauna just communicated on frequencies we couldn't hear.

Other than not barking, Rudy was a dachshund—friendly, sweet, and definitely energetic. And definitely fast. He also was much stronger than other dachshunds, at least from what Keryleyn and I recalled, and training him was, shall we say, a challenge, except for being house-broken and understanding the word "No." So, when he was outside, especially at night, under the double moons, he was always on leash, a short leash, at that.

Even as a puppy, if he didn't want to go somewhere outside the dome, it was a good possibility that there might be molecat pits or fire-spider webs. And that meant I'd have to go out in kevlex later, with a torch or an adze, and take care of the problem. But he didn't bark. He just didn't go there. He'd plant his feet if I tried to get him to move where he didn't want to go, but only when outside.

Rudy certainly enjoyed sniffing around, especially where the ground had just been cleared for a new dome. With his tail wagging and his nose down, it seemed as though he needed to inspect every square centimeter of bare and sterilized soil, although Keryleyn and I both wondered exactly what smells remained in the ground after the sterilization process.

He was incredibly affectionate and less destructive than most dachshund puppies—but that might have been because there really wasn't much to destroy, except for stray plastex scraps, of which there were quite a few as we expanded the domes. Still, if given too much time and too little supervision, he would reduce those scraps to tiny shreds, something that the molecats and the ratlings couldn't, or wouldn't, manage.

Having an essentially unmodified dachshund on Nieuwhuis possibly wasn't the best idea, but he was so warm and enthused to see us; a spot of unforced energy and affection amid the cool business of building what we could while we could. His presence at night, on his little pallet next to ours, if he wasn't on ours as well, was more than welcome. He was warm physically as well as emotionally, and we appreciated it.

I suppose that was natural when you're all strangers in a strange land—or world.

The other pairs on the team often stopped by, more to see Rudy, I think, than to see us, but he did give us all something to talk about besides building the domes for the next wave of settlers—or re-settlers, since some were coming from the mess of the Centauri fiasco.

We'd sit on cushions on the floor in the main room and just talk and watch Rudy. Arlena was his favorite among those who visited. He'd bring her one of his battered and gnawed plastex balls and whine for her to throw it. She'd throw it, and he'd have the ball and be back at her knees in an instant. When Arlena got tired, Rudy would come to me next.

Rudy was a little more than a standard year old when the big flux-flare hit. We all knew that the flares occurred frequently, and that was likely why so much of the animal life on Nieuwhuis dug tunnels, holes, or had dens in rocky area. It was also theorized that was why intelligent life had never developed, but even the astrophysicists and the biologists admitted that was just an educated guess.

Anyway, most times the geomagnetic storms were moderate. We'd only had to shelter, for real, three or four times since we'd been on Nieuwhuis, and compared to the problems other planetary settlements were having, holing up in the domes for a few days every few years was more of an inconvenience.

When the alarm came, I was on the job, installing ventilation ducts in dome nine, the latest dome under construction.

Geomagnetic event. Estimated strength G-9. Shut down and shelter immediately...

Even I knew a G-9 was bad, really bad.

We shut everything down and sprinted for our respective domes. We would have been shielded from the radiation and the flux in dome nine, but not from induced current flows, which were problematic in an unfinished dome. It also would have been damp and uncomfortable, and we'd have been more than a little miserable before the magnetic storm subsided and it was safe to leave .

Keryleyn was waiting for me in the three small chambers we called home. So was Rudy, bouncing up and down at the fact that we were there unexpectedly. I took a few moments to pick him up and let him give me an enthusiastic licking, the dachshund equivalent of kisses.

Then I set Rudy down and turned to Keryleyn, since she was the meteorologist. "How long will this flare last?"

"At least a day and a half, but that depends on whether there's more than one coronal mass ejection. Every once in a while there is, like the historic Carrington Event. This looks to be worse than that."

I took her word for it, although I had no idea what the Carrington Event was or when it had occurred.

Then, as we knew would happen, almost all the power was cut off and the block-points opened to reduce, if not eliminate, damaging induced current flows. That left the limited, and highly shielded, basic emergency power.

We sat down on the floor cushions and spent an hour playing with Rudy, who was confused, because when he went to the door, one of us said, "No." Quietly, but firmly.

His whine was inquisitive.

"Because it's not safe out there, or it won't be shortly," Keryleyn told him.

Rudy looked at me questioningly, then whined again, meaning that we *always* took him out when we came home. He'd use his sand and gravel box, if he had to, but he much preferred the outside, as did we, because it meant much less cleaning.

"As your mistress said," I told him, "it's not safe for us…or for dachshunds." Or in his case, for the only soft-coat wire-haired dachshund on Nieuwhuis, or possibly anywhere off Old Earth.

Later, in early evening, Arlena and Pietro came by, since they had quarters in our dome, if on the other side. He had a deck of old-style pasteboard cards—useful indeed when power was limited. Thankfully, his cards were nearly indestructible, some sort of plastex, kevlex, and synth mix that was also resistant to Rudy's teeth on the occasions when he could grab a card; not an impossible feat, given we were sitting on the floor, under the dim glow of the single emergency lamp, and using my equipment case for a table.

Rudy would watch for an opportunity to seize a card, after which he'd prance around so proud of himself. So, in a way, we all were playing two games at once—cards and get the card back from Rudy.

We laughed a lot…and tried not to think about how much damage the geomag storm might be causing around the domes, but finally Arlena and Pietro left. It was fairly late, and the three of us went to bed, with Rudy ending up next to Keryleyn. It got cool enough I almost wished Rudy were between the two of us.

Almost two days passed before full power came back…if two hours before dawn. I couldn't get back to sleep and finally dressed and got ready to go to work. When Rudy saw me put on my work jacket, even though I hadn't planned to leave for almost an hour, he raced to the door, tail wagging furiously, and offered a series of inquisitive whines that quickly turned to verging on demands.

"Rudy, it's not even that light out yet."

The whines and tail-wagging continued unabated.

Keryleyn looked from Rudy to me, grinned, and then said, "Dom…you've got more than a little time…and he has been very good. Just stay away from the jangle."

With her expression and Rudy's enthusiasm, I didn't see that I could do much else, nor did I really want to. So, we stepped out into the corridor, and Rudy hurried toward the outer door, his short legs moving swiftly. I checked the monitor beside the door but didn't notice anything unusual.

When I opened the dome door, and Rudy and I stepped out onto the walkway, I could see that it was far hazier outside than it had looked through the monitor. Not only that, but there were fire-spider webs all along the edge of the jangle, and silvery lines running from the jangle across the mossgrass and the still-struggling crabgrass, and even across the walkways. Except the lines weren't lines; they were bands, more than five centimeters wide. I'd never seen anything like it, and no one had ever mentioned such a display.

I couldn't help frowning because the monitor hadn't picked up any of that. Or maybe the webs were so fine it couldn't show them. But they didn't look that fine. Both the webs and the bands looked almost solid, with a greenish-silver light of their own in the dimness before dawn.

Then, out of the corner of my eye, I caught a glimpse of something moving, moving fast. I turned to see the largest molecat I'd ever seen—a giant molecat, the size of a cougar, with fangs that would have been right at home on an ancient sabre-tooth tiger, bounding toward us, somehow avoiding the fire-spider webs and the green-tinged, silver-banded paths that wound everywhere.

Before I could say a word, or even move, Rudy barked! Really barked, the way only a determined dachshund can bark.

That one series of barks echoed through the stillness like shots from an antique rifle and seemed to strike the mole-cougar physically—enough that it lost concentration and focus—and one forefoot landed in the middle of one of the silver-banded lines.

Green aurora-like fire flared from the silver banded lines and enveloped the mole-cougar with the sizzling of an electric current jolting through the beast. Even before the dead body stopped twitching, hundreds, no, thousands, of tiny fire spiders appeared out of the mossgrass and converged on the corpse like a silver tide.

I could have hugged Rudy, but I was too worried. I just wanted to get the two of us safely back inside without touching any of those shimmering lines, or before any of the silvery fire-spiders could get inside the dome. Since Rudy had planted himself firmly at my feet, I just scooped him up and withdrew.

Withdrew? Hell… I fled and closed the dome door.

Once inside, I grabbed the emergency comm by the door and immediately broadcast a warning.

Danger! Danger! Shimmering silver lines and webs carry high-energy charges…

I'm not sure I was even that coherent, but I did get the word out, and no one got jolted or irradiated.

The biologic types are still investigating how the local eco-system stores the mag-flux energy, but early indications are that their communications are more electronic rather than sonic. It seems the fire-spiders lay down those bands and lines after large magnetic events, and the mole-cougars have always been around—but they're rare because most prey is small.

Although the techs theorize that the sonic energy of Rudy's bark disoriented the mole-cougar, I still don't know why Rudy barked, But whatever the reason, I'm still alive because a miniature, cream, soft-coat, wire-haired dachshund didn't turn out the way he was expected. And, to this day, how he knew or felt what to do, I haven't the faintest idea.

And I don't care. I'm just grateful… and so are a lot of other people.

Rudy was a dachshund. Rudy was no sham.
Rudy came to Nieuwhuis and made us feel at home.
We're still here on Nieuwhuis, with no need to roam.

Author Bio

L. E. Modesitt, Jr. is the bestselling author of over seventy novels encompassing two science fiction series and four fantasy series, as well as several other novels in the science fiction genre.

Mr. Modesitt has been a delivery boy; a lifeguard; an unpaid radio disc jockey; a U.S. Navy pilot; a market research analyst; a real estate agent; a director of research for a political campaign; legislative assistant and staff director for a U.S. Congressman; Director of Legislation and Congressional Relations for the U.S. Environmental Protection Agency; a consultant on environmental, regulatory, and communications issues; and a college lecturer and writer in residence. In addition to his novels, Mr. Modesitt has published technical studies and articles, columns, poetry, and a number of science fiction stories. His first story was published in 1973. He lives in Cedar City, Utah.

Connect with L.E. Modesitt, Jr. at: lemodesittjr.com/about-the-author/

The Kitcoon

By L. J. Hachmeister

Author's Note: A prequel short story in the world of *Laws of Attraction* and the *Triorion* universe.

Y ou're in danger."
Rex averted her gaze, hoping the old woman would lose interest in her. If she could, she'd have found another place to ride in the cargo hold of the star freighter, but the windowless ship was already jam-packed with other refugees, immigrants, animals, and illegal merchandise. Besides, being crammed between biohazardous drums was better than fighting for a place to stand in the congested, shoulder-to-shoulder crowd.

"You shouldn't be here, especially not alone." The old woman, clinging to the black netting dividing a pile of luggage, looked Rex over with rheumy eyes. "How old are you?"

Nineteen; not a kid anymore. Clutching her rumbling and very empty stomach, Rex muttered, "Old enough."

"I know those eyes," the woman whispered. "Orange-fire, like the sunset. You must be from the southern tribes."

Rex tensed. Seated on the grated floor, she brought her knees up to her chest and double-checked her surroundings. The drunk in the corner, slumped over a barrel, hadn't noticed their conversation. Neither had the mother trying to feed her whimpering infant as the janky freighter rocked and shook in the turbulence of faster-than-light travel. Everyone had their own problems, their reason to be aboard an illegal transport bound for the sanctuary city of La Raja, on Neeis.

Old fears resurfaced: *"You can't escape this life."*

Heart racing, Rex tried to sound firm. "I'm human, like you," she said just loud enough to be heard over the ticking engines. "Just modded."

"Modded?"

"Modified," she emphasized. A lie that had gotten her this far without too much scrutiny. Rex looked human enough, except for her eyes, but if someone looked underneath her jacket and pants, they'd see the marks—

Scars—

Of a monster.

"Mmmm," the old woman replied, sounding unconvinced.

Frail and wrapped in patched robes, the elderly woman didn't look like she'd amount to a threat, but Rex knew not to underestimate anybody. Especially someone suspecting her of being a telepath from Algar based solely on the color of her eyes.

The temptation to let her guard down and unleash her telepathic talent was there, but she couldn't control the terrible thing inside her under threat. And in such a tight space, and with all these people—

She squeezed her eyes shut. *Please, I don't want to hurt anybody—*

(—else.)

Rex let her breath out through gritted teeth. *Get yourself together.*

She thought about how the old woman sounded. Her Common, the universal language of the Starways, was decent, though heavily accented. She probably wasn't from the Homeworlds, or the main planets that comprised the central Starways where most humans lived. But that didn't mean much. Humans spread across the galaxy centuries ago and interbred with countless alien species. That's what made it so hard to tell.

Maybe she's like me, Rex thought. Humanish and poisoned by a telepathic lineage. Hunted by the Dominion military for her supernatural abilities. The enemy of the Starways.

A monster.

(Leech)—

"Shhh, sweet boy," the old woman whispered as something wiggled beneath her clothing. Something small but feisty. A feline head popped out of the upper folds of her robe and let loose a pitiful meow. The skinny critter had a rectangular patch of hair missing at the top of his black-and-maroon striped head with a fresh pink scar running down the center, and big, saffron eyes that bade to give her affection.

The old woman gently pushed the thing back inside her robes. "Kio doesn't like traveling."

"What is it?"

"A kitcoon, native to La Raja. They're considered a nuisance, like rats or pigeons from Old Earth. The Dominion use them in experiments because they're so hardy. He doesn't deserve that."

Nothing deserves that, she wanted to scream. Even street vermin.

Rex eyed the old woman again, not hiding her suspicions. "So, you broke him out of a Dominion lab?"

The old woman's forehead knotted. "I wasn't alone…until now. It's been a rough journey. I'm getting too old for this, you know."

"You're risking a lot for a, uh, pest."

The woman frowned and patted the purring lump lying across her abdomen. "For *Kio*. He's worth all the trouble."

"No way," she murmured as phantom pains lanced her stomach. Hunger pangs morphed into a roiling fire. Holding her abdomen, Rex couldn't think of anything or anybody that would be worth that kind of a gamble. The Dominion's military scorched worlds, used devastating weapons of mass destruction to control any threat, and with their objective set on imprisoning—

Eradicating—

—telepaths, Rex couldn't imagine what they'd do to someone who, even on the smallest level, interfered with their plans.

Sweat dotting her brow, she dug her fingers into her stomach. Even through the clothing layers she could feel the scars burning all over again as needles punctured her skin, pumping poison directly into her organs, tearing her apart—

("No, please, I don't want to be a telepath. I'm sorry! Please, STOP—")

The ship hit a bump. The other passengers cried out as they slammed into the walls, each other, as luggage, containers, and boxes tipped over. Rex braced herself between containers, heart racing, as the overhead lights flickered.

We hit something—?

Her senses screamed otherwise. Pulsating tension, stress, leaked in from beyond the bay doors, from down the corridor, where the cockpit was situated. *Something's wrong.*

"They found us," the old woman muttered, clinging to the netting with shaking arms as the engines whined. Passengers screamed as the ship rocked to port. People shoved and scrambled over each other, trying to get ahold of something anchored into the ship. "It's too late…"

Rex barely heard the old woman as the ship lurched and the engines whined and grated. Cages and boxes tumbled from overhead storage, spilling critters of all sizes into the fray along with plumes of feathers and tufts of loose fur.

"What did we hit?" a passenger cried as the ship's engines shut off. Distant *thumps* vibrated through the ship.

Nothing, Rex realized as smoke plumed from the vents, peppering the air with a metallic tinge. *Those are explosives—*

(—Boarding party.)

Scrambling to her feet, she took the old woman by the elbow.

"Slow down," the woman cried as Rex dragged her through the tidal wave of people fighting to get to the cargo bay door. "Where are we going?"

White smoke made it hard to see, harder to breathe. Rex held the sleeve of her motocross jacket to her nose, struggling to push her way through the crowd and keep hold of the limping old woman.

"Stop! I can't go that fast—"

Rex reared around and pointed at a pile of spilled luggage. "We have to hide."

But as the old lady regarded the mess of clothes, packages, and debris, the cargo bay doors lifted. More smoke, and red emergency lights from the corridor, poured into the bay. Rex tugged on her elbow again, but the woman resisted, eyes as wide as saucers. "It's too late. Take Kio. Protect each other."

The old woman shoved the kitcoon into Rex's arms. "No, lady, I can't—"

"Everyone on their knees!" Heavy boots pounded against the grated floor. Rex glanced back to see sweeping laser sights and armored soldiers, in the Dominion's signature blue and black uniforms, flooding inside. "Passports out!"

The kitcoon bellowed and wiggled out of Rex's grip, scampering away. Out of time, Rex dove behind an overturned cage leaning against the wall. Hybrid chickens flapped and scuttled over displaced luggage. Hopefully the frenzied mess of loose animals—and the rank smell of an uncleaned cage—would be enough of a deterrent for a thorough search of her hiding spot.

Rex's eyes flicked to the old woman. Hunched over and frozen in place, the gray-haired lady didn't move, even when the soldiers started roughing up the passengers, or when a laser sight landed over her heart.

"You there," a soldier called, stomping his way through cowering passengers, his rifle pointed at her chest. "Passport."

Rex curled her toes in her boots and clenched her fists. Hopefully the woman had a passport or a decently faked one.

But the petrified look in the woman's eyes said otherwise.

"You," another masked soldier said, grabbing the woman by the shoulder and shaking her. "Passport."

The old woman's hands shook as she searched inside the folds of her robes and produced a chip tied to a necklace around her neck. The soldier scanned it and grunted. "This expired two months ago and says you're a registered citizen of Crais."

An uninhabitable moon? Someone sold her a bum passport.

"Uh, well—" she said, fumbling with the necklace.

The lead soldier waved his gun, signaling for the soldier with the scanner. Rex recognized the handheld wand that would take a blood sample and analyze her DNA. It wasn't completely accurate in detecting telepaths, especially with all the hack clinics that could mask genes, but Rex didn't think this woman, if foolish enough to use passport that listed her as a Crais citizen and steal street vermin from the Dominion, would have that kind of protection.

You're a telepath, aren't you? Maybe not a Prodgy, like her; maybe one of the other four types that got a bad rap ever since the Dominion military came into power. *Why would you risk this for an animal?*

Gun pointed at her chest, the second soldier yanked the old woman's arm and bunched up the sleeve of her robe.

"Please," the old woman whispered as the soldier waved the blue light of the wand over her upturned wrist. "I just want to be left alone."

Left alone. The sentiment burned through Rex's veins. That's all she wanted. To no longer be hunted, chained down and experimented on; hated for being born with a power she didn't ask for—

"Malfunction," the soldier announced as the wand flashed yellow. "What should we do with her?"

"Bring her back to the lab," the first soldier announced, pulling a shock collar from his belt.

Rex's stomach dropped and she clutched her neck. *No*—

The kitcoon burst out of the rubbish, clawing his way to the top of stack of debris, and gave a demanding meow. The soldiers paused, shining their lights at him, illuminating her hiding spot in the background. Rex shimmied back, out of their line of sight.

The kitcoon cooed, tipping over as it emptied his tiny lungs. He righted himself and whipped his tail back and forth.

"Aw," one the soldiers whispered. Even Rex's pounding heart melted little bit at the sight of the little feline mewing for affection.

"That scar on its forehead," the lead soldier said, pointing with his gun. "That's the escaped lab 'coon."

The nearest soldier straightened up, slinging his weapon over his soldier. "I'll grab it." He dove after the kitcoon, disturbing Rex's tenuous debris hiding spot, and shoving the cage up against her, crushing her ribs.

Chak!

As she squirmed to free herself, the cage slid away. She flattened out, hoping to stay unseen as the kitcoon dodged and darted between debris piles, evading the soldier's grasp, heading away from her.

"Hey!" a soldier shouted. "Someone's behind that cage."

The rest of the soldiers turned to her, their laser sights converging on her forehead.

"Leave her be," the old woman pleaded, trying to stop them as they kicked aside luggage and dug their way through the trash toward Rex. The woman's telepathic echo rang through the cargo hold, but it wasn't strong enough.

Rex wiggled backward. Chickens squawked and flapped about as the soldiers flung aside the cage and came after her. Out of her line of sight, the kitcoon wailed.

No, she thought as the first gloved hand clamped down on her arm and wrenched her forward.

Then, from somewhere deeper, where her pain boiled: *(NO.)*

The soldier grabbing her arm screamed. He arched his back and fell to the ground, seizing, as her invisible force took hold of his body.

"Leech! Leech!" the team lead shouted, holding her by the boot. Rex turned her gaze to him and let the dark power slide through their connection. He grabbed at his neck, frothing at the mouth, and fell to his knees.

The other soldiers, gun tips crackling blue with plasma charge, quickly descended upon her as she dove behind a structural divider.

"Get away from me!" she shouted, her mind blazing.

Passengers screamed and fled the cargo hold into the corridor, trampling over each other. A soldier hit the cargo bay controls, closing the door behind the last passenger, isolating Rex, the old woman, and the kitcoon in the hold.

Why won't you leave me alone?

But that question didn't matter. Only survival did.

Look inside. As she had self-taught in her early teens, when her powers first emerged. *Find the living light—*

—Of every nerve fiber, every cell, in the overlapping space between visual consciousness and extrasensory perception. A place that no armor could protect, no living being could hide, radiating, exposed—accessible.

Got you. With her mind, she seized each soldier at the spine, breaking them at the knees and sending them crumbling to the grated floor. A few fired their guns aimlessly, blasting man-sized holes in containers, luggage—and walls.

"Warning," the ship's computer announced as the internal pressure dropped. Rex clung to the black netting connecting the floor to the ceiling as debris and soldiers were sucked toward the holes, through the phasic distortion of the shields, and out into the twinkling stars beyond. *"Hull breach. Emergency landing."*

Rage scorched her chest, igniting old wounds. The scars on her abdomen, the mutilations on her skin, burned. She righted herself and set her eyes back on the panicking soldiers clinging to anything anchored to the ship.

Thin arms wrapped around her, shaking, desperately holding on.

Rex growled. *YOU WANTED THE MONSTER. HERE I AM—*

"Save Kio—"

The calm of the old woman's voice—

The pitch—

"Find…"

That stupid kitcoon—

"…another way…"

The telepathic pull lulled her mind.

Another way. Impossible. Not after being orphaned, abandoned. Not when countless poisons had been injected into her organs, trying to *cure* her of her Prodgy bloodline madness. Not after using the cursed talent to stay one step ahead for those that would imprison her for the very thing she used to survive. The thing that *defined* her.

But the old telepath's words repeated themselves, draining the heat pumping through her body even as the ship rocketed down through the fiery atmosphere and into the clouds.

Save Kio…

Find another way…

Rex held tight to the netting as the woman held on to her, the wind whipping away the tears from her eyes.

The old woman rifled through and around her jacket, fastened something around her waist. Rex looked down to see herself clipped to the net with a cargo-securing belt.

"What are you doing?"

The ship banked hard. Rex lost her grip but stayed fastened to the netting by the belt as the woman flung away.

Kicking and flailing, Rex wrestled back upright as the winds screamed. Anything not nailed or bolted down banged and bashed its way through the widening holes as the ship dove through turbulent, lightning-streaked storm clouds.

"Hey!" Rex shouted, but the screaming winds stole her voice.

We're gonna die, she thought, spotting one of the five remaining soldiers catching the old woman with one arm while grabbing onto a bolted handhold with the other. Even if the ship landed in one piece, the soldiers would tag and imprison them. *Not without more bloodshed, not without risking—*

Rex squeezed her eyes shut. *I don't want to Fall…*

And become exactly what the Dominion propaganda wanted everyone to believe: That a Prodgy like her couldn't control her powers to heal herself and others, and would eventually descend into maddening darkness, killing everything she came across. But she had no choice. She wasn't going allow herself, or the old woman, to be taken. Even the chicken hybrids, hiding between the piping, didn't deserve to suffer like this.

Or even that stupid kitcoon. Wherever he was.

The heat simmered in her chest. This time she wouldn't give up so easily, not until she'd torn apart the soldiers from the inside-out—

The old woman glanced back at her, rheumy eyes filled with sadness. Then, as lightning flashed, a smile hinted at a corner of her mouth. Pulling herself up onto the same bolt, she said something into the mic by the soldier's ear. A mic that linked the audio to the rest of the unit.

Thunder boomed, white lightning cracked open the sky. Rain fizzled against the shields as the soldiers arched and squirmed.

Rex heard the woman's voice in the telepathic echo, soothing and calm. *(Let go.)*

Powerful. Persuasive. Inescapable. The type of power that should be feared.

Rex let go of the netting. She flipped over onto her back, but didn't struggle, allowing her arms and legs to be taken by the winds as the belt held her fast at the waist. She watched as, one-by-one, the soldiers let go of their holds and were swept out into the maelstrom.

Another peel of thunder rocked the vessel.

Oh Gods—what did she do? Rex thought, coming out of the trance. The old woman clung to the bolted handhold, but bent, arthritic fingers couldn't grip much longer. And the crushing, half ton drum of biohazardous material sliding toward her on a collision course—

"Watch out!" Rex screamed, fighting to turn back over—to somehow get to the old woman—

The old woman took one look at the biohazard drum and then back at Rex. She called out to her, but the storm and turbulence stripped her words.

"Don't let go!" Rex cried. "DON'T—"

The ship plummeted, sending Rex, and everything else, flying upward and crashing against the ceiling. Her head struck metal piping. The pain didn't register, nor the shock of blood spilling down her face, as all went dark.

Rex woke awkwardly sprawled across a pile of luggage, face down, with her left cheek pressed against the grated starship floor. Her first breath came with a panicked heave and cough, as if she'd been gut-punched.

Memories came trickling in along with a lancing pain to the back of her skull. When she rolled to her back, she got a nose full of fur and feathers.

"Get off," she said, batting her hands as the chicken flapped and pecked at her. It landed with the rest of the remaining flock, in the stream of artificial light coming through the gaping hole from the hull. It cocked its head and gave her one last *squawk* before continuing to scavenge through the debris.

Rex's mouth tasted like copper, but that didn't concern her as much as the odor of leaked fuel and smoke. Through the stink, she detected the smell of wet leaves, upended dirt, and a floral miasma.

Where did we crash?

Holding the back of her skull, she surveyed the landscape beyond the hole in the hull: White smoke obscured all but some greenery, colorful flowers, dirt—and a strange, multi-colored glow up ahead. In a break in the clouds and smoke, a few scattered stars twinkled in the night sky.

Rex staggered to her feet, toppling over boxes and leaning on bins until she found her balance. Muffled shouting came from close by. The cargo hold door creaked and groaned, then opened a crack. The voices got louder as red emergency lights flickered. Flashlights peered inside.

"Is anybody in there?" someone shouted. "Help is on the way."

More Dominion soldiers would come. *So many witnesses...*

Her adopted mother's reprimands surfaced in the back of her mind: *"What have you done, Rex?"*

The hunt was on.

Experience kicked in, despite the terror shrieking at her to flee. She grabbed a hooded cloak out of an opened suitcase. As she secured it around her shoulders, the memory of the old woman shoving the kitcoon in her arms surfaced: *"Take Kio. Protect each other."*

She snorted. That little pest had just made things worse.

The old woman's plea entered her mind again: *"Save him."*

With a huff, she gave a quick scan over the mess for the old woman's pet. Reptilian critters and a few hybrid mammals crawled around, but no scrawny kitcoon. Besides, the headache was deepening, spreading from the back of her skull to her temples. *I don't need another burden.*

"You guys witnessed—I tried," she muttered to the chickens as she crawled out of the hole and into the forest.

One of them flapped its wings and cooed.

Her boots crunched down upon broken branches and sank into damp moss as she traversed through a wooded area with hedges and flowered bushes. But her trek didn't last long.

Chak, she swore. Jet engines rumbled overhead as another transport shuttled by. She followed the exhaust trail to the landing pad up ahead. As she stepped over a splintered log, a break in the trees and smoke revealed a sprawling city with lighted skyscrapers that penetrated the low-hanging clouds. Holographic advertisements, featuring oversized models, floated between the buildings, filling every inch of air space. *We landed in someone's garden.*

In the back of her mind, she knew it was a good break, but then again, she wasn't in La Raja, and the Dominion was on her tail.

She hustled to the edge of the greenery, slid through the rods of an iron fence, and disappeared into the sleepless city.

Dominion sirens echoed throughout the city as Rex walked down a street crammed with vendors and cheap hotels. Holographic marine animals swam through a digital ocean a few meters above her head, with an advertisement for a *VACATION OF A LIFETIME* trailing in the bubbles in multiple languages. Another reminder than she needed to get off the planet—

Wherever the hell this is—

—as fast as possible, but her mouth watered at the smell of real food sizzling on homemade grills.

"You gonna just stand there and drool, or you gonna buy something, sweetie?" one of the vendors asked, harsh and impatient, as Rex stared at the meat and vegetable skewers grilling on his cart.

Rex's stomach growled. It would take the last of her cash, but she had to eat. But as she reached under her cloak and into her left jacket pocket, her fingers grazed something fuzzy.

"Oh no *chakking* way," she cursed. The kitcoon stirred, then curled into a tighter ball of sleep. It weighed next to nothing, and when she removed her hand, she could barely tell it was inside her pocket.

She recalled the old woman rifling through her jacket before tying the belt around her. *She must have stowed the kitcoon in my pocket—*

Then, a terrible realization: *And lost my cash!* She checked her other pocket, pulling out lint—

I'm gonna starve—

—and her last crumpled Starways dollar.

The vendor, a skinny gentleman chewing on toothpick, lifted a brow as she offered the wadded cash to him. "That would buy you the skewer. *Just* the skewer."

"Please, mister..."

"You gonna give me trouble?" he asked, holding up his dirty butcher knife.

Rex sighed. Back to old tricks. Things that her old sponsor, Chezzie, a seasoned hustler, taught her when she first hit the streets. Things she didn't want to do anymore; one of the many reasons she ran away from him and her old life—

Invading memories, tricking minds.

Her stomach growled, reminding her it had been days.

"Look kid," Chezzie once said, pointing at a similarly crowded street on a different world. *"Each of these assinos wants something. You just need to figure out what, give 'em some version of it, and then you can take anything you need."*

How about a meal? She thought, eyeing the butcher knife.

With a gurgle, her stomach agreed.

Just this once more, she promised herself.

Rex relaxed her gaze, looking over the vendor's toadish face and the yellow, sweat-soaked bandana tied around his head. He wore an apron over a long-sleeve shirt that he rolled up past the elbow, revealing the back-alley tattoos inking his arms and fingers.

Chezzie's voice surfaced: *"Come on, kid, it'll be easy..."*

"Fine, a skewer then," she said, offering her last dollar.

Shocked, the vendor took the cash. In the exchange, she let her hand rest on his for a split second, long enough for her to sense his thudding heartbeat and overtaxed lungs. He'd been in the city too long, oblivious to the noise, the stench; the congestion of stimulus that drowned out his afflictions.

He's been miserable his whole life, she thought, sensing the deeper pain that carved into his soul. A life of inescapable poverty, with relief that came in cheap habits at the expense of his health. She'd encountered his type before.

"A scoundrel like that scares easy. Just get rid of him," Chezzie would have advised. *"Not like you can escape this life, right?"*

Rex focused on his respirations, how he struggled for each breath, in and out. She could squeeze down on his airways just a little bit, and the stress would make him panic, drop the knife, making him vulnerable and—

The kitcoon popped his head out of the side of her jacket and meowed.

"W-what is that?" the vendor exclaimed, his face brightening. His spit out the toothpick and set down the knife on the counter. "Did'ja get him at the exotic market?"

Jarred, she pulled back her telepathic reach and stared at the kitcoon sniffing the grill. "Um, he's a kitcoon."

Heartening emotions radiated from the man like sunshine.

Rex quickly added, "He's hungry too."

But the man didn't budge, cooing back at the kitcoon, making silly faces.

Her stomach grumbled.

(Frighten him, take the food,) experience bid.

The old woman's voice echoed in the back of her mind, countering: *"Find another way."*

The kitcoon, wiggling out of her pocket, broke her from her thoughts. Rex grabbed him before he jumped out.

"Aw, can I pet him?"

"S-sure," she said, keeping the feline in a secured, two-handed hold.

"What a funny little fellow," the vendor said.

When his hand touched the top of the kitcoon's head, Rex grazed his fingers, injecting the hunger gnawing at her belly into his. The vendor's eyebrows peaked. "He's *so* hungry."

The kitcoon meowed and purred.

A pang of guilt pulled at her heart as the vendor hurriedly picked up the knife and scraped leftover pieces of veggies and meat into a bag. "Don't worry, miss. He'll be okay."

I'm taking… Again.

The kitcoon rubbed his head against her hand, then licked her, his tiny tongue rough against her fingers. Delight coursed through her body. She'd never felt anything so sweetly affectionate.

"Thanks," Rex whispered, sliding the kitcoon back in her pocket before taking the food bag from vendor with two hands, one resting on his wrist. The fresh memory of the kitcoon lingered at the forefront of his mind, the same tender delight soothing his anxieties.

What is this? Something unencountered, different. *Unthreatening.*

The kitcoon purred in her pocket as she gave in to curiosity. Shifting her psychic gaze, she focused on his body's release of bonding hormones. He was already disarmed, but what if—

I made him feel…good?

She keyed into his hormones, magnifying the positive effect. Branching out, she guided the relaxation of his muscles, releasing the tension in his neck and shoulders, lessening the pain signals radiating in his arthritic hip. For a moment, she let him feel nothing but the love for the kitcoon, and the kindness of his act.

When she let go, tears spilled from his eyes, but he was quick to wipe them and sport a grimace.

"Get on, now," he said, voice cracking. Then, more gruffly, "Next customer!"

She hustled away, pulling the cloak's hood over her face to hide her beaming smile.

A dual-passenger hover copter turned down the street, just up ahead, sweeping its lights back and forth, creeping toward her position. Three Dominion soldiers walked underneath the copter, scanning the crowds with the facial recognition cams mounted on their helmets. An automated voice announced in Common first, then in the local dialect: "Show your faces and remain calm."

That language is Voltryken, Rex realized, swallowing the last bite of the vendor's scraps. Which meant they were on planet Kreylis, a Dominion-occupied waypoint for interstellar travelers. *The Dominion hijacked the FTL booster highway near this planet,* she thought, inferring the cause of their doomed flight. Her stomach dropped to her knees. *They're stopping all traffic to Neeis.*

To pick up stray leeches like her.

Anger heated her cheeks and chest, but when she spun around to go the opposite way, she was met with another copter and squad closing in from the other direction. She considered the darkened alleyways, but she wouldn't get far, not with the life-sensors on the copters that could detect a flea mite under a dumpster.

"Meow!" the kitcoon whined, food bits dangling off his whiskers as he begged for more.

She pushed him back in her pocket and ditched the emptied scraps bag atop an overfilled garbage can. "Not now."

Grand Hotel lit up in bright neon lights above her head, a beacon in the cacophony. She glanced again down the block, then headed inside, keeping her head bowed as she wove through people crowded into the front of the lobby.

"When are we leaving?" a woman with a miniature pigdog shrieked and stamped her foot at an exhausted-looking pilot. "I can't miss the presidential inauguration."

"Ma'am, it's the military—"

"And this *place*," she spat, flapping her hands at the dilapidated front desk with a last-century droid manning the counter. "Is all you could get?"

The droid's digitally projected face didn't sync with its vocalizations as it spoke to a customer through a broken bullet-proof window.

"We're not the only canceled flight, ma'am," the pilot sighed. "The Dominion's grounded hundreds of starships. They must be looking for someone."

Or something, Rex thought, placing her hand over the kitcoon in her pocket.

She dismissed the thought. How could one little kitcoon be enough trouble that the Dominion would arrest and ground so many flights? It was an actionable offense, enough to trigger a countermeasure by their rivals, The United Starways Coalition. Maybe enough to start a war.

The sirens outside grew louder. In seconds, the place would be raided, faces scanned, passports scrutinized—

I'm not going back in a collar, she thought, rubbing her neck, remembering the excruciating pain of the last shock collar. The thought of prison, of even being detained, stirred the dark space inside her. *I can't get caught.*

Rex pretended to check the advertisement station posted near the restrooms and stairwell but ignored the holograms for local hotspots. What she really needed was the map on the wall.

Grand suites upstairs, she thought, scanning the floorplan. And by the way the basement was segmented and laid out in grids between power sources, coffins—the cheap sim/stim tubes that resembled the long and narrow boxes for the dead—would be downstairs, in the dark and out of sight.

"You can't escape this life," Chezzie's voice recirculated in her head as Rex ran down the stairs to the basement. A keycard reader guarded the door, but utilizing her lockpicks disguised as dangling earrings, she bypassed the cheap lock in seconds, letting herself into the darkened chamber. *Thanks, Chezzie.*

Rex tiptoed down the lighted pathway through the coffins, listening and looking with more than her eyes and ears. Sentients of all types slumbered in the tight confines of the tubes, drifting through simulations/stimulation routines as a rainbow of chems, dripping from machines mounted on the walls, pumped through their veins. A cheap way to pass the time between long layovers and escape the drudgery of reality. And an opportunity for a data hustler like her—

Ex-data hustler, she tried to tell herself.

—to steal valuable information and to sell to the highest bidder, or use it for personal gain, like stealing a starship—

This is the last time.

Decent coffins were encrypted to ensure the privacy of the users' experiences. But even if they weren't, and most of the knockoff coffins she worked with didn't have any semblance of a security system, data-hustlers still had their work cut out for them. Even the most sophisticated tech couldn't decode every detail of a dream, or, in a hustler's case, extract specific, salable information.

But someone like her—who could look deeper, through the fragile walls every Sentient erected to protect themselves—could find anything she wanted. And here, all by herself without Chezzie watching for security—

Watching me—

—while she went in for an extraction, she didn't have to pretend to need all the tech she demanded from him to keep her cover.

As Rex passed by a row of coffins, a psionic storm boomed like thunder from one of the tubes. Most sim-stims induced positive feelings, pleasure. This felt disorganized, chaotic, painful like—

Trauma.

Rex zeroed in on the source and checked the tube. Inside the glowing blue cylinder, a muscular human male with lots of scars, grafting, and biomech parts twitched in his coffin, his face contorted with pain.

Hell no. She didn't want any part of his messed-up mind. But she couldn't look away. There was something about him, even though he reeked of military with his sweat-soaked white tank top, his dirty fatigue pants, multitool hanging off his belt, and the battered dog tags hanging around his neck.

With a starship key, she realized, spying the blue chip between the dog tags. But it wouldn't work without a code. *Which is in your* chakked-up *head.*

The kitcoon stirred, wiggling around, but she placed her hand inside her pocket and stroked his back until he calmed.

"*Chak,*" she muttered, glancing up at the ceiling. Muffled thumps echoed down. *A stampede—*

Or crowd-control gunfire.

The soldier grunted, arcing his back. She grimaced and braced her temples as his pain blasted across the psionic plane.

So much pain…

"An easy mark," she could hear Chezzie saying.

No, not easy. Maybe for a legit data hustler with gear, but not for a telepath that took on their client's pain. Prodgies "Fall" when the person they try to heal is too toxic, and the damage crosses over to their own bodies, driving them insane. That's why her people never healed another being alone.

I'm not healing, she reassured herself. *Just…looking.*

"Right," she muttered and checked the neural feed streaming on the readout near his head. He was outputting massive brain wave variability even though he had fifteen minutes left in the sim/stim and should be coming down off the high.

Bad cocktail, she thought, flicking one of the clogged IV lines hooked to the infuser strapped to his right forearm. *Bad coffin.*

Which meant he probably wouldn't notice her intrusion.

But his pain could kill me.

The thumping increased in intensity, growing louder. Dust and debris rattled loose from the ceiling, raining down on the coffins.

"Chak," she muttered, kneeling beside his tube. She overrode the safeties and lifted the coffin lid just enough for her to slide her arm inside and grab the blue chip and the multitool off his belt. After stuffing them in her pants pocket, she grasped the soldier's cold, calloused hand. Closing her eyes, she whispered: "Give me a break, soldier."

Gathering into an iridescent swirl of psionic energy, Rex slid down her arm, through her fingers, and crossed the corporeal bridge that separated her from the man. Like fizzing carbonation, she bubbled to the surface, and opened her eyes inside his being. Red blood, white bone, yellow fat.

Rising blood pressure pinged her ears. Ignoring the inflammatory cells clumped around his lungs and liver, she traversed upward, through his spine and into his neural network where the sim/stim chemicals lit up his brain like fireworks. There, she watched as his memories exploded across his mind: Gunfire, soldiers in red and black uniforms.

He's some kind of specialist soldier fighting for the United Starways Coalition, *she realized. Not Dominion, not a telepath hunter—but that didn't make him safe.*

She looked deeper.

Four-winged starfighters blazed across white clouds. Incoming missiles shrieked. Death from above, no escape—

Rex gritted her teeth.

Waking in a muddy trench, covered in soot and flames. So much pain. Look down. Body shredded, leg and arm ripped off—GONE—

Rex shuddered. The soldier's pain surged through like a tsunami, eroding the tether back to herself.

All his comrades, dying, dead. All alone, pain capsizing—

(He's inside you,) *her subconscious screamed as icicles formed along her spine. Self-defense mechanisms kicked in: Cut off the pain.*

(Sever neural connections—)

Cut off the soldier.

(Seize heart muscle, destroy cardiac tissue—)

(Kill him before he kills you—)

"*Meow.*" Something in the distance brushed across the top of her hand, lifting her from the inner vortex.

What's happening?

She remembered the sim-stim coffin. The soldier, his cold hand. Trying to steal his starship codes and—

Herself, Falling.

A gentle paw picked at her fingers, until she loosened her grip on the soldier. The furry thing wedged between their palms, sealing the gaps.

Rex resubmerged back into the electric storm of pain. But in the midst, a soft glow, and a thrumming third heartbeat. New memories surfaced: Barred metal trap, sharp smells. Outside gone. Food in pellets, tastes funny. Can't see well now, ears ringing. Curl up, tail over nose to try and stay warm in cold cage. Shivering, drowsy.

The kitcoon...

Rex tried to pull away, but the memories were too strong, too familiar to her own.

Stuck in a white-walled place with many awful smells. Yellow-gloved giants with masked faces reaching into cage. No energy to fight. Lights in eyes. Drowsy. Wake up, head hurts. Paws fuzzy. Everything wobbly. No more. Can't go on.

Rex resisted, pulling back, but the kitcoon wiggled in her hand, stimulating her senses. More memories flooded in—

Explosions. Fire, soot. Shouting and gunfire. Throwing body against cage. Smoke—sirens—

A hand closed around her throat. Rex jarred back to reality to bloodshot eyes and a menacing growl. She shot up her hands to try and break the soldier's grip around her neck, but he slammed her back against the wall, ripping the cords and lines that connected him to the sim/stim coffin, a rainbow intravenous fluids spraying everywhere.

Her senses screamed, terror and rage converging into madness, firing up her blood and kicking in her talent. The world split in two, allowing her to see the hallucinating soldier in front of him, and the electric panic driving the attack.

(Kill him before he kills you—)

Rex blasted herself through the nerves of his hands, up his arms, and into his brain. Nightmares bled into reality, and she couldn't differentiate her own image from the attacking enemy that stole his life years ago.

"Meow!"

The kitcoon leapt from the coffin onto the soldier's back, wrapping his tail around the man's neck and gave another emphatic *"Meow!"* into his ear.

Another world intersected. The kitcoon's memories spun across the chaos: Human arms, pressed into soft bosom, rushed away from the caged place. People chased. Booming, smoke. Frightened, but strong arms held fast.

The old woman that saved the kitcoon, Rex realized.

Soft voice, gentle touch. Rex saw the old woman's smiling face as she lifted a flap of blanket off the swaddled kitcoon. *"It's going to be okay, sweet Kio."*

The memories fast-forward to a ship's compartment. She saw the old woman petting the kitcoon, felt the kitcoon purring. *No more hurts. Not all giants bad.*

The soldier's hands relaxed, enough to allow Rex a gulp of air.

The kitcoon's memories continued to unfurl: Hand fed. Getting stronger. Sleeping curled against the old woman while traveling to new places. No more white walls. Warm, safe. No more cages. Belly always full. Always comforted. Protected. Trust again.

(Trust again.) The idea repeated in Rex's head, and from the relaxing tension in the soldier's grip, his too.

"Hold it right there!" someone shouted down the room.

Rex glanced sideways, to the back exit she'd used to access the basement coffins. Two Dominion soldiers locked the red laser sights of their rifles on Rex, advancing on her position.

Dark motes dotted Rex's vision as she gasped for breath. The soldier had her at his mercy. The Dominion was coming—and so was the shock collar, the imprisonment, the torture—*experiments!*

Death.

"Do what you gotta do," Chezzie's voice echoed in her head. *"It's kill or be killed, baby."*

(Kill them all.)

The kitcoon crossed over the soldier's arms and rested on her shoulder. The old woman's voice surfaced from memory: *"Find another way."*

"I'm not...going back..." she rasped.

Closing her eyes, she rerouted herself through the soldier, up his hands and arms and into his mind, but this time, as the same battle scene nightmare played out, she projected herself on the field next to him as he bled onto the soil.

"I'm not here to hurt you," she said, kneeling beside him. Tears streamed down his pale face, his body racked with pain, terror, shivering.

"You've already survived this. You're here now, with me, in the hotel," she said, placing a hand on his chest. She sent cooling signals to his hyperactive nerves, calming the fires. The soldier relaxed, color returning to his face. He looked at her, his blue eyes focusing for the first time. *"I'm not your enemy."*

The specialist released her, jerking his hands away, looking back and forth between her and the Dominion soldiers pointing their rifles at them. "What the—?"

"Take this kitcoon," she said between coughs, prying the fuzzball off her shoulder and handing it to the soldier. She returned the blue chip and the multitool, too. "Get out while you can."

"But you...?" he said, brow furrowed.

"Go!" she shouted.

"Hey, stop!" the Dominion soldier commanded as the specialist bolted, kitcoon tucked under his arm and howling.

Rex leapt into the walkway as one soldier broke off and went after the specialist.

Another way, she thought, closing her eyes.

Relaxing her mind, she spread her awareness over the soldiers, blanketing them in the few peaceful memories she had: Running through the wildflowers on Algar. Her grandmother's loving hugs. The first feast of winter. Her father's deep, rumbling voice.

The soldier tracking the USC specialist fired, but his aim drifted to the side, the plasma discharge hitting a wall.

"Get on the ground!" the second soldier shouted as the fire alarm sounded. Sprinklers shot out of the ceiling and doused them in cold water.

Rex tensed, but as she brought up her arm to shield her face, the second soldier stumbled and lowered his weapon.

This...worked? She marveled, stepping around them as they stood there, stunned.

But as she made for the exit, a collar clamped down on her neck. She screamed, electric currents piercing every nerve fiber as she fell to the floor.

"Chakking leech."

Dizzy and disoriented, she made out the black uniform of the soldier who had crept up from behind and collared her. Behind his translucent visor spread a sickening smile.

"You'll pay for what you've done," he said, holding up the shock collar remote.

Rex screamed as she fell, electricity searing her body.

"It's kill or be killed."

But as she reached out and grabbed the soldier's boot, he turned up the dial. White lightning blinded her, and all went dark.

Rex came to in a daze, somehow on her feet, stumbling, handcuffed and collared, as she was being pushed out the main door and down the front steps of the Grand Hotel. Sirens wailed and police and military lights flashed from every direction. People shouted and hollered behind a line of crowd-control Dominion soldiers. She couldn't understand all the competing languages, or the words drowned by Dominion announcements to *"BACK DOWN."*

The darkness inside her shrieked as soldiers led her to a hovering copter, where more soldiers with mechanized armor and bigger guns waited. Only seconds away from a cage—

TRAPPED FOREVER—

The remembered smell of disinfectants and the sting of needles washed over her senses—

Can't go back—

(Kill them all!)

For the first time in years, tears pricked her eyes. *No. No more fighting. No more death.*

"Play your hand or die," she imagined Chezzie mocking her.

She missed one of the steps, but the two soldiers holding her by the arms jerked her up.

Instead of rage and terror, something long ignored surfaced: Fatigue. And on its heels, longing. For the memories she'd recently revived of Algar, of family and home. And of something new; something she'd felt inside the kitcoon's memories. Something impossible, found in the most desperate and painful times.

Trust.

(Connection.)

"Stop the injustice!" someone shouted above the din.

Rex turned her head toward the speaker. The vendor, pointing his machete at the soldiers arresting Rex, screamed: "Stop the Dominion! This is our planet!"

The crowd shifted, fists rising and shouts growing louder. She didn't see who threw the first bottle, but the second, thrown by the vendor, struck one of the soldiers gripping her. He wobbled for a second, strengthening his hold on her.

Stop, please—

Tensions intensified as the soldiers holding the line pointed their guns at the crowd. Instead of retreating, a tidal wave of civilians charged forward, toppling soldiers amidst the gunfire. Hot blood splattered her face, the stink of sizzling flesh filled her nose. The soldiers holding her let go to assist their comrades, but the ones waiting in the copter jumped out and ran toward her.

There was nowhere to run, not as the crowd flooded in, battering her from all sides. Shots fired, singing past her ears, blasting into nearby civilians.

Panic sent her heart into overdrive, but the warning buzz of the shock collar depressed her rising instinct to telepathically lash out. In its place spilled the tears she could no longer hold back.

Please... Rex covered her head, shaking, in the middle of the riot....*no more.*

An unmuffled hovercycle throttled over the crowd, slowing down long enough for Rex to look up. The USC specialist from sim-stim coffin, holding onto the handlebar with his real hand, reached down with his biomech arm, grabbed her by the jacket, and hoisted her up. The black hovercycle tipped as she scrambled onto the pillion. He didn't give her enough time to grab onto him, hitting the accelerator.

Rex screamed.

But he held on to her, his biomech arm contorting farther than any human arm could, keeping her pinned to his back as he angled the bike toward the busy skyway of hovercraft a kilometer above the street.

"Watch out!" she yelled as he wound his way around cars. He released her as she hugged his waist and buried her head into his back to protect herself from the freezing winds.

He's going to kill us.

When he jerked the bike, she peeked from behind his cover long enough to see him jump them into the next level and opposing stream of traffic.

"Or you saving or killing us?"

He grunted.

"*Assino,*" she said through gritted teeth.

Rex shivered as he flew them higher, into the blue, rain-soaked clouds and above the legal skyways. How he didn't react to the cold, especially in only a tank top and fatigues, impressed her. Then again, she knew what he'd been through.

Out of traffic, she relaxed her tense embrace, letting him continue to shield her from the weather and cold. She didn't need her extrasensory perceptions to know that he came back for a reason. One that she could barely yet believe.

A light shone through the clouds, growing brighter as they approached.

An illegal port? she wondered, wiping away the rain from her eyes to get a better look. A makeshift dock and a signal station welded together with parts of old starships and freighters hovered in the clouds on anti-grav boosters. The beacon, alternating white and blue in merc code, rotated at the top of the tower.

As he circled around the port, a black, retrofitted corvette with faded yellow stripes and quad wings came into view. It was an ancient starship, probably from the last galactic war, with lots of patch jobs and exoskeleton rigging to keep it from falling apart.

Unregistered, she guessed. And by the looks of the black boxes affixed to the engines, loaded with anti-scanner tech. *A ticket out.*

A garage near the aft engine opened, allowing him to land his hovercycle in a carved-out space between stacks of computer innards, metal barrels, and unfamiliar tech. *Illegal tech.*

Four large, white articulated robotic arms emerged from the tops of the stacks, each arching toward where he landed his hovercycle. It reminded her of something old. *Familiar.*

Sliding off the hovercycle, she caught her breath as he closed the garage and the atmosphere repressurized.

"Thanks," she said.

He looked at her, his blue eyes not giving away any secrets.

"Are you not going to talk to me?" she asked as he went to the storage compartment at the end of his bike. He lifted the trunk to a loud *meow.* The kitcoon shot out, jumped off his chest, and landed on the ground in a frenzy.

But when the kitcoon saw her, he crawled up her pants, claws digging into to her flesh, until she plucked him up and held him in her arms.

"Thanks for helping us," she tried again. The kitcoon purred and wedged into her elbow.

He stared at her for an uncomfortable length of time, then whispered: "Remy."

"Rex," she said back.

He approached her, staring at her neck. She backed up into a stack of computers until he made a motion with his hand around his own.

"The collar?" she asked.

He nodded.

"Hell if I know how to get it off."

The soldier blinked, then grabbed the recently-stolen-and-returned multitool off his belt.

Not like anything I've seen, she realized, getting a closer look. Something he must have customized.

With a few quick motions and a *pop,* he had it off her neck.

"Thanks, I—"

He pushed her behind him and flung the collar into a metal barrel. The collar exploded, sending sparks and fire a meter high. As it fizzled out, the stink of burnt plastic and fried electrical parts permeated the air.

"Thanks again..."

Remy nodded, wiping his hands off on his fatigues before returning the multitool to his belt and heading toward the docking bay door.

"Wait, what's next?"

Placing the kitcoon back in her jacket pocket, she followed Remy. The docking bay door led down a cramped hallway with more mechanical hardware, forcing her to slide sideways. When she reached the cockpit at the other end, Remy was sitting in the captain's chair, punching in coordinates and revving up the engines.

"One minute," he said.

"Until what?"

"More trouble."

"*Chak,*" she muttered, strapping into the co-pilot's chair.

As he rebooted the holographic nav systems, she chimed in: "I can navigate on star charts. And I've flown A-2200s," she said, referring to the junked-out star cruisers from the interior.

Remy lifted anchors and locks just as the first Dominion fighter broke through the clouds.

"Hang on," he said, hitting the accelerator. Rex's stomach lodged in her throat as he launched them into the upper atmosphere. Enemy fire scorched the dash screen, punctuated by cannon blasts. Rex gripped her chair's armrest with one hand and braced the kitcoon inside her pocket with the other.

"Watch out—" Rex yelled as Remy narrowly dodged oncoming Dominion fighters, sending her jerking forward and to the right, testing the strength of her harness.

We're surrounded, she thought just as another blast hit the aft shields, knocking them down to critical levels.

Rex glanced over at the soldier. Remy was sweating profusely, eyes glazed over and breathing heavily. He didn't respond to the oncoming fighters from the rear, or the incoming transmissions flashing red: *"Stand down and prepare to be boarded."*

No response, not even when a second volley of plasma fire knocked out the rear shields. Internal alarms sounded and all four engine lights came on. Still, the soldier didn't move, breathing rapidly.

"Remy," she said, shaking him by the forearm. "REMY."

His shoulder twitched. Something between a grunt and a wheeze came out of his mouth.

Take control, she thought. But even a cursory glance of his modifications and manual overrides to normal starship controls was enough to kill that idea.

She checked the starships pinged on radar. Even if she could reach that far with her telepathic talent, she could never affect all twenty or more fighters surrounding them above the blue and red planet. Not without devastating consequences.

Rex closed her eyes and projected herself through her physical connection with the soldier's shoulder. *Remy. Come back.*

She slid into his consciousness, finding the same battle scene unfolding in his mind: The surprise attack, blacking out. Waking to chaos, pain, and terror. Blood, gore. Everyone's dead—

Rex partially withdrew her consciousness back into her own body, enough to carefully pull out the kitcoon from her pocket and place it on Remy's arm. The furry critter yawned and licked his hand gripping the nav stick.

Placing her hand back again on his forearm, she sank beneath his skin.

"I'm here, Remy," she said, putting herself in the middle of the battlefield with him. *"You already fought this battle and survived. Be here, with me."*

She pulled his sights up with her own, showing him the incoming fighters, and the shields failing.

Dipping back down into his psyche, into the pains and hurts of a long-lost soldier, she offered him the sound of her heartbeat, and the rhythm of her breathing.

"You're not alone in this. You never have to be alone again."

Remy jerked back. The kitcoon leapt off the dashboard and onto her shoulder, anchoring his tail around her neck and meowing.

"*Chak,*" he muttered, inputting something into the computer.

"Remy," Rex said, her voice just above a whisper as a black battleship came into view from the starboard side, its tractor beams deploying in shimmering distortions. The starship rocked and creaked as they were pulled into the belly of the battleship.

"Where are you going?" she asked as he unstrapped from his chair and unbuckled her harness.

"Wait, what's happening?" she exclaimed as the red-striped soldiers with their shock wands, waiting on the battleship's deck, came into view.

He pulled her up by the arm. The kitcoon scampered down her jacket and dove into her right pocket as Remy took her hand and guided her back through the junk-filled passageway and into the garage.

As he switched on his hovercycle and motioned for her to get on the pillion, she scoffed. "I'm not about to rampage through the decks—or take a very short, *very* cold trip outside."

"Get on," he said, shoving a stack of old motherboards, network/graphic cards, and wiring aside to access a wall-mounted interface. The white robotic arms she'd noticed earlier lit up with blue and green tracks, and a glowing white circle appeared around the hovercycle.

"Where to?" he asked, punching in numbers into the interface.

As the Dominion battleship's locking clamps took hold that she blurted: "La Raja, Neeis."

He ran back and mounted the bike as orange and red sparks from laser cutters melted through the garage door.

"Hold on."

When she didn't hold him tight enough, he held one of his hands over hers. His strength surprised her, but not as much as intense vibration of the robotic arms or the tingling sensation crawling up her spine.

"Remy, what did you—?"

The garage door crashed to the floor. Dominion soldiers poured inside, shock wands sparking.

"Stop right there! Don't move—"

Rex closed her eyes and went rigid, anticipating the pain of the shock wands. Instead, her entire body lit up from the inside out with exploding stars, and the vibrations of a massive earthquake. She yelled, but she didn't have lungs or a mouth—

—Not until they rematerialized in a dingy, half-lit parking lot under a light-polluted night sky. Her voice came back, and she screamed until her lungs emptied and the surrounding sparks and static fizzled out into smoke.

"You can stop screaming now," Remy said, this time with a sentence long enough she heard his drawl. He got off the bike, his legs unsteady, but offered her a hand.

She took his hand and half-fell off, catching herself on the side of the hovercycle. "W—what was that?"

"Algardrien teleportation tech, an FTL booster, and a few other mods and tweaks."

"Algardrien tech? How'd you get that? Most of the planet is..."

She couldn't say the rest out loud: *Destroyed.*

Remy's face remained hard set, but his words were gentle. "Helped a few Algardriens once."

She didn't know if she could believe him. The entire galaxy hated telepaths.

"Guess it beats an escape pod," she whispered.

He nodded, scratching the stubble on his jawline. "Yup."

Rex eyed the sizzling remains of a Dominion soldier's arm and a piece of a boot. "Are they going to track us here?"

As Remy stretched and drew out his response, she surveyed the empty parking lot. An abandoned warehouse, covered with graffiti and moss, crumbled to the north, next to a billboard advertising a casino on the main drag.

In Rajan.

Which means they were in La Raja, Neeis. *We made it.*

She tilted her head up toward the night sky and inhaled the warm air, detecting the fruit trees and flowers within the miasma of city smells. For the first time in a long time, she smiled.

"Blast radius'll take care of it," Remy finally acknowledged.

"Mmm. So, what's your deal? Ex-marine gone tech rogue?"

He shrugged. "You?"

She shrugged back. "Just another girl trying to find a way to get by."

"Not just another girl..." he said coolly.

Her shoulders knotted, and she moved her right foot back, into fighting position. "You gotta problem with that?"

The soldier's face went stone-cold, his blues eyes locked on hers. "No."

The kitcoon crawled out of her pocket, up the front of her jacket, and perched on her shoulder before giving a loud *meow* in her ear.

"I know you're hungry," she said, pulling him off and scratching behind his ears. "I'll get you something soon."

"What?" she said, reading Remy's disapproving expression. "At least he volunteers what he's thinking."

"What'd the Dominion want with that thing?"

"His name is Kio."

"Looks like a street 'coon."

"He's more than that," she said, brushing back Kio's raggedy fur. Her heart softened. *Much more.*

Worth saving.

(Like me…?)

A part of her, buried deep down inside long ago, eased.

Remy pulled out his multitool and clicked on a blue light. With her holding the kitcoon still, he scanned over the fresh scar and showed her the readings projected in holographics out of the side of the gray handle. "That's sim/stim gear jacked with high-caliber reverse coms."

"Meaning?"

Remy cocked his head to the side, analyzing. "It's a sophisticated neural input/output device. If I had to guess, they were trying to replicate…"

He went silent.

"Telepathy," she whispered. "An old woman gave him to me. She said that she and many others risked rescuing him from Dominion labs. I think she meant the tech, not specifically Kio. With all the military's obsession with telepaths, all the imprisonments—in the end, they just want our talent. But why? What's the endgame?"

Remy shook his head. "I'll get it out, but it'll break the tech… Unless that'd make him *undesirable* to you."

His inference made her wonder: How much could she get for him from the USC or black-market buyers?

Probably enough for seven lifetimes.

The kitcoon meowed loudly, reminding them of his hunger, arcing his head back and adding to the dramatic effect.

Rex's heart melted, her emotions softening. *Wait…is the effect magnified by the tech?*

All this time, was the kitcoon, as sweet and endearing as he was, projecting—and influencing—thoughts?

He saved our lives. But her stomach knotted. *What kind of weapon could the Dominion make with that?*

"Get it out. Make sure it's destroyed," she whispered, stroking the kitcoon's back. "I think he's ready to move on."

Remy cleared his throat. "Yeah. I get that."

The kitcoon made a chortling sound and sniffed the air, excited. Rex delighted in the spark in his eyes, and how furiously he wagged his tail.

"It's just a parking lot, silly boy," she whispered to the kitcoon. But to him it was a place with familiar smells, sights—

Home.

"I can't believe he still trusts after all he's been through," she said as Kio crawled up onto her shoulder again.

Remy checked the batteries on his hovercycle and then angled his gaze toward the curved skyscrapers and twisting rail systems to the south, at the heart of La Raja. His voice wavered, speaking each word carefully. "Not just anyone."

Kio licked Rex's cheek, then whapped his paw into her temple with another insistent *meow.*

"Ouch, okay," she said, prying him off her shoulder and putting him back in her pocket. "I'm starving, too. Let's find something to eat." As Remy kicked on the hovercycle, she slid in behind him.

When she wrapped her arms around Remy, he relaxed. He tilted his head back, pressing against hers.

"You meant what you said back there?" he asked, barely audible above the rumbling hovercycle.

"What?"

He didn't move or offer an explanation. But she felt the ache radiating from his heart, and the quickening of his pulse as he awaited her response.

Listening with her deepest senses, she recalled what she said to him in telepathic limbo: *"You're not alone in this. You never have to be alone again."*

A telepath, tech rogue, and a kitcoon. I wonder what kind of trouble we'll get into? The kitcoon wiggled in her pocket, protesting his entrapment. She reached inside and let him nibble on her fingernails. *Thanks to you.*

"Yeah," she whispered back. She pinched him on the stomach through his tank top. "Just get me something to eat before I change my mind."

Remy grunted, his equivalent of a laugh, and sped them toward the city.

Author Bio

To read more about Rex's adventures, check out: *Laws of Attraction*.

Amazon bestselling author L.J Hachmeister writes and fights—although she tries to avoid doing them at the same time. The world champion stick-fighter is best known in the literary world for her epic science fiction series, Triorion, her LGBTQ+ sci-fi romance, *Laws of Attraction*, her bestselling anthology, *Parallel Worlds: The Heroes Within*, and her equally epic love of sweets.

If you would like to learn more about L.J's work as an LGBTQ+ and science fiction/fantasy author, please visit triorion.com.

All book sale profits are donated to Lifeline Puppy Rescue (lifelinepuppy.org). Read books and save lives!

A Cry in the Night

by Lucienne Diver

I let myself into Spirit's enclosure, as I did at the end of every day, needing to soak up the love after a shift spent with people and paperwork, only he didn't come running.

"Spirit, it's me," I called, as though he didn't know. As though the big, gray wolf-dog couldn't smell me coming from a mile away and hear me from, literally, ten times that distance.

But Spirit, and his skittish mate Frost, had been acting strangely, which was why Thompson, our biologist, was with me. When I did our tours, I always said Spirit was over eighty percent wolf and one hundred percent love, which was a miracle after the way he'd been treated.

One of my neighbors, in the wilds of Colorado, had decided it would be amazing to have a wolf-dog to impress his friends, but he hadn't done his research, and took all his own failings out on Spirit. A mix of more than fifty percent wolf was unlikely to ever be domesticated. They wouldn't learn to wait for walkies. They would never be comfortable living within walls without clear sightlines of anything coming at them. The poor animal would stress and act out because of it. Gavin reacted by beating and starving Spirit, taking it like a challenge to his manhood and trying to "break" the animal, leaving Spirit chained out in the yard in all kinds of weather.

Which was where I came in. Gavin took off on one of his long hauls, leaving Spirit bolted down with a single bowl of food and water and a major storm threatening. Well, wolves were outdoor creatures; they could survive in the wild, but there they had the freedom to seek food and shelter. Spirit had no freedom at all. Until I arrived with my trusty bolt-cutters after listening to him howl for too long and deciding to do something about it.

I had a fenced in yard, blankets to spare, and a large faux-wooden playset that my son Luke had outgrown. Spirit spent his nights sheltered beneath it. When Gavin returned and tried to bully the "little lady" I laughed in his face. Then I showed him the pictures I'd taken of Spirit before and asked him if he really wanted to argue that the beautiful beast growling at him from behind me was the same animal, because I'd happily see him in court for abuse. He decided that neither of us was worth the trouble.

Spirit had been worth *all* the trouble. And then some. One rescue had grown into two. Message boards, training, more rescue work. The need to move to a larger facility.

Three years later, the Wolf Rescue and Rehabilitation Center was going strong.

Only Spirit hadn't made an appearance today. He was keeping to the edges of his spacious enclosure, hiding from visitors, and I was worried.

He was one of our ambassadors. He loved to greet people. He was the first to join in the group howls. Was he nursing a wound? Had someone thrown something dangerous into his enclosure or, worse, tried to cut through it?

No matter how much we educated people, some still didn't understand. We didn't put up fences to imprison our wolves and wolf-dogs, coy-wolves, coyotes, and foxes, as some suggested rather virulently, but rather the fences were there to protect them. Some had gotten too comfortable wandering into towns or feeding off livestock and were likely to be killed or weren't fit to live in the wild for one reason or another. Others were only being held pending release once laws and preparations were in place.

Wolves were endangered and were, even now, mostly allowed to be hunted where they *did* exist in the wild. It didn't help that they had such bad PR, that we were taught to see them as evil from the cradle, from *Little Red Riding Hood* and the *Three Little Pigs* up through *The Wolfman* and *American Werewolf in London*. Farmers shot and killed them on sight for fear of losing livestock with no thought given to how much natural predators were needed as part of an ecosystem.

"Spirit," I called again, that line of thought spurring me on.

Finally, I heard a whimper.

"Lacey," Thompson said and pointed in the same direction I'd already turned.

Wordlessly, we headed that way. We'd worked together for five years, and could do silence as easily as words now, and while there were one or two times when more might have been said, when I might have invited him to stay after hours for a drink or conversation, there was always Luke, my nearing-twenty-year-old still living at home.

It would have been awkward. Or maybe that was just my excuse. I was bad with change. Bad with people. Good with animals. I could have suggested we go out, yet I never did. My house was on the grounds; it was important to stay in every night, in case the animals needed me or someone who thought we weren't doing enough, or were doing too much, tried to start something. Besides, I was Thompson's boss. Maybe that was why he never asked me either.

Spirit looked over his shoulder at us as we skirted a bush left in the enclosure to give the wolves privacy. His golden eyes met mine, full of meaning, as though he could convey it to me mind to mind, then he gazed back out into the darkening evening. I looked where he looked but couldn't see a thing.

"What's the matter, hon? What do you see?"

His body language was stiff, tail out like a flag behind him, hair raised, but not to full-on alert. More like concern.

Something was out there. Not an immediate threat, maybe, but he didn't like it. Didn't want to look away. In case… In case what?

I approached slowly, knowing I didn't want to box him in and limit his options.

"Everything's okay. It's okay. You're safe. Where's Frost?"

Spirit backed away from the fence. One step, then two. Backed up to where he was beside me, then finally looked away and bumped me with his head, almost knocking me down as I'd started to go to one knee but hadn't yet settled.

Wolves were big, far bigger than people realized unless they'd seen them in person. Even wolf-dogs, as Spirit was— eighty two percent timber wolf, eighteen percent husky. We'd had him tested. But he looked all gray wolf— varying shades of gray and white with black detailing, especially around the tips of his ears and around his eyes, as though someone had ringed them with kohl. He had tan in there too, lower on his sides. Standing, he came to the low/midpoint of my ribcage, and I was no tiny tot.

I caught my balance and ran my fingers through Spirit's ruff, scratching just so and muttering nothings until he calmed. Until he turned and licked my face, his big tongue taking up my whole cheek. It was magical the way my tension melted away.

Seeing Spirit stand down, Frost came out of the trees at the back of the enclosure to nudge Thompson's hand with her nose, much like our German shepherd, Beau, did with Luke and me at home. Thompson dropped to a knee, like I had, to scratch her behind the ears. She rolled to give him her belly, winter white like the rest of her. I'd seen her do it before, but only for Thompson. He seemed to have a special gift. The wolves had chosen their humans. And as much as my knees were starting to ache, I didn't dare shift and ruin the moment.

The wolves were fine, and whatever lurked in the deepening night must have moved on.

I was exhausted by the time I got home. I'd finished off the last slice of cold pizza—all my son had left me—while standing at the kitchen counter, and had poured myself a glass of merlot when the phone rang. I seriously considered letting it go to voicemail, but it was forwarded from the office line and might be an emergency, and so I answered with the name of our rescue.

"Lacey?" My best friend, Sarah, sounded…odd. It didn't make sense for her to call the office line at this time of night. Not when…I cradled the phone between my shoulder and ear and patted myself down for my cell before cursing internally. I'd done it again—pulled it out of my jeans pocket when it impeded mobility, set it down somewhere and forgot all about it. It could be anywhere from my office to an enclosure. Sarah knew that if she couldn't reach me on my cell, she had only to call the rescue. As a former volunteer, she probably had the place on speed dial, especially with as many times as she'd had to call out to take care of her husband during his cancer treatments, and then afterward.

"Guilty," I said. "What's up?"

"I really don't want to bother you, but I didn't know what else to do, and… Tell me if you think I'm just crazy and I should check it out on my own."

"Check what out?"

"Okay, first you have to know that my mother just sent me an article about all the ways predators use to target people, particularly women—looking up obituaries to see who's newly widowed, playing sick or injured like Ted Bundy did, faking car trouble or lost pets, playing recordings of crying babies or women in distress to lure someone out of their home…"

I took a sip of my wine, swallowing it too quickly when I realized she wasn't going to continue without encouragement. "And?" I choked out. "Not crazy so far."

"And…I keep hearing a crying baby outside."

I set my wine down. "I'll be right over."

"You don't think I should check it out?"

"You live on two and a half acres on your own." Since Joe's death, which had recently been in the obituaries. "Where would the baby have come from?"

"Someone could have abandoned it. It could be scared. Or hurt. The crying… It's breaking my heart. And we do have coyotes in the area, even some feral dogs…"

"I'm on my way now. If you're concerned about dogs, turn on all the lights, put on some loud music. That should scare away man or beast, but *wait for me*. If someone wanted to abandon a baby, a church or a hospital would make more sense."

"Maybe there's too much surveillance there or too many people, too much chance of being seen. Maybe—"

"*Wait!*"

I'd already grabbed my keys off the counter, and my shepherd, Beau, hearing them, was pawing at my leg, asking to come. He'd heard the tension in Sarah's voice straight through the phone. Or maybe in mine, and he wasn't letting me go alone.

"Get your leash."

He did a half spin and took off to where I left it hanging on a hook with his harness as I ran down our short hall to let Luke know where we were going. I had to yell twice to penetrate his ever-present headphones, but I finally got through, and by that time, Beau was bumping my hand with the leash and harness in his mouth. I got him into the harness, scratching him quickly as I went and telling him what a good boy he was, but neither of us lingered. We were both up and running for the door as the last snap clicked into place.

After that, our only brief pause was for Beau to water the path twice on the way to the car, either to refresh his marking of our territory or because Luke had forgotten to let him out earlier. Either way, it didn't keep us long, and we were rumbling in my Jeep down the steep drive to the actual roadway in no time.

As anxious as I was to get to Sarah, I didn't put my pedal to the metal. Our crazy Colorado weather—freezing and thawing, often in the same day, the sometimes drought followed by flash-floods—and the volume of our visitor traffic took a toll on our paved drive. Cracks, potholes, erosion at the edges. At night with only headlights as a guide, the drive could be a hazard, but with no oncoming traffic expected, I stayed to the center and drove as fast as I dared.

I carved ten minutes down to nine, glad Beau was strapped into his doggy hammock in the back, so he wasn't shaken around. He whined only once and put his head up to make a vee in the sling so that I could see him if I looked over my shoulder or angled my rearview mirror. I didn't, but I could feel him there.

As soon as we pulled into Sarah's drive, though, he went crazy, as though he could pull himself out of his car seat by force of will. He threw himself at the door. He'd never done that before. Quickly, I got myself out and went around to get *him* out, but that put my back to the night, and I didn't like it. My own hackles rose in reaction—hair on the back of my neck, up and down my arms, all over my body standing on end. My t-shirt, flannel and jeans suddenly felt like flimsy protection against whatever was out there.

And something *was* out there. Just as Spirit had sensed earlier.

As Beau sensed now.

I freed Beau from his car seat and jumped out of the way as he flung himself out of the car, snarling and barking and ready to chase down Sarah's intruder. I grabbed the end of his leash just in time to get my shoulder wrenched as I tried to hold him back.

At my command, Beau quieted, except for low growls to let me know there was still something out there, as though I couldn't feel it. But I needed to hear what Sarah had heard, what I thought I'd heard even over his ruckus: a baby crying, screaming for someone to save it. No one with a heart could resist. It was eerie. Haunting. Horrible. My mind had already sorted through all of Luke's baby cries, and this wasn't like any of them. It wasn't one of want—food, changing, comfort. It was one of desperate, immediate *need*. One of terror.

With my cell gone, I couldn't let Sarah know we were there, but when I looked toward the house, I saw that Beau's barking had done that already. She was silhouetted in the window beside her door, looking out into the night. She raised a hand, and I gave a nod back. Then I turned my full focus onto the trouble.

"Find it," I told Beau. "Go. Good boy."

He didn't need to be told. His ears were already back, and his body tense, spine rigid, tail low. His nose was pressed to the ground, scenting. He strained at the leash, pulling us forward, and I wasn't at all surprised when the trail took us toward the baby's cries, which seemed to come from the bushes beneath Sarah's bow window.

The closer we came, the louder the baby's cries. The more I wanted to grab it up, cradle it in my arms. Save it. I almost launched myself into the bushes. Beau seemed to sense that, and stopped short in front of me, quivering, tacking right and left to block me as I tried to go around him. I had no choice but to stop or fall over him. Try to see what had him on alert.

At first, I couldn't make sense of his behavior. The light from the house didn't extend out over the hedges. All I could see was that they were overgrown. Trimming them had been Joe's job, and the least of Sarah's worries after his death, but thorns and brambles wouldn't set Beau off like that.

And then the shaggiest part of the bush *moved*, and I realized that those weren't jagged leaves or branches at the top. They were matted fur and raised hackles, a ruff or a mane or... I couldn't even make sense of what I was seeing. The thing in the bushes was far bigger than a wolf; bigger than any predatory animal we had here in Colorado except the black bear, and this was no bear.

It turned toward me as I stood stunned, its dark eyes flashing in the night, and my arms and legs suddenly felt as though they were made of clay, heavy and hardening. Terrified, I tried to reach for the ever-present treats in my pocket so that I could throw them far afield, divert the thing long enough to grab up the baby and run, get it and Beau to safety, but I couldn't move. Not a muscle. My stunned paralysis had become all too real.

All I could do was look my fill, but that didn't help with the horror. This was like nothing I'd ever seen. It was more of a size with a male lion and had a mane like one as well—or like a hyena, since it was dark and spotted. That mane continued in a ridge down its back as far as I could see. And its teeth... My mind sputtered. Not teeth. Or yes, one on top, one on bottom, but each arcing the entire jaw. One singular ridge of bone sharpened like a butcher's blade.

Truly terrifying.

Beau lunged, and the beast rose up, its shadow falling upon Beau, and his rigid spine seemed to become fused. He was frozen. A block of Beau.

But the thing's movement had released me, at least for now. I wanted to drop to Beau's side, assure myself that he lived and breathed, but that would leave us both vulnerable. I had to defend him. And get to that baby...

And that was when I realized the cries had stopped. Had there even been a baby? Was it all a ruse? Bobcats were said to sound like babies crying, but nothing like this.

This was another level. And the paralysis... I'd heard of basilisks and cockatrices, but in mythology, not in reality, and anyway, they turned things to stone, didn't they?

I was out of my depth. This was completely beyond my experience. I didn't want to go for the knife in the sheath at my belt, the one I carried with me everywhere in case I had to cut one of my rescues loose of something or finish taking down branches felled by our weather.

But I reached for it now, and when the thing's attention swung back to me, I avoided it and dove for the bushes. My plan wasn't to kill the beast—not if I could help it—but I would if I had to in self-defense. Otherwise, I would find a way to subdue it and take it in. Maybe it had been driven out of its territory. Maybe it was a species so endangered we didn't even know it still existed, or a cryptid someone was searching for. Either way, it deserved a chance. And if Beau didn't come out of his paralysis, this thing might have the answer for that too!

But not looking dead on made it hard to fight. The bushes cut and scraped at me, and the beast itself immediately caught me in the chest—two sharp blows just above my breasts, like paddles to either side of my heart, only a helluva lot harder. I went down, my knife falling useless at my side.

Vaguely, I heard Sarah's door open, and a cry of "Lacey!" and the sound of a shotgun going off. There were shadows and scuffling, and a second later, Sarah's face appeared above me, her hair falling like rain all around.

"I found Joe's shotgun. He even kept it loaded. You okay?"

I mumbled something I meant to be yes, though I wasn't so sure, and she gave me a hand up. I went to sitting first, making sure nothing in my chest was broken before I tried standing. It hurt like hell but felt like bruising rather than a break. I thought I was okay, especially when Beau came up and nosed my hair, licking my cheek and catching the corner of my eye. Aside from us, the night was silent. No crying baby.

I looked down at myself to see two prints as clear as mud on my flannel. Cloven. Definitely not canid. The thing had kicked me in the chest, and I had fallen. If Sarah hadn't come out with Joe's shotgun, it probably would have torn me apart with those teeth next.

"What the hell was that thing?" I asked.

We all looked off into the night as though it held answers. "I was hoping you knew," Sarah said.

I shook as I drove back up my drive with Beau curled protectively around himself in the backseat. He peed on his way into the house, but quickly—so much so that he never got his legs firmly set and went off balance before he was really finished, but it didn't seem to matter.

He scooted inside like his tail was on fire, cutting me off and looking back with apologies. He didn't pause for me to take his harness off. Or to offer his nightly minty chewstick.

He ran straight for the back of the house. At a guess, to leap onto the side of my bed he'd claimed as his own, to nose himself under the covers and hide out there as he did during thunderstorms—the only thing he was afraid of.

Until now.

I locked the front door, bolted it, checked the back door as well, and all the windows. Then I grabbed my laptop and brought the cordless phone into the bedroom in lieu of my cell, just in case... I knew I wasn't going to sleep for a long, long while, but Beau preferred to have me next to him when he was scared, and if I didn't show soon, he might go scratching at Luke's door, and Luke slept like the dead.

The thought sent chills over me, and I slipped under the covers rather than settling over them to work. That could have been us tonight. Me and Beau—dead. He sidled next to me under the covers, settling his warmth against me. I stroked his head resting on my 'guest' pillow as I waited for my computer to boot up, telling him over and over that he was safe.

Once I had my browser up, I struggled with what to search. *Big hyena that freezes people* didn't get me anywhere. I tried *hyena with cloven feet*, and that got me something really odd, a creature called a *leukrokotta* said to come from Ethiopia and written about by Greek and Roman historians. It had the body of a stag, a mane like a lion, cloven hooves and that sharp continuous ridge of teeth—er, tooth, in the upper and lower jaws.

My beast was nothing like a stag, but it was so close that I kept reading. Not because I believed it. I mean, this was crazy. A mythological beast written about by historians in first and second centuries A.D. and certainly not widely sighted since or I'd have heard about it!

But every fiction, fable, and fairy tale started with a kernel of truth, a point to the telling. I just had to find it. And *ah ha*— or sort of, anyway—the leukrokotta was related to another beast called the krokotta, or crocotta, which was a hyena-lion hybrid and maybe from Ethiopia or maybe from India, and either way, known to mimic human speech to lure victims, which explained the piteous sounds of the baby crying.

Oh, yeah, and if they looked at a person—generally thrice—the person was frozen in place, and if their shadow fell on a dog, they were struck dumb. Or a bit more, as we'd experienced.

In other words, they were apex predators. Everything about them was designed to lure, subdue, and savage prey. Maybe they weren't reported because so few lived to tell the tale. If that was the case, and if this one had decided to move in on our territory, as Spirit and the other wolf-dogs' agitation seemed to indicate, there was a good chance that this one would be back.

Despite Beau's heat, chills ran up and down my body, and it was well into the night, edging toward morning before I fell into an exhausted sleep.

Part of my sleeplessness the night before was going round and round in my head about how to bring the subject up with Thompson without having him think me mad. But I had to put him on alert. And find out if he'd ever heard of such a creature or any way to trap or defeat it. I couldn't have it coming for Sarah again. Or for me and Beau. Or Luke or Thompson or any of my volunteers.

I was fairly sure my wild wolves and all the others could fight for themselves, but what if they couldn't? The folklore I'd read had said that the krokotta's shadow struck dogs dumb, but instinct or *something* had frozen Beau in place, and most of my wolves were part dog. I didn't know what would happen with the wolf side. Or coyote. Or fox.

Most people thought that because wolves and dogs were genetically similar enough to breed, they were the same, but they were so, so different, from when they begin to socialize to when certain genes turned on to the stronger reliance on scent. Coyotes and foxes were even farther afield. There was no telling what a krokotta would do to them until tested, and I'd be damned if I'd let things get that far. Not with my animals. Not on my watch.

So, I kept an eye out for Thompson's truck, and when he arrived, I ambushed him right there in the parking lot.

He didn't look at me like I was crazy, but then, he hadn't yet heard what I had to say. As I was saying it, he started out looking deeply into my eyes, as though he could see straight through them into the inner workings of my mind. At a certain point in my story, I watched his eyes widen, and he gave up our staring contest to look me all over, checking for any damage I wasn't reporting. Finally, those green eyes with the crinkles at the corners rolled skyward as though headed for a mental search bar to browse through any outlandish experiences he might have archived.

When his gaze met mine again, he only said, "Everyone thought the New Guinea Singing Dog was extinct until just recently. Maybe this is something like that. Some nearly-forgotten evolutionary offshoot—"

"That you and I have never heard of? One that stopped me and Beau in our tracks? That can sound like a crying baby?"

"The bobcat has been known to sound like a crying baby."

"I thought that too, but this was no bobcat," I said, trying not to get irritated. He was only going through the very same process I'd gone through myself. "They have short tails. This one was long. Lion-like. And it had hooves, not paws. Listen, I know how this sounds. Just be on guard, okay, especially around the other animals, because if this thing is in their territory, they'll have their hackles up. I did some research last night and found an old, old reference that sounds a lot like what we saw. It's mythological, but there's often a little truth in fiction. I'll text it to you, but if you see anything, or know anyone you can ask who won't have you committed, let me know, okay?"

He agreed that he would, and we parted ways, a full day ahead of us, though my day would be spent mostly in the office. I was the proposal writer for grants and other funding, but I backstopped our educational outreach administrator. We basically worked the office, handled questions, wrote up articles and content for the website, fielded interviews and Q&As, or arranged them where our biologist or vet or others were called for. I did other fun things too, like bill-paying, spread-sheeting, scheduling, and troubleshooting. It was a relief when I occasionally took a break to participate in something like the afternoon wolf encounter.

Some rescues were entirely no contact, and I completely got that. Most of our animals were off-limits except to be viewed in their enclosures. But a few were more social, and we allowed limited visitors who signed up, and were vetted in advance, agreeing to our strict rules and accompanied by our staff, to visit with our animal ambassadors. But we were *not* one of those places who constantly bred baby animals for photo ops and tore them away from their mamas.

When the time came, I stretched out the hours of sitting in my office chair, listening to my vertebrae snap, crackle and pop, then went out to mix in with the back of the tour group I'd be accompanying. Our volunteer, Jenny, started up the group wolf howl, encouraging the tour to howl with the wolves, and it warmed my heart, as it always did, when the wolves, wolf-dogs and coy-wolves across the rescue took up her call. Our entire woods were filled with the joyful, communal sounds of pack, of being recognized and reinforced. It was heartening. Bolstering. Bracing.

I almost forgot all my fears. Until the howls started to subside, and in the last echoes, something entirely other came back at us. Laughter. Entirely preternatural laughter that said *you can't touch me, for you are in there, and I am OUT HERE.*

It dared all to follow and be lost.

The humans on the tour looked at each other for reassurance at the primal fear they felt. Their howls cut off, but the wolves took up again, answering the challenge. More than a few fences were tested as wolves flung themselves at the perimeters.

Thompson came home with me that night, loaded for bear. Quite literally. I didn't keep guns on the property, even with the threats we sometimes received. Threats to property weren't worth a potential loss of life, and who was to say my animals wouldn't get caught in any crossfire.

I didn't like guns. I'd seen the damage they could do. Tranq guns, though, were a different matter. They took a target down but not out, and that was the plan. Whatever this thing was, it had been evolutionarily designed that way. It was obeying its instincts. I didn't have to like them or submit to them, but I was against the death penalty for people or animals. If we could keep this thing alive, we certainly would.

I just hoped that 'loaded for bear' would be enough. Maybe he should have come 'loaded for moose.'

I'd sent Sarah to her sister's. Hopefully, that meant the beast would be coming for me. I was equating the imitation of human speech with human intelligence, which might be a mistake, but many animals were so much smarter than we gave them credit for. And predators in particular could be wily. They had to be, especially if they hunted alone.

Luke, after a chin 'sup of acknowledgement, a raid of the refrigerator, and a retreat to his room, gave no thought to Thompson's presence and asked no questions. We were left alone in my cozy living room/kitchen combination to sit catty-corner to each other over coffee, him with the tranq gun resting against one leg and Beau hard-leaning against the other, as if I never gave him any love at all and Thompson could scratch behind that ear all night, thank-you-very-much.

I tried not to enjoy the sight too much.

And then I heard it. It was soft at first. I sat up straighter in my seat, as though that might help me hear. Beau pulled away from Thompson, whimpering, ears perking forward. He heard it too.

A cry—my name, Sarah's voice.

"Lacey!" Out of breath. In pain. "Lacey, help me!"

It was a trick. It had to be a trick. I'd sent her out of town. She promised to go.

"Help!" A scream this time, as though whatever was after her had taken her down and she was seconds from death.

I ran for the door, grabbed for the walking stick I kept beside it, and wrenched it open. Thompson was right behind me. Beau tried to get out between his legs, but our biologist kept him back.

"Not this time, buddy." He closed the door in Beau's face, and I heard his barking and scratching behind us, desperate to join and protect us despite what had happened the last time. I was relieved that he was safe. That Luke with his headphones would never even hear the commotion.

"Lacey!" It was otherworldly, as though Sarah was choking on blood as she screamed.

Thompson outpaced me, which made me angry, somehow, and I poured on more speed until we were side by side. The uneven ground of the rescue tried to trip me, but momentum kept me upright as I raced, vaguely aware of the howling and fence rattling all around me. My animals were restless. They knew there was an invader in their midst. Whether Sarah was in trouble or not, this *thing* was here. Right here. In my territory. Their territory. Thompson and I were all that stood between it and my rescues.

As we ran past Spirit and Frost's enclosure, a shadow launched out of nowhere, landing on Thompson's back and biting into his neck with a crunch I could *feel* as though it were my own pain. He went down with a cry, arms going wide, tranq gun flying off into the night. I raised my walking stick like a club, leaping in to bash it over the beast's head, desperate to get it to release, to save my friend. If it got Thompson's jugular… I thought of that sharp ridge of teeth I'd seen in my Internet search. I didn't know how well it would cut, but it seemed like a chopper, like something out of a butcher's shop. Terribly effective. And that spurt of blood…

My brain wouldn't stop with that until the monster—the krokotta—turned on me, jaw running with blood. Its lips pulled back from the teeth and there was no gum at all, just that ridge of bone straight down to the jaw, razor sharp and cutting. It looked like a horror version of a hyena, but pride lion sized, a sense reinforced when it flicked its lion-like tail my way as though swishing at a fly. It leapt off of Thompson's body and started to come at me.

No, not off his body. He *had* to be alive. I had to draw the thing away. Had to put it down before it could double back to finish him.

It came slowly, sinuously, casually, as though it had all night. As though it was *enjoying* this.

I jabbed my stick forward; it snapped at it like it was nothing more than a twig. I pulled back quickly, afraid that it wouldn't stand up to those jaws. Suddenly, it seemed a flimsy thing, and yet it was all that stood between me and death.

I angled so that I could redirect myself, try to get at the tranq gun that had skittered off, but the thing's eyes flashed in the night, as if with sudden insight, and it pounced at me, striking out with its hooves, knocking my walking stick away and driving me to the ground. I rolled before it could take me, but I came up in the wrong direction. It was between me and the gun. And my stick was too far away to grab.

It laughed. That same mocking, horrible laugh from earlier that day, and a howl went up around the camp, a rattling of fences, especially close by. I'd recognize Spirit's vocalizations anywhere, and he was snarling and throwing himself so hard I was afraid he'd hurt himself. I made the mistake of turning to look, an instant of inattention to the threat before me, and the krokotta pounced.

Only to be met in the air by a one-hundred-pound gray wolf-dog determined to rescue me as I'd once rescued him. How he'd gotten free I had no idea, but—

"No!" I cried, terrified the krokotta's shadow would fall across him as it had Beau, and he'd fall frozen to the ground.

But Spirit was a force of nature. He hit with everything he had, knocking the krokotta away from me and tearing into the beast's neck. But it was bigger and more powerful. It gave a horrible cry, still half-sounding like Sarah, and bucked to tear itself loose of Spirit's jaws. It twisted, as though its spine were elastic, side kicking Spirit with its hooves, like a horse or a mule, pummeling him hard enough to break bone to get him to release. I couldn't stand by and watch him be brutalized.

I ran for the tranq gun and heard Spirit give a sudden sharp whimper as though it had caught him in the chest. In an instant, their positions shifted, and the krokotta was above him, free of Spirit's jaws and going for its own bit of flesh. And then suddenly Frost was loose as well, a blur of white against the darkness, crashing into the krokotta's side, sending them all rolling across the packed earth. She wasn't as large as Spirit. Or as powerful. I had to hurry. Together they might stand a chance. But with Spirit down…

But Spirit didn't stay down. He rose with a snarl, making sure the krokotta knew him for the bigger threat, making it face him. It leapt to its feet and backed away a pace to face the two wolf-hybrids, snarling and bristling and ready to defend their territory and the people they considered their pack.

I almost stumbled over Thompson and heard him groan. My heart gave a leap. He was alive. Oh, thank the god I wasn't even certain I believed in, he was alive.

I fell to my knees, not to pray, but to feel for the gun in the scant night lighting of the rescue, and I found it.

I lifted it from my kneeling position and sighted in. The krokotta was between me and my wolves. I prayed to the maybe-deity that it wouldn't move, and I pulled the trigger.

Nothing.

Dammit, I'd forgotten the safety. Even tranq guns had safeties. Wouldn't do to shoot oneself full of bear tranq. I quickly scrabbled for it, toggled it off, raised the gun again.

But now the krokotta was engaged.

Both wolves were on the beast. Or it was on them, as they scrapped, recovered, rolled, tore. I ran toward the snarl. I had to save my wolves. They couldn't die on my account. They couldn't.

Tears were streaming down my face as I ran toward the fight. It wasn't a long run, but it was long enough. When I reached them, Spirit and Frost stood, bloody but triumphant over the even more bloody and bizarre creature out of myth, panting and exhausted. Bleeding, but not dead. I shot it anyway, not wanting it to rise. It was just tranquilizer. It wouldn't kill it. But it would make sure it wouldn't kill us.

Then I dropped the gun and got down on one knee.

"Are you okay, my heroes?" I put out an arm for each of them for them to decide whether they wanted to be touched, scratched, loved on. They were wounded. They might feel vulnerable, might want to go off and lick their wounds. Frost gave my hand a lick and backed away, then went to check on Thompson. Spirit came in, face to face, and then rested his chin on my shoulder. I brought my hand up to scratch his ruff, and we stayed there a moment. It was Spirit's version of a hug, and I drank it down. Then he limped away a little bit to lick at his wounds, and I, too, went to check on Thompson. He was completely unconscious but breathing as I patted him down for his phone to call 911 for an ambulance and then animal control for the beast. But as I looked over between one call and the next to make sure that the krokotta was still out and we were all safe, the creature began to fade away. There, and then going, going, gone until it was as though it had never been, returned to the annals of myth or off to plague some other place or time.

I blinked and then blinked again, as though that would change anything.

I wasn't thinking about how it would simplify my night, only about how it would complicate my world. An accident on rescue grounds involving what was clearly an animal attack and the shooting of a tranq gun—the first conclusion anyone would reach was that things were out of our control. Our *animals* were out of our control. Investigation would be required. Spirit and Frost were clearly blooded. Even if I could clean the beast's blood from them before authorities appeared— and I had other priorities—I couldn't hide their wounds. How would we ever satisfy an investigation?

Quickly, quietly, with apologies to Thompson for leaving him, I brought Spirit and Frost back to their enclosure and begged them to stay, even though I could see where they'd bowed and torn the fencing enough to allow themselves to slip through. Then I phoned our on-call vet and asked her to pay them a visit on the QT, explaining as vaguely as possible and promising more tomorrow before collapsing beside Thompson to wait for the ambulance and the unanswerable questions to come.

"So, what was it that did this?" Sergeant Martinez asked.

I was pacing the waiting room while Thompson was in surgery. Not normal for animal bites, but the krokotta had done major damage. There was internal bleeding that had to be stopped, blood vessels that had to be stitched back together or cauterized or whatever they did. He was up-to-date on his shots, but...

"I'm sorry, what?" And the x-ray had shown that the collar-bone had been broken...

"I said—"

"Oh right, go through it all again." Because I had babbled something to the paramedics when they'd asked, stunned at the damage, and now I had to remember what I'd said and stay consistent. Although really, I hadn't said much, had I? They'd been happy to move me quickly along to his insurance and medical history.

I kept it simple—wolves acting oddly, asking Thompson to stay behind, having the tranq gun loaded up in case there was something stalking the preserve. We didn't really get a look at what attacked. When Thompson dropped the gun, I picked it up, fired it off at the intruder.

It stumbled off into the night. End of story.

It seemed as though there were going to be a lot more questions. Sergeant Martinez— or Cami, as I knew her from the monthly poker games that mostly took place around my kitchen table, since I didn't like to leave my rescue—was onto my tells. But then two things happened at once. A tall woman all gowned up in surgical scrubs came out and called my name, and a man and a woman decidedly not in hospital garb walked through the outer doors into the waiting room of the surgical center, making a bee-line for the Sergeant. I hesitated for an instant before answering my call, because there was something about the duo that radiated *power* and *presence*, and I had a feeling I wanted to hear what they had to say.

"Tori Karacis, P.I. and Apollo Demas—" the woman said, flipping open a wallet with some kind of identification to show the Sergeant.

Cami's eyes went wide. Even I recognized the second name and, now that I was paying attention, that face. Apollo Demas...the actor? What on earth? But I went on my way. I'd get the full story later. Right now, I had to know what was going on with Thompson.

"Miss Guerrera?" the surgeon asked. At least, I presumed she was the surgeon who'd been working on him.

"Yes," I answered, breathless. Thompson had me listed as his medical proxy, as I found out when we got to the hospital. Otherwise, I wouldn't have been allowed to know anything at all.

"He's going to be fine, as long as we keep the wound infection-free, and we're doing all we can on that, of course. We have to leave it open for a few days to drain and clean it, and we'd prefer to do that here before we close up. And a collarbone break is more a matter of slinging than casting, so he's going to need care once we send him home to make sure that he's not doing too much for himself."

"I've got that covered," I said with relief. More relief than the situation warranted, probably. I was terrible with change. But rescue. I was amazing with that. Not that I'd ever frame it in those terms to Thompson. He could come home with me. And if he chose to stay, become part of my pack, well, that would probably work out just fine. We'd see how it went.

"Are you okay?" the surgeon asked, reaching a hand out for me. I realized then that I was shaky with relief. Or maybe the released adrenaline of the whole damned night.

"I'm good, thank you. I think I just need to sit down. Or lie down. Maybe go home and sleep. Someone will call me when he wakes? I assume he's still under anesthesia?"

"I'll see to it," she said, and turned back for the surgery center.

I let her go and turned back, but the strangers were gone, leaving just Cami staring after them. My legs carried me only so far as a chair I could collapse into, and Cami collapsed into the one beside me.

"What was that all about?" I asked. It came out more or less coherently.

She gave a bark of a laugh. "They're here on behalf of a high-profile client, who asked that his name be kept out of things. Apparently, his 'dog' got free. He sent them for a private retrieval, which has now been accomplished, and they wanted to assure us that there'll be no more trouble. There's no reason to open an investigation or hunt down the animal. They're going to cover all of Thompson's medical bills, by the way—and they'll be back around in the morning to talk to you about a donation to your rescue."

"Oh, good," I said, or almost. A yawn split my face before the words were entirely out.

"Good? I thought you'd be hopping mad. Someone's keeping a dangerous animal that clearly got loose and savaged Thompson. That seems like the sort of thing you'd want me to investigate."

If this was a lion or tiger or some other exotic animal, she'd be exactly right. But the krokotta was on another level entirely. Something about it fading away as I watched, freezing me and Beau in our tracks said it wasn't entirely of this world. And I didn't think that my people or the Sergeant and her force were equipped to deal with it. If this Tori Karacis was, so much the better. But I'd be asking some hard questions of the P.I. when she came to visit, and if I wasn't satisfied... Well, now that I knew such creatures as the krokotta existed, I could hardly let them go running amok. Or allow the beasties to hurt others. Or be hurt or hunted themselves.

I hadn't known a lot about wolves or wolf dogs before my first rescue. If need be, I could launch a whole new crusade.

But I had a very strong feeling that the two who'd arrived had things well in hand, and I'd be more than happy to get back to my pack and my son. And maybe, once Thompson was ready to come home, a new normal.

Author Bio

Lucienne Diver is the author of the Latter-Day Olympians urban fantasy series, featuring Tori Karacis, P.I., who makes a cameo in "A Cry in the Night." *Long and Short Reviews* gave the series her favorite pull quote of all time, "a clever mix of Janet Evanovich and Rick Riordan!"

Lucienne has also written the Vamped young adult series—think *Clueless* meets *Buffy the Vampire Slayer*—and young adult suspense novels, including *Faultlines*, *The Countdown Club*, and D*isappeared*. Her short stories have appeared in *Kicking It,* ed. by Faith Hunter and Kalayna Price, *Strip-Mauled*, and *Fangs for the Mammaries*, ed. by Esther Friesner, Faith Hunter's Rogue Mage Anthology *Tribulations*, and more.

On a personal note, Lucienne lives in Florida with her husband, daughter, the two cutest dogs in the world, and enough books to someday collapse the second floor of her home into the first. She likes living dangerously. Wolves are her spirit animal. If not agenting and writing, she would run off to work at a wolf rescue. Or become a dryad and guardian of the forests, but, so far, no opening has become available.

The Kindness of Cats

By R.R. Virdi

Author's Note: This story is from the series Tales of Tremaine and takes place between the events of book one and two.

To learn more, read *The First Binding*

This is the story of one of the most important things in all of Brahm's creation.

Myself.

The people of Ghal have called me many things: nuisance, thief, miscreant, stray, and disaster. But my first real friend called me Shola.

The shy one, at least as far as he understood it. But in truth, it means the flame. I suppose we are both alike in that regard, though he doesn't understand it himself. Then again, he doesn't understand a great many things. But how can he? After all, he's only human. Not everyone can be blessed with the uncanny knowing of all things.

It is a gift I possess.

Because I am a cat.

The world has worsened in its cold and uncomforting climate. Taking to more snow than the appropriate amount, which happens to be none. It makes it a discomforting prospect to go about my morning necessaries with the accumulation of ice. A terrible design, if you asked me.

But perhaps if the creator of all things had bothered to consult a cat, the world would be a more orderly place, and make better sense. Brahm could have at the very least given me more direction in what to do with my charge.

The boy is young, and currently sits huddled on the floor of his room before a flickering candle. Its glow washes over him and brings its brightness and color to the light brown of his eyes. He stares at it, searching for some answer, but he's rather blind to the one it casts along the lines of his face.

I suppose that is the nature of people. They look so hard for answers everywhere other than within themselves. But, even with all the things

Ari happens to miss, I am fond of him. He gets the important things right.

Such as kindness.

He remembers this, even when he is caught in a weary torpor, like now. A stillness gathers around him just as much inside. Moments where the best of him is silenced and weighs on him like a mantle of lead. I worry for him, and the wounds he carries so deep inside he cannot see them.

But it is not so easy a task to make a human aware of these things, most especially when they lack the skill to understand the other creatures of the world. So, it is our duty to speak to them in simpler ways and remind them of the things they overlook.

A single bound from his bed brings me to one of Ari's legs. He sits with them crossed, hands resting in his lap as he regards the candle. His eyes flicker to one side as he notices me, then return just as quick to the flame.

I would sigh if I possessed the ability. Instead, I thump my head against the meat of his thigh, drawing his attention.

"Hm?" He turns his head, long dark hair coming to hang before his eyes. A brush of a hand sends it all back and he looks at me—the candle's orange still burning through his gaze. "What is it, Shola?" His fingers come to touch my skull and gently run along it.

You are doing it again, Ari. Sitting and sulking. Souring yourself. You should leave the candles be for a moment and move. Better yet, feed me, and perhaps yourself. There is little that cannot be fixed with food. He hears none of this, of course. "Mrrp."

Ari nods as if he understands me, though I know that is far from the truth. But, a small smile breaks across his face regardless. "Maybe so. I just… I can't make sense of it. I was so close—Brahm's blood. The fire, the binding. I had it!" He lets out a heavy breath and his hands ball into tight fists.

I tap him twice on the leg with a paw, delicately pointing out that he had not come close at all. He had been closer to cooking himself. And then who would tend to me? A terrible oversight on his part, really. "Mrow."

He sighs again. "Now it's just so far. It's all slipping away from me. What am I supposed to do between now and the next season's start? Half the Ashram thinks I'm a damn monster after what happened with Nitham." The smile from earlier returns and now grows into something crooked—cunning.

But I recognize it as the fake smile many humans adopt when

masking a hurt.

"Maybe I should let them think that. Brahm knows Nitham will try to get back at me twice as hard for anything I've done to him. But they might avoid me if I start letting more people think I'm some kind of monster, hm?" The grin he holds is a hollow thing. A disguise worn by someone who in truth is rather lonely and puts on the kind man's face to not worry others.

I know it, because I have been where Ari has, and he was the one to pull me from that. I have not forgotten, and I will not let him forget. But first, the damnable candle taking his attention.

I move around his leg and approach the third flame in the room.

"Shola—*hsst*—no! Stay away from that. You remember what happened last time—"

I do indeed, but all the same, my paw darts and I snuff the flame from existence. Its heat pricks my skin and I wince. The audacity of fire lets you know just how much Brahm had a hand in shaping it. Rude. Inconsiderately bright. Harmful. And always giving off that unpleasant smoke. I voice my disdain, and moment's pain, to Ari. "Maow!"

He grinds a palm to his forehead and uses his other hand to slide the candle away. "Brahm's tits, cat. What did you think would happen?" A heavy sigh leaves Ari, and he reaches out with both hands to take my palm in his grip.

What I thought would have happened was that you would leave the candle be and give yourself a moment's break. Brahm knows you needed it. I tell him this, though he doesn't have the ears or skill to hear me. "Mrrp."

"Yes-yes, you'll be fine, Shola." His fingers gently rub my skin, though he is utterly blind to the fact that I am not hurt. Only irritated. What else could I be when dealing with a boy so thick? Even so, I love him for the kindness he offers.

It is what made me accept him as my ward. The one to watch over. If only he was a better Listener.

But working on your human takes time, and I must better learn to be patient.

I catch his eyes darting back to the snuffed candle, and their desire is plain enough for me to see. He wishes to rekindle it and resume his practice.

I lunge, my paw striking the waxen-stick, sending it skittering along the floor.

There are times for patience, and then those moments when you must simply bat your problem away.

Ari shuts his eyes and rubs a few fingers against the bridge of his nose. "Brahm's. Blood. Shola." He rises and makes his way toward the door. "Maybe we'll both be less moody after a bite, hm?"

The first sensible thing he's said. "Mrrrl."

"Of course, your majesty. A double portion of meat. How could I forget?" He laughs to himself and slips out of the room, leaving me to myself for a time.

I lose track of how long it has been since Ari has left, but the pains in my stomach let me know it has been quite the while. Long enough that any other lesser animal, which is to say, all of them, would have perished from starvation.

The door opens and he moves through it—a tray rests in his grip. "Back. Miss me?" He gives me a smile that should mollify most of my displeasure.

It does not.

A cat can be kept many things, but never hungry. "Mrrr."

"Uh-huh. Thanks for asking how it was, by the way. Everyone's looking through me rather than at me." His shoulders slump and he soon follows, sinking to the ground. "It's like no one can stomach seeing my face after what happened at the festival. I didn't even see Aram or Radi in Clanks."

He folds a piece of flat bread and mops it through a thin pool a color close to my own fur. Tiny peas float through its surface, though he avoids picking them before taking his bite.

"What if they changed their minds about being my friends? What if—"

I bump my head firmly into one of his legs, taking his attention from the bothersome thoughts. Besides, there are more important things to focus on. I inform him of this as I eye one of the drumsticks resting in a sauce of spinach and butter.

"What—oh." Ari grins and rubs a hand against my head. "Here." His fingers take a piece of the chicken, tearing a lump free. He is quick to ensure it has little of the green filth stuck to its meat, and more of the butter instead.

Sometimes he is much smarter than he looks. I take the piece and set to work, sharing the pleasurable meal and silence together. My company buoys him as he frets over his other friends. But it is the least I can do: letting him know that no matter what, he will never be truly alone.

We eat in continued peace before he gets to his feet and unlatches the window resting above his bed. "All right, out you go. I'm taking this back to Clanks, hm?" He gives the tray a little wave.

"Mrrmp."

He blinks, then realizes his error. "Right. Sorry, distracted."

I'll say.

Ari drops the tray and takes me in both his hands, raising me to the window before easing me out. "Don't stay out too long with your business, *ji?* It's cold, and the snow's getting heavier."

I weathered worse winters before you took me into your home, Ari. "Marow."

"And don't lick any snow—I swear, cat. You were stuck wincing half the day last time."

Nonsense. An utter lie. And I was simply showing my displeasure at how horrendous snow happened to be. "Mrrl." He does not listen to my reasoning and instead places me on a cushion of soft winter's ice.

"I'll be back soon." Ari leaves as soon as that, and I set off to do my business. Though, I don't imagine any human has an understanding of what that might really entail.

The place known as the Rookery has many secrets all its own. Forgotten paths laid into its stone and along its height. The perfect place for birds to perch and be ignored by the many human eyes too dull to see anything they are not concerned with. But it is the perfect place for a cat.

There are ledges and ways for the quick of foot to reach the Ashram grounds, even with the snow and ice. It isn't long before I am astride the courtyard, then just as soon, the city of Ghal.

Streets I know well. Just as much as the cruelty they can carry.

I keep to shadowed paths under buildings' heights, all ensuring the wrong stares do not find me. Not all people have Ari's heart.

Snow crunches underfoot and I move with all the grace and speed I can muster. I reach the cornerstone of the structure closest to me. The sound of footsteps loudens, and I peer around the edge to see who draws close.

She is nothing more than a child. Younger than Ari by a good handful of years if I am any judge of humans. And I happen to be a masterful one. Her hair is bird's nest tangle and done no favors by the sharp cold today. Stress has dulled the blackness of each strand and a hollowness hangs in her eyes. It is one I have known too.

The emptiness that comes with hunger.

And loneliness.

All the weight and sorrow of an orphan. Like I once was.

She brings a thumb to her mouth, biting at the skin around her fingernail. Then, catching herself in the nervous act, she stops. Her gaze flits to the warmth of a stone pit and the fire that burns within it. Then, just as quick, she turns to watch a man turn a thin mass of dough that is still cooking atop a metal sheet. The girl thumbs the collar of her robes, the color of which has come to be a gray only found in things that have given up their original shade to time and stress. The clothes carry more lines of thread and patches than any child's ever should.

She shakes, then her shoulders lose what strength they had moments earlier, and she slumps.

I move closer but do nothing to betray my presence. I have long since mastered the art of moving unseen by the clumsy in Ghal.

"Cat!" A child's voice carries through the otherwise quiet street.

I whirl to find someone no more than five, jabbing a pudgy finger my way. They repeat their declaration as if to inform anyone else who had thought me to be something other than what I am.

"Cat. Cat. Cat."

Yes, very good. You're twice as smart as you look, which isn't that smart at all, doubly so when considering your limitations as a human. I tell him this but remember myself and let a touch of grace flood my voice. "Maoooow."

He frowns, furrowing dark brows and losing what spark had taken his brown eyes moments earlier. Then, a madness seizes him, and he reaches for me with an open hand.

I hiss and move with a speed only rivaled by beings in stories. My paw darts and bats his hand several times. *Away! Back! You've no right to touch me, little dullard.* "Maow!"

The child reels, clearly overwhelmed by my ferocity, and falls into the snow. Their face twists and tears follow. His voice cracks and fills the air with a young boy's cry.

Oh, Brahm's breath.

I close the distance and reach out with a paw. He shies away from the touch at first, bawling twice as hard as before. I let him know that it is fine, and I am only trying to comfort him. "Mrr."

My touch makes its way across the top of his head and, for a moment, he ceases his tantrum. Assured that he will no longer sound an alarm to my presence, I tear free from the place, searching for the young girl I'd seen moments earlier.

I catch a passing sight of her as she turns past one of Ghal's rounded buildings. The cold hasn't reached me deeply yet, but I feel its grip against my muscles. Still, I bound after her, keeping an eye on one of the city's overlooked.

I have lived too long in the same way to let the same suffering befall another. Just as Ari once did for me, I'll do for her. At least in some small manner.

My run brings me past the flatbread maker she had been eyeing, but there is no time for that now. She moves to another merchant. A man stacking cutlets of freshly cooked meat. The smell of it is touched with sharp spices and of charcoal. His hands move and several pieces of lamb are skewered and then folded within a sheaf of parchment.

The young girl fiddles in the folds of her robes, drawing out two bent pieces of tin. She motions at one of the pieces of meat and the man blinks. Then he laughs, head thrown back and a hand waving her off. She shrinks further into her clothes and the money vanishes back inside the tattered cloth. The child does not linger, knowing well enough to harsh truth of the orphan's life.

There are few places where we are welcome for long. And fewer still where we are wanted at all.

So, she shuffles onward, and I walk her path, prowling just far enough behind to keep from being spotted.

I am the truest embodiment of stealth, and—

"Oi, what's this?" The man's voice holds as much smoke and coal grit as his cooking pit.

He is lean with features brought out even harder by the thinness in his face. His foot blurs and I recognize what it means. I move just as the tip of his boot sails by where I had been moments ago.

"*Hsst*, move-move. *Gutiya*. Stray. You'll drive away customers." Another motion of his foot, but this time it is only a deterrent—no lashing kick.

I bite back the urge to hiss or lunge at the man. Fool that he is, I have need of his goods. *I require but just one piece of your offerings, cook, and I'll be on my way. You can spare that much.* "Mrowl."

The man turns his eyes to focus on everywhere but me, now realizing I will not be brushed aside. "Hot skewers. Goat, lamb, and some sheep. Spiced and fresh and still hot-hot!" He cups his hands to his mouth, making his voice carry.

You have more than enough to give scraps to an orphan, fool! "*Maaaow.*"

Another movement of foot and a current of snow sails my way, but

259

I am the pure shape of deftness itself. So I leap, the torrent of snow…still brushing my sides.

I hiss, leaping at his legs. My paws strike with a fury and speed unrivaled by anything short of the gods.

"Ackh!" He shakes one leg, trying to dislodge me.

But I will not be shaken.

His hands clamp to folds of skin at the back of my throat and he heaves me up.

Unhand me, you cussed, callow, heartless—"*Mrrow!*"

My world teeters as he shakes me. Old instinct takes hold and my paws move to take action. And I am free as quick as that.

The man reels, his hips brush against the flat metal surface atop the flame. It tilts, and charred meat falls to the snow.

"Brahm's Blood!" The cook grabs the flesh of his hand, now welting fresh red from where my claws savaged him. He does not have the grace to thank me for my mercy, for I could have just as easily cleaved him to ribbons instead of just some scratches. Instead he spits curses.

I ignore him and take a rolled parchment of meat between my mouth.

"Thief!"

I am at that, and a marvelous one, just like my ward—Ari. My legs carry me far from his protests and a look over my side reveals the man retrieving what meat he can from the snow.

Serves him right. There are many forms of poverty in the world, but no few so bad as those poor in heart. The ones unable to give but even a piece of it to someone else in so desperate a need of its touch—its warmth. There is a special place in the bottom of the world for men like that, but it is not for me to judge. Well, mostly not for me. I happen to be a marvelous arbiter of character. So Brahm has shaped all my kind to be.

The girl comes into view ahead and vanishes just as quick. Her threadbare robes flutter at the edge of a corner I barely catch sight of. But it is enough.

I set chase again and keep from the throng of tangling legs and awkward shuffling steps only humans can take. Utterly without care, grace, or the eyes to see what moves before them. If I had the time, I would give them the sharp side of my tongue and point out all they do wrong. But they wouldn't have the ears for it anyhow.

I reach the turn she's taken and move along it, coming to a space between the many domed structures in the city of Ghal. There is a point where three buildings meet to form a nook of sorts. Attached to the roofs of others is a canted structure of wood. A hovel by all accounts, stretching far into the alley and supported by beams that look close to giving way. But it is what lies under it that catches my attention most.

A bed, fashioned much as the structure around it. Shoddy wood barely kept together. Blankets that are closer to rags than their namesake. And the elderly woman beneath them. By her side rests the child I have been following.

"It's fine, *mama.*" She runs an affectionate hand over her mother's brow, wiping away the beaded sweat.

It is near the full of winter's cold and the woman is flush with sweat. That tells me enough.

I approach, making no effort to hide my coming.

The young girl notices and flicks a gaze towards her ill mother. "*Tsst.* Go away." She motions with a hand, trying to shoo me.

But I do not stop, nor heed her wishes. Instead, I come as close as I can and lower my head to the ground. The sheaf of parchment with meat skewers falls, and she sees this. I back away and motion with a paw, making my intent clear.

She eyes me—wary. It is the outcast's look. The untrusting stare that views all kindness suspect, and it can only be earned through a life of hurt and being shunned.

I have known it well and worn that same look many a time. And now I hope to help her find her way out from it.

But it begins with a shared kindness. Of building trust. I know this, and I know its touch. It came my way when Ari first crossed my path. And now I carry the tradition—the kind man's helping hand.

She edges closer, reaching out to take the parchment. Her fingers brush against it then close—hard-fast. She recoils as if afraid I might move again for the bundle. But I do not, and she realizes this. Her fingers move and she has opened the wrapping. She blinks, then trades a longer look with me.

It's food, quite obviously, for you. And I suppose for your mother, if she has the stomach for it. I watched you with the merchant. I have been following you since, but you clearly were unaware as you do not have the eyes to catch something like myself stalking after you. "Mrrow."

"Um, thank you." She does not wait before tearing into a piece of the meat. Her eyelids flutter and her mouth spreads into a wide smile of the pleasure only found in someone starving freshly given a piece of something tasty. She takes another chunk out of the meat.

"What is it"—a hard and dry cough racks the old woman's body—"what is it, Sarika?"

The girl, Sarika, turns halfway to her mother. "*Billi*, a cat!" She takes a step toward me, then looks over her shoulder again. "It brought us meat."

She coughs again, just as harsh. "It did?"

The old woman's eyes finally turn on me—cold, and hollow. Someone closer to the Doors of Death than the fresh breath of life. There is little warmth in the brown of her gaze, and my heart aches. I know the sorrow and fear that now holds little Sarika. And I do not know if there is much at all I can do to spare her that.

But I will try.

It is all any of us can do in the end. To try to be there for those that need a hand—or a heart.

I come closer and reach the girl's side.

Her leg moves and I recognize it as the fear of someone all too used to being shooed away. The cautious flinch of someone ready to be chastised—maybe struck. Something else I have come to know.

I keep this in mind before I speak, knowing this will settle the young girl's heart. There is nothing to fear. *While I may look rather fearsome and have the full fury and color of flame itself in my coat, I am rather friendly.* "Mrrow."

My words steady her, and it is clearly due to the calm and reassuring basso notes found in my voice. Soothing.

"It's cute, *mama*." She kneels and reaches out with a hand to brush my head.

I inform of her of her error. *Technically, I assured you that while I look fearsome, you have nothing to fear. But I understand the limitations of human ears and understandings—a simple translation error on your part. And a cat is nothing if not patient—*

Her fingers dig into my fur and runs her nails against my skin, scratching more than an affectionate pet.

Not what I had hoped for...or permitted. But the kindness she required demanded me to weather the minor misunderstanding. But the moment passes, and I place a paw on her hand. This informs her that she is to stop, and that I in turn offer a gentle touch to soothe her.

You should give your ailing mother some of the meat, if she has the strength for it. It will help her. Though you should consider some kind of soup. I have seen many of your kind turn to it during the colder turn of climate in Ghal, and most especially when you are sick. "Mrrip."

She doesn't heed my words, though. So I must show her. I saunter past, leaping up the rickety assembly of wood that serve as rotting steps. The makeshift floor of the shack is nothing more than scrap, long-assembled by hands that never knew what they were doing. It serves its purpose, however, and that is enough.

Sarika's mother looks down at me. "And who do you belong to, sweet thing?" Another cough shakes her and takes what little strength she has. Her body sinks further into the motley pile of rags and strips of old clothes that act as poor blankets.

I belong only to myself, but Brahm placed me on this good world, like all cats, to eventually take a charge under my guidance. To shape him with our wisdom, and to of course look after the best of god's own creation. Myself, I mean. "Mrrl."

"Yes-yes." The old woman smiles, clearly understanding and agreeing with what I have said. One of her hands moves from out under the various garments keeping her warm. It is frail, with the skin holding tight and thin to her bones, revealing veins that must be suffering in Ghal's cold.

I save her the effort and move to meet her touch, laying one of my paws atop hers. *It is all right, old one. It will be fine. I am here now.* "Mrr." I eye her, making it clear what I intend to do, and wait for her silent permission to go ahead.

She smiles, and I take that as my invitation.

As with all things—kindness and care—touch, and warmth, they must be agreed to. Welcomed. Consented.

And she has given me this.

So, I make my way with all gentleness atop the mountain of clothing, making sure no step of mine causes the old woman further grief. Once atop her chest, I curl tight and bring to her the best of my soothing assurances. It is a noise of bottled thunder—the promise of lightning to come. The rumbling susurrus of a river in storm. And all the comfort of a cat's purr.

It is the smallest kindness I can give to her today. But soon, I will give her all the comfort a cat can bring.

Sarika's mother rests in the deep sleep of one who has gone long without, as well as spent much strength giving life to a body that has little left to it. But the young girl has found little respite herself. The crumpled remains of paper sit discarded in the snow, and nothing is left of the lamb once wrapped within. Sarika licks her lips, and I recognize the look of an orphan in want of more food than they have, and the weary resignation that follows.

The next thing I can offer her then. A piece of knowledge. The working of how to fend for herself. Something a cat is all too aware of.

I only have Ari tend to my needs because he offers and is ever willing to meet my every request with the utmost enthusiasm. To deprive of him of that pleasure would be a cruelty.

"*Tch-tch.*" Sarika motions at me with a few fingers, beckoning me closer.

I have half a mind to inform her that I am not something to be called at whim. Brahm shaped us to teach and guide the simpler things of this world, not be their servants.

Her mouth pulls downward and the disappointment spreads clear.

I swallow the urge to sigh and make my way over to her touch. It is not so bad, I suppose, as she runs her hand over me. Though she lingers too long in doing so, and I remind her of this, staying her motions with one of my paws. *That is enough, youngling. There are things to show, and knowings you must have. Follow me, and I will show you where to find hidden kindness.* "Ma-wow."

"Yes, it gets cold here. *Mama* and I have enough sometimes to stay warm, but we need more, just to be safe. I can get food sometimes. Some people are nice and give alms. Tea is easier. People share that a lot. It helps."

That was not what I made mention of, but I suppose your conversational skills are limited. You are young, after all, and so it is mostly forgivable. "Mrr."

I do not wait for her to try to make further talk, instead, taking down the alley in where she lives. She follows and I quicken my pace, leading her down the many paths I learned to walk before Ari came into my life.

I bring her first to a merchant I remember my first kindness from. He takes wool and warm fibers, banding them together into rugs and blankets to sell. It was in his hands that I first experienced a touch of consideration from another human.

He stands behind a small stall, weathering the cold, all before a domed shop of modest size. Strips of fabric and some woven shawls hang for inspection. They carry all the colors found in gemstones and summer evening skies. "Oh-ho, and who is this marvelous little thing." His face, kept fresh from the cold and lack of sun, breaks into a wide smile. The brown of his eyes is the same dark as his skin, but they brighten on seeing me.

You've met me before, merchant-sahm, but you seem not to recall. "Mrow."

"Yes, it is quite cold for a little thing as you and—" His attention leaves me as Sarika comes racing behind. "And who's this then, ah?"

The girl stops and clasps her hands together. "Apologies, *sahm*. My kitten ran away. I'm just trying to get him back. I don't want to make trouble for you, and I promise to have him back to my *mama*." At mention of this, the merchant frowns and gives Sarika a longer look.

I can see the same thoughts running behind his eyes as once did me. The state of her clothing, and how freely they hang from her body.

"And your mother, girl? She is…well? Your father?" He offers her the first kindness many should to one another, but often forget. A true and honest smile. An invitation, of sorts.

She shakes her head. "*Mama* is…tired. She gets more tired every day. She doesn't leave bed. I don't know why. *Papa* left long ago."

Left. Not passed. But left. I have no words or the right sympathies to offer her. But I know a similar pain, as does Ari in what he has confessed to me. Sometimes there are no things you can do to set an old hurt right. All you can do is listen, and simply be there for the one in pain. It lets them know that, at the very least, they are not alone.

"Oh, Brahm's breath and blessing wash over you, girl." The man means every word of it, and it rings clear in his voice. His hands reach out toward her, but Sarika shies away. The merchant realizes this and stops himself.

"It's a hard life, that. Come here, child." He motions her closer. "Come, come." One of his palms presses against a thick shawl. Its color is crushed sapphires and strung with silver moon thread in patterns of racing ivy. "This is good wool. Thick and will keep your *mama* warm." He takes it between both hands and presses it toward her.

She recoils again. The wary-eyed look of someone who has been hurt before fills her eyes.

I know what I must do and move in kind. My body crashes against her leg to take her attention away from the merchant. *It is all right. This man has done me a kindness before. His heart is that of gold. And now he gives you a piece of it. Learn to take it.* "Mrrl."

One of the forgotten pieces of kindness is that one must be open to receiving it. To have the open space to take it. And so many of us learn to shut our hearts to that gift for fear of a pain that may never come. All because we have felt its sting once before.

But that is the way to shut the doors of our hearts to one another, and with that comes a cold and lonely life.

Sarika reaches out, fingers brushing the fabric. The cloth passes from his hands to hers, and she clutches it as if it is a treasure. She shoots the man a look and it asks a silent question. Will he change his mind? Will she be forced to give this piece of kindness back?

But the smile that stretches wide along the merchant's face gives the answer clear.

No.

She returns the expression and inclines her head. "Thank you, *sahm*. Thank you."

He waves her off, but a touch of color floods his cheeks are her appreciation. "It's nothing, little one. What would the world be without a little kindness, *ji-ah?*"

"*Ji!*" She presses the cloth close to chest, almost if wanting to press it deep into her own body.

The man watches this, and I see his eyes flicker to me, then back to Sarika. He knows there is more to her misfortune than just a lack of warmth. "Your mother...is well cared for with food? A hundred apologies, but you look..." He doesn't need to finish. Her state of life is clear enough to him.

Sarika says nothing. Instead, her eyes slowly turn to look anywhere but at the merchant.

Whatever other words the man has to offer die in his throat. He knows enough to see that he has pushed too far. And there is limit even to the generosity one heart can accept from another.

A shame to be certain, but another of life's truths as well.

So, it is time again for me to take charge and show her another of the world's certainties. I bat at her legs until her attention comes back to me.

"What is it, kitten?" She reaches toward me, but I move from the touch.

Follow me. "Mrp."

I take off down the streets of Ghal, Sarika well in tow. We pass through another space of squat buildings, all shaped to shrug off the snow. There is the scent of fires that have burned too low to be rekindled, and some fed too well, now pluming the sky with smoke. But between it all lingers the smell I am searching for.

It is of soft spice and warmth. Of promised sweetness, and a much needed reprieve.

"Where are you going, cat? Slow down." Sarika's breath comes twice as hard as before.

I do not stop, though, and wind my way through an alley that leads to my goal.

The place is not like many others in Ghal. Its roof is canted sharply to one side, but it serves well enough to keep the snow from piling.

More windows line the shop than necessary. This is especially true considering they only face back down the way I have come, and there is little to see but an icy street. But an inviting smoke filters out from the chimney, and that is why we are here.

I require you to open the door, Sarika. "Mrr." My paw brushes against the way in and she takes my meaning. The pair of us enter together and we are greeted by scene of crowded tables and bustling people. Painted bowls are placed before customers and spoons follow. Drinks are served and all gather close to share in the delight of soup.

And I remember a time a starving kitten came looking in search of warmth and kindness, and he found it in this place.

I move to brush against the legs of one of the men passing a customer a bowl. *You, I need a moment.* "Maow."

He looks down at me. The man's face holds a good amount of mass, well-fed, and the lines along it concentrate along his mouth and eyes. Someone who smiles a great deal, and he gives me one then. "Oh-ho. What's this, ah? Where did you come..." He trails off as he sees Sarika standing behind me. "I can sit you in a moment girl. This your cat?"

She glances at me, then shakes her head. "I found him." Which is not an answer, but it is enough to placate the man.

"Ali, you're not paid to stand like a sack of lentils, *ji-ah?* Move." The voices from behind the server. A woman in her middle years, proportioned the way you'd expect of a prosperous cook. Round in face and in body. Dark curls frame her aspect and bring out the curves in her cheeks. She bustles past the man then sees Sarika.

I remember her, and the night she tended to a lonely kitten very much in want of something fresh to eat.

"Did you say something about a cat, Ali?" The shopkeeper gets her answer a second later as she spots me. "Brahm's breath. I've seen you before, little one, *ji-ah?*" She stoops to scratch the side of my head.

I allow it, knowing this is not the time to take umbrage. Not with Sarika's needs still unmet.

"Here for another bowl?" The woman's eyes drift back to Sarika. "And what's with you, little one?"

The girl has no words, this time merely pointing my way.

It is Ali then who fills the silence with an explanation. "She came in with the kitten, Maanvi. But, look at her. She's in rags. And doesn't look like she's eaten a good bit in sets."

The woman looks Sarika over and realizes Ali speaks truth. "Come here, girl. We'll get you sorted, and your kitten." She speaks in the voice of someone who is never argued with and does not expect that to change any time soon. Maanvi turns and moves toward the kitchen, and I follow.

Sarika, however, lingers behind. Doubt once again clear along her face.

A heavy hand lands on her shoulder and jars her a bit. But it is Ali's touch, and he gives her a gentle shove forward. "It's all right, girl. Maanvi sounds meaner than she is." He grins and grabs one of his earlobes, pulling on it in a manner many do when indicating a light joke. "But she is a good cook, and we make soup to spare, ah?" One of his hands claps to his belly, giving it a heavy pat. "Though, maybe some of us have a bit too much of it." Ali laughs, and it brings Sarika to smiling.

She follows as the server leads the way to the kitchen. We come into a place packed far past comfort. Elbows brushing elbows, and fires fed full to warm to pots of soup and stew. A woman grabs a bowl and ladles it full before leaving.

Maanvi moves past another server, eyeing two women preparing ingredients. "Two bowls. Goat, sides of rice, and extra spice!"

A chorus of, "*Ji,*" greets her back. Maanvi does not stop, though. She moves to a pot, tasting its offering before addressing the room once again. "More star anise, and white pepper!"

Once again, "*Ji,*" echoes through the room.

"Tables are full, customers are waiting. Move-move."

"*Ji!*"

Several people leave the room giving Sarika and I the space for privacy with the shopkeeper.

The older woman rounds on us and thrusts her chin up. "So, what is it, little one? Why do you look like you haven't had a good meal in a while?" Maanvi doesn't wait for an answer, though. Instead, she gestures to two large pots that have been simmering away. "One is stew: chickpeas, lamb, mountain rabbit, and spiced enough to keep the cold from your bones for many nights." She smiles. "The other is a lentil soup: turmeric, cumin, coriander, and more. It's light and filling. Very good. Which would you like?"

Sarika shuffles from foot to foot, her gaze falling to the floor. "I can't pay."

Maanvi gives the young girl a mother's smile with all the warmth and patience as well. "I didn't ask if you could, sweetling. Now, which will be, hm? Oi, Ali, why are you standing there watching—ah? You're not paid to do that. If you're going to linger here, get the girl a bowl and get a ladle, *ji?"*

The man knows enough not to say anything other the appropriate response. *"Ji-ah!"* And he moves to do as he's been ordered.

"Then the lamb, please. It has meat, and that means..." Sarika's words fall apart, but she manages to look my way, making her intention clear.

"Oh, don't worry about this one, *ji?* I remember this little flame." She reaches down to brush the knuckle of one finger against my nose. Not a place I particularly enjoy to be touched, but given the kindness she is showing Sarika, I will permit it.

Humans are often ignorant of boundaries, and more so on matters of invitation, but they have hearts of kindness if you give them chance to show it. And for that, they are mostly tolerable.

This is one of those moments.

Ali brings a bowl of lamb stew and sets it on the counter near us. Maanvi all the while picks meat from another bowl, shredding it fine with her nails before placing it atop a wooden board.

"I think I have some clotted cream here as well." The shopkeeper fetched that as well, pouring the contents of a shallow pan into a bowl. She laid the assembly of food before me and reached out for another affectionate touch.

Given what she has offered, I feel an acceptable exchange. Her nails dig into my fur just behind my throat and she scratches somewhere that needed soothing. "Now, tell me what is wrong..." Maanvi stops short, leaving the question hanging in the air. The obvious invitation for Sarika to offer her name.

And the little girl does just that. "Sarika." Her name comes out nearly mangled as the girl struggles with a piece of all too hot meat.

I, knowing well enough the proper order of things, try the cream first. It is more than satisfactory. *My compliments, cook.* "Mrrrl." The shredded lamb it just hot enough for me to nurse a small worry of burning myself, but its taste makes up for any discomforting heat.

"So, what is it then, Sarika?" Maanvi fixes the young girl with a mother's stare. A weight of inquisition as much as gentleness.

Sarika swallows and takes a breath. "My *mama* is sick. I don't know what's wrong, or how to make her better. We don't have much. Not since *papa*..." Her words fall apart, but Maanvi understands what goes unsaid.

"Oh, child." The shopkeeper crosses the distance and wraps her arms around Sarika, holding her tight.

I know Maanvi's heart, and though many people are not given the chance to show the fullest of theirs, this is a moment when hers will shine through. I know it. And it is why I have brought Sarika here. To prove to her a hidden truth I have learned.

That despite the cruelties that man can be capable of, there is a warmth of love within you lot as well. It just takes the right people to show that to you.

And in a world as large and wide as ours, there are always the right people. You just need to know how and where to find them. Which of course I do. After all, a cat is nothing if not discriminating in finding the perfect things no matter the situation or need.

"Before your mother took ill, was she a good cook? Did she work needle and thread?" Maanvi fetches Sarika a mug of something warm and spiced, promising to take any chill away.

The young girl bows her head. "Good cook. But she never—"

Maanvi doesn't wish to hear anything further. That answer is more than enough for the matron of the soup-shop. "Never you mind, Sarika. Wait here. I have some customers to speak to. Customers I've given much love to and never asked a spare chip from for any extra consideration. Now there's something I need to bend their ear for." The woman marches off at that, and I follow in tow.

Though my stomach and palette yearn to savor more of the food, I cannot leave Sarika's future unknown. So, I must hear what is happening next.

We make our way back among the crowded tables where elbows jostle, soup splatters at times across wood, and someone occasionally laughs.

"Oi-ya." Maanvi's puts a hand to her mouth, ensuring her cry echoes far through her shop. "Is Mender-*sahm* here? Where's Mender Katar, huh? Where are you?"

A man rises. He is the sort of lean that is much apparent with just how much his winter robes hang off his frame. The man could be someone's grandfather with how white his hair has gone, and the lines along his face, but there is a brightness in the gray of his eyes. An invitation and warmth that matches this place—the same as Maanvi's.

"Yes, Maanvi, what is it?" The mender folds his hands, looking at the now silent crowd as if hoping to glean a silent answer from them as to what is happening.

"There is a woman that needs looking to. No-no"—she motions him to stay as the mender moves closer—"sit and finish your meal. After. Her daughter is here, and sad shape that one's in. I've been good to you, and Brahm Himself knows—"

The mender clasps his hands together tight. "Yes-yes, Maanvi. Brahm knows it. I've never said anything otherwise. You want me to look in on this woman, I'll do so."

She doesn't waste time listening to another word, rounding instead to face the other side of the shop. "Where's Sneha, hm? You're always in here on a cold one like today. Always with the order of *thori* with extra butter, and a good hot soup. Hm, where are you—stand-stand!"

A woman rises at the snap of a call. She is dark of eye and of hair. A long braid hangs to her waist, drawing my eye.

And I might nurse the overpowering urge to give it a good batting, but there are more pressing matters at hand.

…perhaps later, though.

"What is it, Maanvi?" Sneha adopts a similar gaze to the mender from earlier, looking as if she expects trouble and an equal chastisement.

"You and your father are doing slow business this set, no?"

Sneha shrinks but inclines her head. "Yes…but that doesn't mean I cannot pay. I have—"

Maanvi waves her off. "So you and your father have spare rooms—warm ones, all open for the taking, hm?" The way she asks the question makes it clear she knows the answer.

Sneha licks her lips and bows once again. "Yes, Maanvi. We have many spares. But why?"

Another heavy wave of a hand. "Never you mind that. How many times have I brought your father a hot bowl, in the cold, no less? At no charge, because I know how late he works tallying ledgers, and tending to travelers—some of whom have less manners than they have coin, trying to skimp you lot on a debt. How many times, girl?

"No, don't answer. Finish your food, then you and Mender-*sahm* will come with me, *ji-ah?*" Maanvi's tone makes it all-too clear that will accept a singular response.

"*Ji,*" says Sneha.

And it is as simple as that. The shape of Sarika's future seems to brighten—to clear. But she doesn't know it yet, and it is a poor thing to keep a surprise from someone for too long.

So, I leave, making my way back to the young girl in the kitchen.

Her lips now bear the marks of meat juices as much as a mulled fruit beverage. "Hello, cat. Where did you go?" She smiles and bends to brush my head.

The amount of touch I have received might be more than any of my kind has had to bear in so short of time. The many sufferances a cat must endure in our duty to look out for humans. Though it certainly wears after a while.

But I am ever the model of patience and dignified.

That will be enough, little one. You may stop now. "Mawow." I smack a hand to hers, moving it away.

It isn't long before Maanvi returns, interrupting the conversation I wish to have myself with the girl. "Are you done? How was it?"

Sarika beams. "It was good. Thank you. But...I told you, I can't pay. *Mama* and I don't have—"

Maanvi shakes her head and lets out a heavy sigh. "And I told you, little one, I didn't ask. Next time, clear the oil from your ears, *ji-ah?*" But she says this with no malice, only a wide smile. "Now, we are going to wait a little bit while some customers finish their food, understand? Then I want you to take us to see your *mama.*"

Sarika frowns, the old urchin's worry plain across her face again.

This is where I must intervene and play the cat's part. I move and bump the whole of my mass against her leg, rubbing hard against her in what I know will take her attention and give her comfort.

And it works. Sarika does not reject the offer. Instead, she smiles.

We return to the snow-swept streets of Ghal, now with a group tight to our sides. Maanvi, the shopkeeper. Sneha, the attendee of her father's inn, and the mender, Katar-*sahm*. Sarika leads the way through the winding streets back to the hovel in which her mother lays.

"Oh, Brahm's blood." The curse leaves the mender's mouth before he realizes he has spoken.

Maanvi rounds on him, slapping a meaty hand to his chest. "Oi, no speaking of Brahm like that. Not in front of the girl."

The mender's eyes widen. "Of course, Maanvi. Right. Let me go have a look at the girl's mother." Mender Katar rushes off to do just that. A leather satchel rests in his grip and he lays it flat near where Sarika's mama rests.

The elderly and ill woman raises her head to regard the man peering down at her, but he gently hushes her. "I'm a mender—studied at the Ashram many years ago. I'm here to tend to you."

Sarika edges closer, but Maanvi's hand stays her. "Let the man work, *ji-ah?* Katar-*sahm's* mind might wander at times, but he has a good head for his work. He will see to your *mama.*" Her tone brooked no room for argument.

The little girl bows her head, accepting the elder's wisdom, but she continues to watch with the quiet worry of a child.

I brush against her once again, offering my steady and reassuring presence.

After all, there are few things that cannot be made better by the intervention of a cat. And none that cannot be improved if that cat just so happens to be me. But, alas, not all can be blessed to have myself as their watcher.

Such is the way of things.

"How long do you think you can house the girl and her mother, Sneha—no dickering, *ji-ah?* Just give me the answers. And, if it will cost?"

The young attendant shakes her head. "No-no, Maanvi. We can at least keep them for a set comfortably. But food and—"

Maanvi dismisses her. "T'ch. Food. I can do that well enough myself, and you see if I can't. I need them warm and safe. Once her mother is—"

Sarika pulls on a length of the shopkeeper's robe. "What do you mean? What do you want to do with *mama* and me?" Her mouth pulls into a frown that wishes not to betray what she is feeling within.

But I can see it plain enough. A deeper dread that comes with uncertainty, and now it involves her mother. That is not something Sarika can bear to have go wrong. Not after everything she has endured. And so she keeps to silent hope that things will be all right.

It will be all right, child. "Mrawow." I put a paw to one of her legs, pressing hard until her attention is on me, and not her fears.

But Maanvi speaks then to better assure her. "Nothing, sweet one. We are going to find you and your *mama* a home. Then, Mender-*sahm* will keep checking in and make sure she is doing well. Won't you, Katar!" Her voice now carries the crack of thunder, making it clear this is no question, but an expectation. "And I don't want to hear a piece of how many chips it will cost, *ji-ah?*"

"*Ji-ah*, Maanvi. She is weak. Malnourished. But the worst is a *jahaam* in her chest. A tightness—a thickness. It is not good, but I can help her. But we must bring her somewhere warm."

Maanvi snaps her fingers. "Then get to it. Go back to my shop, bring Ali here. He is good for more than just passing bowls to customers. We will carry her mother to your inn. Have them both settled, then we will see what comes next."

Something I too wonder about, but it is Sarika who voices the question.

"What do you mean?" She looks up at the older woman, waiting for an answer.

Maanvi rests a hand on Sarika's shoulder, giving her a gentle squeeze. "First, we're going to find you and your *mama* a new home for a while. Once you're warm and settled, and she's better, we will see about work. I can always use another cook, and there are always leftovers." She smiles, and it is one Sarika returns.

I stay by her side as time passes and the mender does his work, assuring us her mother will be fine. For that is a cat's duty. To be by your side, even when you are too limited to understand us.

And we know another secret truth of the world. That not all stories need legends and lies. Or action and adventure. Sometimes the best stories are of quiet companionship, of kindness lost and to be found.

...and, of course, the comfort only a cat can bring.

This is one of those stories.

This is mine.

My name is Shola.

And I am a cat.

Author Bio

R.R. Virdi is a USA Today Bestselling author, two-time Dragon Award finalist, and a Nebula Award finalist. He is the author of two urban fantasy series, The Grave Report, and The Books of Winter. The author of the LitRPG/portal fantasy series, Monster Slayer Online. And the author of a space western/sci fi series, Shepherd of Light. He has worked in the automotive industry as a mechanic, retail, and in the custom gaming computer world. He's an avid car nut with a special love for American classics.

The hardest challenge for him up to this point has been fooling most of society into believing he's a completely sane member of the general public.

Connect with R.R. Virdi at: rrvirdi.com

Junkyard Rex

By Sam Knight

Author's Note: This story, the first Abandoned Lands story to be published, takes place approximately twenty-five years before the upcoming novel, *A Girl and Her Velociraptor.*

WE ARE THE ABANDONED LANDS! Hugh Sanchez, sitting at his kitchen table, shook his head at the newsfeed headline on the cracked screen of his NetTab. He didn't need to read the article to know what it meant: there was no longer any hope of help coming from anywhere. The whole damned country had fallen apart, broken up by petty squabbles and stupidity. Some people were calling it the Social War because they thought it had all started on so-called social media, which, as far as Hugh was concerned, was nothing more than a modern-day propaganda machine. Hugh called it the Stupid War because people were stupid with a capital D for dumb. But the truth was, this was just the latest in a long string of different kinds of conflicts, both within what had been the States and without. He didn't have a GED, and even he understood that.

Texas and California had declared themselves independent countries—like they hadn't pretty much been that already—and a bunch of the East Coast states were calling themselves New America. And now some of the other states were calling themselves the North American Alliance or some other nonsense crap. But none of them were sending any kind of help to what was left of the central western states.

Why would they? Who had time for a bunch of empty prairie land decimated by a climate change-induced drought and infested with prehistoric creatures when there were lies to be told, wars to be fought, people to be killed, and money to be made?

Disgusted, Hugh tossed his NetTab down on the old Formica-topped table. He took a giant gulp of coffee, draining the stained mug down to dregs that hadn't had time to cool, and got up to put it in the stainless-steel sink. He'd eat later. Maybe at lunchtime. He didn't have the stomach for it now.

The Abandoned Lands sounded about right, he thought, picking up his straw cowboy hat and jamming it down over his thinning black hair. Kudos to whichever talking head had come up with that one. He kissed his fingertips and tapped them to the smiling faces in the photo hanging in the entryway where he could see it when he came in every night. His wife and two girls had been taken early in the wars by what was suspected to have been a man-made virus, before common folk even knew it was a war, back when things were just starting to get good and stupid.

He took a holstered .357 Magnum pistol from the shelf under their photo and clipped it to his belt, just behind his right hip, then he added a sheathed machete to his left side, adjusting the handle so it wouldn't hit his hand as he walked. Opening the front door to an early morning, he squinted into the barely risen sun, knowing it was going to be another hot one today. They were all hot ones anymore.

Hugh stepped out onto the three wooden steps leading up to his trailer home's door. He lifted a scuffed boot and stomped down hard on the peeling blue paint, sending dust billowing out around the ankles of his faded jeans. The hollow sound from the wooden box echoed out across the junkyard in front of him like a gunshot.

Nothing came running out from under his feet this time, and he grunted with satisfaction as he closed the door behind him. He couldn't hope to get rid of all the little prehistoric bastards, but he'd finally managed to put a dent in them with rattraps.

Stepping down into the dust, he kicked the top of the steps with the toe of his boot, knocking them over, and looked down at the trap he'd put under there. The not-lizard it had caught was long dead with dried blood around its head. It had probably been caught minutes after he'd reset the trap last night. A couple of flies were crawling over the filmy eyes and buzzing around the black tongue lolling out between rows of tiny, razor-sharp teeth.

And it stunk.

The only thing he could compare the nasty little bastards to would be a long-necked, featherless roadrunner that thought it was a t-rex, worthless little arms and all. Except these arms didn't end in hands; they came to a strange, one-claw point. And the only thing he could compare the stench of the reptilian vermin to was rotten chicken, which prevented him from even considering eating the nasty things.

Hugh did his best not to get a snootful of the stink as he dumped the sixteen-inch-long demonic critter out of the trap and into a plastic bucket.

He reset the trap with a piece of moldy chocolate granola bar from his pocket and put it back on the ground. As far as he could tell, it didn't matter what the traps were baited with, or that they had been reused over a dozen times and were stained with blood, these stupid little nippers would try it. He righted the stairs, covering the trap, and picked up the bucket, heading into what had once been the greatest junkyard in eastern Wyoming.

Hugh's grandfather, in a moment of brilliant inspiration, had bought a bunch of worthless land just outside the county landfill and set up shop as a junkyard, paying people for their scrap metal instead of charging them for it. It had worked out well, supporting the family for nearly seventy years. Until people stopped going to the dump. Until people had all but fled the country.

The Abandoned Lands.

That name fit well. Hugh nodded to himself as he checked the trap set between the twelve-foot-tall stacks of wooden pallets. He fished out another tiny dino or whatever it was, tossing it into the bucket on top of the other one and resetting the trap. Some folk, experts he supposed, but who the hell knew with all the bullshit on the Net, said the creatures weren't really dinosaurs, that their DNA had been messed with for military experiments.

Hugh picked up the foul-smelling bucket and headed for the trap set up in the row of old washers, dryers, ovens, and refrigerators.

It didn't matter if all of the weird things running around through Wyoming, Nebraska, Colorado, and Kansas were real dinosaurs, wooly mammoths, saber-toothed tigers, and thylacines or not: the bastards were dangerous, and they had spread quickly. Too quickly to keep them under control. Most people had fled the central western states over the last couple of years. Losing dogs and cats was one thing but losing kids was a different ballgame. Not to mention all the idiots who missed and shot other people instead.

Which had led to a new kind of lawlessness not seen since the Old West. And a failure of government and utilities. Food and water were scarce, gas and electricity even more so. And there was no help coming.

The Abandoned Lands.

Hugh couldn't shake the name from his thoughts. It fit too well. So well, it made him wonder if he oughtn't to have packed up and left long ago as well.

The trap inside the washing machine was empty for what Hugh thought was maybe only the second time ever. He didn't know if that was good or bad. It was tougher to reach, but then, the little bastards seemed to eventually get everywhere.

When he finished his rounds, the bucket was full. Tails, tiny-clawed feet, and sharp snouts stuck up above the rim, and he couldn't help but smell the stench now. He would have gagged, but he'd almost gotten used to it over the last couple of months, since the ankle-biters had finally taken down his dog, Junker, and started roaming the junkyard at will.

One of the little monsters was easy enough to deal with. Hugh could stomp a loner down with his boot if it didn't move fast enough, and Junker had easily chased them off in ones and twos for nearly two years. Five or six of them, though, became a problem, as they were fearless in a pack. As near as he could tell it had taken over a dozen of them to take down Junker, who, judging by the body parts Hugh had found, had taken at least seven of them with him.

The idea of getting another dog had only briefly passed through Hugh's mind. For starters, he didn't know if there were any dogs within a three-hundred-mile radius anymore, and, even if there were, he didn't think it would be fair to put another dog in that position. Not to mention the occasional ruined rattrap didn't tear Hugh's heart out the same way. The place had gotten awfully quiet and lonely after that, though.

Hugh reached the back end of the junkyard where the twelve-foot-high chain link fence sat atop a low ridge. His grandfather had always figured the drop-off was the hundred-year high-water line. Just inside the fence was a series of walls made up of stacks of crushed cars, extending a hundred yards in each direction. Hugh climbed a series of short wooden ramps leading up the piles of junked cars. Some cars were crushed into cubes, others pressed flat. A few had just been placed on top because his father had dreams of restoring them or thought they might be worth something someday.

Moving progressively higher until he was twenty feet up, Hugh walked to the edge and looked out over the fence. Across the dusty valley he could see the thin, winding line of trees following the near-dead river almost a mile away.

The rising sun was just hitting the low-lying trees, and the greenery was bright against the gray prairie. Hugh used to love this view, used to love to get out here first thing in the morning and sneak a cigarette and watch the sunrise before everyone else was up. He'd done it countless times as a boy, and then later, after he'd been caught and deemed old enough, with his father. But there were no more cigarettes now, no more father, and no more anyone else.

But there was the stench.

He swung the bucket out, tossing the contents over the fence, where they fell, slapping, and bouncing into the growing pile of rotting things below, startling other little nippers cannibalizing from the pile. At least eight of them, he thought. It was hard to tell. They were quick, darting into the shadows and blending in well. At least one squirmed its way deep into the pile of bodies like some kind of snake, disappearing impossibly fast, and Hugh wondered if they used those little toothpick-arms to pull themselves along somehow. That might explain where all the prairie dogs had gone.

The smell, already wafting up from the pile as the day warmed, would become a wall of stink, rising up like a tsunami when the heat of midday hit it, washing away the normal junkyard smells of old oil, rubber, and steel. Hugh needed to fire up the tractor and dig a hole and bury the mess again. He'd already done it four times since he'd lost Junker, moving the hole farther away from the junkyard each time as, even buried, it still seemed to attract more of the little demons.

But the more of them there were at the pile, the fewer there were in the junkyard.

He looked back out to the greenbelt in the distance, trying to find even half a moment of solace, of what had once been. But it wasn't there.

Maybe he should leave. Maybe he, too, should abandon the Abandoned Lands.

After a moment, he spotted something moving slowly in the distant brush and trees. At first Hugh thought it was a man with a giant backpack, but he'd stood in those bushes, and they were head-high on a man. They were only waist-high on the dark figure slowly stalking through.

Hugh squinted, trying to see better. He'd heard stories and seen photos of all kinds of monsters in the last couple of years, but, other than the pre-historic demon-rats, he'd only ever seen a few small, not-a-triceratops things and a wooly mammoth move through here. Everything else he'd ever laid eyes on had been already captured or killed and brought into town when he was there getting supplies.

This didn't look like any of them.

Twice as tall as a man, he was guessing, and maybe on two legs. But he couldn't make out a head or tail as it moved through the trees and thickets. Until it turned sideways to him.

The hair on the back of his neck rose, and Hugh stared, stunned, convinced he wasn't seeing what he thought he was. He wished he'd brought his binoculars or even his scoped rifle up with him, but he hadn't done that in months. Game had become scarce; he hadn't seen an antelope in over a year, and memories of hunting with his father haunted him if he sat up here too long.

But that did make him think of something.

He sat the bucket down and worked his way across the top of the pile of cars, toward the highest spot, the one his father had preferred. At the apex he found the red convertible his father had favored, had never had the heart to crush, thinking someday, when they had the extra money and time, they'd pull it down and fix it up. Memories of stargazing from the open top filled Hugh's mind as he stepped down into the mess of rat nests, rotted cushion foam, and rusty springs that were all that remained of the seats. The first time he and his wife had kissed had been here.

Somehow that felt properly reflected in the way things were now, too.

He jabbed his finger at the rusted, once chrome-plated button that opened the glovebox, finally giving up and smacking at it with his palm to make it let go. The glovebox door fell open to reveal a small pair of binoculars with an ancient pack of cigarettes on top of them. He pulled them both out and sniffed at the pack of smokes, unable to guess how old they were. He shoved them into his shirt pocket anyway and lifted the binoculars to his face. A small, square, foil packet stuck to the bottom of them scratched at his fingers and made him want to both laugh and cry as he peeled it off and saw the ring-shape under the wrapping. He flipped the no-longer needed trash out over the fence like a tiny Frisbee and raised the binoculars to his eyes again.

It took him a moment to find the creature and another to bring it into focus.

Hugh's jaw slowly gaped open as he stared through the lenses.

The creature's long, stiff tail was now clearly visible, and though he couldn't make them out individually, so were the six-inch, dagger-like teeth. When it turned, and he saw the tiny arms, there was no longer any doubt in his mind as to what it was.

He watched, fascinated, as the tyrannosaur haltingly picked its way through the trees and brush, occasionally stopping and cocking its head to the side like a robin looking for worms in a lawn. Hugh had no way of knowing if this was an actual rex or some other member of the family, but he knew it was big, and that they were rare. As soon as their existence had been confirmed, giant bounties had been placed on them by the government, for the protection of the people, and even bigger bounties had been offered by private citizens and companies.

The end result was the same. All, or apparently nearly all, had been wiped out.

Hugh tapped his wristphone to life and pulled up the camera, wishing he had the pocketphone with the better camera, but he hadn't carried it, or needed it, for two years. He held the lens up to the eyepiece of the binocular and started recording, watching the screen and trying to keep the beast in frame. There was a good chance he could make some money off the video, or maybe even selling information on where a hunter could find the tyrannosaur. He'd once read about a man who'd made over a billion dollars on one by selling parts on the black market in China. Information on where to find another one had to be worth something.

Intently watching the tiny screen, pointing the binoculars at the distant creature, Hugh did something he hadn't done on top of the car piles since he was a drunken teenager, thirty years ago: he lost his footing.

His boot slid forward on the slick, curved body of the convertible, and he windmilled his arms, leaning himself backward over the car, trying not to fall twenty feet onto the fence below. The binoculars flew from his hand, out somewhere into the junkyard behind him. Feeling his footing going out from underneath him, he lifted his knees to his chest, forcing himself to fall ass-first into the open well of the convertible, landing in the remains of the mangled seat, his shoulder slamming against the steering wheel.

The sound of the car horn blared out as pain shot through him, startling him, and it took Hugh a moment to overcome the shock enough to differentiate the two. He gasped, twisting to get himself off the steering wheel, and the noise finally stopped. His ears rang as he straightened out and tried to assess the damage to himself. He had a couple of sore spots, and a cut on his palm was bleeding pretty good for how small it was. It was probably from the rusty wireframe of the seat. At least it wasn't a puncture wound. He'd have to make sure he cleaned it out well. The last thing he needed out here was to get Tetanus.

As he wiped his bloody hand on the leg of his jeans and caught his breath, his eyes fell upon the newest part of the old car, a fifteen-year-old cigarette lighter sticking out of the dashboard plug, and he started laughing. It was a novelty item that had no real reason for existing. His father had installed the silly solar-powered accessory years ago, and it had never occurred to Hugh that the tiny trickle charge it made could have possibly kept a car battery alive for all these years.

He pushed the lighter into the socket and fished in his shirt pocket for the old cigarettes. He pulled one out and sniffed it. It was too dried out to smell, but the thought of tobacco was there, and it made his mouth water. He licked the seam as though he'd rolled a fresh one and then stuck it between his lips. When the lighter popped, he took it from the dash and held the glowing end to the cigarette and puffed, making the desiccated tobacco crackle as it caught and burned.

The pungent smoke filled his mouth before he inhaled it. It was harsh and burned his throat and he nearly choked on it, but the memories of what once had been flowed through him and he smiled. He took another puff and raised the cigarette to the morning sky. "Here's to you, Papi." Hugh took a long drag and laid his head back, blowing the smoke up in a white column and, despite the pain, feeling…okay…for the first time in a long time.

A strange snuffling sound broke his reverie.

Hugh sat up and leaned over the side of the convertible to see two large golden eyes, set deep under thick and menacing brow ridges, not more than a foot down from his own face. They looked back, laser-focused upon him. The rex—and Hugh was sure that's what it was now—was standing nearly straight up, easily towering over the twelve-foot fence and most of the lower stacks of cars.

Hugh swallowed, hard, but held still, his heart fluttering against his ribs like a moth trying to escape a screen door.

The monster inhaled deeply, nostrils opening wide, pulling in Hugh's scent. It lifted its head farther back, giving him too good of a view of its wicked teeth, and Hugh tensed for it to roar and attack, slamming against his tower of cars to knock them, and him, over.

Instead, it sneezed.

Hugh jumped—throwing himself back—and watched in slow motion as blood and the cigarette flew from his hand and spattered across the rex's snout, leaving dark, wet spots and sending up a shower of glowing sparks, making the monster blink in surprise.

Panic and thoughts of the creature having his scent literally in its nose spurred Hugh into movement, and he hopped out from the well of the car and raced back the way he'd come—the only way down the stacks of cars without jumping twenty feet.

Hugh could feel the rex pacing him, snorting and running right beside him at the fence line, and he feared being snatched out of the air with every stair-stepped block he dropped down. He flew past the plastic bucket and jumped wooden ramps, not daring to look back. When his boots hit the dirt, he found himself instinctively running for the trailer home, but some part of him realized it wouldn't stop that beast. The thin metal sides would tear like paper under that thing's massive jaws.

Changing direction, Hugh raced for the garage, wondering if dowsing himself in oil or gasoline would hide his scent. He knew his machete would be worthless, and the .357, even if the first three rounds hadn't been loaded with varmint shots for the little nippers, would just piss that thing off.

The garage door, sensing his approach, opened just in time for him to duck and roll in under the big door. Spotting that the tractor still had the forklift attachment on, Hugh suddenly had the mad idea of impaling the creature upon the forks before it could get to him, and he swung himself up into the cab and started the motor in one smooth motion.

A black cloud of exhaust floated down in front of the cab, billowing through the morning sunlight streaming in through the garage door. Hugh drove the tractor forward, hoping to take the tyrannosaur on before it got clever and circled around him or something. He broke out into the yard at full speed, wishing the tractor moved faster, and squaring up toward the way he'd come while raising the forks to what he guessed would be chest high. He slammed the brakes and waited, listening for the monster to come plowing through the rows of scrap metal after him.

The tractor's air conditioning kicked on and the motor dropped and then revved back up to compensate, vibrating the whole cab.

Hugh twisted his sweaty palms against the dirty rough spots of the otherwise smooth steering wheel. When he realized the radio was on, he jabbed a finger at the knob and turned it off, so he could listen for anything crashing around outside.

Though the motor rumbled, Hugh felt he was sitting in a dead silence. There was nothing moving outside the tractor. There was no sign the giant dinosaur was pursuing him.

He rolled the tractor forward, trying to get a better look through the rows of stacked cars. One of the little nippers, squawking like a scared blue jay, came running around the corner, looking more like a roadrunner than ever, and raced off toward the main gate.

Hugh tensed, waiting for the pursuer.

After a moment, when it didn't show, he pushed the accelerator and crept forward more, turning the wheels slightly so he could see farther down the rows. At the end, just beyond the fence, the tyrannosaur was nosing at the rancid pile Hugh had dumped there.

Hugh watched for a moment, heart racing. The size and sheer lethality of the creature was hard to comprehend. And the scars it bore, long jagged white ones to smaller lumpy spots Hugh assumed were from being shot, covered the length of its body from snout to tail tip.

After what felt like forever, Hugh's breathing calmed, and he put the forklift into reverse and slowly backed out of sight, hoping the rex would forget all about him and leave the area when it got done snacking on dead nippers.

Hugh slung the .30-06 rifle over his shoulder and adjusted the machete handle so it wouldn't hit the stock. He kissed his fingers and touched them to his family's photo. With a deep breath, he steeled himself and opened the front door into the morning sun.

He stood on the top of the wooden steps but couldn't bring himself to stomp down on them. As near as he could tell, the tyrannosaur had wandered off yesterday morning after eating its fill, but Hugh hadn't pushed too hard to find out. Instead, he'd spent the rest of the day sitting very quietly in the trailer and reading up on what was known about rexes.

There had only been eighteen of them confirmed to have existed—and killed. No one thought there were any more, and the occasional rumored sightings were disregarded as either exaggerations of what had become known as stalkers—man-sized troodonts, ambush predators, that walked on two legs and hunted in packs of two to five—or outright lies intended to bring hunters and money into dying towns. There weren't even official government bounties offered on them anymore.

There *was* a hundred-million-dollar reward offered by a private company for anyone who could bring them a live Tyrannosaurus rex.

Hugh walked down the wooden steps, self-conscious of the noise he made for the first time in years. A hundred million was a lot, but it might as well have been a reward for flying to the moon with construction-paper wings for all the chance he had of taking that thing alive on his own. He didn't want to take it on at all.

He drew his machete, not wanting to risk the sound of a gunshot, and lifted the wooden steps with the toe of his boot but didn't let them fall over. Nothing came rushing out, so he quietly dropped it back down, tapped it with the side of his blade a couple of times and lifted it again.

Still nothing.

Kneeling and, against his better judgment, but not willing to make noise, Hugh lifted the steps with his hand and peeked under. The trap was undisturbed. He set the steps down and walked into the junkyard, listening to the crunch of gravel under his boots and wondering if it had always been so loud and what he'd been thinking about to not have noticed it in the past.

The trap at the pallets had caught another one. The giant mousetrap design seemed perfect for nabbing long-necked lizards as they reached in for a bite of food. He left it be and didn't bother to check any of the others, instead heading toward the back of the junkyard where he'd left his bucket on top of the car stack yesterday. He sheathed his machete when he got there, flexing sore fingers that had been gripping it too tightly, and quietly began ascending.

At the top, he found his bucket. Next to it were a couple spots of blood he must have dropped from his hand as he'd run by. He'd cleaned and bandaged the wound yesterday but hadn't thought to clean up the rest of the mess. What if the rex came back and ate the damned tractor because the cab smelled like his blood?

His chore list suddenly gained a new priority.

Hugh looked down to where he'd been dumping the buckets. The remnants of the pile were still hidden in the early morning shadows and hard to see. As far as he could tell, it had been nearly cleaned up, and the smell was gone but replaced by something a bit mustier and more pungent.

A crater-like depression in the dirt indicated a large amount of liquid had been dumped there, and Hugh hoped the rex hadn't been marking its territory. The footprints all around the area reminded him of turkey prints—if the turkey had fat, size two-thousand feet.

Turkeys were something else Hugh hadn't seen in a long time. The thought made him sad. He didn't know where the pre-historic creatures had come from—military experiments, if the rumors were to be believed—but the effects, even beyond the people fleeing the country, were obvious.

Looking out to the river, he wondered if the rex was still out there, somewhere, hidden in the trees. How far away was that? A mile? And when Hugh had accidentally sounded the horn, it had made it to him in, what, less than a minute? And Hugh hadn't heard a thing until it was damn-near sniffing his hair.

The thought chilled him.

Without the pile to keep them distracted elsewhere, and maybe because of the new smell outside the fence, the ankle-nippers were in the junkyard in force, and Hugh finally began setting the traps three times a day to try to keep the numbers down. He wasn't sure what they were eating, if anything, that kept them coming here. Maybe they just liked the artificial shelter, as the mice, rats, and rabbits once had.

But mice, rats, and rabbits didn't jump out and try to bite him as he worked to strip metals from the old machinery, and Hugh hated the little bastards. They'd gotten him a couple of times in the past, and their bites always seemed to get infected. Needless to say, finding a quiet corner to take a leak was a thing of the past.

His dump truck was almost full now, and he'd make a trip in another day or two to trade the copper wire, circuit boards, catalytic converters, and other miscellaneous precious metals and parts for supplies. More rattraps were on the top of his list, as well as some kind of perimeter security. The one he had now couldn't tell a car from a cow, not that he'd seen either out here in nearly a year, but he wanted to know what he was dealing with before he went outside if the rex ever came back. It wouldn't be cheap, but at this point sleep wasn't exactly coming cheap either.

Between rampaging thoughts of the rex and wondering if it was just time to give up and pack up, Hugh felt lost.

He'd heard a new trading post had sprung up near Cheyenne, which would be twice as far, but it would be an easier drive, and supposedly it paid better because of the direct route to Denver down I-25, so he was considering trying that, though he was a bit worried about bandits and pissing off his established contacts in Rapid City. But if it paid well enough…maybe he would just keep right on driving afterward. Spend the night in Denver, and then, who knows. Maybe continue on to whatever the hell Texas was calling itself now. Or maybe Mexico. There weren't any dinos in Mexico yet, as far as he knew.

Bucket full again, he made his third trip of the day to the top of the car wall and poured the floppy contents out into the growing pile. The late afternoon sun was brutal, and in his eyes, so his view of the river trees was limited, but he stared out at them anyway, knowing it was silly, knowing he would always look to see if the rex was there now, despite the fact a creature that large couldn't possibly stay in one place and support itself on the meager hunting available in such a small area.

He sat the bucket down and fished into his shirt pocket for the ancient pack of cigarettes. There were only three left now, and a new pack was the third thing on his supplies list. He hadn't expected to enjoy them so much after years of not smoking, but each one seemed to carry with it a bit of a memory, seemed to bring a tiny bit of peace to his soul that he hadn't ever expected to feel again, and made him feel closer to his father.

Besides, he was pretty sure his chances of dying of old age out here were close to nothing.

He put the cigarette in his lips and the pack back into his pocket and walked the rest of the way up to the convertible and the folding lawn chair he'd set up over the ruined seat to watch the sunset last night. Stepping down into the car, he pushed in the lighter and waited for it to pop out before lighting his smoke and settling into the chair with the rifle across his lap.

After a couple of puffs, and blowing a smoke ring that broke apart in the still air, he assessed himself. And he didn't like it. His calm serenity, his acceptance of what was, of having lost what had been, was gone. It had been replaced by a constant, nagging fear that the rex was going to tear through the side of his mobile home at any time in the middle of the night, looking for the chewy center.

Hugh hadn't thought much about his own death up until now. After his family had died, he'd carried on as best he could, knowing they were watching him from above and that he'd be with them someday. So, he'd kept on doing what he thought was right: living his life and waiting for his time to be with them again. But now he was haunted by the thought that maybe it was time to go, time to leave the family legacy—what there was left of it—behind.

Between that and the rex… This was different from the quiet life he'd been living. This was like having been led to the gallows and waiting for some unseen person to show up and pull the lever at some random, unknown time.

As he sat there, his quiet fear turned into frustration and then anger, simmering in the sun until it boiled over. "Shit!" He picked up the rifle and slammed the butt against the steering wheel, cursing the horn that had lured the rex here. The horn sounded as he hit it, and hit it again, and a third time.

Rage spent, and feeling more stupid than angry now, Hugh laid the rifle back across his lap and took another drag off the smoke. He wasn't normally prone to anger, let alone outbursts, and his ears burned with shame under his straw hat as he wondered what his wife, his daughters, would think of him now: an angry coward ready to quit.

The silence became oppressive. Even the flies seemed to have been chased off by his behavior.

He reached out to the dashboard and flipped open the old ashtray. Crushing the cigarette out in it, he dropped the butt on top of the other ancient butts, most smoked by his father, and felt the emptiness inside of him grow from being so close to something touched by one of his family, but still being so far, so impossibly far away from all of them. Tears welled in his eyes. He didn't bother to wipe them away.

After they dried on his cheeks in the afternoon heat, he stood up, carefully holding the hilt of his machete so it wouldn't catch on the arm of the chair, and climbed out of the convertible. He took two steps before he saw the rex feeding at the pile.

The sinewy muscles down its back rippled and moved like steel cables under its dappled hide as it nosed the pile and gingerly picked nippers up with its teeth. Hugh didn't know much about anything when it came to dinos, but looking at all of the scars and the defined shapes of ribs on its sides, he figured this creature had been through hell and back and had come out malnourished

It raised its head slightly, still chewing, and glanced at him, as though it had known he was there all along, before it bent back to scoop up the last of the pile. When it had downed the small mouthful, it snuffled around the ground for a moment and then stood tall, meeting Hugh's eyes.

Hugh held still, assuming that if he ran, the predatory instinct would kick in and it would chase him, just as dogs did.

The rex took one step closer, unblinkingly holding Hugh's gaze with its golden eyes. Unlike the cold, black eyes of the nippers, the rex's glittered with an intelligence Hugh hadn't expected. It sniffed at him, snorted, and then turned to slowly amble away, not looking back.

"PRESS GANGS ROAM THE ABANDONED LANDS!" The NetTab headline had to be clickbait, but Hugh followed the link anyway as he sipped his coffee. If there were really press gangs, surely he'd have heard something about it when he'd been to Dino Town to trade goods yesterday.

The article was nothing but rumor and speculation about people who'd disappeared possibly being forced into the Texas Army. But people disappeared all the time, most just up and leaving, and Hugh regretted wasting his time reading it.

On the other hand, driving all the way to Dino Town, as the pop-up trading post was being called, had not been a waste of time. It had been a great success. The town had been there longer than he'd thought and was well established, which made him wonder if the traders in Rapid City intentionally never talked about it. Which made sense, as they were business competitors, of a sort.

He'd gotten nearly twice as much as he'd expected for his haul and had come back loaded with supplies. And a new security system.

It had been tempting to take the money and go, but the better earnings made him think twice. If he could pocket the extra money from four or five more trips, he'd have enough to establish himself somewhere instead of throwing his fate to the wind and hoping for the best. Not to mention he'd met a dino farmer—someone who was raising them and selling them—who was doing all right for himself. Well enough to make Hugh consider whether it would be feasible out here as well.

Though who the hell would buy nippers, which was all he had, he couldn't begin to guess.

He closed the uninformative article and opened the new security app. Thirty small vids appeared on the NetTab screen at once, each too small to make out what they were showing, but each showing a different part of the junkyard, both inside and out. One vid flashed a yellow outline, and he tapped on it to expand it to fill the screen. It was a high view of the trailer home and the garage, taken from a camera he'd placed up on an old power pole. A little nipper, slowly walking out from behind the garage, had its outline highlighted as the AI tracked it and listed its size, estimated weight, speed, distance from Hugh, and, to Hugh's surprise, its species: *Parvicursor remotus.*

Hugh tapped the name and a pop-up gave him information on what was known of the feeding and nesting habits, as well as its currently recognized range and a warning of danger if they were in a pack. It also asked if he wanted more information and if he wanted to report it or call for assistance.

A grin crept across Hugh's face. His family had never been able to afford a household AI, and while this wasn't really one of those, it was the closest he'd ever come. It made him feel affluent to have such a luxury, and he continued to watch as the AI tracked the nipper around the junkyard and then picked up and followed the motions of two more as they approached the junkyard fence line.

Sliding the app from the NetTab to his wristphone, Hugh marveled at how smoothly it placed him on the map of the junkyard and showed where the three nippers were in relation to him, still tracking their movements.

He took a deep breath and let it out, feeling tension go with it. He was going to walk out the front door without fearing for his life for the first time in nearly two weeks.

The pile of dead nippers was getting big enough Hugh was considering getting the tractor out. The size of the heap wasn't the real problem though. The smell was starting to waft all the way to the house and, in the evenings, not having the windows open to cool the trailer home was not an option.

He sat the bucket down and looked out to the treeline, wondering if the rex was out there somewhere. An idea crossed his mind, and he worked his way up to the convertible. Taking a seat, and lighting a fresh cigarette from a new pack, he settled in and pulled up the security app on his wristphone.

Yellow dots, four of them now, slowly moved around the tiny map of the junkyard, but none were anywhere near his own blue dot at the edge of the screen.

Hugh took a long drag off the cigarette and then reached out and pushed the car horn button on the steering wheel three times. Chuckling at how quickly the yellow dots scattered, he folded his hands across the .30-06 resting in his lap and waited.

He hadn't seen the rex since he'd installed the security system, and there was no reason for him to believe it was still anywhere nearby, but this was a win-win situation, he told himself. If it was still around, maybe it would clean up that mess for a third time. If it wasn't, well, honestly, that would put him more at ease than the new security system had.

Finishing the cigarette while he waited, Hugh saw nothing out on the prairie, and nothing appeared on the wristphone screen.

Both relieved and disappointed, he got up and worked his way down the wall of cars. His wristphone beeped once and flashed to get his attention. One of the nippers was moving in a path, projected by the AI with a dotted yellow line, that would intersect his own, a blue dotted line, if he kept heading in the same direction.

He neared the bottom of the car wall, getting ready to head for the tractor, and he drew his machete anyway, oddly excited to have the cautionary information. Musing over the idea of using the app to hunt down the nipper, Hugh wiped sweat from his brow and decided it was too hot to play silly games. The traps seemed to get them all eventually, and it would be nice to not have the house stink tonight when he opened the windows to try to get a breeze moving through.

As he moved toward the garage, and the projected paths no longer crossed, the warning on the wristphone winked out. He sheathed the machete.

Thinking about resting in the air-conditioned tractor cab and cooling off for a few minutes after the job was done, he decided to grab a water bottle. Before he'd even changed directions to the trailer home, the wristphone alarm went off again, this time silently, but flashing and vibrating on its strongest setting. Hugh glanced at it. A giant, red exclamation mark inside of a triangle flashed on the screen. He tapped it and words quickly scrolled across. WARNING: REX NEARBY. SILENT MODE ENGAGED. QUICKLY AND QUIETLY SEEK SHELTER.

The words began to repeat, and Hugh, heart racing, quickly tapped the screen and pulled up the map. The rex wasn't marked anywhere inside the junkyard. He pulled up the grid of tiny vids and found one flashing with another red exclamation mark. Expanding that, he spotted the rex, outlined in red by the AI, running toward the junkyard from a distant part of the greenbelt. Information, in text almost too small to read, followed it: TYRANNOSAURUS REX: 3.7M H X 12.2M L: EST. 6100.34KG: 34.3KMH: DISTANCE: 2.5KM (-).

CALL FOR HELP? repeatedly flashed in red at the bottom of the screen.

Hugh watched, shocked and amazed at the rate the rex was closing the distance to the junkyard. He'd read they couldn't properly run because they were too large, but it moved fast enough it really didn't matter what technical term its gait had.

Another red warning flashed across the screen: DISTANCE: 2.2KM (-). CALL FOR HELP?

Hugh hesitated. There wasn't anyone out here to call for help, and he didn't want to hurt the thing anyway. It wasn't like it had been stalking him. He was the idiot who had called it in.

Just in case, he ran to the tractor, fired it up, and raised the forks to chest-high on the rex. He slowly pulled out of the garage until he could see down the aisles.

When the rex showed up at the pile, Hugh could have sworn it was wagging its tail.

The security system recordings of the rex were way beyond anything else Hugh had seen on the Net, and he was sure he could make a decent amount of money with them. The quality and resolution were good, and the rex stayed well in frame for long periods of time as it fed on the nipper pile.

Watching the vids through for the umpteenth time, Hugh became convinced that three things were not his imagination.

First, the rex *had* been wagging its tail. But it was not a friendly, excited thing, like a dog. It was a reflex, likely designed to distract other predators and protect the rex while it was feeding. This was evident at how much faster and wider the tail swung about when a couple of live nippers tried to sneak up to get bites out of the pile. Quick as they were, the rex still managed to snap one out of the air as it tried to leap to safety.

Second, the rex was definitely malnourished. Though he knew next to nothing about rexes, and there was little to be found about their health, other photos and vids he found did not show such prominent ribs. And, now that he wasn't nose-to-nose with the beast, the vid showed him that its hipbones stuck out way too much for any healthy animal, no matter what it was.

As interesting as those things were, it was the third that bothered Hugh the most: the rex's response to the cameras. It didn't just know where they were, it seemed to know *what* they were.

Hugh watched the vids one more time, tracking how the rex had circled the junkyard and stopped to look directly into each perimeter camera—even the ones located highest up on the old power poles. Each time, the beast bowed its head low, scraped an enormous furrow into the earth with its right foot, and then looked back into the camera before moving on.

The whole thing gave Hugh the heebie-jeebies. Was it thanking him, or was it showing him it knew where his territory was, and he'd damned sure better stay inside it?

Hugh honked the car horn, lit a cigarette, and waited, looking out toward the trees. The pile of nippers below him was covered in a white, dusty coating of powdered vitamins. He'd purchased them from the dino farmer he'd met during his previous visit to Dino Town. He'd had to ask around a bit, but it hadn't taken long to track the man down and get some well needed, if circuitously asked, advice.

The worst part had been the extra couple hours it had added to the drive in order to reach the farmer's "dino ranch," which had been on past the ruins of Laramie a bit. But that had worked out well in the end, as evidenced by the four-hundred pound protoceratops carcass lying on top of the nipper pile. Hugh had arrived just as the farmer had been about to bury it. Killed by a pack of stalkers before the ranch hands could get there, the 'ceratops was no longer fit for human consumption.

But it was perfect for Hugh's needs.

When Hugh's watch vibrated, he was surprised to find the rex coming in from the other side of the junkyard where there was nothing but prairie for miles on end. Tempted to get down and go watch remotely, or hide, he chided himself, Hugh instead took another drag off his cigarette and stood his ground, waiting.

It hadn't been a hard decision to try to help the rex. Sure, he'd wrestled with the idea of money—and it was a possibility of a *hell* of a lot of money—but basic decency had won the argument even before he'd really given it a good thinking on. Hugh couldn't, in good conscious, lead hunters to the creature. Judging by the scars, they'd found it several times before.

Nor could he ignore the fact that it didn't seem well. Starving maybe. Something else wrong maybe. There probably wasn't a whole lot he could do about any of that, but he could try.

The rex rounded the edge of the fence and immediately stopped, locking eyes with Hugh. Hugh could feel in his soul that he'd been seen. He wished he'd run back to the trailer to watch from the vidscreen when he'd had the chance, but it was too late now.

Cocking its head, the rex took a cautious step forward. Hugh slowly raised his cigarette and took a drag. After a moment the rex came slowly forward, sniffing at the air, moving more quickly as it neared the nipper pile with the 'ceratops on top of it. At the edge of the carrion pile, it sniffed at the white powder all over everything. It snorted, raised its head, and caught Hugh's gaze again.

Hugh could feel the accusation in the piercing eyes. How a giant lizard monster could have feelings behind its eyes, he couldn't say, but there it was.

"It's vitamins," Hugh said, feeling his shaky voice sounded puny and lost as it floated down from the top of the cars toward the imposing rex. "Good for you. You should eat it all."

The rex held frozen for a moment, as if shocked Hugh had spoken to it, and Hugh wondered if anything ever intentionally made noises around a t-rex.

The rex snorted again, dropped its head, and slowly gouged a long furrow into the ground with its right foot before looking back up to meet Hugh's eyes.

Hugh swallowed hard and nodded back.

The rex leaned over the pile and nosed the 'ceratops. Suddenly, with a quick snap of its massive jaws, the rex bit the calf-size 'ceratops in half and began to eat greedily.

Hugh, listening to the bones snap like twigs and thinking how stupid he'd been to allow the rex to get anywhere near him, quickly and quietly worked his way down the car wall and back to his trailer.

The NetTab, the vidscreen on the wall, and Hugh's wristphone all flashed to life at the same time, blinking red warning symbols, filling the dark bedroom with flashing light and a buzzing warning tone. Hugh jerked upright in his bed, heart suddenly racing. He'd been dreading this moment for weeks, waiting for the rex to come skulking about in the middle of the night to rip open the trailer home and snatch him out of his bed, shaking him apart like dog with a ragdoll.

He'd been a fool tempting fate and feeding the monster, teaching it there was food to be found around the junkyard. He was out of bed, pulling on pants, and then grabbing for guns when the buzzing stopped and the screens all dimmed, nearly leaving him in the dark. A warning began scrolling across the screens. He stepped closer to read it. WARNING: FIREARMS DETECTED. MALICIOUS INTENT POSSIBLE. SILENT MODE/DARK MODE ENGAGED. QUICKLY AND QUIETLY SEEK SHELTER. CALL FOR HELP?

Hugh frowned and tapped the vidscreen to enlarge the camera feeds while avoiding the call for help button. Finding the vid feed outlined in red, he expanded it. If it weren't for the AI's glowing yellow outlines, he wouldn't have realized the swirling mess he was looking at was two vehicles coming down the road with normal headlights off and several infrared spotlights sweeping back and forth like stiff, wooden legs on a giant spider. Rifle barrels, sticking out of the passenger windows, were outlined in red.

DISTANCE: 1.6 KM (-). CALL FOR HELP?

Ignoring the text, Hugh finished clipping the .357 and the machete to his belt before grabbing the .30-06. Feeling a bit calmer now that he knew it wasn't the rex, he headed for the front door, grabbing a pair of night-vision binoculars off the shelf as he went by and out into the stifling heat of the still night.

Dino hunters were rare but not unheard of, though there hadn't been any passing through here in a long time. Scavengers were rarer, as there wasn't anything out here to take for miles and miles, but they were more dangerous, often willing to kill to take people's property. He wasn't worried about that, though. Scavengers rarely traveled at night, spotlights or no. It was too easy to miss the treasures of abandoned things in the dark and too easy to stumble upon a nest full of things with nasty teeth.

Hugh could hear the motors of the approaching vehicles in the distance. He broke into a jog, hoping to get up on top of the garage, where he could get a good look at them on the road as they went past. He was halfway to the garage when his wristphone vibrated. Glancing at it, he saw the warning that he was on an intercept course with a yellow dot; one of the nippers. He drew his machete and kept moving.

The map on the wristphone turned out to be very accurate. It zoomed in as he got closer to the yellow dot, enlarging the immediate area around him until his blue dot became recognizable as a human figure and the yellow dot looked like a skinny, long-tailed chicken.

Hugh slowed at the corner of the garage, where the little nipper had stopped moving, apparently waiting to see what was coming toward it instead of fleeing from the sound of his approach.

A lightning-fast shadow flashed out of the dark, lunging at Hugh. He barely saw it coming, despite knowing it was there, and swung the machete out at it. He felt it connect near his hand, almost at the pommel, knocking the little monster down. With a kick against Hugh's boot, the nipper silently ran off into the night, vanishing somewhere around the old car crusher.

Hugh paused a second to take a deep breath and calm himself. Without the security system AI watching over him, he would have likely lost a finger that time. He'd never seen a nipper that aggressive singly, but then, he didn't usually wander around at night.

Checking the wristphone and seeing that no more were near, he sheathed the machete and took a step forward, feeling his boot kick something and send it rolling.

He paused to look down and spotted the nipper's severed head lying in the dust, its mouthful of nasty teeth gleaming in the dark and still opening and closing. Looking toward where the body had run off to, Hugh wondered how far it would get. Something to think about some other time, he chided himself and resumed his jog to the ladder.

The metal ladder, bolted to the outside wall of the garage, creaked and popped under his weight as he pulled himself up, trying not to let the rifle butt bang against the aluminum siding. The last thing he wanted was to make a bunch of noise and attract attention to himself. He couldn't hear the motors of the vehicles anymore, which meant it was likely they had stopped nearby and would easily hear any loud noise he made.

Having been distracted by the nipper, he wasn't exactly sure when he'd stopped hearing the motors, but he assumed they had to be close. Maybe even at the front gate.

He hadn't seen anyone out here in months, and no casual passers-by in over a year. And with those guns and spotlights, the only thing Hugh could think of was that they were dino hunters and they'd somehow heard about the rex, although he didn't know how. He hadn't said anything about it to anyone and didn't think there was anyone else around this area to have seen it. He was also pretty sure the AI wouldn't have reported it unless he had called for help, but then, there were a lot of people who didn't trust AIs.

Other than the rex, there was little reason for dino hunters to have stopped at his place, which added credence to the scavenger theory, which meant they might be more dangerous than he'd hoped. Unless they were stopping to ask him if he'd seen the rex.

Hugh shook off the worthless circular thoughts and pulled himself up onto the roof, staying on his belly, and crawling his way to the peak just in case anyone was watching the junkyard through infrareds and decided to take a pot-shot at something moving. Worse and stupider things had happened in the last few years. Especially out here in the *Abandoned Lands*.

He checked his wristphone again. Two red dots were now situated in a place Hugh knew seemed to be a blind spot when you drove up, and it made him wonder if they were trying not to be seen.

He lifted the night vision binoculars to his eyes and searched in the direction the map had showed them to be. All the infrared spotlights were off, which surprised him, but what surprised him more were the men, in leg irons, hopping down from the backs of what appeared to be large, armored trucks. Other men with rifles, looking and acting like prison guards, were helping as much as pushing the prisoners out of the trucks. When the captives—all nine of them—were lined up along the fence Hugh's gut tightened in fear at the thought of what he was seeing happen.

A voice, one of the guards Hugh assumed, carried angrily, forcefully through the night, but Hugh couldn't make out what was said. His wristphone gently vibrated, but he ignored it.

When the line of prisoners began fumbling at their pants and urinating on the fence, Hugh felt tension flow out of him. He didn't know why he'd thought it was going to be a mass execution, but he had.

Turning his binoculars to the trucks, Hugh looked for any markings that might tell him who these people were, but he couldn't find any.

More gruff words, and the prisoners began hurrying to finish and forming lines back into the trucks. One of the prisoners slipped off the tailgate and fell back to his knees. A guard cursed and slammed a rifle butt between the man's shoulder blades, knocking him the rest of the way over. The cry of pain carried clearly through the night. When the man didn't stand back up quickly enough, the guard kicked him in the ribs, sending him tumbling out of the way of the other prisoners.

Hugh's wristphone vibrated again.

The guard's voice was rough and his motions quick as another prisoner tried to intervene and got a rifle butt to the face for his trouble. Gesturing with his gun, the guard harried the others back on the truck. When they were all aboard, he turned back to the last two prisoners, the first of which had just gotten himself off the ground. The guard drew a pistol and Hugh's night vision binoculars flashed white with too much light.

The report reached Hugh's ears and the image returned just in time for Hugh to see the prisoner topple backward and lay still.

Hugh's wristphone began vibrating wildly, but he ignored it. His heart was pounding even more violently. He'd never seen a man killed before. And that was in cold blood. Unprovoked. Without reason.

He didn't know who these men were, but they certainly weren't dino hunters or scavengers and, for all the terrible things he'd heard over the years, he didn't think any prison guard or lawman would have done what he'd just seen. Not even out here in the Abandoned Lands.

Three other guards, coming running from around the sides of the trucks, guns ready at the sound of the shot, quickly converged on the shooter, who was shoving the remaining prisoner back into the truck. Angry and confused exclamations reached Hugh's ears. The shooter put his pistol away and waved the others off, his replies too low to hear. One of the other guards, tensed with angry body language, stayed in the shooter's face and angrily pointed back toward the body.

No, Hugh realized, he wasn't pointing to the body. He was pointing to Hugh's house.

Hugh lowered the binoculars from his eyes so he could look out over the whole area. He couldn't see anything in the night, but his wristphone began vibrating in S.O.S code. He looked down at it.

DANGER: RESIDENTIAL BREACH DETECTED. GUNSHOT DETECTED. HOMICIDE SUSPECTED. MALICIOUS INTENT LIKELY. CALL FOR HELP?

Hugh tapped the screen to pull up the map and was shocked to see a red dot inside his trailer home. One of the men had invaded his home. He zoomed in until the dot looked like a man, and the man looked like he had a gun drawn and was going room to room, searching.

A sharp whistle caught Hugh's attention and he looked back to the trucks. Unable to see them in the dark, he lifted the night vision binoculars up and was confused to find only a white screen. It only took a second for Hugh to realize someone had an infrared spotlight on him, but it was a second too long.

The bullet stuck his shoulder, knocking the binoculars from his hands and sending him falling back, sliding down the slick metal roof.

His right arm numb, Hugh desperately scrabbled with his left hand for something, anything to grab onto, but he kept sliding. A sudden, sharp blow to the back stopped him, snapping something on the rifle across his back and spinning him around at the top of the ladder, leaving him gasping as he caught the top rail and found himself hanging off the edge of the roof.

Running footsteps crunched gravel in the darkness, and Hugh knew he only had seconds until someone arrived.

He swung a foot until he found a ladder rung and then put his weight on it. When he tried to use his right hand, his arm moved, but it didn't move right, didn't have any strength, and he couldn't control it. Using only his left, he went down the ladder two and three rungs at a time, heedless of the noise. His grip slipped and he fell the last six feet.

The footsteps were almost upon him.

Hugh sprinted deeper into the junkyard, away from the approaching footsteps, and into the darkness where he hoped their infrared spotlights didn't reach. He dodged squat washing machines and pallets of alternators, running by memory more than actually being able to see, trying to figure out where to go, how to get away.

He couldn't stay in the junkyard. Though he knew the layout, they had the advantage of numbers, time, and, in the dark, those infrared spotlights. Sooner or later, they would find him.

There were only two gates out of the junkyard, one near where the trucks had parked, and one on the other side of the yard, neither of which Hugh could reach without going back toward the men. That only left the fence. He would have to climb it and hope he could escape into the night before they realized where he'd gone

Pressed up against an old shipping container he used for storing tools, he paused to tap his wristphone, pulled up the home app, and opened the garage door, hoping to buy a few minutes by making the men think he'd somehow gone in there.

CALL FOR HELP? flashed across the screen. HOMICIDE SUSPECTED. MALICIOUS INTENT LIKELY.

Hugh was tempted, but he had no idea who the AI would or even could call for help, and for all he knew, these men were supposed to be the new local help.

He closed the app and did his best to move silently and, he hoped, invisibly toward the fence, using the rattling sound of the opening garage door as cover. When the door silenced, Hugh could still hear people moving around, and some whispered voices somewhere behind him, but nothing sounded close.

Reaching the rows of stacked cars, he picked an aisle and headed down it, trying to make sure there were no straight lines of sight between him and where he thought the men were. He changed rows twice and then froze when his boot hit something, kicking it across the dirt with a scuffing sound.

He'd picked up all the loose odds and ends years ago, clearing the path so tires wouldn't get punctured, so he was surprised to have kicked something in the dark. He leaned closer, trying to make it out. It was the binoculars he'd dropped from the convertible weeks ago.

They weren't night vision, but they'd come in handy when he was trying to decide if it was safe to come back. He scooped them up with his good hand and hurried on.

The feeling was returning to his injured arm, and it hurt like hell. By the time he reached the fence, he was sure it wasn't a major wound. The bullet seemed to have grazed him between his neck and his shoulder, which led him to believe whoever fired the bullet had been going for a headshot. But the wound was still enough to stop him from climbing the fence. He just couldn't pull himself twelve feet up with only one arm.

Frustrated, hearing more voices and movement, he knew he had to get out. He was sure they'd figured out he wasn't in the garage by now and were searching the junkyard. He was just as sure they'd kill him, if for no other reason than they knew he'd seen one of them kill a prisoner.

There weren't any weak places in the fence to push through. He'd spent too much time fixing and patching it, which he now regretted for the first time. He would have to get over it somehow, and the only way other than climbing was to jump over from higher up.

He changed direction and headed for the ramps up to where he dumped the nipper bucket every morning. The wooden ramps creaked under his weight as he worked his way up, eyeballing the top of the fence in the dark as he got higher. He would have to jump out three feet and try to catch himself on it, and it would be a twelve-foot fall if he missed the fence, but he'd be over it and out into the night.

The junkyard floodlights came on, and Hugh froze midstride across a crushed car, nearly blinded. The men must have found the switch in the garage. Hugh hadn't used them or even thought about them in forever; they took up too much of the battery reserve.

Shouts filled the air, followed by gunshots and Hugh reflexively crouched, expecting bullets. But the sounds were moving away from him.

He stayed low and climbed higher, watching for pursuit. He spotted men with rifles running back toward the trailer home, and then there were muzzle flashes from beyond, out where the trucks were parked. He heard the reports from the gunshots a moment later and searchlights, white ones this time, came on from the vehicles.

Prisoners, hobbled in their shackles, were trying to escape out into the prairie. A spotlight found one and stayed on him until a shot rang out and the man went down, shot in the back. The spotlight swung wide and searched for another. When the light found a prisoner, the hobbled man froze and threw his hands up into the air in surrender.

A bullet tore through his back before he could turn around.

Hugh grit his teeth, his soul becoming a black acid pit. He didn't know who these men were, but they'd invaded his home and shot him first, and he couldn't stand by and watch them murder any more people.

He unslung the .30-06 and brought it around to shoot. The scope was smashed, useless. Worse, it prevented him from sighting down the barrel. Holding the rifle between his knees, he tried to work the damaged scope off with his good hand.

Another gunshot rang out, and Hugh looked up to see the spotlight on another man who was already face down in the dirt.

Hugh slapped at the scope, trying to break it off, but it was solid. He gave up and raised the rifle, trying to see if he could even guess how to aim around it. Before he could find a target, a hissing sound flew by his head, quickly followed by the distant report of the shot. He spotted the man standing on the blue steps to the trailer pointing a rifle up at him. The muzzle flashed and Hugh threw himself down into the shadows cast by the wooden ramp.

A bullet cracked into the metal somewhere near him, sending a small shockwave through the crushed car. He couldn't see the gunman anymore, but he couldn't stay hidden here either. Another bullet hit. Voices shouted. Footsteps moved toward him.

Hugh looked out at the top of the fence, brightly lit in the flood lights. It was three feet away and, if he stood, it was at head height. He could make that. If he hadn't been shot in the arm. If they didn't already know where he was. If it weren't lit up.

If it weren't lit up.

Hugh turned to his wristphone, ignoring the suggestion to call for help, and opened the home app again. Another bullet hit. A voice, the words clear now, called out, "I've got him pinned down!"

Footfalls came quickly, closing in.

Hugh found the light controls and shut the floodlights off.

Even as the bright lights still faded, he jumped up and scrambled higher up the cars. Someone else's feet hit the bottom wooden ramp, the sounds like pistol shots into Hugh's heart. There was no way he was going to outrun them. Even if he jumped the fence, they'd still be right on top of him now.

But what if he didn't jump the fence?

With a grunt of pain, Hugh tossed the worthless .30-06 out into the dark, as far out over the fence as he could. It landed with a satisfying thud and bounce, and the footfalls behind him stopped. Holding his breath, and trying not to make a sound, Hugh tossed the binoculars after the rifle. The sound of it hitting was quieter, but farther away.

"He jumped the fence!"

A metallic clanging filled the night, and, as Hugh's eyes finally began to re-adjust to the dark, he spotted a man going over the top of the chain-link fence.

A small flashlight flickered on, and the man waved the beam back and forth until it landed on the rifle. "He went this way," the man said quietly. "I need infrared over here."

Hugh, crouched down and trying not to so much as breathe, assumed the man was speaking into a microphone.

After a moment, the man spoke again, saying "Roger that," and then turned off his light and squatted down in the dirt.

Quick footsteps approached from within the junkyard and then stopped at what Hugh figured was the fence line. "You climb this, Ty-man?"

"Like a monkey. Hurry up, he's got a lead on us by now."

"Screw that. Ain't climbin' no fence."

Clipping sounds filled the night.

"You takin' the time to cut the damned fence, Junior?"

"You want help or not?"

The noises stopped and a second figure appeared outside the fence, walking toward the squatting man. "I can't believe Sunflower shot that guy."

"They don't call him Mr. Happy for nothing."

"Yeah, but there ain't no way we're headed back to Texas without a full load again. That's gonna add another couple of days to find another conscript at least. By the way, what's all the shootin' back there? Family in the house?"

"You don't want to know. Come on. Which way?"

The little light snapped on again and fell right on the binoculars. "I'd say that way, but it's gonna be hard in the dark."

"The others will be here in a minute."

Hugh watched the two figures move out into the darkness of the night, following their tiny beam of light.

Another gunshot sounded from the other side of the junkyard.

Quietly moving farther up the pile, hoping to get as far away from where they were looking for him as possible, Hugh's mind worked over the word he'd heard the man say: conscript.

He'd never heard that word before, but he'd read it. Recently. That story about a press gang apparently hadn't been a load of shit after all. These men were kidnapping people to force them into the New Texas Army—and killing them at the drop of a hat instead.

The white spotlights in the distance seemed small and far away as they speared out from the trucks and into the darkness looking for another enslaved man to kill, but they felt like hot irons burning across Hugh's soul. There was nothing he could do to help those men. There wasn't even anything he could do to help himself.

He risked a glance at his wristphone to see if anyone was near him. The red dots were all outside of the junkyard. Two on this side and five on the other. Gray dots had appeared where men had died, six of them. Hugh didn't know if that meant there were still three survivors, or if they had died outside the security system's reach.

CALL FOR HELP? flashed across the screen.

Hugh wished he could. There wasn't anyone out here. No one who would respond. And if someone actually did, it wouldn't be for a day or two. Or three. Maybe they'd just come to see if there was anything to salvage for a couple of bucks. There wasn't anyone to call.

He reached the convertible as that thought still echoed through his skull.

There was only one thing out here Hugh was capable of calling anymore.

He looked down at the steering wheel, barely visible in the gloom, and then back out to the spotlights searching for men in the prairie. There was a good chance he wouldn't survive this night, but maybe he could help one of those last three men get away. And, if they did, maybe they could warn others that it hadn't just been a click-bait story, that people had to be careful and protect themselves, protect their families from this new threat.

Hugh looked up to the sky and wondered what his own family would think of him now, and how long it would be until he saw them. Then he honked the horn three times.

The bullet shattered the convertible's low windshield. Hugh dove down into the seat well, pushing the lawn chair out of the way. It had taken only a second or two for them to lock in on him, and he wondered if it was AI assisted sound targeting, something he'd read about. One of the many things AIs were considered unethical to use for.

He was still in darkness but assumed there was an infrared spotlight on him.

Another bullet hit, and he felt it shake the car. White spotlights found the car. Another bullet put a hole through the door at his feet and a shaft of light shone through and sent him scampering, curling up into a ball under the steering wheel. He had to get out of the car. Fumbling at the door latch with his good hand, he tugged and pushed, hoping to get it open without falling out.

Shouting, coming from the direction of the vehicles, grew louder, and he knew they'd be on him soon.

He tugged the latch again, fighting twenty years of disuse, and pushed his good shoulder into it. The door gave with a wretched creak of rusted metal that carried out into the night. Hugh found himself looking out over the fence toward a small bobbing light that was approaching quickly.

There was a flash next to the light and a moment later a bullet struck the car.

Trapped, Hugh drew his .357 and quickly fired the three varmint-shot rounds out toward the flashlight, knowing they wouldn't have any effect from this distance but hoping it would at least make them slow.

The tiny light bobbed, and Hugh imagined he could see the two men dodging. He took the chance, dropped his pistol to the ground twenty feet below, and then rolled himself out of the convertible's door even as more bullets hit the other side and more shafts of light appeared through the door.

Hanging from the edge of the foot well, Hugh said a silent prayer that he wouldn't land on the fence or eviscerate himself on a jagged piece of crushed car, and he let go.

He landed on his feet, knees buckling under him, and rolling him into the fence. Cracks of bullets hitting above him made him flinch, and he twisted around in the three feet between the stack of cars and the fence, moving himself deeper into the shadows created by the spotlight spilling through gaps in the wall of cars.

His hand fell on the gun he'd dropped. He grabbed it and raised it up, steadying his weak arm with his good one. Grimacing with the effort, he aimed at the bobbing light out in the dark prairie and fired.

The return fire was near instantaneous, and the world around Hugh exploded into a hot spray of dirt, steel, and lead. Hugh covered his face with his elbow and folded down into the dirt.

The hail of bullets stopped with a distant scream. More shots were fired, but no bullets hit, and Hugh cautiously raised his eyes to look out through the fence.

The light was gone, and something moved in the darkness. Something big.

The roar of a motor pulled Hugh's attention to the far end of the junkyard fence. One of the armored trucks, having circled the property, came into view, spotlights piercing the night, shining up the fence line, following the row of cars. It only took seconds for the light to find Hugh, huddled at the base of the wall.

He scrambled to his feet, ignoring whatever was wrong with his knee, and ran for all he was worth, trying to thread the needle between the sharp edges of crushed cars and the jagged spurs on the old chain-link fence snagging at his sleeves. A bullet hit in front of him, throwing metallic flecks that shone in the spotlight. Another hit behind him, feeling to him like it had narrowly missed his head. And the then spotlight left him.

Barreling full speed, he stumbled as the light moved out ahead of him and on to a tree trunk. Even as he irrationally thought there were no trees here, the light moved up to reveal the golden eyes of the rex.

Bright red blood covered its serrated, six-inch teeth and dripped from its jaw.

Hugh heard the truck slide to a stop in the loose dirt as the spotlight wavered and then found its way back to the behemoth.

"What the fuck!"

The voice was right in front of Hugh, right where the other gunman had cut through the fence, and Hugh dropped to the ground and pressed himself into the shadows.

Gunfire erupted from the truck.

The three men appearing from the break in the car wall, transfixed by the rex, never looked toward Hugh.

"Jesus Christ! Is that what I think it is?"

"Stop yapping, start shooting!"

The rex was already charging the armored truck when the men opened fire, shooting at its back, following it as it lowered its head, bellowed, and attacked the truck.

Hugh gripped his pistol and swallowed. He couldn't let them kill the rex. He'd called it here. Raising the gun, he stepped out of the shadows. "Drop your weapons!"

One man turned and rolled his eyes at Hugh.

"Drop them!" Hugh yelled.

"Yeah, yeah," the man said as the other two turned to see what was happening.

The first suddenly jerked his rifle up at Hugh and fired. Hugh shot back, throwing himself to the side, not knowing if he hit the man or not. He fired two more times as the men shot at him.

He felt a sledgehammer pound into him, and the earth shook under him, but he continued to shoot back until the magazine emptied.

One of the men vanished under a blur of motion as a giant foot came down upon him, shaking the earth again. A second disappeared into a dark maw of impossibly big teeth. The third turned man and fired twice up into the belly of the rex before another giant foot came down and ended him. The impact vibrated Hugh's teeth.

Hugh gasped for air, unable to move, his body in shock. He knew he was shot, but he couldn't tell where or how many times. And he didn't want to know.

The rex stepped closer, dripping things off its foot, and brought its horrid, bloody face down to Hugh's face. The smell of hot blood washed over Hugh and he gagged. The rex dropped its nose to the dirt and tilted its head to look Hugh in the eyes.

He met its gaze for a moment and then nodded. He closed his eyes and turned his face up to the heavens. It was finally time to be with his family again.

The rex nosed him, as it had the 'ceratops, and Hugh felt its wet breath dampen his shirt. A calm came over him and he relaxed his body and waited.

The rex took a deep breath…and sneezed.

Hugh opened his eyes. The darkness ahead of him was broken up by streaks of light from spotlights in the junkyard casting long shadows out into the darkness. The rex's form dappled as it slowly passed through the light beams, and Hugh could see several trickles of blood from wounds on its flank before it silently vanished into the night.

Moving slowly himself, not wanting to know how badly he was hurt, not wanting to guess how long it would be until he bled out, Hugh fumbled at his shirt pocket and found his pack of cigarettes, crushed. He worked at it with the only hand that would move, the one that had been worthless earlier, and managed to put a broken cigarette in his mouth. He didn't have anything to light it with, but that didn't matter. It smelled good.

He raised his eyes to the night sky, to the billions of stars, and sighed. "Here's to you, Papi."

His wristphone vibrated, and he lifted his arm to look at the flickering, cracked screen.

Traumatic injury detected. Please remain calm. Calling for help.

Hugh silenced the notification on his new wristphone and picked up the new NetTab off the kitchen table. He tapped the screen to see the vid and was glad to see the approaching truck and trailer right on time.

Finishing his coffee, he put on his hat, kissed his fingers and touched them to the photo of his family, and adjusted the sling holding his right arm. He tucked his crutch under his left arm and stepped out of the trailer home to meet the truck as it pulled through the front gate. The truck stopped in a cloud of dust and the passenger window rolled down revealing a young boy.

"Where do they go?" the driver called.

Hugh pointed past the garage where he'd built a corral out of scrap metal posts, pipes, and I-beams.

The man waved to him, rolled the window up, and turned the truck around in the yard, expertly backing the livestock trailer up to the make-shift fence. The truck shuddered and went quiet, and the man and boy got out.

"Good morning, Mr. Sanchez," the man called, putting on his hat. "Pleasure to see you again."

"And you, Mr. Williams," Hugh said, limping down the wooden steps. The men met in the middle of the yard and nodded to one another instead of shaking hands.

"This is my son, Roger," Mr. Williams said.

"Pleasure to meet you, Mr. Sanchez." The boy held out his hand and then shyly grinned as he looked at Hugh's sling.

"And you, Roger." Hugh grinned back at him.

"You're looking good," Mr. Williams said. "Healin' up nicely."

"Slower than I'd like but getting there."

"And how'd that dino first-aid kit work for you?"

"That worked perfectly. The sedative took longer to work than I would have liked, but it other than that, the patch-up paste was perfect. I should get another one from you, just in case there are any future incidents."

"Another one?" Mr. Williams laughed. "That should have been enough for a dozen dinos!"

"Well…" Hugh kicked at the dirt. "Maybe I didn't know what I was doing."

"We're all learnin' out here. It's a different world."

"Ain't that the truth."

"Well. C'mon, son," Mr. Williams put his hand on Roger's shoulder. "Let's unload Mr. Sanchez's 'ceratopses."

Hugh followed and watched as they herded four waddling, three-foot tall protoceratopses out of the trailer. The animals looked like miniature triceratopses, without the horns, and they grunted and hooted as they entered the corral.

"You really want four of these every week?" the boy asked.

"Well, we'll see how it goes," Hugh answered, "but yeah."

"Must be some barbeque you're gonna have!" Roger's eyes were impossibly wide, and he nodded enthusiastically.

Hugh couldn't help but enjoy the boy's passion. "I'm hoping it works out. If it does, maybe I'll be able to invite you guys someday."

"That would be great!"

Hugh turned back to watch the protoceratopses exploring their new pen, hoping it would work out that he could have the boy come watch someday. He wondered how wide the boy's eyes would get when he saw a rex coming out of the prairie to get its own private barbequed 'ceratops.

Probably not as wide as Hugh's had gotten when, after he'd tracked the sedated rex back into the trees, waiting for it to fall asleep so he could patch its wounds, he'd found the nest and three eggs.

Something about the eggs, open and vulnerable in that giant nest, had finally settled Hugh's soul. This land wasn't abandoned. It was just going through a change in demographics.

And some of the new neighbors were a lot more worthwhile than others, willing to lend a hand when needed. It hadn't taken Hugh long to decide to stick around and return the favor.

Author Bio

Sam Knight is the owner/publisher of Knight Writing Press (knightwritingpress.com) and author of six children's books, five short story collections, four novels, and over 75 stories, including three co-authored with Kevin J. Anderson.

Though he has written in many cool worlds, such as Planet of the Apes, Wayward Pines, and Jeff Sturgeon's Last Cities of Earth, among his family and friends he is, and probably always will be, best known for writing *Chunky Monkey Pupu*.

Once upon a time, Sam was known to quote books the way some people quote movies, but now he claims having a family has made him forgetful—as a survival adaptation.

To learn more, you can find him at samknight.com.

Nine

By Seanan McGuire

Cats have nine lives, they say. Cats come back nine times, and our lives follow a strict pattern. Three to stray, three to play, and three to stay. And then, they say, it's over. No eternity for Cats, oh, no, but nine lives should be eternity enough for something small, and soft, and swift. Nine lives should satisfy our souls.

The people who say that don't account for the ones we love, the ones who walk more slowly, the ones whose hands are soft but whose skin is as rough as a paw-pad, the ones who tower over the world. We are their hearts gone running wild through the places they cannot see, and to say that we don't deserve anything more than nine is to say that our Humans must go to their own eternities without their hearts.

I would never have known how little Humans loved themselves if not for the way they spoke of Cats.

But nine is a well-accepted number, among the people who like to say such things. Somehow, those are never the ones who sit down and do the math of how long a Human life is, and how short a Cat's life can be, when our Humans are unable to care for us as the ancient compact demands. They fail to do the accounting which shows that as Humans have grown better at tending to their own needs and extending their own lives, they have done the same for us.

Nine is the number of times a Cat comes back, and nine is the number of times we will find our Human waiting for us when we return. Nine is the distance between a kitten and a child together, running through the grass with no understanding of the perilous and persistent future, and an elder of each kind, withered and weighted with the ghosts of those long-lost summers, sitting together in a final sunbeam, ready to embark on one last trip into the dreaming dark. Nine will get us from here to there, in almost all circumstances. Sometimes, when the world is not kind, it is far more than nine. Sometimes, when the world is either *very* kind or *very* cruel, it is fewer. But nine is the average.

Three times to stray, through the wild and fickle hours of youth. Three times to play, when spirits have settled but fire yet remains. And three times to stay, mellow as a moment, curled beside the people we adore, choosing the hands we have known before.

There is no great office which assigns the hearts of Cats to their Humans, and some Cats, seeking a Human heart to tether to, find themselves greeted by fallow ground, cruel words and disinterest. When this happens, they go looking elsewhere, for the lives of straying are still in flux: they can change allegiance. There is yet no investment in the Human, no reason to stay loyal. We are not dogs, to give ourselves so easily. Dogs need but a single life to become totally devoted.

So, this is the first lie they tell themselves: There is no true limit to the number of times a Cat may stray, in the search of the home where they belong. We try on Humans like Humans try on shoes, checking their fit and then discarding them, until we find the right one. This is not always due to cruelty. At times, a Human and a Cat simply do not suit each other, and both can be best served by moving on. So, we quest, and we consider, and we ponder. If a Cat is so fortunate as to find their home quickly, they may cut the lives of straying short, may choose to move straight along to playing. This is most common when the Human is older, already grown enough to live in harmony with themselves, already secure enough to provide a harbor.

A Human is a harbor, if nurtured right, if trained by the proper deeds and whispers and nudges. A Human can be a place of safety and unending affection, where there is no need to fear cold, or hunger, or the tearing teeth of predators larger than ourselves. A Human can also be a source of endless sorrow. For we measure our time in the number of lives it should take for us to match their time in flesh, but Humans are as temporary as we are, if on a somewhat longer scale. At times, the count is wrong. At times, they reach the end of their time while we still have miles to go on our own, and they must go first into the clearing that awaits us all, when our count of nine is finished.

It is a sad thing, to see a Human go on ahead, unaccompanied and alone. It is a glorious thing, for it tells us the counting time is finished. When next we shrug off flesh and fur for the space of wind and starlight that waits beyond, there is no need to struggle with the question of return, whether our Human has the time to need us again, whether they will be too deep in mourning to accept us if we chance to come before them. We can simply go, onward to what waits beyond, which neither Cat nor Human can know with any certainty. We exist; we end; we go to the clearing at the end of the path, to wait a time before we return to help our heartless Humans along, and when we find ourselves there together, we must decide together.

Should they choose to return to the world they've left, we go with them, to serve another nine as their roving hearts, their small and vulnerable pieces of the world. And should they choose to follow the pathway that leads from the clearing into whatever waits for weary spirits tired of flesh and fighting, we go with them there as well, and we are never seen again, neither Human nor heart, neither custodian nor Cat. We find our endings in that hollowed, hallowed space outside of everything, and we are content with this way of things.

I have seen Humans in the clearing who never knew their hearts were in the world, or knew but didn't care, or found their hearts in other forms, and were waiting for them still. I saw them, and I knew them, and I knew which they were, whether the companions for which they waited were Dogs or Horses or—in a few rare, terrible cases—nothing at all, whether they had lived their lives so outside the possibility of love that they had never found comfort outside the sanctums of their skins. Those Humans, who have never learned to love anything other than themselves, find only one route from the clearing, and it leads back to the world they left. They have to go again, to run a life the length of our nine, in hopes that their return will teach them love.

That alone makes me look forward to the day when I will take my last trip to the clearing. There is no promised paradise that I have ever seen, only the clear and quiet green at the ending of the longest road, but it only allows those who have learned love to continue on. Whatever comes next, whatever form it takes, we go together, and we go knowing the shape and the substance of love. That is a powerful thing.

But they count our lives in nines, and that is a good and useful thing, because it tells us from the very start that we must continue to return until we have finished. Until we have led our Human home.

I can see that you do not understand. Don't worry, child. Soon enough, you will. These are things you must know, before you take to flesh for the first time, things you must understand: Kittens are very skilled at the art of dying. It is not a thing that anyone will teach you, nor should they have the need: It is a thing you will understand as soon as you feel the tension of blood and bone settle over you. You will want to live, for all things yearn to survive, and if fortune is on your side, you will have the opportunity.

If it is not, as it will not always be, you will end your one and return here, to speak to those who linger, before you undertake your two. If you do return quickly, do not think that you have failed in any way: It is common, to return swiftly after a first outing. No one expects you to find your Human immediately, nor will shame you if you are not among the lucky few who accomplish such a thing.

You may run through all nine of your lives in searching and find them when they are elderly and tired and you are much the same, weary of the going and returning, ready to remain. Or you may find them swiftly and settle by their side. That is not for you, or for me, to know.

Their world is large, and we are small. Our spirits can be large as anything, but our bodies are not the same. You may spend several lives searching. They will not always be easy ones. For every kitten born into warmth and comfort, wanted and wished for, there are a dozen born into the great, cold wild, hungry and afraid, fighting to survive.

Those kittens, when they survive to grow strong and swift, are still at the mercy of a world so much larger than themselves. Some Humans will want to help them, and others will wish to do them harm, and they will not always look different from one another.

You may meet some of these Humans, in your time. They may end those lives before you're ready. You must be quick and clever to escape them, but you must not let their existence close you off to the promise of your own Human, waiting somewhere in the world for you to find them.

I have sometimes wondered whether the cruel ones were those whose own roving hearts had been broken before they could ever meet, and so now they seek to deny other Cats their chance to find their homes.

Time will be your friend and your enemy, and it is very likely you will go before your Human, even if you find them swiftly, even if you return to them again and again and again. We have the potential to outlive them by so very long, if we take our full ration of nine, but potential and reality are not always acquainted.

You will very likely die and leave them living, mourning you for the rest of their long days. Mourn with them, but do not hurry back unless you are sure—truly sure—that they have long enough to not leave while you are once again living, trapping the pair of you in separation. The clearing waits for us. It is good here, and green, and comfortable. You can be content here until they arrive.

And oh, when they come! When they come walking down that path, grief in every step, sure that you have left them forever, for that is the lie the Humans tell themselves—that they are forever, and Cats are only temporary—only imagine the joy in running to their sides! Only imagine their surprise, while they are grieving their own deaths, to find that you have waited for them, however long it took, that you have not gone on ahead! They grieve the temporary, so that we can help them rejoice in the eternal.

There: those are three things you should know, one for each triad of lives you have yet to live, all the wonders that are yet ahead of you. It will be hard. The dangers will be great.

The rewards will be greater still.

So go, kitten: go and begin your counting down. Go and begin your living. Find the Human whose heart you were always intended to be and keep them from becoming cruel in your absence.

I will be here when you return. My Human has yet a little time left to her—not so much as once she did; not enough for another life together—and I will wait until she comes. You will all but certainly return before she reaches me. I will see you in the pause between numbers, and I will remind you, each time, that it's worth it.

They're worth it.

All nine times we have them, they're worth it.

Author Bio

Seanan McGuire is a native Californian, which has resulted in her being exceedingly laid-back about venomous wildlife and terrified of weather. When not writing urban fantasy (as herself) and science fiction thrillers (as Mira Grant), she likes to watch way too many horror movies, wander around in swamps, record albums of original music, and harass her cats.

Seanan is the author of the October Daye, InCryptid, and Indexing series of urban fantasies; the Newsflesh trilogy; the Parasitology duology; and the "Velveteen vs." superhero shorts. Her cats, Lilly, Alice, and Thomas are plotting world domination even as we speak, but are easily distracted by feathers on sticks, so mankind is probably safe. For now.

Seanan's favorite things include the X-Men, folklore, and the Black Death. No, seriously.

She writes all biographies in the third person, because it's easier that way.

To learn more about Seanan, go to: seananmcguire.com/index.php

A Memory of Witches

By Patricia Briggs

Author's Note: This story takes place during *Storm Cursed*.

While most of his werewolf pack were milling around aimlessly—or catcalling at the sight of their Alpha kissing his newly arrived mate—Sherwood Post watched the witch's house.

Architecturally speaking, it was a lovely, two-story mansion with an interesting roof that sported skylights. If he were a poet, he might say that it sprawled out in the afternoon sun like a sleeping cat. The exterior was a warm cream stucco, a substance that withstood the extreme heat of the Tri-Cities better than wood and more stylishly than mason board or vinyl. The house was surrounded by extensive gardens and those were surrounded by acres of agricultural land. This edge of the Tri-Cities was mostly comprised of houses on acreage—some of them huge upscale places, some of them moldering mobile homes set side by side in a sort of quiet class warfare. Or possibly class assimilation.

This particular house was large and expensive, but witches came from families and those families served the witches in the same way the pack served the werewolves. Elizaveta Arkadyevna Vyshnevetskya's family was large and included a lawyer and a doctor. And they all lived...*had* lived...in that house.

Now they were dead, all of them except for Elizaveta, who had been in Europe being wined and dined—and paid—by the Lord of Night himself. The witches were dead and everything he had seen in that house said the family had been killed by black witches who had moved in and taken over—possibly shortly after Elizaveta had left. And no one had noticed.

Adam wanted answers that couldn't wait for Elizaveta's return. Witches who killed fourteen witches in their own home, might be able to kill werewolves as easily.

"You okay to go back in?" Zack had been watching Sherwood for a few minutes before he broke though the invisible barrier separating Sherwood from the rest of the pack. "Witches can't be your favorite people."

He was being tactful. Doubtless he could smell Sherwood's stress.

"I don't remember anything about the witches," Sherwood said because he couldn't say he was okay without lying and because his lack of memory was well known to anyone in the pack. Probably anyone in any werewolf pack. Amnesia was something that most werewolves didn't survive. Unstable werewolves—and amnesia—made containing the violent nature of a werewolf difficult. That Sherwood had survived, even though his memories had not returned, was unusual enough to be gossiped about.

"Sometimes, some memories are imprinted in your skin, though," Zack said softly. Visceral." He hesitated and gave him a perceptive look. "Or your wolf."

Sherwood gave a short nod. It wasn't a lie. His wolf did not want to go back into that house in a way that was not based on today's experience alone.

Stupid, agreed the wolf. *We don't remember how to protect ourselves from magic.*

But the wolf knew that at one time they—*he* could have kept himself safe from what awaited in that house, which was more than Sherwood would have guessed.

"Five years of memories," said Carlos, following Zack, as many of the wolves had a tendency to do—especially when their submissive wolf came too near Sherwood. It was as if their protective instincts understood Sherwood was a threat. He sounded friendly enough, but he put his body subtly between Sherwood and Zack. "I don't know what I'd do if all I could remember was the last five years."

Carlos had been born in Mexico around a century ago and now worked for Adam, their Alpha, in his security business. That was most of what Sherwood knew about him. Sherwood had avoided becoming too close with anyone in his pack. He thought Carlos's instincts were pretty good because Sherwood considered himself a threat, too.

Until last winter he'd accepted that his memory loss was due to his long captivity in the hands of witches. The Marrok, into whose care Sherwood had been brought, thought that the horror of being tortured to the extent that his left leg would never regenerate—something that just didn't happen to werewolves—had given Sherwood traumatic amnesia. But if that were true, he shouldn't still be losing memories.

We aren't crazy, his wolf asserted with more confidence than Sherwood felt was due.

It had taken him a while to notice because he wasn't losing years or centuries worth of memories—not that he had those to lose anymore. No one remembered every minute of every day—but he was losing the wrong moments, the *interesting* ones.

There was something broken in his brain—and he didn't know what it meant—other than it made him unpredictably dangerous. That was why Sherwood had asked the Marrok, he who ruled the werewolves in this time and place, to send him away. The Marrok had been too likely to see what was going on. Though Sherwood agreed *in principal* that unstable werewolves had to be killed, he did not particularly wish to die.

Maybe the witches are stealing our memories, the wolf suggested, not for the first time.

That seemed like a possibility. Sherwood had spent the last few years studying witches in an effort to make his affliction make sense. There were a few of the witch families who knew how to feed off the emotional energy of traumatic memories. The idea that he was still somehow tied to the witches who had taken his leg made his skin crawl.

His revulsion didn't feel like something new, something built over mere decades. It felt bred into his bones.

Yet you volunteered to go back inside, growled his wolf.

Mostly the really old werewolves could talk to their wolves. As if being linked to a human for so long gave the wolf access to speech in the same way their human halves gained access to the wolf's instincts. He knew that, just as he knew that the sunset over the Parthenon was breathtaking, though he could not remember how he knew either one of those things. He was sure that he was very old because when he thought of the Parthenon, it looked a lot different from modern photos he'd seen.

"I heard Darryl say that you were going to escort Mercy," said Carlos. "Why isn't Adam doing it? Hell, why isn't the whole pack going in?"

Carlos wasn't as stupid as his question sounded. The whole pack had become a lot more vested in their Alpha's mate's safety since Sherwood had joined up. Partly it was because they recognized that she—a coyote shapeshifter—was a lot more vulnerable than a werewolf. Part of it was because she was directly responsible for giving the whole pack a higher purpose, a purpose that made them into heroes.

And Carlos thought Sherwood was a threat.

Even though the other wolf wasn't wrong, Sherwood felt his eyes narrow. Carlos took a step back, bumping into Zack, who steadied him. It was the question in Zack's face that Sherwood chose to answer.

"It's a crime scene," Sherwood reminded them. "The fewer of us who go in, the more Mercy will be able to discover. Adam asked me to go in because I found the witch's traps."

Both Carlos and Zack frowned.

"You don't do magic," said Zack with certainty. "Not even pack magic. What do you know about witchcraft?"

What do I know about witchcraft? Sherwood echoed the question silently because it was a good one. He didn't like the answers that suggested themselves because he wasn't sure regaining his memories was safe. A small dark voice in the hidden depths of his mind told him that magic was dangerous. It didn't tell him why.

"I thought you didn't remember the witches," said Carlos in a tone that tried very hard to be neutral. "All you have is the memories after you were freed."

That wasn't quite true.

Sherwood had a few scraps of the time before he'd spent those years—maybe decades—a captive of witches. They were bits and pieces of memories, though—foggy at best. He had a vivid one of being on the deck of a storm-tossed ship, watching one of the sailors be sick on the deck. Seawater boiled over the ship and washed both sailor and spew into the sea, making Sherwood wonder if his decision to travel to England in search of who he had been mortally stupid. In that fragment he was in human form, and he had two good legs but no memory of his past. He might have gone into the sea after the sailor. But maybe not, because werewolves don't swim well.

What *was* true was that he had no memories of being among the witches. Carlos was right again—there was no reason that he'd been able to spot the traps they had laid inside that house. Though he had done. There was reason for him to believe he could keep Mercy safe while she used her quirky relationship with magic to look for clues about who killed Elizaveta's family and, possibly more importantly, how it was done.

We can keep her safe, but we could protect her better if you freed our memories, suggested his wolf slyly. *Some things are lost, but—*

The wolf might know language, but it spoke more often and more clearly in images and impressions. It chose now to share the weight of the knowledge, the memories, that lay beyond the solid barrier in his mind.

How could his memories, all that he had been, lay behind that barrier if he was continuing to lose memories? Did the barrier itself eat his thoughts like some parasite? Or was there something lurking in his brain that had nothing to do with magic?

You could take down the barrier, insisted the wolf. *Are you a coward?*

Afraid to know what you—what we once were?

The wolf fought him for the memories sometimes. Recently, Sherwood had found them leaking out in small ways—it had started before he'd come here. Another reason he'd asked to leave the Marrok's pack. Some memories disappearing while others returned unbidden did not seem like something he could have hidden from the Marrok for long.

"Sherwood?" asked Zack.

"I can protect Mercy in that house," Sherwood told them, believing it to be true.

He'd kept Adam and Darryl safe already. He could keep Mercy safe.

"Darryl says it is bad in there," Carlos said.

"Elizaveta is a grey witch," said Zack.

"Darryl says that there are signs the black witches had some time to play, maybe since the day Elizaveta left." Carlos said darkly. "The basement cages…"

Sherwood nodded. "It is bad. I will keep her safe."

The laboratory of a grey witch didn't look much different from the laboratory of a black witch. Both witches fed on pain and suffering. The difference was in the willingness of their victims. Because of that, grey witches tended to treat their victims better. And they didn't torture animals. There were animal cages in Elizaveta's basement.

His pack bond flared. Sherwood looked toward Adam. He wasn't surprised to see that his Alpha was looking at him. As soon as their eyes met, Adam nodded. Sherwood left Zack and Carlos to their worries and made his way to where his Alpha and Mercy waited, now a little apart from the rest of the pack.

A photo of Adam Hauptman would show a man of average height and movie star good looks. It could not capture the fierce personality that made even Sherwood's stubborn knees want to bend a bit in his presence in an old-fashioned gesture of obedience. Adam's innate power had nothing to do with the magic that had made him a werewolf. It was the kind of charisma that had allowed Alexander the Great to conquer most of the known world before he was thirty. Thankfully Adam had no ambition to conquer the world, he just wanted to keep his pack and those under his protection safe. He was a very strong Alpha.

We are stronger, said Sherwood's wolf, but Sherwood ignored it because both of them, wolf and man, knew that they would not be able to keep their pack safe the way that Adam could. Stronger did not make one a better Alpha.

"Sherwood?" Mercy asked, glancing at the house and then back to him. She sounded worried for him.

Like Adam, she was average in height and unusually fit—the second being a byproduct of being a shapeshifter. He'd heard her father was a Native American. He'd also heard her father was Coyote—but that could have been an attempt to elevate her status. Having a coyote shapeshifter as the mate of their Alpha could have been a political liability for the pack. Naming her Coyote's daughter, even fictionally, made her sound cool.

Her hair and skin agreed with the Native American, Sherwood was still making up his mind about the Coyote part. He hadn't detected a whiff of the divine about her, but trickster gods could be subtle. Today her shoulder-length hair was working its way out of her usual French braid, and she looked tired. She'd been out hunting zombie goats.

Adam answered her before Sherwood could. "Sherwood knows the dangers better than anyone else here. I trust him to keep you safe."

Sherwood's wolf thought rude things aimed at Sherwood because he still believed they could keep Mercy safer if Sherwood freed the parts of himself he was keeping imprisoned. And unless he did that, the wolf was very much afraid they would die in the spiritual darkness of the black magic that dwelled in the basement of the house. The wolf was, Sherwood knew, viscerally afraid of going back in—but he wasn't trying to get out of going. They both knew, with very little real evidence, that they could protect Mercy better than anyone else here.

Mercy frowned at Adam, then looked at Sherwood. "I thought you didn't remember anything of your captivity?"

He thought of Zack's assessment and said, "Apparently some things are imprinted in my skin. Like that—"

He thought of the basement laboratory that felt so familiar in its black malevolence, the place that threatened to send his wolf into paroxysms of terror.

Adam made a subtle gesture and Sherwood remembered that Adam wanted Mercy to go into that house without any idea of what she was walking into. He needed her unbiased opinion. That was the main reason Adam was staying outside. He and Mercy were true mates. It was entirely possible that Adam's opinions would influence her if he were the one to go in.

So instead of continuing, Sherwood shook his head and said, "Never mind."

Mercy glanced at Adam then gave Sherwood a rueful look and a shrug.

"No sense putting it off," she muttered and started stripping off her clothes. Her coyote was better at sensing magic and identifying people than her human self.

Politely, Sherwood looked elsewhere until his nose told him that she'd shifted into her other form.

The little coyote's nose for magic was better than any wolf's in the pack. Adam needed her to glean whatever information she could get from the crime scene inside that house. She was the best the pack had, but all she had was a nose for magic and a chaotically occasional immunity to the same. She'd just been cleaning up a mess left by someone working black magic. Odds were that the zombie goats and the dead witches were connected, but it would be good to get confirmation of that.

But, more importantly, Adam was counting on her to confirm a hunch. That was the real reason why Adam was staying out. He didn't want her to pick up on his reactions. Sherwood hadn't felt the need to explain that to Carlos and Zack. What he had told them had been true enough.

Sherwood caught Adam's worried expression before his Alpha hid it. If whoever had killed the people in that house came back, Mercy, herself, had very few defenses. Even a werewolf wouldn't be much use against this kind of magic.

We could do this for her, insisted the wolf. *Keep Mercy safe by doing this in her place.*

Sherwood liked Mercy, and he knew her better than most of the rest of the pack. She was tough and funny and held her own in a pack of werewolves when her coyote wouldn't have been much more than a mouthful for one of her packmates. She should have been a liability—but she wasn't.

If we had our memories, our power back, she would not have to risk herself.

This time he wasn't sure it was his wolf speaking or his human half. But the deathbringer here was gone and had already feasted on the deaths. It was unlikely the killer or killers would return.

What if, he suggested to the wolf, *I take that barrier down and whatever is still feeding on our memories eats it all? We would have nothing and our enemy would be enriched by what it steals?*

He could feel the wolf pause, tasting his questions and finding merit in them.

The barrier tastes like you, the wolf said. *The Marrok thought so too. He thought you should rip it away and regain all that we have lost.*

What do you think? Sherwood asked. *If I put that shield around our memories, do you think it is a good idea to take it down? The Marrok thinks I am hiding from those memories—but it doesn't feel like that to me. It feels like I did it to protect those memories—and whatever else I have hidden.*

The wolf was silent a moment, then suggested, *We could go hunting. Find whoever it is who is stealing our memories and kill them.*

Sherwood chose not to argue with the wolf. *Right now, we have to keep Mercy safe*, he said instead.

Let me come out. A wolf would be better protection for her.

Someone needs to open doors, Sherwood told his wolf. It would take too long to change—fifteen or twenty minutes sometimes. And he didn't trust his ability to control the wolf in the basement if he were wearing his wolf shape.

He felt his inner beast consider that and agree with the faintest whiff of condemnation for Sherwood's lack. Sherwood controlled a huff of inappropriate laughter.

Unlike a werewolf, Mercy didn't take long to change. Between one blink of the eye and the next a coyote stood where the woman had been. Mercy shook out her fur like a dog emerging from a bath and stretched. Then she turned her eyes toward the house.

Sherwood gave Adam a nod—which was a promise to keep her safe—then headed toward the house, the little coyote at his side. Adam kept the rest of the pack well back so they would not interfere with Mercy's senses.

Sherwood's prosthetic leg thumped on the imitation wood of the porch. He could move silently when he chose, but there was no reason here. He opened the door and the darkness he could perceive but could not see made him hit the light switch.

The coyote gave him a puzzled glance. It was still daytime, and this part of the house had vaulted ceilings that rose to the full two-story height and sported a pair of skylights as well as large windows. But the sunlight streaming into the room did not touch the darkness he felt—not that the artificial light could help with that.

Still.

"This house is dark," he told her. "A little light doesn't hurt anything."

She walked in ahead of him and, aware of his Alpha's intent stare, Sherwood pulled the door closed behind them.

Trapped, said his wolf.

Mercy hadn't made it very far in. She stood in the middle of the room, the light from the windows showing the multitude of colors that made her coat look almost blond. The hair along her spine was raised and she sneezed at the foul scent of death—and maybe whatever else she could feel that he could not.

"I know," Sherwood told her. "But you get used to it."

The oily magic that had killed Elizaveta's family had left the house reeking of black magic so strong that he thought even a mundane human would smell the rot. Fourteen witches lay dead within these walls, but the magic worked here had been more lethal than that. Every mouse, every bug, every house plant was dead, too.

Mercy sighed and headed into the kitchen where the closest corpses lay. From her flattened ears, the dead bothered Mercy more than they did Sherwood. But she did not shirk from exploring the bodies. Her tail drooped and tucked a little when she saw that one of the bodies belonged to a young woman—Adam had known that one, too.

Sherwood followed, hanging back a little, as Mercy moved from body to body, then room to room. He spoke as little as possible, letting her concentrate. She was thorough and she noticed every trap, though he couldn't tell if she caught scent of something or if she was sensing the magic. Even though most of them were scribed with runes, he was pretty sure that she wasn't picking up on them by sight because a lot of them were in obscure places.

Obscure enough places that he had no idea how *he'd* found some of them. They'd seemed obvious at the time but looking at them again he realized that they had not been.

Too much magic in here, observed the wolf. *It's calling to the hidden part of us.*

He rubbed his fingers together and felt a faint tingle in the air. He was very much afraid that the wolf was right. Uneasily, Sherwood followed Mercy up the stairs.

This part of the house held a long hall with six bedrooms. The dead lay below them, and he'd discovered no traps up here when he'd explored it earlier. He told Mercy that and waited in doorways while Mercy tracked through the rooms. The last and largest room belonged to Elizaveta. Mercy took her time here, ears pinned in unhappiness. She wiggled under the bed and emerged a few minutes later a little dusty. She sneezed twice, looked around and then nosed Elizaveta's closet open.

Sherwood frowned at Mercy's disappearing tail as she pushed under the tightly packed hanging skirts. He hadn't checked the back of the closet. He was already striding into the room when the deadly magic flared to life.

Sherwood was a dominant wolf whose instincts were to protect. Mercy had been given into his care. He didn't even hesitate.

He ripped off the protective barrier that blocked his memories—*his magic*. As knowledge flooded him, he threw up his hands and wiped the structure of the witch's warding so that the magic that charged it drifted harmlessly into the ether before it had a chance to touch Mercy.

The enormity of his lost memories—not just centuries but millennia—and unexpected power flooded him with staggering force. Cold sweat ran down his face and he struggled to breathe through the storm.

And at that moment, when his defenses were down under the influx of power and information—his enemy struck, engulfing him, swallowing everything it could in huge gulps.

He knew this enemy. *Remembered*.

A divine spark had awoken in the wilderness, a nascent god waiting to become whatever its worshipers conceived. Usually, without a civilization to feed it, such things fade away. But this one had lured a small group of people to it, had fed them beauty and consumed them in return. And so it had starved more slowly than it should have, growing into something twisted and wrong.

Sherwood—or the person he'd been before he'd been Sherwood—arrogant and sure of himself had gone in to…to do something. Save the people it held captive. Destroy it. Maybe. Probably.

He couldn't sort out the memories from the tangle they were in. But this he knew, the mortals that divine thing had lured had been crumbs that kept it from dying immediately. But if it consumed Sherwood, with his years and his magic, with his ties to pack, that would be different. A feast. More than a feast.

If it ate Sherwood, it might have the power it needed to BECOME. The world would have a new god, the kind of being this modern world had no way of defending itself against. Even at his best he had been forced to lock his memories, his powers, away so that he could not access them either. Off-balance and vulnerable, Sherwood could not defend himself against it now. He would need some great artifact or solid faith to call upon another divine being to defend himself. The gods no longer walked the earth as they once had—and if Sherwood had ever had faith enough for summoning the God of Abraham or in one of the lesser gods, his memories were too jumbled to help him.

It was not his nature to give in, though. So, he fought with all the magic he had, all the knowledge he could pull out of the tangled skein of his mind. But it was useless against the thing that fed upon him, growing more powerful with every mouthful of Sherwood it gulped down.

It was his wolf, hunting for any weapon at hand, who found it, a small bit—a small *memory* of divinity that lingered nearby. Sherwood had no time to question how such a thing could be found in this house of death. He grabbed at it rudely and used it to coat the incipient shields he was trying to build from the shards of the old barrier he'd destroyed to protect Mercy. He pulled that remnant of divinity over himself like a child using a blanket to hide from night terrors, once more barricading his core–power and memories inside a vault.

Sherwood stood, breathing hard, in the witch's bedroom and wondered how he'd moved from the doorway to the middle of the room without remembering it and why his body felt sore, as if he'd fought a battle. Under a bright pink ruffled skirt, Mercy's tail stuck out just about as far as it had when he last remembered seeing it, so he couldn't have lost much time. Even so, the sour smell of his own sweat and the way the back of his shirt felt clammy indicated that whatever had happened, it had been something big.

Yes, agreed his wolf. *We have our magic back.*

The wolf was right. Sherwood rubbed his fingers together. He could feel it now and the magic felt familiar and comfortable, as if he'd always had this connection.

Dangerous. That wasn't the wolf, it was stark knowledge.

That he had magic was bad, something hadn't been fixed right and it meant they were vulnerable. Abruptly pain laced through his head, sparking behind one eye and then the other. *His attacker giving one last frustrated, rage-filled attack—*

While he tried to figure out what had happened in the time that had been stolen from him, Mercy reemerged and shook herself briskly. She gave him a bleak look that distracted him enough to wonder what she'd found in Elizaveta's closet, then headed for the stairs at a trot. He paused long enough to get a feel for the magic that lingered in Elizaveta's room.

Adam had been right—the pack's trust in one of its oldest and most useful allies had been betrayed. If he'd been on his game, he would have stopped Mercy then, because there was no need for her to go to the basement. But she was quick and, by the time he realized he might save her a few nightmares, she was down one flight of stairs. He caught up to her halfway to the basement.

He almost said something but rethought. He didn't know what she'd found or how much she sensed. He didn't know if she was suspicious or certain. She needed to see the basement so that Adam would be sure. Sherwood was certain—but Adam would believe Mercy.

So, Sherwood followed the coyote to the basement, hitting the light switch at the bottom of the stairs. The basement laboratory hadn't changed in the past few hours. It was still a huge rectangular room strewn with cages of dead animals and tables and chairs to which living creatures could be attached. With his new sensitivity, it was worse than it had been the first time. The witches' bodies didn't bother him—there were seven of them, mostly in bondage positions that indicated they were actively being tortured when they had been killed. He did not feel sorry for any of them.

Because now that he could feel the magic, he could tell that every one of the dead witches in this room—with the possible exception of one—was a black witch. Just as Elizaveta was a black witch. Oh, her room hadn't smelled of black magic—she must have some way of hiding the scent of it. But he didn't need his nose to identify the greasy, clinging foulness.

Adam was fond of Elizaveta.

Sherwood couldn't imagine being fond of a witch, even if she were a white witch. He rubbed his fingers together and then wiped them on his jeans as if that would clean them. There would be no cleansing until he was out of this place.

He paced back and forth between the pressure washer and the sink—torturing was a filthy business literally as well as figuratively. He tried to ignore the nearby racks of cages filled with the bodies of brightly colored frogs, turtles and a scattering of lizards. The alligator in the bottom cage was only two feet long—many of the creatures were babies. The young—of any species—had more power to harvest whether the villain was a witch or a fae.

We remember more about magic, observed the wolf.

That was true.

I remember more than you do, continued the wolf thoughtfully. *I remember more about a lot of things than you do. I wonder why you did that?*

The familiar smell of death combined with black magic was making his skin crawl.

I wonder, said his wolf, *where I found a bit of divine—remnant you called it—just when we needed it.*

That thought made Sherwood pause. He remembered that part, now that the wolf mentioned it—remembered using it to save himself.

A remnant is what's left behind when a god works a miracle, the wolf told him.

He froze. If he had used such a thing to protect himself…

Then the creature hunting us is divine, agreed the wolf unhappily. *A minor such being, or we would already be dead.*

The gods didn't walk the earth much anymore—there was a reason for that he couldn't remember. He had no idea why a miracle had been worked here, or why the memory of it had remained, unconsumed, in this dismal and spiritually filthy place. But the next time whatever hunted them attacked, he would be unlikely to find another divine memory to save himself.

Mercy's urgent yip reminded him that his job was to keep her safe—not be distracted by his own doom. His job, as long as he was still alive, was to protect those in his care. He strode over to the cages of dead mammals and opened the one Mercy was staring at. There were two half-grown kittens in it. The orange tabby was limp and lifeless, but the black kitten…

"We missed this," he said.

He tried to be gentle as he extracted it from the cage, but it twitched back from his hold and tried to move away. The kitten stank of urine, feces and old blood—Sherwood could feel its spirit weakening. He was pretty sure it was dying—and maybe that would be a blessing for it.

Maybe it would have been a blessing if Sherwood had died in the hands of the witches, too.

He didn't know—other than that obvious comradery of both surviving captivity by black witches—why the little survivor was suddenly important to him. Sometimes connections like that are made without warning or cause. But he found himself stripping off his shirt to wrap the little cat in to keep it from moving more in case it had broken bones, and also because his shirt was warm and softer than the floor. He had to set it down on in order to search the rest of the cages again.

If they'd missed this kitten the first time through, they might have missed another animal. But nothing else was alive.

The spell killed every living thing in this house except that kitten, said his wolf. *I wonder how that happened.*

A remnant of the divine is left when a god performs a miracle, Sherwood thought, arrested. He knelt on the floor beside the bundled kitten and brought it to his face.

He couldn't feel it, but his wolf did.

Yes. He felt the wolf's attention switch from the kitten to the coyote with sudden interest.

Coyote, the wolf said.

Sherwood knew it wasn't talking about Mercy—and that the possibility that the stories about who Mercy's father was might be more accurate than he'd assumed.

He considered the kitten again. It was struggling weakly in his hold—afraid of the wolf, possibly. But given that it had spent time in this place, it was likely frightened of everything.

He accepted that the wolf remembered more of magic than he did. But he looked at the dying kitten he held, touched by Coyote, and thought of the presumed god that waited to consume him.

He became aware that Mercy was staring at him.

"Missing an eye," he told her soberly.

She whined in sympathy and then closed the distance between them. She licked the kitten's filthy fur—grimacing at the taste—but the little creature relaxed under Mercy's attentions. When Mercy stepped back, Sherwood stood up with the kitten held as gently as he could.

"Have you seen enough?" he asked Mercy.

She padded over to a metal door set in one corner of the room. Sherwood put himself in her way.

"No. You don't want to go into the freezer. There are some things you don't need to see. We should go."

It had been the thing in the freezer that had made Adam think that Elizaveta had given herself over to black magic. Between Elizaveta's room and this basement, Sherwood didn't think that Mercy needed more convincing.

Mercy flattened her ears at him and looked pointedly around the room at each of the bodies. He'd told her there were fourteen bodies here, hadn't he. She was one short. But that wasn't in the freezer.

The kitten had given up fighting and lay limply in his hold, mouth open and panting a little in distress.

"This should only take a minute," he assured it—him—Sherwood's nose told him. He wasn't sure that the time mattered, though. He doubted the kitten would live. The kitten had survived whatever had killed every living thing in this house of horrors—by a real miracle. But his senses told him that it was dying now. It seemed like a waste of a miracle.

Sherwood took Mercy to the large bin that held the last body. There had been one witch in the house who *hadn't* been working black magic. Possibly because he had no way to do so. He pried the lid off and showed her the body. Mercy looked at it and displayed her fangs in distress.

"Adam said this was Elizaveta's grandson and that likely Elizaveta had done most of the damage to him herself."

Mercy sighed and inspected that body—for what, Sherwood could not tell. Then she went from body to body, sniffing carefully at fingers and faces. When she'd finished, she shook herself and trotted up the stairs. Sherwood had no trouble keeping up with her—but the smell clung to all three of them—Mercy, the cat and him—as they escaped out the front door and into the fresh air.

Sherwood rode in the back of Adam's SUV with the kitten on his lap. He'd rearranged his shirt to be a bed rather than a straitjacket, but nothing was going to make the kitten comfortable. After a few miles it started making soft mewls of distress. He'd sort of curled into Sherwood and had started shivering. It probably wasn't a good thing. The cat's noise attracted Adam's attention. Sherwood could feel it, even if his Alpha kept his eyes on the road as he drove.

"He's dying," Sherwood told them, feeling the malaise of that house creep further into his bones. The little cat had saved him—at least for the moment. He wished he could return the favor.

"He made it this far," Adam said. "It's just a mile more to the clinic."

Because his wolf thought it might help, Sherwood slipped his hands under the limp body and pulled the cat up to his face, careful not to hurt it. He took in its scent—its real scent, not the filth that matted its fur—and gave the cat his own. If the cat breathed his last here and now, he'd know he was safe from the witches.

Witches.

"Did you know?" he asked Adam. "About the black magic in that house?" He wasn't talking about the magic that had killed today, he was asking about the older magic that permeated the walls. Elizaveta's magic.

Adam shook his head. "No. I'd have put a stop to it. I had no idea."

Sherwood nodded. He'd known that from Adam's reaction earlier. He'd just needed to hear him say it. Adam was a straight shooter and saw things mostly in black and white. Good and evil. He didn't know why he'd needed to ask.

His wolf said, *I remember the witches.*

The wolf asked Adam, using Sherwood's voice, "And what are we going to do about it?"

"*We* will do nothing," Adam said. "This is something for me to do."

The wolf wasn't sure he liked that answer. That was the sort of answer that people gave when they were working out how to save a friend from the consequences of their own actions.

"There will be no black magic in my territory," Adam said, his voice very soft.

That soft-voice implacable rage settled over the wolf, and Sherwood felt his shoulders relax a bit.

No black magic, purred his wolf.

They stopped at the emergency vet hospital in Pasco. As soon as he walked in, Sherwood felt the tension in the air: grieving families, worried pet owners and terrified animals. The emergency vet wasn't where you took your animals to get vaccinated.

The kitten, who had mostly stopped making noise, let out a frantic sound and struggled a bit for the first time since he'd brought it up from the basement. It attracted the attention of everyone in the room. Sherwood saw the people take notice. The kitten was a rack of bones. They didn't have werewolf noses to smell the filth on the cat's fur, but they could see it. The dogs in the room quieted and a few of them showed their bellies to the werewolves. Cats hissed from their carriers.

He also realized that he didn't have a shirt on. Sherwood was mostly indifferent to clothing, but he usually made some kind of effort to blend in.

Adam chose that minute to say to the receptionist, "My friend's cat needs to be seen."

Ownership implied responsibility. Sherwood had to admit that anyone responsible for the state this kitten was in should get the kind of looks that were being turned his way. Sherwood wasn't exactly sure when the kitten had become his cat. But he wouldn't have given him up to anyone else at this point, either.

"Adam Hauptman," said a woman in the scrubs that seemed to be the vet's office uniform. "You're Adam Hauptman the werewolf?"

Adam smiled and nodded—and that smile swept through the room, breaking the tension in the air.

"I am," he said. The dogs relaxed and even the cats settled down at the sound of an Alpha wolf's voice.

"I thought werewolves couldn't have cats as pets," said someone else.

Sherwood moved past Adam, who was answering questions for his rapt audience, and spoke to the receptionist himself.

"We found the cat like this," he told her. "He's in rough shape."

Adam had his back to her, so she hadn't gotten the full effect of the smile. She was still suspicious.

"It looks like it's been tortured," she said.

He nodded. "That's what we thought. And starved."

The cat made a sad noise and Sherwood blew gently on its face to reassure it. The cat tried to purr.

The receptionist stared into his eyes for a few seconds—which was pretty good. Sherwood wasn't an Alpha, but he was dominant. There weren't many people who could meet his eyes at all.

She nodded and looked away, using the excuse of taking his information down. She finished her paperwork and assured Sherwood that someone would be out to get them as soon as there was a room free.

"Would you do that again?" The woman who'd recognized Adam waved a cell phone at Sherwood.

Sherwood lifted an eyebrow because he had no idea what she was asking. But the kitten mewed again, this time more quietly. He wished he thought it was because the cat was less scared, but he was afraid the softer volume meant it was getting weaker. He raised the kitten to his face and, when it raised its battered, one-eyed face to his, he kissed its nose on impulse.

"That's even better," said the woman, and he'd realized she'd taken a photo. "Do you mind if we use that on social media?"

He shrugged.

It didn't take long to get called back to an examination room. Sherwood wasn't sure if that was because the cat was so obviously in distress or if it was to keep the waiting room from becoming a social media circus. The cat was whisked away for x-rays and blood tests, then returned to Sherwood's care looking even more limp than it had before.

"We can try," the vet said after explaining all the damage they'd found. "But it's likely to be painful for him and expensive for you. He'll have to stay here a while and that eye needs surgery—though not until he's stronger. Even with everything we can do—I put his chances of survival low. It might be easier and more humane to let him go now."

The news wasn't anything that Sherwood hadn't expected. What he had not expected was the coyote who casually walked in through the half-open door that led into the depths of the clinic, toenails clicking on the hard floor. Sherwood thought for one incredulous second that it was Mercy—but no one else, not even Adam, reacted to it at all.

That's not a coyote, said Sherwood's wolf.

The coyote smiled at Sherwood as though he'd heard the wolf speak.

"Would you leave me alone with the cat for a minute?" Sherwood asked, his eyes on the coyote that apparently only he could see.

"Of course," said the doctor. "Just knock on this door when you know what you want to do."

He slipped back through the door the coyote who was not Mercy had entered through and closed it.

"I'll be in the waiting room," Adam said. His face bore a touch of puzzlement.

Sherwood understood. Werewolves were not afraid of death—or of suffering either. Whether or not to put the kitten to sleep was not a decision a werewolf should need privacy for. But Adam didn't push.

As soon as they were alone, Coyote unfolded into a human form—appearing to be a wiry Native American man about a foot shorter than Sherwood. His smile was charming—and much less reassuring than the one Adam had used in the waiting room.

"You won't remember our last meeting," Coyote said coyly.

Sherwood just watched him.

"*And,*" Coyote drew out that word, "if you could remember it, you wouldn't be happy with me."

"Why does this cat bear your mark?" Sherwood asked, tired of the trickster's games already.

Coyote hopped onto the empty exam table, landing in a crouch. He stayed there and leaned forward to run a light finger over the cat cradled in Sherwood's arms.

"They call that color tuxedo," Coyote said. "When all four feet are white it's supposed to be a good luck sign."

"I found it in a black witch's lab," Sherwood said dryly. "How lucky could it be?"

"Possibly good luck for you," said Coyote. "You shouldn't have wandered around in a witch's house when you were trying to hide yourself. Without that exposure, your safeguards might have held out another month or two. But you aren't going to keep the Singer out of your head with that mishmash you've cooked up now. He'll have you consumed in a few days."

The Singer, said the wolf. *I remember the Singer.*

Sherwood didn't say anything. He was pretty sure that Coyote was right.

He is, agreed the wolf.

And Sherwood was also pretty sure that asking questions about "the Singer" would be engaging with…not an enemy…but a trickster god. That never went well for the questioner. Coyote would tell Sherwood what Coyote wanted to tell Sherwood. Questions weren't going to make it go any faster.

"But," said Coyote when Sherwood didn't say anything. "But. *But* you were harmed watching over Mercy. *But* you were harmed originally hunting down the Singer because I told you about him. *But* it doesn't suit me that the Singer moves on to the next phase of godhood."

He caught Sherwood's expression and grinned sharply. "Oh, he wouldn't be all powerful. There are gods and there are *gods*—" he gestured to himself "—and then there is Apistotoke."

He frowned at Sherwood. "Gitche Manatu. Wakan Tonka?"

He made a sound of mock-frustration. "You used to know things. I forgot you are stupid now and need a translation. The Creator. God-All-Mighty. Allah."

"Got it," said Sherwood as Coyote took a breath as if he were going to run through even more names for God.

"Good." Coyote nodded his head. "So, not God or *god*, but even such a weak new thing as the Singer could become is enough to throw off the balance of the earth and cause—well, not chaos, I *like* chaos—but damage. Eternal damage. Damage to eternity. Something bad anyway."

Coyote peered up at Sherwood, one hand in front of him on the silver exam table, the other resting on a bent knee. After a moment Coyote leaned back and sighed. "I liked you better when you understood what I was telling you."

The kitten made a sound and Sherwood comforted it. It snuggled against him.

"I had…have—" Coyote paused, considering, then said, "—*will* have had a use for the kitten. But more importantly, for this conversation at least, I think you should have a use for him, too."

Familiar, suggest the wolf. *If we have a familiar who has been touched by the divine, I can use it to keep us safe. Actively keep us safe.*

"Exactly," said Coyote.

"*Witches* use familiars," Sherwood said.

Coyote gave him an encouraging nod.

"I am not a witch." He bit out the last word as if it tasted foul on his tongue.

Coyote sat down properly and swung his feet a couple of times. "That's true enough. Or rather it isn't, and it is. There's no proper word for exactly what you are anymore. But you were witchborn—"

Sherwood felt his lips twist in a soundless snarl and fought to control his expression.

Coyote waved a dismissive hand. "Witchcraft can be useful—but I am not here to dictate your morality or lack thereof. I am here to tell you that I will have made use of that cat. That means that making it your familiar will give you—" he paused and peered at Sherwood.

"Well, that's different," he said. "Why did you do that?"

He considered it and said, "Oh. That was smart. I think. Your wolf might be able to keep you safe. Maybe. Thus, keeping everyone safe. Maybe for long enough. I have plans for the Singer. Hopefully they turn out better this time."

When Sherwood didn't respond, Coyote said, "You could think of the kitten as a reward and an apology—"

Sherwood grunted.

Coyote looked at Sherwood's hands, cradling the tired, dying kitten and said, in an oddly gentle voice, "—to him. If you make him your familiar, you will live and so will he. I owe him."

"I don't know how to do that," said Sherwood, knowing it was capitulation. Witchcraft. He was uncomfortable about how much of his willingness to do this thing—and anything that touched on witchcraft repulsed him to the bone—was because he did not want the kitten to die. It was important to him that it survive what was done to it.

I know how, said the wolf in a voice very like the one Coyote had just used.

"Touch and go," Adam said to Mercy as they got into the car. "Lots of broken bones, some of them half-healed incorrectly. Lots of superficial and not so superficial damage. Minor skull fracture. Dehydrated and starving. They have him on IVs and have treated everything they can treat. It's up to him now."

"They thought it was us who had tortured the kitten," said Sherwood to change the subject. He wasn't as certain as Coyote had sounded that the kitten would make it. Coyote wasn't the sort of being who inspired a lot of trust.

Mercy looked over the back of the seat at Sherwood, but it was Adam who spoke. "Until a lady in the waiting room recognized me and got so excited. Sometimes the publicity can be useful."

Adam's distaste for being a celebrity colored his voice.

"There will be headlines," suggested Sherwood. "Werewolves rescue tortured kitten."

Adam flashed Sherwood a grin in the rearview mirror. "Spotlight will be on you this time. That useful lady took a picture when you kissed the kitten's nose."

Sherwood snorted. "I posed for her."

"Sure, you did, softy," Adam said in dry tones. "That photo will be all over the social media sites by morning."

"Werewolf contemplates dinner," said Sherwood. "Dinner contemplates werewolf back."

Mercy gave him an uncertain look.

She was right, it wasn't like Sherwood to play verbal games. Coyote must be contagious.

Sherwood closed his eyes. If he concentrated, he could feel the little cat's weakened heartbeat.

"I hope he makes it," Sherwood said. He should have been worried because his survival could depend upon the little creature living. But he that wasn't why he was worried.

It's a survivor, his wolf told him with something near affection. *Like us.*

Author Bio

Patricia Briggs is the #1 *New York Times* bestselling author of the Mercy Thompson series and has written twenty-eight novels to date; she is currently writing novel number twenty-nine. She has short stories in several anthologies, as well as a series of comic books and graphic novels based on her Mercy Thompson and Alpha and Omega series.

To learn more, go to: patriciabriggs.com

To Our Readers

By L. J. Hachmeister

Thank you so much for purchasing this anthology. 70% of book sale profits are donated to Lifeline Puppy Rescue (lifelinepuppy.org), a no-kill shelter for puppies in Brighton, Colorado. Each $20 raised means that one puppy is saved from a kill shelter or other dangerous situations. So, thank you, from the bottom of our hearts for helping us share great stories and save lives.

A special note—this anthology would not be possible if it weren't for each of these authors contributing a short story. I'd like to thank each one of them, but most of all, Sam Knight. Sam is the associate editor on this project and did the majority of edits on "Instinct." He's not only a fantastic editor and author, but also a good friend. Thanks, Sam!

I hope that after each story you give your own furry, scaly, and/or feathered friend a hug, for they are truly the ones that, in the end, rescue us.

Made in the USA
Middletown, DE
15 June 2024